Catch a Dream

by

Cynthia Breeding

Catch a Dream

Cover Art by *Teddi Black*

The Wild Rose Press, Inc.
PO Box 708
Adams Basin, NY 14410-0708
Visit us at www.thewildrosepress.com

Publishing History
First Edition, 2026
Trade Paperback Print ISBN 978-1-5092-6470-4
Digital ISBN 978-1-5092-6471-1

Published in the United States of America

Other Books by Cynthia Breeding from The Wild Rose Press, Inc.

The Templar's Woman
Knight of Rosslyn
Bedroom Blarney
Night Prey
Cruising along Nostalgia Lane
The Last Pirates
Highlander Unleashed
Highlander Untamed
Highlander Unconquered
Christmas Dreams
Knight of the Red Rose
Gunslinger
Looking for Love
Summer of Love
The Love Beat Goes On
The Viking's Yuletide Woman
Glasgow Rogue

Chapter One—The Twain Shall Meet

Caught in a web of dreaming, Elizabeth O'Malley fell, glided through mists, and hurdled downward, the air getting darker until all was pitch. She reached for something to grab onto, but met only swirling vapors as she spiraled on. A speck of light dawned ahead, silhouetting the shape of a flame-haired woman dressed in white leather. The vision became engulfed in a web of blue and green strands as Elizabeth rushed forward. She put her hands out to brace herself and swept right through the mesh, landing with a solid thump onto a wooden floor, bumping her head in the process.

"Ouch!" Rubbing her forehead, she slowly opened her eyes. She was lying face down in a pile of fresh hay. Her nose twitched. The smell of horses filled her senses. A stable? She must be dreaming, but this felt so real.

Behind her, a horse gently nickered and stamped a hoof. Elizabeth rolled over and sat up in front of a box stall. The dappled gray who looked at her had large intelligent eyes set in a broad forehead between well-placed small ears now cocked forward as he leaned over the half-door to nuzzle her.

Trembling, she stood and stroked his muzzle. The horse felt real, but she often dreamed of horses, or at least she had until sexy men began appearing in her night visions, and she always dreamed in vivid color.

She looked down. She was still wearing the black

bra and thong with the chiffon wrap her traitorous fiancé would never see. She certainly did not need to relive finding Edward in bed with a Barbie look-alike. Not that she should have been surprised, she grimly reminded herself. Edward was drop-dead gorgeous and had enough bad-boy attributes to make him alluring to any female. Better she had found out about his promiscuousness now than later.

Elizabeth fingered the leather strap on her wrist from which a Native American wood-carved fetish dangled. Her history students had given it to her yesterday, before the start of the Christmas holidays, along with a beautiful dream-catcher. The kids loved to tease her about her passion for the Old West, but they'd gotten caught up in the era after she'd brought in vintage John Wayne films and Clint Eastwood's spaghetti westerns. The fetish probably wasn't the right accessory for her black lace, but she had not wanted to take it off. Just as she started to close the chiffon wrap, not that it covered much, she heard a sound. She whirled around and gasped.

A half-naked Indian teenager stood not two feet away, close enough for her to see a slight bead of sweat on his upper lip. It was uncanny how authentic this dream felt—probably the result of seeing too many of those western films. He wore a breechclout and leather leggings. Colored beads hung around his neck and his bare chest. A hawk feather was braided into his long hair and he had the blackest eyes she had ever seen. He looked like a hungry wolf stalking its prey. Instinctively, she took a step backward.

The Indian took a silent step forward. "I could have counted *coup*, you know," he said. "Touched you without your knowing I was here. But I wanted you to know."

Elizabeth drew another shaky breath and tried to cover herself more fully. Why in the world would she be nearly nude in her own dream? The Indian's glance traveled from her face to her breasts and a small smile played on his mouth. A hard mouth, thin-lipped and straight-lined. She took another step backward and bumped against the wall of the stall. Trapped. The wall felt real, too. Some dream.

He came closer and reached over to touch her copper hair. "Fire Woman. You must have much magic. Your eyes are the color of our forests—a blessing from the Earth Mother." He touched the diamond solitaire at her throat with a finger. "A shining star from the heavens. Yes, you have much magic."

Elizabeth held herself still, hardly breathing. This would be a really, really good time to wake up. "I don't have magic. Where am I? Who are you?"

Drawing himself up, he said proudly, "I am called Swift Hawk. My father is a Comanche chief." He twisted a strand of her hair around his finger. "To my people, a woman with flaming hair has much power. Many even fear her."

She smiled weakly. Good Lord, a Comanche? She had conjured someone from the fiercest of all the Plains Indians to dream of? The finest light cavalry in North America, some said, and the most dangerous fighters. They loved to fight and feared nothing. Well, except maybe a woman with red hair. Feeling ridiculous to be so deep into the dream, she raised her chin.

"Take your hand off me if you don't want to feel my wrath."

Swift Hawk laughed and his hand dropped to her shoulder. “I said many fear you, Fire Woman. I do not. I am the son of a chief. I will claim you as my woman and have much honor and power among my father’s people.” He grasped her head in his hands and leaned forward to kiss her. She pushed against him, hard.

“Don’t you want to know where I came from?” she asked, trying to stall him.

He looked surprised. “The Great Spirits sent you. I do not question them.” He glanced down at her breasts again. “I like what they’ve clothed you in, too.” His hand slid down to stroke a breast.

She needed to do something to stop this—closing her eyes, she screeched at the top of her lungs.

Suddenly, he was yanked away. Elizabeth felt cool air surrounding her. Slowly, she opened her eyes and then quickly closed them again. She could not have seen what she thought she had. Clearly, her mind was bent on fantasies tonight.

Tentatively, she peered out from behind her tousled hair. The man—her rescuer, she assumed, for the Indian boy was gone—was breathtakingly handsome. Far too good-looking to be real and very much like the delectable man she’d encountered in her sleep a couple of nights ago. She might still be dreaming, but this was much, much better. The stranger’s blackish hair curled just above the collar of the open neck of his shirt and a part of it fell across his forehead, giving him a roguish appearance. She almost reached out to brush it back for him. His eyes were warm brown and deep-set above high cheekbones and a straight nose. He had the most sensuous mouth she had ever seen. Definitely kissable. Well, of course he would. She was dreaming! He was tall, well over six feet, and with broad shoulders. With the sleeves of his white shirt rolled up, she could see tan, well-muscled forearms. Her gaze traveled to his tight-fitting jeans and she tried to ignore the bulge lodged there. She focused on his well-developed thighs. Big mistake—better to look down. The boots were hand-tooled. Cowboy boots. Real ones. She *really* had to stop reading romance novels about the Wild West. Cowboys and Indians. Her students would get a real laugh!

"Who are you and how did you get into my barn?" His voice was deep and resonant and held a note of authority. A man would think twice about crossing him, she thought, and almost giggled. She certainly had conjured up her perfect cowboy. And all man. She couldn't resist extending her dream-fantasy just a little longer…

"Elizabeth O'Malley," she said and gave her dream man her best smile, the one her best friend, Brooke, said made her look alluring. "And you are one hot fantasy."

The man blinked and let his gaze travel slowly over her body and back to her face. A corner of his mouth twitched. "Happy to oblige. My name's Miguel."

Elizabeth became uncomfortably aware of how much of her body was exposed. She drew her wrap closer, which caused her fantasy to grin. It was a lopsided grin, giving him a definite bad-boy look. Obviously, her dream-mind hadn't quite learned its lesson about bad boys. But it was only a dream—

"How did you get into my barn?" he asked again. "You don't look like you're from around here." His glance lingered on her breasts. "Are you a working girl?"

Working girl? Did he mean prostitute? This dream was taking an ironic direction, given the fact that at twenty-four she was the oldest virgin she knew. Her fantasy man sounded dangerously real. She could almost feel the heat radiating from him. She crossed her arms over her breasts. "I'm a teacher."

His eyebrows went up. "Ah. Well, teachers seem to be changing. You don't look like a schoolmarm."

Schoolmarm? An Old West term. She frowned slightly. "Where am I?"

"You're obviously in my barn," Miguel said with a glint in his eye. "And since I'm —hot, did you say? That means desirable, *verdad*?—we may as well get acquainted." He took a step toward her and put one hand on either side of the stall she still had her back to, effectively trapping her with his muscular body. He bent his head toward hers.

This wasn't going like it should. Somewhere she had lost control. She could inhale the scent of him. Soap and leather and *man*. Elizabeth felt a moment of panic. "Where am I?"

He hesitated, those luscious lips barely an inch from hers, and gave her a quizzical look. "You don't remember how you got here?"

She began to feel desperate, all too aware of his closeness and an almost irresistible urge to taste him. "I don't know where *here* is. I'm dreaming, I think."

"Well, if you are, so am I." Miguel straightened and took her hand, intertwining their fingers. "See? Warm flesh and blood. Now, how did you get here?"

"I don't know." The hand that held hers was strong. She could feel the roughened palms, but his touch was exquisitely gentle. Elizabeth tried to ignore the pleasant sensation that was seeping up her arm. Miguel certainly *felt* like a real man. She pulled her fingers loose and tried to close her wrap. "Please tell me where I am."

He dropped his hand. "All right. I'll play your game. You're on the de Basque ranch—my ranch—just southwest of Johnson Station, Texas."

Johnson Station? That was the original name for Arlington, back in the 1800s! It couldn't be. "What year? What month?" she asked suspiciously.

Miguel grew wary. "December. 1849. Now, if we're through with your game, I'm willing to share one of mine." His eyes smoldered and he caressed her cheek lightly with a fingertip. "It's a little more exciting than yours, I think."

His touch was as soft as silk and sent a river of warmth flooding her veins. Her knees went weak. Elizabeth braced herself against the wall and looked around wildly. By all the saints, this was real—the sunlight pouring in the door, dust motes riding on its shafts, the horse shifting his weight from hoof to hoof in the stall behind her. The scents, the sounds—all of them were real. Somehow, she had traveled back to the nineteenth century. How was that possible? And this man—her hot fantasy—was propositioning her! Not that she minded his luscious mouth mere inches from hers, but he really thought she was a hooker. Her Irish temper began to simmer. She'd think later about how she got here. She thrust her chin up defiantly.

"I'm not that kind of girl. If you had any decency, you'd find me something to wear instead of looking at me like that."

He grinned indolently. "It's not often I find an attractive woman in my barn in the morning. And a scantily clad one, at that. What do you call this?" He slipped a finger under her bra strap, slipping it off her shoulder. "It certainly is an improvement over those danged corset laces that get all tangled up."

Elizabeth quickly pulled the strap up. Flame seared through her shoulder where his hand had been. Her breasts suddenly felt heavy and ached for his touch. She had never had this reaction with anyone, even that cheating disaster from Dallas she'd thought to marry.

Turning her back on Miguel, she nearly hit her nose on the wall. He chuckled and then walked away from her, but soon returned and she felt him behind her. A part of her wanted to lean back, press against him, feel the length of his powerful body against hers. The other part of her wanted to cower in a corner.

He leaned over her shoulder, his breath warm on her ear, and put his arms around her. Something soft fell on her shoulders. She reached up to gather the edges of a saddle blanket and, for one moment, his hands covered hers. Then his fingers grazed her neck as he lifted her hair from under the blanket and settled it over her back.

Elizabeth forced herself to remain still and not give in to the shudder of delight building within her. How could a man have such an incredibly light touch? Did he have any idea of how her body tingled? Her blood chilled suddenly and her thoughts stopped. Of course, he did. Bad boys were so good. That's what made them bad. He knew exactly what he was doing. Just like Edward. Like every good-looking man. God help her, she'd almost fallen for one again. Obviously, she hadn't learned her lesson about gorgeous men who were born to break women's hearts.

When she turned around, he was several feet away, leaning with one arm against a stack of hay bales. "Now, why don't you tell me where you're really from?" he asked.

Would he believe her? That somehow she'd time-traveled? She was still having trouble accepting that herself. Maybe it was the fetish. That must be it. Somehow, her students had gotten hold of a real artifact. Maybe if she rubbed it, she'd wake up in her own bed. Quickly she closed her eyes and tried. Slowly, she opened one. Nope. Fantasy man was still there. She swallowed hard. "I'm from Arlington, Texas."

He frowned. "I've never heard of it."

Elizabeth took a deep breath. "You know it as Johnson Station."

Annoyance flickered across his face. "Another game, Miss O'Malley?"

"No." Elizabeth hesitated and then plunged on. "Johnson Station will be renamed Arlington. In 1876."

He arched an eyebrow. "Really? And I suppose you are the Spirit Woman Swift Hawk thinks you are?"

Elizabeth squelched her temper. "Don't make fun of me. By the year 2000, Arlington will have nearly 300,000 people living there."

"Uh-huh."

He didn't believe her. Well, wait until he heard this. "I don't know how I got here, but I'm from the twenty-first century."

"Not possible." Miguel slipped a sliver of hay between very white teeth. "I say you've come to work at Miss Lily's over by Fort Worth and got off the stage one stop too soon."

Elizabeth looked at him suspiciously. "Who is Miss Lily?"

"The madam who runs the finest bordello north of San Antonio and west of New Orleans," Miguel answered languidly. "She only hires really attractive ladies."

Elizabeth felt her face flush. "You still think I'm that kind of girl?" His eyes glanced over her body and she felt as though he could see straight through the thick blanket.

"You're not dressed for much else." A corner of his mouth quirked up. "Not that I mind. In fact, if that's how women dress from this place you call Arlington, maybe you could take me there."

She pulled the blanket tighter. The man had a one-track mind. "I told you I don't know how I got here, but I'm not a hooker."

"A what?"

"Hooker. Prostitute. Whore."

"Oh." His dark eyes narrowed and he studied her. He stepped closer and lightly touched the bruise on her forehead. "Is it possible you hit your head on something and can't remember where you came from? I've heard tell that can happen."

"I *know* where I'm from. The twenty-first century—a hundred and sixty years into the future. We have cars and smart phones and computers—"

"I don't know what you're talking about," Miguel interrupted, but for the first time he looked undecided. "I think I should take you to Fort Worth to see the army doctor there. Maybe he can give you something to help you remember—"

"No! If you won't believe me—and you found me in your barn like this—what makes you think another person will? He'll think I'm crazy."

Silence met her remark and she looked up to find Miguel regarding her. "You think I'm crazy, too! That

I've just invented this whole story!" Fear suddenly struck her. She was truly powerless here, stuck in a time warp. "I've heard what the insane asylums were like in this century." She fought to control a rising hysteria bubble in her throat. "I don't have any relatives here. No one to vouch for me. I'll be locked away and end up rotting somewhere." She started shaking uncontrollably.

Miguel put steadying hands on her shoulders. "All right. Calm down. Working girl or not—and I don't have anything against them—I won't send you off to rot, Elizabeth."

He'd used her first name. Why did that seem important? Whether it was that or the fact that she suddenly felt safe in his arms, as though she'd known him before. The trembling subsided. She looked up at him with troubled eyes. "What am I going to do?"

He released her and began pacing. "I don't know. You seem sane except for this foolishness of being from the future. You're welcome to stay here while I send out inquiries or someone comes looking for you." He hesitated. "Are you sure you're not trying to hide from someone? Are you on the run? Or in danger? You can tell me."

"No! I told you—" A shadow falling across the floor interrupted their conversation. She looked toward the door to see a pretty Native American girl about sixteen standing there. At least Elizabeth thought she was Indian. Her skin was golden, and she wore her raven-black hair in two braids, but her dress was conventional: a high-necked calico with a fitted bodice and loose skirt. The tips of her shoes showed below the dress and Elizabeth could see that they buttoned up the front. Just one more fact that confirmed she really was in the nineteenth century.

"Cactus Flower. What are you doing here?" Miguel asked.

"Swift Hawk told me we have a guest," she answered in a soft voice. "I came to see for myself." She walked toward Elizabeth, her eyes focused on the red hair. "It is as he says. You are Fire Woman. Welcome."

"Her name is Elizabeth," Miguel said with a slight hint of irritation. "She's—lost. A blow to her head, I think. She doesn't remember where she came from."

Elizabeth glanced sideways at Miguel, but for now she was willing to go along with the story. No use in telling another person she was from the future. Native Americans might think her a true witch then. She tried to remember if any witches had been hanged in the old West or if that stopped with Salem. She had the distinct feeling she knew how those victims had felt. The more she tried to proclaim the truth, the less she was believed.

Cactus Flower looked at Elizabeth, her brown eyes sympathetic. "In time, you will remember." Glancing at the leather bracelet with its small fetish, she said, "See? The spirits of our ancestors sent you. It is all we have to know for now."

Miguel gave a small groan. "Why don't you take Elizabeth to the house and find her some clothes? She—uh—was waylaid by *banditos*, I think. Got bumped on the head and when she woke, they had taken all her things."

In spite of the situation, Elizabeth almost laughed. He was the worst liar she had ever met. But why argue? Clearly, he would not accept her story. Besides, it might be better not to press the point. He did have the power to have her locked up somewhere if she kept talking like a lunatic. She had no means of defending herself against that, much as she hated to admit it. She needed time to think and let reality sink in. Then she definitely had to find a way to return to her own world.

As Cactus Flower led her away, she wondered what Miguel would do with her. Involuntarily, heat shot upward through her body like a fiery sword as she remembered his sensual touch and those erotically full lips just inches from hers. He'd almost kissed her! Then she bit her own lip. Because he thought she was a hooker. To be used.

Far, far better—and safer—to stick to her original plan. Elizabeth O'Malley had sworn off good-looking men. But did Miguel de Basque have to be the hottest hunk of Texas cowboy she'd ever met?

Chapter Two—Where The West Begins

Miguel grinned as he watched her walk across the yard, her long, nude legs swinging enticingly beneath the saddle blanket. Elizabeth was certainly one spirited woman, nothing docile there. Nor was what she was wearing. Some frilly see-through thing—and those undergarments! Hardly scraps of cloth! The strap he had played with had an easy stretch, nothing he had ever felt before. His fingers itched to have played with the lace edging that covered her full breasts, tugging it lower to expose a pink nipple, teasing it to tautness…

He stopped smiling and frowned slightly. Why hadn't she been willing to let him kiss her? Women in her trade were used to it; most of them expected some sort of foreplay. Even the pretty ones—and she was one of the most alluring women he'd ever seen, with that wild, flame-colored hair—didn't usually play hard-to-get unless that was the man's pleasure. How many evenings had he listened to Lily patiently explain the more practical details of operating a bordello?

His frown deepened. Miss O'Malley had been screaming desperately when he'd run in and seen Swift Hawk trying to kiss her. Granted, she might have been frightened by an Indian if she were from the East, but she didn't sound Eastern. Something about her seemed vaguely familiar, as though he'd met her before. He shrugged off the feeling. He'd check with Lily tomorrow and find out if she'd hired anyone new.

Miguel opened the door to Diablo's stall. "One thing's for sure," he said as he led the dappled gray Andalusian out, "Elizabeth is no schoolmarm. Not dressed like that."

His collie, Brina, settled on the hay with her head on her paws and watched as Miguel began to brush the stallion. The horse nudged his arm.

Miguel laughed. "Okay, Diablo. Treats first." He dug into his pocket and brought out two lumps of sugar.

Diablo arched his neck gracefully and accepted the offering, his muzzle softly sweeping Miguel's palm.

"You're spoiled rotten," Miguel said affectionately as he briskly curried the silky coat. He wondered if the flame-haired woman in his house was spoiled rotten too. Memories of his late wife filtered through his mind. He'd given his heart to the beautiful Elena, even though it had been an arranged marriage. She came from the same Spanish nobility of Navarre that he did. Her father had brought her to New Orleans and they had married there. But Elena had hated the wide-open space and sky of Texas when he brought her back. She'd refused to help his housekeeper, Olga, with any chores and detested being pregnant. Elena had let him know he would not be touching her again. Unfortunately, her wish came true in a macabre way—she'd died in childbirth. He'd resolved there would be no more wives after that.

Resolutely, he pushed thoughts of her away and turned back to the stallion. "You and I have been together a long time." Diablo was the last foal born of the magnificent Andalusian stallion imported from southern Spain eight years ago when his father was still alive. Ten mares had accompanied that horse, and over the years, more stock had been bred, but only the best colts were not gelded. Above all else, the bloodline must be kept pure and strong as it had been since the 1400s. More than that, though, Miguel knew he loved Diablo for his intelligence, courage, and loyalty. The two of them had shared many a long ride when he needed to get away from Elena's shrill complaining.

As Miguel turned the horse out into the corral, he heard hoofbeats. They hadn't had snow yet this year, so the gravel crunched under the steady cadence. He closed the gate and went outside, Brina at his heels.

Lt. Colonel Middleton Tate Johnson of Colonel Peter Bell's Ranger regiment dismounted. From the looks of his dusty blue uniform, he'd ridden all the way from Fort Worth, although his horse didn't look blown.

"Come on in to the house," Miguel said as they shook hands. "Trouble?"

The lieutenant shook his head. "Can't stay. Just wanted to let you know that on my way back home, I saw a lot of fences torn down."

"Comanche?"

"Most likely. We've had an uneasy peace since the '41 Village Creek rout. They don't like the sod-busters."

Miguel nodded. "I can't say I blame them. Several hundred families from Peter's Colony moving in right after that. The Comanche own thousands of horses. They need the land for grazing."

The colonel looked at him. "You don't fence your stock, except for those beautiful Andalusians you breed. Don't you ever lose cattle?"

"A few," Miguel answered, "but when my family was granted this land it was with the understanding New Spain and the Indians could live together." It was an unusual alliance, but Miguel's great-grandfather on the French side of his ancestry had backed Spanish Charles during the Revolutionary War. Instead of interest, his great-grandfather had asked for 100,000 acres of untouched land in the New World. "Anyway, I let them graze their horses, and they leave my cattle alone. Rustlers fear the Comanche a lot more than they do swinging at the end of a rope, so they don't bother my herds."

The colonel nodded. "You still have the hostages, too?"

Miguel grimaced. "I try not to think of them that way. Cactus Flower and Swift Hawk could very well be the bridge we need between our people. They are being educated in the white man's ways." Briefly he thought back to when the shaman's daughter and the chief's son had been taken in a raid several years ago and nearly murdered—the Comanche went on the warpath. The Rangers intervened and saved the two children, but were in a quagmire as to what to do with them. If they gave them back, there was no guarantee Chief Jim Ned wouldn't continue his raiding out of revenge. That would bring in the full army and ignite a Plains war. Miguel had negotiated to foster them until they were twenty-one.

Johnson looked skeptical. "Well," he said, "keep an eye on them. You know a Comanche can count *coup* before his enemy even knows he's there."

Miguel grinned. "I know. Swift Hawk tried it on me several times when he first arrived here, but he's grown out of it."

The colonel mounted. "Still scheduled for dinner tomorrow night?"

"Yep." The small group of Rangers, Army officers

and businessmen rotated their monthly meeting place. "Olga's looking forward to it."

The colonel paused. "You know, it wouldn't hurt you to think about getting married again."

"No, thanks. Once was enough."

"Raul could use a mother."

"He's got Olga." Miguel grinned suddenly to ease the moment. "Anyway, if I got married, I'd break Miss Lily's heart."

Johnson laughed. "If anyone could, it'd be you." He touched two fingers to his cap by way of salute and cantered toward the road.

Miguel tipped his hat back and stared after the man while he absently scratched the dog's ears. He didn't even know what he'd do with the girl who showed up so unexpectedly in his barn. But he was sure about this: a woman complicating his life was the last thing he needed.

Swift Hawk was brushing a white mare when Miguel returned to the stable. The boy's long, straight hair glistened raven-blue in the shaft of sunlight filtering through the door. Miguel remembered suggesting once that he cut it and received such a look of outrage he hadn't brought the subject up again. He'd even given up on trying to get the boy into conventional *vaquero* clothes. Swift Hawk insisted on wearing the traditional leather breechclout and leggings. Except for the coldest days, he wore no shirt either. After all, he would remind Miguel, he was a chief's son and would never accept the white man's ways. Still, it would have made it easier for him to fit in with the other young men who lived in the bunkhouse and worked at the ranch. Most of them resented him. Not that Swift Hawk seemed to care. He cared only for the horses, as all the Comanche did. Cactus Flower was of a much gentler nature.

"When you're finished with the mare, there are a couple of fillies that need halter-breaking," Miguel said.

Swift Hawk flashed a brief smile that didn't quite reach his nearly-black eyes. Along with his aloofness, his looks made him enticing to the girls, a fact he was very aware of. More than once, Miguel had caught sight of him with one of the maids or the daughter of one of the ranch hands. If the girl was of age, Miguel didn't interfere. He felt some sympathy for the boy. He was eighteen. As an Indian, he couldn't very well go into Johnson's Station and proposition a saloon girl or even visit Miss Lily's. Not without getting a noose around his neck.

Thoughts of the fiery and very skimpily dressed woman who was now his guest almost blurred Miguel's vision. If she were a working girl—ummm. He didn't want to become a regular at Lily's, although they were good friends. He felt a familiar stirring inside his jeans as he thought of Elizabeth writhing beneath him begging for mercy, of him taking his sweet time in granting her request, building the passion, and then plunging into that warm, wet wonder between her legs and— He stopped. He was thinking like a schoolboy. Damn. Maybe a trip to Lily's would be a good idea, after all. Unless— if Elizabeth actually were willing—

Swift Hawk was watching him. "Which fillies did you want me to work with?"

Reluctantly, Miguel left his fantasy. "I'll get them for you." He considered jumping into the cold water of the horse trough as he left the barn.

****

Cactus Flower hurried across the yard and Elizabeth breathed a sigh of relief as she was bustled up the back stairs of the hacienda. No one had seen her, wrapped in only a saddle blanket, thank goodness. It was going to be hard enough to convince Miguel she wasn't a hooker.

She hardly had time to notice the highly waxed, inlaid floors with the thick carpet runners over them or to stop to study any of the ornately framed oil portraits of what must be Miguel's ancestors hanging along the corridor.

"In here," Cactus Flower said as she opened a door and took a quick look up and down the hall before she closed it behind them.

The room was one of contrasts. A china wash basin and ewer stood on a delicately carved dresser that matched a small table near the window. The velvet brocade chair was feminine too, but the bed had a woven Indian blanket of bold reds, blues, and yellows spread across it. A completely white dream-catcher hung above the headboard, reminding Elizabeth of the beautiful blue-and-green one that had been her students' gift. Her breath caught in her throat. Would she ever see it—or them—again?

"Here," Cactus Flower said as she handed her a garment. "You can begin by putting those on."

"These are actually bloomers!" Elizabeth held the pair of frilled cotton trousers up in amazement.

Cactus Flower looked up briefly from rummaging through the clothespress in her bedroom. "Yes. Of course."

Elizabeth felt herself blush. She was supposed to know about bloomers.

The young Indian girl inspected the homespun dress

she took from the wardrobe. "This is the longest dress I own, but I'm shorter than you are. I'm afraid your ankles are still going to show."

Elizabeth almost laughed, but remembered that in the 1800s, showing an ankle was something decent women didn't do. Well, she'd certainly showed more than an ankle this morning. She felt heat flush her face at the memory of Miguel's more-than-casual lingering gaze at her body.

"Come." Cactus Flower tugged at the horse blanket before Elizabeth could clutch it tight, and slipped it off. She stared. "What are you wearing?"

How to explain a thong from the future? "Uh—it's a new fashion— in the East. Ladies wear this…uh…to keep their bloomers clean."

"And this?" Cactus Flower pointed to her bra. "Does it keep your corset clean?"

"Ah—well, actually, we don't really need a corset if we wear this."

Cactus Flower tilted her head to one side and considered. "It is practical. Maybe *Don* Miguel could order me one, if you'll tell him where you got it. He doesn't usually expect us to wear corsets."

Elizabeth barely refrained from exploding. "*He* doesn't expect…? What business is it of his? Your body is your own!" She suddenly remembered his remark in the barn about struggling with corsets. Did he try to seduce every woman who was a guest in his house? "How would he know?" For a brief moment, she felt his fingers lightly graze her cheek again. If those strong hands went around her waist… "He doesn't touch you and actually feel for it, does he?" she asked in alarm as she slipped the chemise over her head.

The Indian girl giggled. "Of course not. Only when he has to entertain the Army officers and their wives he asks that we dress properly."

Wives. Did Miguel have one? "Do he and his wife do much entertaining?"

Cactus Flower shook her head. "His wife died before I was brought here. *Don* Miguel doesn't like formal dinners. We're having a small one tonight, though, which is why you haven't met Olga yet. She's busy with preparations."

"Olga?" Elizabeth pictured a leggy, blonde Scandinavian beauty. After that near seduction in the barn this morning, it would be just like him to have someone like that as his paramour. "Is she his lady friend?"

For a moment the girl looked puzzled. "No. Olga basically runs the place and everyone on it. We all love her and her husband, Olaf. She is the one who taught me so much of the white man's ways. I have good manners, do you think?"

Elizabeth smiled. "Yes, you do. It's just too bad that Indian boy doesn't."

"Swift Hawk? For him, it has been hard. He thinks he will fail his people if he accepts the white man's ways."

"He certainly didn't have any trouble behaving like a white man this morning. He practically tried to rape me," Elizabeth said sardonically.

A worried expression came into the girl's eyes. "He touched you?"

"Yes." Elizabeth nodded. "He had my hair in his hands and he was trying to kiss me when Miguel—*Don* Miguel—came in. I've never been so frightened in my life." The look on the young girl's face was not settling her nerves any. "Why?"

Cactus Flower studied her silently for a moment and then she said, so softly that Elizabeth had to bend over to hear, "He has claimed you. It is our way. To him, you are his woman."

Elizabeth snorted. "That's ridiculous. I'm not going to be anyone's woman."

"You have strange ideas, wherever you come from," Cactus Flower answered, "but I would tell *Don* Miguel. Stay close to him while you are here. He will protect you."

As hysteria threatened to bubble to the surface, a wild idea skittered across her brain that she would probably need more protecting from Miguel than by him. "That's silly," she said shakily.

Cactus Flower shrugged. "I will talk to Swift Hawk." She walked to the door and turned before she left. "I've never known him to take back his word, though. It would mean disgrace among our people. Be careful."

Elizabeth sat on the edge of the bed and rubbed her temples. So much had happened in such a short time. Last night—at least she thought it was, but how did time-travel happen anyhow?—she had planned to give her virginity to a man who loved her. Ha. Instead, she'd drunk herself into a stupor and awakened in the nineteenth century.

Would anyone miss her? Brooke, certainly. Her mother? Jacqueline O'Malley was on leave from her professorship at the university and in the south of France trying to establish a link about Templars. When her mother was on a research project, she was like a small terrier with a bone. Nothing would deter her. She wouldn't even know her daughter was missing for months.

Her police-officer father would have been frantic if he were alive. Elizabeth swallowed a big lump in her throat. Even though it had been ten years since he'd been killed in the line of duty, she missed him horribly. It was the promise she'd made to him to wait for true love that kept her still a virgin at twenty-four.

But she needed to focus on the present predicament. Elizabeth fingered the fetish again, feeling its smooth, polished wood. It had to be the key. Somehow, her students had gotten an authentic Indian artifact and somehow, she had activated it.

What had she said? Elizabeth remembered using several choice invectives describing Edward. Her father would have washed her mouth out with soap. She remembered thinking—somewhere around a half-empty bottle of wine—that cowboys of the Old West were honest, honorable, and respected women. Ha! She'd managed to find the one man in Texas—probably the entire nineteenth century—who thought she was a hooker. Some respect! He was stubborn and wouldn't believe her. Arrogant, too, just assuming she'd let him have his way with her. Never mind that she nearly went into meltdown at his touch. Who did he think he was? *"The owner of this place?"* a small voice inside her head inserted reasonably, *"who's given you a place to stay?"* The annoying voice then added, *"and the most divinely sexual man you've ever met?"* Elizabeth tried not to think about the pure animal magnetism that radiated from him when he had her nearly pinned against the stall. For a moment she thought she caught his soap-and-leather scent. Deep within, muscles contracted, sending coiled heat scorching delicate nerve endings everywhere. Sweet Mary! How could she be attracted to a man who though she was a hooker? Just one more reason she had to find a way back. Miguel was danger, spelled in all capitals.

"Please," she said as she stroked the wood, "I want to go home." Nothing happened. She tried to think if she had invoked any kind of Indian curse while she ranted at Edward. Nothing. Going to the window of her room, she looked out into the darkness. As her eyes grew accustomed, she became aware of the Milky Way, looking like a ribbon of diamonds against the black velvet of the sky. In her time, the stars were barely visible in the city. It was a beautiful sight she would remember when she returned to her time—if she returned to her time.

Elizabeth sighed and opened the drawer of the bedside table and dropped the fetish inside. No sense in encouraging the half-naked Indian boy by wearing it. Claim her as his woman, indeed! Male chauvinism crossed cultural lines, it seemed.

However she'd gotten here—and for now, she had to accept that she *was* here and this was reality—this century was going to be challenging. Until she could figure a way to go back, she would have to play along with the amnesia ruse Miguel had brought up. Still, two men who thought they could tell her what to do? Elizabeth lifted her chin. They were about to meet their first feminist, twenty-first-century style.

Chapter Three—Schoolmarms

Miguel's son, Raul, was waiting for him when he got back to the house, uncharacteristically quiet and subdued.

"What are you doing home early from school?" he asked.

Raul studied the floor as he handed his father a note from the new schoolmarm, Miss Parsons. Miguel sat down and read it quickly. It simply asked that he come by today to discuss Raul.

"This is the last day of school before Christmas," Miguel said. "You couldn't behave for one more day?"

Raul hung his head. "I didn't do anything, *Papá*."

Miguel eyed him suspiciously. When he acted meek, it was usually bad. "You didn't put a snake or a frog in the teacher's desk like you did with Mrs. Higgins last year, did you?" He remembered having to face Mrs. Higgins; the elderly widow had nearly swooned with fright.

"Oh, no! It was just…"

"Just what?" Miguel tapped the tips of his callused fingers on the oak table, dreading to hear the answer.

"A spider," his son whispered. "Just a little one. It was crawling along the floor…and Gus dared me…"

Miguel sighed. Gus was Raul's best friend, if that term could be used for one who aided and abetted his son's shenanigans. In the rare event when Raul behaved,

Gus easily thought of something to reverse that. The problem was, he reflected, that he had been just as bad at that age. Only instead of tormenting his teachers, he teased the girls. Then older girls. Miguel's thoughts began to roam. Teasing took on a whole new concept, especially when they let him know they liked it. He'd lost his virginity at the delicate age of thirteen to a girl five years older.

He took a deep breath. Somehow the presence of the strange woman from the barn this morning had addled his brains. He couldn't concentrate on anything except the vision of her nearly naked with all that luscious smooth flesh just waiting to be caressed. He wanted to bring her alive beneath his touch, to see her green eyes darken with passion and hear her breathing come fast and shallow. He wanted to tease her with kisses—abruptly, he forced himself back to the present.

There wouldn't be any teasing at this meeting with Miss Parsons. He'd have to be respectably serious and stern. And he'd have to create an impression on Raul, too. He stood and motioned to his son. "We might as well get this over with. Tonight, when you get home, you can look forward to a switching."

Raul winced, but to his credit, he didn't cry. "Yes, *Papá*." Then a light flickered in his hazel eyes and he grinned mischievously. "But you should have seen the look on Miss Parsons' face!"

****

Miguel felt like a fool, standing in front of the schoolmarm's desk, his hat in his hands, listening to her explain what had happened and how disappointed she was in Raul's behavior. Raul had already apologized, and it had even sounded sincere, although Miguel knew that would be only until the next time something caught his son's attention, which could be anything that would create a diversion from his studies.

"Are you listening to me, Mr. de Basque?" Miss Parsons asked.

He refocused. She was standing with her hands on her hips, her eyebrows arched delicately. She was a pretty-enough little thing, her blonde hair piled high on her head with those little sausage-looking curls around her face. The neckline of her dress was a little low, even though a white tucker edged the top of it. It fit snugly, accentuating the swell of her breasts and her small waist. His mind flitted to Elizabeth. What would *she* look like in clothes?

"Yes, ma'am." He bowed slightly. "He'll get a switchin' as soon as we get home."

Her expression changed instantly. She looked at Raul, who was wearing a perfectly angelic expression on his heart-shaped face. She turned back to Miguel, her eyes round and her voice soft. "I didn't mean that you had to hit him. I don't believe in striking children."

Miguel groaned inwardly. He was going to have to do some serious talking with his son tonight. "Then what would you like me to do with him?"

She considered Miguel for a moment, head perched to one side, perfectly still. He had the distinct impression that she was about to pounce, much like a mountain lion. And he was the prey. He'd seen it often enough. The sudden stillness of the big cat, the slow, low crouch, the switch of the tail—briefly he wondered what was under the huge bustle that she wore—and then the spring. And here he was, cornered. In a manner of speaking.

Then she gave him a brilliant smile, which he didn't

trust, and put her hand lightly on his arm.

"Sadly, Raul has no mother. Perhaps I could spend some individual time with him. Being his only parent, I think you might need some help." She added, "If you would stop by after school on a weekly basis, I would be more than willing to work with you." She looked demurely down, her eyelashes touching her cheeks before she looked back up at him. Ever so lightly, she squeezed his arm before she dropped her hand.

The corner of his mouth twitched. If there was one thing about women he did understand, it was when one wanted him. But Miss Parsons had a predatory air about her, and he'd learned long ago to stay away from women who were planning to be the mother of his next child. Translated, that meant wife. There wasn't going to be another wife.

"Ma'am, I think…"

"Call me Abigail, please, since we'll be working together for Raul's sake." She smiled prettily and took a small step toward him. "May I call you Miguel?"

He felt like she was a cougar moving in for the kill. Even her eyes were golden like the big cat's. He had to be careful not to jeopardize Raul's education.

"I reckon I'm not going to have time to be payin' visits at school, Miss Parsons."

Momentarily she looked hurt, then she rallied. "Perhaps you'd permit me to call on you at home, then. That might be better. I'd have a chance to see what your home is like and make some suggestions…" Miguel raised an eyebrow and she quickly said, "You know, little things, like where does he do his homework? Is there a quiet place for him? He really does need to concentrate more on his homework…" Her voice trailed off.

Miguel found himself holding onto his temper with an effort. There was nothing wrong with how he ran his home. He had Olga there to see to it. And for some totally illogical reason, he didn't want to insult Elizabeth by bringing a *real* schoolmarm into his house. He'd probably be in for another lecture on being a parent if Miss Parsons knew he had a lady-of-the-evening staying with him. He almost laughed at the irony. If Miss Parsons weren't a schoolmarm, he'd think her one of the brazen hussies who stood in front of the saloon doors in San Antonio. Somehow, though, he couldn't picture Elizabeth in the same way.

He put his hat on and tipped it to her as he turned to go. "Ma'am," he said, "I'll keep that in mind." He could almost see her claws retracting as she smiled. For a moment he hesitated; he hated turning down an easy opportunity for sex. Then almost imperceptibly, he shook his head. This one would be clingy, and Katy had done enough damage. He'd not let a woman get close to him again, except in bed. Just let one try.

****

As Miguel unsaddled Diablo, he realized how much he was looking forward to seeing Elizabeth again, even with clothes on. Having seen the rounded ivory mounds of her breasts and the satin expanse of her smooth hips and thighs, it would be intriguing to see her in clothes. And imagine taking them off—slowly.

So he was disappointed when he arrived in the dining room that evening, freshly bathed and clean-shaven, to find her chair empty.

"Where's Elizabeth?" he asked Cactus Flower as she joined him and took a seat.

"She asked to be excused this evening. She said the bump on her head was hurting and she needed to rest."

Miguel frowned. "If she's in that much pain, I should take her to the army doctor in the morning." He saw Cactus Flower grimace at the idea. Indians didn't place much store in the white man's medicines, and Cactus Flower dabbled with healing herbs. "Do you have something that would work?"

"I can make a poultice," she replied, hesitating, and then, "but I don't think that's why she won't come to the table." She looked down, refusing to meet his gaze.

Was the little vixen trying to stir his blood further by withholding her presence? Clever of her. She put the bait under his nose this morning and then pulled it away once he'd caught the scent… Her scent, he remembered, slightly exotic yet comfortingly familiar, like cinnamon and vanilla blended together. Yes, very clever of her, indeed, to let him glimpse so much lovely, silken flesh and inhale her fragrance and then keep herself hidden. He wondered where she had received her courtesan training. In Europe, perhaps? Her accent was strange. Two could play this game, and he was more than ready. "So," he said with a grin, "does she wish for me to take dinner to her?"

"You'll do no such thing," Olga scolded as she bustled in from the kitchen bearing a large platter of roasted meat. "If the poor girl doesn't know where she came from, the best thing for her memory is peace and quiet. I'll take her some broth and fresh bread later."

Miguel opened his mouth to protest that this was his house, but the stern look Olga gave him let him know she knew exactly what he really wanted to do. He had never been able to fool her, even when his own mother was still alive. And Olga was the only one who could make him feel like a small boy caught with his hand in the cookie jar. He turned to Cactus Flower.

"And where is Swift Hawk?"

For a moment she didn't answer, then she said softly, "I told him to stay away."

Miguel raised an eyebrow. Since Swift Hawk rarely joined them unless coerced, the question had been rhetorical, more of a cover-up for his lustful thoughts. "Why would you tell him that?" She didn't answer immediately and he was about to repeat the question when she spoke.

"He's the reason Elizabeth is staying in her room."

"What? Why?" Surely, she couldn't be so sensitive—given her likely profession—that she took so much offense at the boy trying to kiss her earlier. Miguel was sure nothing more had happened.

"He has claimed her for his woman, *Don* Miguel. She fears him."

He almost laughed but stopped when he saw her serious face. "He has no right to do that, Cactus Flower. You both know it."

She shrugged. "White man's laws are different from ours. The son of a chief can choose for wife any woman he wishes. Even a married one, though he would have to fight her husband for her."

A momentary vision of himself fighting with Swift Hawk for Elizabeth filled Miguel's mind and he quickly dismissed it. Where had that thought come from? He didn't want a wife, damn it. But he would put a stop to this notion of Swift Hawk's.

He went looking for the boy as soon as they had finished their meal. Usually, Swift Hawk could be found in the barn, crooning to the horses in his native tongue or sometimes just sitting silently near one of the stalls. But tonight the barn was empty, as was the room off the stable where Swift Hawk kept his pallet and a few personal items.

Miguel sighed. He knew the boy was honor-bound not to run off, for it would bring disgrace to his father, but there was other trouble that a lone Indian could get into if he fell into the wrong white man's hands. His talk with him would have to wait, but he'd make sure Elizabeth had no cause for fear. It was the least he could do.

Chapter Four—Sparks

"What do you mean, you didn't hire her?" Miguel crossed his long legs in front of him and leaned back in the well-padded arm chair in Lily's private chambers the next day. He accepted the brandy one of the girls brought, but declined both the invitation of her nearly exposed breasts and the proffered cigar.

Lily arranged the soft woolen shawl around her shoulders and adjusted her spectacles so she could look over them at Miguel. "Just that. I've not even interviewed a new girl in a long time. It takes so much time to train them to my standards."

Miguel grinned. Her candor was one of the things he liked about Lily. He'd met her in New Orleans, where she'd owned a brothel for nearly fifteen years before she moved out here. She managed this bordello like any man would run a business. Straightforward and up-front. Her clients knew exactly what they could do and not do. No young Army recruits bedded her girls without a talk with Miss Lily first.

"Then why is she here? If you could have seen what she was wearing…"

Lily held up her hand. "So you've told me. Three times. I don't know where she got that clothing. Maybe you should ask her. Some of my girls would be interested."

He knew what Miss Elizabeth O'Malley would say.

They're from the twenty-first century, just like I am. He hadn't even had a chance to talk to her since she claimed to be ill and Olga had robbed him of his chance to see the newcomer last night. This morning he'd ridden out early to get to Lily's. Now what was he going to do?

"What do you make of her crazy talk about the future?"

"I don't know." Lily stirred her tea in its china cup and looked thoughtful. "I had a girl who worked for me in New Orleans who thought she was a queen from another lifetime. She was quite sane except for that notion. She called herself Gwen. Short for Gwenevere, I think."

"King Arthur's wife?" Miguel laughed. "How ironic. There were some who called her Britain's Great Whore."

Lily shrugged. "I don't know the story. She insisted that one day a man would come for her and take her away from this."

For a minute, Miguel allowed himself to be sidetracked. "Did someone?"

"Well, yes, now that I think of it." Lily sat up straighter. "A tall, dark stranger. No drifter, though. His eyes were too penetrating. We thought he was a lawman, probably. I remember he wore a military sword as well as a sidearm."

In spite of himself, Miguel was intrigued. An oddly similar incident had occurred following the massacre of the Council House meeting in 1840. Chief Buffalo Hump had gone on the warpath, raiding and burning all the way to the coast, then turned back and fled north. He was finally routed at Plum Creek, but the interesting part was that a tall, dark-haired man wearing a uniform no one recognized and brandishing a sword had come to the aid of the army just in time to save General Huston's life. The man had disappeared before anyone could get his name. Looked like a lawman, everyone had said.

"What happened?" Miguel asked Lily.

"The stranger stood in the doorway and scanned the room, like he was looking for someone. Several of the girls went over to him—actually, he drew them like a magnet—but he didn't even notice. He just stood there like a statue, commanding silence without saying a word." Lily closed her eyes and smiled. "I remember Gwen appeared at the top of the stairs. "I knew you'd come," she said and walked right down the steps like she was floating. Their eyes never left each other. He just put his arm around her and they walked out the door." Lily opened her eyes. "I'd forgotten about that. It is kind of romantic, isn't it?"

Miguel tipped his brandy back. "Did you get his name?"

"No. By the time we'd recovered and gone to the door, they were gone. She left all her things, but I never heard from her again. Why?"

Miguel felt a small chill quiver down his back. It couldn't be true. First of all, no one had ever been able to prove that King Arthur or Queen Gwenevere had ever existed, although his own French ancestors certainly claimed Lancelot as one of their own. Even so, they could *not* have travelled through time from the sixth century. It wasn't possible.

"Miguel?"

He frowned. "Lily. Do you think maybe Elizabeth is telling the truth?"

"Sweet, I think you're the one who's insane if you

believe that." Lily patted his hand and stilled his tapping fingers on the table. "More than likely, she left some wagon train headed for California's gold. Maybe some young man lured her out, maybe she needed to attend to nature. You know how the Comanche trail those wagons. However it happened, Elizabeth was probably raped and knocked unconscious. Either of those things could cause her not to remember and certainly to be frightened of Swift Hawk."

It made sense. Olga had said Elizabeth had a knot on her head, although he hadn't seen any bruises and he had definitely looked over almost every square inch of her. Having been abducted was more rational than time-travel, as she called it. He breathed a sigh of relief. No one was crazy, after all.

"What are you going to do with her?" Lily asked.

"I have no idea. I told her she can stay at the *hacienda* for a while. Maybe she'll remember something."

"You can bring her here if you like. If I think she's trainable, I'll give her a chance. You know my girls don't have a hard life."

The image of Elizabeth, nude and writhing beneath some soldier or ranch hand, seared through his mind like a branding iron. Another man's mouth on her soft, sensual lips, another man's hand caressing the fullness of her breast—it was too much. He clenched his fists.

"She must be awfully pretty."

"Why do you say that?" Miguel forced his voice to stay calm.

A knock on the door interrupted them and Lily smiled and stood. "I've haven't ever seen you look so besotted. Usually you don't take your women too seriously."

"I'm not taking her seriously. I just—"

"Maybe you should go home and take care of your woman." She patted his arm and opened the door.

"She isn't my woman," he called after her, but all he heard was her laughter. He was irritated momentarily and then he grew thoughtful. Maybe what Elizabeth needed to bring her memory back was a man with a slow hand. He grinned suddenly, remembering the hours he'd spent in bed making sure his various lovers had their pleasure. No woman had ever accused him of rushing the moment of her release.

****

Olga had brought Elizabeth buttered toast and fresh milk this morning, but Elizabeth knew she couldn't hide in the guest room forever. Tentatively, she wandered down to the kitchen near noon, hoping she would—or would not—see Miguel. She wasn't sure if she was—or was not—disappointed to find out he wasn't there.

After much clucking and fussing on the housekeeper's part, Elizabeth realized how ravenous she really was and ate enough roast with gravied potatoes and homemade bread to equal any of the ranch hands who passed through the kitchen. She'd gain thirty pounds if she kept this up. Well, she wouldn't be here that long—she just had to figure out how to use the fetish right.

She tilted her face up now to catch the late afternoon winter sun as she walked through Olga's garden, the collie padding silently beside her. At least she had one friend here. She let her hand travel along the soft fur of the dog's coat and was rewarded with Brina leaning against her leg, tail wagging.

The garden was a pleasant spot behind the main house, tucked away from wind and noise by thick adobe walls. A graveled walkway, lined with sturdy holly, bright with red berries this time of year, led through the arbor entrance. To her left was the plot for the spring vegetable garden and to her right stood a profusion of purple ligustrum and pyracantha hedges enclosing flowerbeds, creating almost a maze. Honeysuckle vines hung along one of the walls and what looked like orange trumpet vines along another. To the far back was the rose garden. In the summer this whole garden would be fragrant with scent.

In the center of the massive outlay rose a huge stone fountain, its marble centerpiece a rearing Andalusian stallion. It reminded Elizabeth of the one she had seen in the barn on her arrival. She sank down on one of the benches facing the fountain. How she'd love to ride one of those fantastic horses!

"Who are you?"

Startled, she turned to see a young boy staring at her with wide, hazel eyes. His dark hair hung over his forehead and he was, more or less, covered in dirt. Even his face held smudges. Whoever his mother was, she would not be pleased with the condition of what looked like new clothes.

"My name's Elizabeth. I'm a guest here."

The boy gave her a mischievous grin and moved closer. With that smile, Elizabeth knew she must be looking at Miguel's son.

"Are you Miss Katy's replacement?" he asked.

"Who's Miss Katy?"

"Miss Katy was supposed to take care of me, but she ran away. At least, that's what *Papá* said. I'm Raul." He gestured proudly, one dirty hand sweeping the landscape. “My father owns all of this.” He turned back to her. “Are you going to take care of me?”

“I don’t know, Raul. I may be here just a few days.” Surely, she’d be able to figure out what happened soon.

The boy raised an eyebrow, the gesture looking so like Miguel. “*Papá* doesn’t usually bring pretty girls home. I heard Miss Olga scolding him once when he did, a long time ago.”

Elizabeth smiled. The boy couldn’t be more than seven. “Long ago” might have meant only a few weeks. Still, she was pleased for no reason that Olga had lit into Miguel. He should know better than to bring around one of his “working girls.”

“Except for Miss Katy,” Raul said. “He liked her.”

Katy. Elizabeth was beginning to suspect Katy might have been more than just a nanny. Still, why had she run away from Miguel? Could he possibly be really dangerous? Or even cruel? She shivered a little, and then memories of Miguel’s touch yesterday morning sent a thousand tiny pricks of heat piercing her skin, and her face burned as she pictured his mouth just inches from hers when she’d stopped him. His hand had been so gentle… She was so not going there. Definitely not.

Raul plopped down beside her. “Where are you from?”

Elizabeth hesitated, her mind reeling. She certainly couldn’t tell him the truth, and she hated lying. “A place that you probably haven’t heard of. It’s called Arlington.”

He frowned momentarily. “I don’t like geography.” A sly expression came across his face. “Do you want to see what I found today?”

Elizabeth nodded, thinking he really was a pleasant, friendly child.

Raul reached into his pocket and quickly pulled out a small, striped garter snake, which he dangled in front of her. He laughed as she involuntarily shrank back. "Shucks, it ain't poisonous. I like snakes, don't you?"

"Raul!" Miguel thundered as he strode through the arbor toward his son. "Throw that thing away right now and stop scaring the lady. Then you can go find your own switch for your swats. And make it a strong one."

Raul turned pale and he looked like a fallen angel. Elizabeth's "teacher mode" took over. There had been too many times, when she had been a substitute teacher, that students had tried to find her weak points. A few had even tried to intimidate her.

Briskly, Elizabeth reached for the snake and curled it in her hand. Raul's eyes widened and even Miguel stopped in mid-step. Now if she could just keep her own skin from crawling at the scaly feel… She clenched her teeth momentarily, forcing herself not to think about the creature.

"I don't think there's any need for a spanking. As you can see, Raul didn't scare me." Deliberately, she put the snake on the ground where it gratefully slithered away. She resisted the urge to wipe her hand on her dress. She turned to Raul. "However, don't try to scare me again. Is that understood?"

He nodded mutely, his eyes still huge.

Miguel placed a firm hand on his son's shoulder. "I didn't hear you say you're sorry. Apologize to the lady. And mean it."

"I'm sorry. I really am." Raul looked into Elizabeth's eyes and respect began to grow in his. "You really weren't scared, were you?"

"That's enough," Miguel answered. "Go to your room and stay there. You may have been saved from a switching, but you're still going to be punished. Go."

They watched him run toward the house and then Miguel sat down on the bench beside Elizabeth. Instantly, she was aware of the maleness radiating from him, even though a respectable space was between them.

He grinned. "Good acting on your part. Maybe you've been on the stage?"

Elizabeth bristled. "I was not scared. Just a little surprised."

"Is that why your hand shook?"

"It did not."

"It did." Miguel reached over and picked up her hand, turning it over. He pulled his bandanna from around his neck and wiped the palm clean. Then he placed a soft kiss in it before releasing her hand. "There. All better."

Elizabeth grasped her hand with the other one, to keep them both from shaking uncontrollably. If the man ever got any idea of how she reacted to him— well, he'd never find out. Still, his strong fingers holding hers, the gentle pressure of his other hand—and his lips, brushing her skin, lingering just long enough for the sensation to spread…

Miguel watched her with an almost amused expression on his face. She had a sneaking suspicion he knew exactly what kind of effect he was having on her. She looked down in embarrassment.

He leaned forward. "For what it's worth, you did a good job handling Raul."

Elizabeth nodded, and hoped her voice would not

squeak. “I’m a teacher.”

A slight look of annoyance flickered over his face. “You still think you’re from another century?”

She looked straight into his eyes. “I know I am.”

Miguel stood. “You’re not. Lily thinks you got—kidnapped, maybe—from some wagon train and got a bad blow to your head.”

“Lily?” Elizabeth stood, too, her temper rising. “You went to a *madam* and told her about me? Why?”

“Lily is an old friend. I wanted to know if she’d hired you.”

“I told you I’m not that kind of girl!” Elizabeth was so furious she wanted to stamp her foot, but she was a grown woman. Still! Did nothing penetrate this man’s skull?

“Hard to prove, given what you were wearing, waiting for me in the barn.”

Elizabeth reminded herself she was a guest in his house, but her temper flared anyway. “I was not ‘waiting’ for you, you arrogant bastard!” She put her hand to her mouth too late…the word had slipped out.

But Miguel laughed. “I can assure you that a bastard is one thing I am not. My father’s lineage dates back to medieval Spanish royalty and my mother’s bloodline to the Templars.” He shrugged. “I’ll give you arrogant, though. Maybe.”

“Maybe? You’re the most—”

His mouth twitched. “You really are beautiful when you’re mad, Red.”

Of all the infuriating things to say! And to call her “Red”! No one had dared to call her that since she was a child and that one had carried a black eye for days. Her hand swung up instinctively.

He caught it. His grip, although not painful, felt like steel. "That's one game you don't want to play with me."

His voice was flat, devoid of emotion. Looking into his eyes, Elizabeth knew he meant it. She could sense the animal power in him. The danger if she pushed him too far. But she was seething inside and not ready to be rational. He still thought she was a whore. That hurt. Nothing could be further from the truth, but obstinate as he was, he wouldn't believe her. He had to be the most infuriating man she had ever met. She lifted her chin. "What would you do?"

For an instant, surprise flickered in his eyes and then they turned even darker. He released her arm suddenly and leaned close, his breath tickling her ear. "Do you really want to find out, Red?"

He turned and walked away, leaving her to stare after him. What did he mean by that? A thrill of excitement pulsed through her as she wondered. She felt she was treading a very precarious path. Just how far could she push him?

And where did she get the idea she wanted to push him? She didn't know, but the shiver that went down her spine had nothing to do with the weather.

Chapter Five—Questions

"Ouch!" Elizabeth gasped, tears stinging her eyes as Cactus Flower gave another hard pull on the laces of the corset as they prepared for a dinner that included guests. "How can you stand wearing these things?" She hung onto the bedpost, the whalebone painfully digging into her sides.

"Here." Cactus Flower lifted the blue satin gown over Elizabeth's head and tugged it down and then frowned. "You're so much taller than I am. With the crinoline, your entire ankle shows."

The dress was a snug fit for Elizabeth. Her breasts, already pushed up alarmingly by the effects of the corset, strained against the bodice, threatening to pop out. Miguel would think she was a hooker, for sure. "I can't wear this."

Cactus Flower held up a yellow redingote. "This is worn open with an under-dress, but I think it's even shorter." She laid the coatdress on the bed. "Those are the only two gowns I own. *Don* Miguel really doesn't entertain much."

Elizabeth considered. The garment would cover more of her shoulders, but it was cut lower than her present dress. She sighed. It was bad enough that Miguel thought her a prostitute; she certainly didn't want Army officers thinking the same thing. She would just have to keep her feet under the table and breathe lightly. She doubted whether she could eat at all, with the corset lacing her in. A vision of Scarlett O'Hara having Mammy tug her corset tight for the Twelve Oaks picnic flashed through her mind and she grinned. There was an Irish girl who would know how to handle Miguel.

"What's so funny?" Cactus Flower asked.

She shook her head. "I was just thinking of a story character from the Civil War…" She trailed off, looking at the Indian girl's puzzled face. *My god! The Civil War hasn't taken place yet! These people have no idea of how this nation will be ripped apart. Brother against brother…* A part of history she didn't particularly want to relive. She had to stay calm. There must be a way back. "I meant…uh…the War of 1812. I'll tell you about it someday."

Cactus Flower looked puzzled. "You say some of the strangest things. I think, though, that we should go to the dining room and get you seated before the guests arrive."

Elizabeth agreed whole-heartedly. The less of her that could be seen, the better. She would have been happy to stay in her room, but Miguel said too many rumors would start if he didn't present her tonight. She hoped she'd have time to relax first.

But one person was already waiting when they got to the dining room.

****

Swift Hawk turned from the window as they entered, his black eyes resting their gaze on Elizabeth's breasts. Dressed in his usual leggings, he had added a long leather tunic edged with fringe. He wore soft moccasins on his feet and had braided his hair with a dangling hawk's feather. He scowled at Cactus Flower.

"I see you adopt the white man's ways all too well."

She lifted her chin. "And you refuse to adopt them at all. *Don* Miguel has bought you a suit. Why don't you wear it?"

He ignored her and turned to Elizabeth, reaching to touch her hair. "Fire Woman. It is only because of you that I agreed to come to this table tonight. You will sit beside me."

She tried not to shrink back from him visibly. A menacing power emanated from him, almost the opposite of the magnetism she felt around Miguel. This was raw need and survival, like a lone lobo.

She took a slight step to the side, away from his touch, which only made him smile and step closer. This time, his fingers gripped her arm like steel talons. She repressed a shudder. What would Scarlett O'Hara do? Her head came up and her eyes flashed green fire. "Take your hand off me."

"You heard the lady, Hawk. Do it."

Elizabeth whirled at the sound of Miguel's voice and then inhaled sharply. If she'd thought he looked good—and she did—in Levis and a work shirt, the man striding toward her now was beyond the wildest fantasy she'd ever had.

He was dressed in black, except for a dazzlingly white starched shirt, which only set off his tan and dark eyes and hair. The roundabout jacket hugged his broad shoulders—she hadn't really noticed before just how broad they were—and tapered at the waist, just above his taut flat belly. Soft leather pants fit his thigh muscles like a second skin, flaring enough at the bottom to fit over hand-tooled boots. The leather rippled as he walked, leaving Elizabeth aching to run her hands over it and—

what? Unzip his pants? She felt herself blush. The men she conjured up in her dreams were hot enough, but Miguel was making her sizzle and he hadn't even touched her. What was wrong with her?

And then he was beside her, smelling of fresh soap and a slightly spicy after-shave. Even clean-shaven, there was no denying the shadowy darkness where the stubble would be tomorrow morning. She wondered what his cheek would feel like against hers.

"You'll sit next to me," he said and took her elbow to guide her towards the head of the table.

He pulled out the chair for her, and as she sat down, the crinoline's hoop caught and pushed her skirt up, exposing her thighs.

Miguel's mouth twitched as he blocked Swift Hawk's view with his body and pushed down the hoop. "For my part, you could hike your skirt to your hips and I'd be pleased, but I'd better get you some dresses that don't pose such a danger. No sense having our guests know you're a working girl. I'd rather that be our little secret."

Her lust turned its heat into hurt and she jerked her skirt away from him. He would never believe her. Even if he did shield her from Swift Hawk's view, he was only being nice because he thought he could bed her, like one of Lily's girls. "I won't be staying."

His eyebrow went up. "And where will you go?"

"Home. Back to the twenty…"

He leaned toward her so quickly that her nose burrowed into his hair as he whispered in her ear. "Do *not*, repeat *not*, bring up this craziness tonight. These men are officers. They *do* have the power to have you locked away." He straightened, his eyes intent on hers.

Elizabeth swallowed hard, her nose still mesmerized by the softness of his hair and its fresh, clean scent. Did the man have to be so sexy? He was right, although she hated to admit it. He was trying to protect her—if only he would just believe her.

"All right. I have amnesia; I don't know what happened to me or where I'm from." She looked up at him suddenly. "So am I going to stay here then, until I 'remember' something? Are you going to keep me?"

His eyes flickered with amusement, although he did not smile. "Keeping you, Red, is exactly what I plan to do."

****

God, she was lovely, especially when her eyes flashed in anger. Miguel enjoyed goading her just to see it. Such passion. He wondered how wild she would get in the throes of lovemaking. He wanted to find out. First, to taste her nectar, then to suck on the nub, bringing her to the peak of ecstasy. She'd wrap her legs around him, arch her back to take him, beg for more, and he would honor that request, drawing out her pleasure until her body trembled and shuddered in his arms, every nerve ending crying for release. An unusual sensation surged through him—he wanted to make her forget every other man who'd ever bedded her.

Or even flirted with her. Seated at the dinner table, he watched as the lawyer from Virginia—Tate Johnson had brought him along—talked to her. He didn't like at all the way the man's eyes kept glancing at her breasts. Miguel frowned. Those breasts were too exposed. Thank the gods the wives hadn't attended this dinner. He hoped Elizabeth wasn't being taken in with all the flattery the dandy was passing out. Christ, he hadn't heard such flowery speeches since he'd attended a Shakespearean play in New Orleans with Elena on their honeymoon.

"You not only have a beautiful face, Miss Elizabeth, I find your mind fascinating," the lawyer, Beauregard Cartier, was saying. "Imagine thinking the South could do away with slavery!"

"But they will," Elizabeth said earnestly. "In a few more years—"

Miguel reached under the table and placed his hand on her thigh, shocking her into silence. He longed to let his fingers glide upward, but this was not the time.

She gave him a sideways look and then turned back to the lawyer. "What I meant was that perhaps it is somewhat inhumane to own other people. Don't you think black people have rights?"

"Blacks?" he asked. "You mean darkies?" He laughed. "No, ma'am. We've always bought, sold and traded them, just like livestock."

Miguel could see the warning signs in her eyes that he was becoming accustomed to. He squeezed the soft flesh of her leg through the satin dress in warning.

Her breathing hitched and he felt her hand trying to push his away. He managed to keep from grinning as he caught her fingers and intertwined them with his. She tugged once, but then returned to her conversation. She was tenacious, he had to give her that.

"They're humans. You don't have the right to own another person."

Colonel Johnson leaned forward across the table. "Miguel tells us you don't remember where you're from, but ma'am, I don't think you understand slavery. I've got a cotton plantation that needs those people to work it. I treat them well, I provide for them. They have food.

They have clothes. When they're sick, a doctor attends them. Why, they wouldn't know what to do if I freed them. And who would pick the cotton?"

Elizabeth was ignoring the pressure Miguel was putting on her hand. He had to admire her. The woman was stubborn if she believed in something. And she obviously felt strongly about the slaves. His great-grandfather hadn't taken to the idea of slavery either, and they'd never owned any, but they weren't farmers. They were ranchers and he paid his *vaqueros* for their work. The Mexicanos from south of the Rio Grande were a proud people who had come freely to him.

"You *hire* people to pick your cotton. You *pay* them. Free your—darkies—and pay them, and I'll bet you'll get more production and more yield per acre," Elizabeth declared.

Silence met her statement and Miguel groaned inwardly. Colonel Johnson was a powerful man and not used to being dressed down, especially by a woman and, it seemed, an intelligent one. How did she know anything about crops? She probably consorted with more than one rich landowner. He didn't dare squeeze Elizabeth's fingers any harder, afraid he'd break one of them, but he had to get her to cease this line of conversation. For her sake.

"Fire Woman is right," Swift Hawk said from the far end of the table.

All heads turned to him. The Indian was rarely seen when the soldiers visited and he talked even less. Even now, he nearly sneered at them.

"She is right," he said again. "My own people fight for their freedom to stay off the reservations the white man provides. It, too, is a form of slavery."

"Now, son," Colonel Johnson said firmly, "that's not the same at all. We have made treaties with your people."

"You have taken our land," Swift Hawk answered.

"It's the government's land. First Spain, then Mexico, and now the Republic of Texas. We have provided for you to remain on it."

"It was our land before the white man came." Swift Hawk leapt to his feet. "It will remain forever ours. Our ancestors' spirits sent Fire Woman here. She is right. You will see." He turned and walked from the room so swiftly he seemed to have vanished into thin air.

Miguel released Elizabeth's hand with one more squeeze. He hoped she would remain quiet. Enough damage had been done.

"Gentlemen," he said, "May I suggest we retreat to *la sala* for French cognac and cigars?"

As the men nodded their heads and pushed back from the table, Miguel bent down to Elizabeth. She stared at him defiantly.

"I did nothing wrong."

He cupped her chin in his hand. "You and I are going to have a long talk. Later." He let his thumb graze the contour of her cheek lightly before he straightened. "So either you wait up for me or I'll come to you wherever you are."

****

Elizabeth took a deep breath, glad to be rid of the corset. Cactus Flower had assured her the soldiers would not expect either of them to reappear for the evening and the meetings that went on behind closed doors lasted well into the night, so Elizabeth had changed into the plain homespun she had worn earlier.

As much as she wanted to explore the huge *casa,* she didn't think Miguel would want her to bring any more attention to herself by wandering around. Still, this was a magnificent home, a far cry from the chinked and daubed double-room log cabins and shotgun houses she'd seen in the history books. The dining room furniture had been real mahogany Chippendale. To her surprise, the house even had indoor plumbing, although bathwater was still hauled to the large wooden tubs in the dressing rooms. She had noticed a pump by the kitchen sink earlier, too.

She took a back staircase and let herself into a room near the rear of the house and looked around. Miguel's study. Oil lamps burned softly in each corner. A huge fireplace filled most of one wall and bookshelves lined the other three. A large lamb's wool rug covered most of the hardwood floor. In the center of the room stood a huge black walnut desk, polished to a sheen. Behind it was a well-padded leather chair and, in front, two overstuffed horsehair armchairs.

Elizabeth wandered along the shelves of books and stopped in front of a shelf that had to do with Indian tribes. Some of the books were historical, regarding territories and conflicts that had arisen since pioneers had begun moving westward. They would make for interesting reading, having been written from a late-eighteenth-century viewpoint. She took down a slim volume simply titled *Legends*, opened it to a story of the dream catcher and began reading.

I am the maker of dreams and the weaver of spells.

Once, a young, white woman was captured by the Comanche and brought to their camp by a handsome young warrior named Black Eagle. Meant as a prize for his father, the shaman, her hair was the color of copper, reflecting the life force of Fire. Such a woman would bring much power to a man. But this was an ill-fated match, never meant to happen.

The shaman had other ideas. Bad ones. Mingling Fire with Earth would please the Great Spirit and their tribe would be blessed in keeping their land and not be forced onto a reservation. He laid the girl on a herkee, a brush arbor frame made of poles, binding her hands and feet and slashing them, so her blood might drip slowly into the ground, solidifying the bond. She lay all day under the grueling sun.

Black Eagle had fallen in love with her while she was his captive and tried to ease her pain and bring her drink. He was beaten for it.

Hers was an ancient soul. Weakly, she called me by the name her Celtic ancestors knew: Brighid. Swiftly, I found Black Eagle. "Go to her again," I said, my voice just a whisper on the breeze that gently brushed his face. "If the shaman wants fire, I shall provide it."

The sun dipped then, its slanting rays emblazoning the maiden's head, sparking flames which sprang to the ground, the fiery tongues forming a circle around the bier.

"Go," I whispered again. "The flame will be cool, 'tis but an illusion."

Black Eagle didn't question me, although I was unseen. The wall of fire produced much smoke, hiding their escape. I watched as they rode away, satisfied these two, who had known each other in other lifetimes, would finally fulfill their love. What is intended must be.

And then I brought the rains down, heavy and hard, sloughing the road into a murky quagmire, making pursuit impossible, even for the swift-footed Comanche.

To this day, women with hair the color of fire are held both in awe and fear.

Comanche still see me in the smoke of the sacred pipe and the sweat of the Medicine Lodge. Dressed in white leather, with my own flame-colored hair braided, I come to them in peyote-laced dreams. In those dreams, wishes can come true. That is why I am known to them as Dream Catcher.

Elizabeth had not read that myth before, only thinking of dream-catchers whose webs were supposed to keep bad dreams from children. She smiled as she closed the book and placed it back on the shelf. It would make good reading for another time.

She continued looking at titles on the shelves. Some of the books were practical: cattle and horse breeding, architecture and building. She stopped again when she came to the second wall of leather-trimmed books. Miguel had classics here: Shakespeare, Homer, Chaucer, Cervantes. More modern writings too: Jonathan Swift, Alexander Pope, Robert Burns. Poetry? It seemed that *Don* Miguel was an educated man. Interesting. She had thought he only had a one-track mind that focused solely on women. Or, more precisely, bedding them.

She moved on and then stopped again. Sir Thomas Malory, Chrétien de Troys, Lord Tennyson. Arthurian legends. She smiled. These made more sense. Miguel shared the same sensual qualities that Lancelot, the ultimate Bad Boy, did. And the lesson, she reminded herself soberly, was to avoid such dangerously appealing men.

Elizabeth turned away and rubbed her arms for warmth, for the night was turning chilly, and then noticed the kindling already laid for a fire. She walked over to the hearth and picked up the tinderbox. How did they start fires in the mid-1800s? Surely not by still using flint! To her relief, she found wooden matches, but what to strike them on? She experimented on the tile with no luck. She tried again on the rougher adobe brick of the fireplace; the match broke. On her third attempt, a spark sputtered and then flamed. She grinned triumphantly and ignited the kindling beneath the logs, watching it catch, spreading upward with crackles of blue and yellow and orange. A faint pine scent filled the room, and then she saw the pinecones thrown in with the wood. Olga's doing, maybe? Anyway, it reminded Elizabeth that Christmas was just a week away. Would she be back in the twenty-first century by then?

She moved over to the credenza next to the fireplace. A bottle of French cognac and a crystal goblet stood on a silver platter next to a tiered candelabra. She considered lighting the candles but decided not to push her luck with lighting another match. She undid the stopper on the brandy, poured herself a generous portion, and then nearly choked on the first swallow, the fiery liquid burning a searing path to her stomach.

"Swirl and sniff, then you sip," Miguel said from the doorway.

She whipped her head around. Miguel leaned against the doorframe, one leg bent, the foot crossed over the other. His shirt was open at the throat and he had his jacket flipped over his shoulder, hooked on one finger. Strands of dark hair fell down across his forehead. Elizabeth inhaled sharply, ignoring the heat flaring through her body that had nothing to do with the brandy. She couldn't help but think Lancelot would have met his match with Miguel.

He moved into the room, tossing the jacket on one of the chairs and came to her. "Here." he said as he covered her hand with his and swirled the golden liquid lightly. "Now, sip slowly."

She wasn't sure she could swallow, as conscious as she was of his touch. How could his hand be so hot? Then she caught his look of amusement and reminded herself he knew exactly what he was doing. She wasn't about to be seduced. No way. She took a gulp. Tears sprang to her eyes but she kept from gasping.

Miguel shook his head and took the glass from her and set it on the table. "You don't have to fight me on everything, Red."

"What do you mean?" Her voice was raspy, her throat raw from the liquor.

He gave her a lopsided smile. "I can tell when a woman is attracted to me."

Her face flamed and she was very glad she had her back to the fire so she was in silhouette. Was she that transparent or did he expect women to fall at his feet? Probably. With an effort, she ignored the remark and moved toward the bookcase. "I must say, I'm surprised at your collection."

He came to stand behind her and reached around her shoulder to tap the leather trim on the Shakespearean book. Although he didn't touch her, Elizabeth could feel his seductively mesmerizing presence. Too late, she realized she was trapped between the bookcase and his incredibly muscular body.

"These were my mother's books," he said. "She used to read them to me when I was a child."

"Your mother read Shakespeare and Homer to

you?" Elizabeth turned around in surprise. *Whoops. Bad move.* Their bodies brushed against each other. She swallowed. "Most children grow up on Grimm's Fairy Tales."

"Whose?"

She bit her lip. *Another twenty-first century thing.* "You wouldn't know. They haven't been written yet."

Miguel sighed. "You're going to keep up that pretense? You almost said too much tonight at dinner. The colonel is a straight-thinking man, not given to foolishness. You need to be careful."

"Well, I'm sure you won't mind groping me again if I say something inappropriate," Elizabeth said with a trace of sarcasm.

He ignored her tone. "Did you like it?"

She turned back to the bookcase. No way was he going to know how much she had enjoyed having his hand on her thigh and those strong, callused fingers intertwined with hers. And when he'd rubbed his thumb in her palm— "Did your mother read the Arthurian legends to you, too?"

"Of course. I even had a wooden sword I played with. I would run around the place shouting, 'I'm King Arthur and this is Excalibur!' to anyone who would listen."

She looked up at him, trying to envision him as a child. "Arthur? You mean Lancelot, don't you?"

"Why do you say that?"

As if he didn't know! Elizabeth refrained from rolling her eyes—she did owe him some courtesy. "Because you're every bit as much of womanizer as he was."

Miguel shook his head. "I think Lancelot has been

much maligned by history. I doubt he chased women at all. His love for Gwenevere was too strong. More likely, Arthur, being king, tumbled a wench or two when he felt like it."

She tilted her head, considering what he'd said. Suddenly, she laughed. "And you thought you were Arthur? I rest my case."

A glint came into his eyes and she knew she was in a danger zone. That sensuous mouth was only inches from hers. In a near panic, she turned her back to him and studied the books again. "When I saw these, I thought you were an educated man."

"I am. Harvard. Didn't cotton to the Easterners, though. I like Texas and the wide open spaces."

Elizabeth inhaled sharply as he stepped closer to her and put his hands lightly on her shoulders. Dear Lord, what was it about his touch that inflamed her body so? She felt as though a hundred tiny arrows had pricked her skin. Then he laid his head beside hers, his breath warm in her ear.

"There's some education that can't be learned in school," he whispered and let his hands glide slowly down her back and rest at her waist.

Elizabeth's knees went weak and for a moment she thought they wouldn't support her. Sweet Mary! Was she going to swoon like ladies did back in the 1800s?

He encircled her waist and pulled her back against him. "I like experienced women who know what they want. Let me make love to you, Red," he said as he lightly nibbled her ear and then softly kissed the nape of her neck.

She shuddered in response, her traitorous body not obeying her mind. How had he known that was her most vulnerable spot? Good thing he was holding her, for her legs had definitely given out. He had taken an open stance, one of his thighs on either side of hers, and nudged his hard erection between her buttocks. *Was all of that him?* She tried to wiggle free, which was a mistake. A really big mistake. He slid one of his hands over her belly, pressing her to him. She felt a sudden gush of wetness between her thighs and trembled in his arms.

"Ah," he murmured and laved her ear. "I knew you'd like this. You'll probably even remember who you are."

Who she was? Or what she was? Elizabeth felt as though she'd been doused with a bucket of icy water from the horse trough outside. She had almost forgotten he still thought she was a hooker. Nothing more. With an effort, she pulled his hands away. "Stop. Now."

"What?"

"You heard me." She turned and put both of her hands against his broad chest and pushed. "Get away from me. You think I'm a whore."

Annoyance flickered over his face, but he stepped back. "Fine, Red. I don't force myself on any woman, even a working one. By the way, I don't think of them as whores. But what else could you be, with what you were wearing this morning?"

Elizabeth could feel the tears welling up in her eyes. "I told you I was a teacher and I don't know how I got here! All I want to do is get back to my own life and my own time!" She turned and ran for the door. "Why won't you believe me?"

****

Miguel rubbed his jaw thoughtfully as he watched

her go. Confound it, but the woman was confusing. He knew she'd wanted him; she wasn't trembling because she was cold. He'd felt her melt against him. So what was the problem? It wasn't like she was some vestal virgin from one of his mother's books—not with that tiny black see-through underwear.

But she did talk oddly, and she seemed perfectly convinced that the South would free the slaves. As if plantation owners would actually pay their workers. She had given the year Johnson Station would change its name and whoever that grim fairy was, as if fairies existed. Most of the time, though, she didn't sound crazy. But traveling through time?

He thought back to his conversation with Lily about the girl who thought she was Gwenevere. What he'd said tonight was true. His mother had loved the Arthurian legends and spoken of Merlin's magic.

He'd heard a Buddhist monk once, at Harvard, talking about reincarnation. Could the kind of love Lancelot and Gwenevere had pass through time? If it could, was time-travel possible?

He shook his head and finished off the brandy. Lily was right. If he started thinking like that, then he was the one who was crazy.

One way or another, he would find out who Elizabeth O'Malley really was.

Chapter Six—Mistletoe and Holly

Elizabeth opened one eye and squinted at the morning sun streaming through her window and across her face. Slowly, she turned her head. The porcelain chamber set stood on the hewn oak dresser along one wall, an empty wardrobe beside it. On the other side of the room were a small table and two chairs and a brazier. The coals had gone out during the night and the room was cold. She pulled the patchwork quilt up under her chin and snuggled down into the big four-poster bed.

This was the second morning she'd awakened here, still in 1849. This was no dream. By the time she'd gotten up yesterday morning, Miguel was already gone. A part of her felt relieved since her mind, not to mention her senses, went into total confusion when she was around him. Yet she really wanted to see him again. Could any man be that sexy? Maybe she had just out-fantasized herself. Her brain was probably addled with whatever had taken place when she time-traveled. Most likely, Miguel was just an ordinary-looking man. She had to admit he was also kind.

One person wasn't a fantasy, though. Swift Hawk. She'd gone to the barn to look at the magnificent Andalusian stallion again yesterday, and the young man had come up behind her so stealthily she didn't know he was there until he stroked her hair. If the foreman hadn't come in right then, she didn't know what would have happened. The Indian's black eyes held a lust that promised his retreat was only temporary.

Again she wondered how she'd gotten here. And how she'd get back. She picked up the fetish from the bedside table. Was there magic here? Could she use it?

A knock on her door interrupted her thoughts. Olga entered, accompanied by two of the housemaids. One carried coal for the brazier and the other a steaming pitcher of hot water for the basin.

"You'd better wash up and come downstairs," Olga said. "Yesterday we let you sleep in, but life on a ranch begins at dawn, and Miguel's been waiting on you for an hour. He's got the buckboard ready."

Elizabeth laid the fetish down, sat up, and swung her legs over the edge of the bed. "Waiting? Why?"

"He's taking you into Johnson Station for some ready-mades. I told him to let you pick out the material for some dresses. Lord knows what he'd come back with." Elizabeth padded across the wooden floor to the basin of hot water and lifted the soap from its dish, surprised by its smooth texture. She'd read that soap in the 1800s was made with waste fat and lye, a product derived when rain seeped through the ashes that were deposited in a hopper outside. She sniffed appreciatively. No lye. "I didn't know soaps were scented in the 1800s."

Olga gave her an odd look and shooed the maids out. "Miguel told me you have odd ideas about where you came from. More than likely, it's the knock on the head you took. Still, it'd be better not to talk like that." She turned and moved to the door. "I'll save you some deer sausage and biscuits with sawmill gravy."

Elizabeth quickly washed her face and hands and donned the homespun she'd worn the past two days.

Maybe she could get some jeans and work shirts at the store. She wasn't used to wearing all these layers: hose and garters and bloomers, a chemise and then the dress. She held up a long narrow strip of linen. Cactus Flower had told her it was a binding cloth, used to hold her breasts up when she wasn't wearing a corset. She grimaced. Her lace bra may not be that practical, but it was a lot more comfortable. She tossed the material aside and hurried down the stairs.

Miguel sat by the kitchen table, drinking coffee from a clay mug, the fingers of one hand drumming the table. She caught her breath. No fantasy on her part after all. This morning he wore a chambray work shirt, the pale blue setting off his tan even more. Could a sculptor have crafted a more perfectly chiseled face?

Elizabeth hesitated in the doorway, recalling the way those tapping fingers had slowly and sensually slid down her back last night and how she had felt in his muscular arms. Her knees turned wobbly and then she remembered. He thought she was a prostitute. It was the only reason he had taken such liberties with her. Better to remember she'd resolved to stay away from good-looking men too. Thank goodness he'd been in Fort Worth all day yesterday on business and she hadn't seen him until dinner. And then later, in his study—

"Time's wastin', Red. Are you going to come in?"

"I'm not really hungry. We can just go, if you want. That way you can get back to your work." She knew she sounded stiff, but what else was there to say?

He shrugged and stood. For the first time, she noticed he had a gun strapped to his thigh. She hadn't noticed one the day before.

Miguel opened the door and they walked out to

where the horses were harnessed to a real buckboard with long benches that ran the length of the wagon. At least seeing authentic items on this adventure was gratifying. Briefly, she wondered why they had not taken one of the buggies that stood near the barn. She raised her foot to the running board and promptly snagged her bloomers on the braking stick, causing her dress to slide up. Embarrassed, she tugged at the skirt and took hold of the back of the driver's seat to scramble up.

"Ouch!" She slid back down, a splinter in her finger. She sucked the drop of blood off.

Miguel's gaze lingered on her finger in her mouth before he reached for her hand. "Let me see."

Gingerly, she rested her hand in his, trying not to notice the warmth already spreading up her arm from his touch.

He squinted and then gently applied pressure, working two of his fingers up toward the splinter. "Sorry. This may hurt," he said and then with a final push, the splinter popped out.

It did hurt, but only a little. Elizabeth quickly pulled her hand from his as he began to raise it to his mouth. No way was she going to be able to stand his sucking at her finger without her knees buckling. She was already acting as helpless as one of Scarlett O'Hara's mealy-mouthed sisters.

She turned and reached for the seat. Did the step have to be so high? Her skirt was hiking up again and this time Miguel laughed. No doubt he'd like to see her entire thigh, too! She blushed, remembering he'd seen a lot more than that.

"Allow me," Miguel said as he put his hands around her waist and lifted her into the driver's seat. He climbed up beside her. "I do want to get you back and forth in one piece." He looked up at the sky and frowned. "Cloud bank rolling in from the north."

He lifted the reins and the wagon lurched down the road, causing her to fall against him. Did he have to feel so rock-solid hard? She had no idea these wagons were so unsteady, rolling from one side to the other. She bounced off him again. Miguel looked straight ahead, but a corner of his mouth twitched. He was probably laughing at her, well aware of what this wagon would do. She clung to the side of the seat, resolved not to lean into him. But God, he felt good.

****

So this was Johnson Station. Arlington in her day. Elizabeth craned her neck as Miguel stopped the horses in front of a sign that read General Store. Across the street were the public stables and smithy. Farther down the road, leading out of town, were a sorghum mill and a gristmill. Beyond that, a cotton gin. She remembered the Colonel saying he owned a cotton plantation. She turned in her seat to look in the other direction. A saloon sat squarely on the corner and farther out she could see rows of log cabins, neatly laid out along dirt streets.

"Where's the mineral well?" she asked.

"What mineral well?"

"Arlington has a well in the middle of town." She turned, sensing her directions and then pointed north. "That way. It was supposed to be a town well, but the mineral water was therapeutic."

Miguel frowned. "Are you talking about the future again? That bump on your head must be worse than I thought."

Elizabeth sighed. "I'm trying to make you see. Is

there a cemetery?"

"Nope. There's a Boot Hill near here, at Marrow Bone Spring."

"Well, there will be a cemetery at the corner of Cooper and Mayfield. It's still there in the twenty-first century." She could tell by the look on his face he thought she had totally lost it, but she doggedly went on. "Do you know a woman named Elizabeth Robinson?"

He stared at her. "Yes. Do you? Is your memory coming back?"

She shook her head. "No. Mrs. Robinson's marker is the oldest one still standing. From 1863."

Miguel pushed his hat back. "You tell fortunes? Is that what you did with some traveling show?"

"No! I'm telling you—"

"Don't." Miguel stepped down from the buckboard and turned back to her. "Your mental condition will only get worse if you continue to make up these stories." He held out his hands. "Let me help you down."

"I can do it myself."

"Probably, but I'd rather not see you sprawled in the mud," Miguel answered.

Before she could stop him, she felt his hands go around her waist again, lifting her as though she weighed nothing more than air. She slid down the length of him as he set her on the ground and he made no effort to release her. Sweet Mary! Here they were on a public street and he was making full body contact with her. And he was hard *there*. For just one second, she closed her eyes in bliss and then opened them and pushed away from him. "Behave yourself."

He grinned. "What was I doing?"

Ignoring that, she turned from him and marched up

the steps to the general store, leaving him to follow in her wake, chuckling.

She stopped inside the store, dazed. It was crammed full, from floor to ceiling, with only narrow walkways between the wares. Food goods, from blackstrap molasses to bins of pinto beans and barrels of pickles, were to her right. Salt, sugar, spices, flour, tea, coffee. On her left were tools, everything from hemp rope to shovels and saws and axes. In one corner, inside a locked glass cabinet, guns were displayed, and along the far wall were the dry goods. Bolts of materials and sewing supplies covered several tables. Behind them hung men's working clothes and boots and the "ready-mades."

The mingled smells were enticing. Tart vinegar from the pickles, spicy cinnamon and the heady scent of sage by the condiments, and a delightful aroma near the coffee beans. A slightly acrid smell from near the rope and a more musty odor near the dry goods. A real "General Store." It had everything.

The store lacked ventilation, and dusty rays of sunlight danced through the door as Miguel followed her in.

"Okay, Red. Shop away. You'll need enough material for several dresses and something for Sunday. Pick out a couple of ready-mades, too."

"What I really want is some Levis, a work shirt and a pair of boots."

"You want what?"

"Pants," Elizabeth said. "They're so much easier to move in."

"Ladies don't wear pants in these parts," Miguel answered.

"I'm not from—"

"Stop it. All right. Get the pants." Miguel looked around as if to see if anyone had heard. "One pair. And you wear them only when I say you can."

She rolled her eyes. "I'll wear them when I want to. Like horseback riding."

He sighed. "You're telling me you ride astride like a man?"

"Yes." Suddenly, Elizabeth smiled mischievously. "If I'm going to be stuck in this century, I want to learn to herd cattle, go on the roundups, attend the branding—"

"*No*. Absolutely not."

"*Yes*. Absolutely."

He scowled at her and then turned and walked away. Elizabeth grinned to herself as she selected two dresses, some undergarments, and fabrics. Maybe he was a softy under all that macho? Anyway, she loved horses. Why not make the most of living history?

The clerk was wrapping her items in brown paper and tying them with string when Miguel reappeared. He had a copy of *Godey's Lady's Book* with him. Opening it, he flipped it around for the clerk to see.

"Order this. In red."

The young man's eyes popped and his cheeks turned color. She pulled the book toward her and gasped.

The woman in the drawing was wearing a satin evening gown, its bodice fitted to her, the waist nipped in, the skirt clinging to her hips. And it was cut low. Very low. More than half of her breasts were exposed as were most of her shoulders.

"I can't wear that," Elizabeth said. "It's indecent."

Miguel smiled, a glitter in his eyes. "The pants are indecent, too. Wear the pants, you'll have to wear the dress too. I get to say when."

Elizabeth sighed. She had been wrong. Male chauvinism was alive and well in this century. But she was his guest and it was his money. She needed those pants. Let him order it. He couldn't force her to wear that dress. Could he? The idea of his stripping her, then dressing her himself left her almost gasping for air. She recovered.

"Two pairs of pants," she said to the clerk.

Miguel grinned and flipped the book back. "Order another one of these in black."

****

When they returned from their trip, Raul was waiting for them, hopping from one foot to the other in excitement.

"I thought you'd never come home! Are we going to go and get the tree now?"

"Tree?" Elizabeth asked.

"It's Christmas, remember?" Miguel said. "Family tradition. We all pile in the buckboard and go find a pine tree. There's some piney woods east of here, about halfway to a little settlement called Dallas."

"Little?" Elizabeth asked. "You should see it—"

He cut her off with a glance, then looked at the sky again. The horizon was an ominous charcoal. "Looks like we're in for a blue norther. We'd best dress warm."

They ate a hurried lunch and then everyone—Olga, Olaf, Raul, Cactus Flower—climbed into the wagon. Even Brina managed to jump in, her tail pounding enthusiastically on the floorboards. To Elizabeth's dismay, Swift Hawk came too, managing to sit next to her on the long bench. For once, she wished Miguel had asked her to ride shotgun, but his son was in the seat next to him, bouncing happily.

The ride took nearly two hours, most of it over rough dirt and caliche roads. This time it was Swift Hawk who kept sliding against her and she was pretty sure he was doing it on purpose since she had seen how gracefully he could move when he wanted to.

Olga started singing Christmas carols, her voice a soothing alto. Olaf joined her and so did Raul. By the start of the second song, Miguel had added his rich baritone. Shyly, Elizabeth began to sing, hoping she would remember the words. Her own family didn't ever do this. Her father usually worked the streets since crime was high during the holiday season, and her mother was too intellectually involved with whatever project she was working on. "Christmas is all about commercialism," she'd said more than once.

Only Swift Hawk did not join in. He closed his eyes and began to rock to some silent rhythm of his own. Cactus Flower looked worriedly at him and then at Elizabeth, but Elizabeth ignored it. She was beginning to have fun.

When they arrived at the woods, Raul jumped down and ran excitedly to the trees, examining first one and then another. The adults climbed down more slowly, Olaf helping his wife down. Cactus Flower leapt nimbly to the ground—were all Indians so lithe and limber?—and Miguel held out his hand to Elizabeth, but before she could take it, she felt Swift Hawk's arm encircle her waist and her legs dangled in the air as he stepped down with her. His arm was like iron and she felt like a sack of flour. Furiously, she righted herself and planted her feet on the ground, but he didn't release her.

"Fire Woman. You are mine."

Miguel's eyes glittered dangerously and he took a step toward them, but she managed to push away from Swift Hawk. "I am not yours. You're young enough to be one of my high school students."

He looked puzzled. "What is high school?"

She opened her mouth to reply, but Miguel took her arm quickly. "Let's go look for a tree."

Just then, a whoop came from Raul. "I've found one, *Papá*! This is it!"

Everyone but Swift Hawk hurried over to him, Olaf bringing the ax, and the incident was quickly forgotten in the excitement of examining the tree from every angle. Everyone gave their opinion on it before Miguel took the ax, felling it in three strokes.

As they were returning to the *hacienda,* the norther blew in with the full fury of a brutal winter storm. Dark clouds scudded across the sky, dipping menacingly lower, as the wind picked up and howled. By the time they reached home, it was starting to sleet.

"Brrr!" Elizabeth said, rubbing her hands together as Miguel built a fire in the hearth of the main *sala.* Olga went to work making hot chocolate while Olaf put the tree in its stand.

Cactus Flower and Raul hauled the ornaments in from the storage shed, allowing some of the cold air to enter whenever they opened the door. Soon, though, the room was bustling with everyone stringing cranberries and popcorn on the tree, laughingly arguing about where each ornament should go. Olga decorated the mantel with holly. The fire leapt up, dancing in flames of red and blue, warming the room with its glow. Outside, snow began to fall as twilight descended.

Elizabeth watched Miguel with his son, hoisting him

up to put the angel on the top of the tree. He really was a good father. She thought again about how different this family was from hers. And they were a family—she could feel the love that Olga and Olaf had for Miguel and Raul. Even Cactus Flower seemed to enjoy being included. Luckily, Swift Hawk had gone back to the bunkhouse, so there was nothing to break Elizabeth's good mood. She basked in the sensation of togetherness, something she hadn't had since her father had been killed.

The next few days passed quickly, and presents began to appear under the tree. Some even had her name on them. Miguel had gone to San Antonio and Swift Hawk took full advantage to be at her side, sitting beside her at dinner, even though Olaf kept a watchful eye on him. He'd followed her to the barn again, too, and she decided the horses would have to wait until Miguel returned. Instead, she helped Olga bake cookies and found she actually enjoyed working in the kitchen. She couldn't recall her mother ever baking cookies.

Miguel returned home late the afternoon of Christmas Eve, just as the snow began again, this time falling softly in big, wet flakes. After supper, they all gathered together and lit the candles on the tree and sang more Christmas carols. For their final song, they stood in a circle, holding hands, Miguel on one side of her, Cactus Flower on the other. Elizabeth did not think she had ever heard "Silent Night" done so beautifully as from that little group of people who all loved each other. She felt happy tears building. This was what Christmas was supposed to be about. The 1800s were beginning to feel a lot more comfortable. After all, what did she have to go back to at home? She began to wonder if her stay would be permanent.

****

Miguel was sitting in front of the glowing embers of the hearth when Elizabeth walked into the room after helping Olga finish the dishes.

"Join me," he said, patting the seat beside him on the sofa.

Elizabeth hesitated. The evening had been so pleasant and he had been such a gentleman. She didn't want to start sparring with him again. Not tonight.

He held up a second glass of red wine. "I bought this in San Antonio. It's imported from Spain. Quite mellow. You'll like it better than the cognac."

She sat down gingerly on the edge of the sofa and accepted the glass. Miguel gave her a lopsided smile.

"I won't bite unless you want me to."

The idea of being bitten by him was titillating. "Really?" the woman in her whispered, *It would depend on where—* She felt herself blush and was glad the light from the fire only cast her in shadow. It seemed her mind ran in only one direction lately.

"I bought you something," he said and slid out a package from behind him.

"We're not supposed to open our presents until tomorrow morning," Elizabeth said. "Raul will be furious if he finds out."

Miguel arched an eyebrow. "I don't think Raul needs to know about this one."

She looked at him suspiciously as she picked up the package and undid the wrapping. Black lace and silk. She lifted the garment up by its thin straps and then gasped and dropped it back into its wrapping. It was an exquisite, delicate sleeping gown, sexy beyond words.

"What were you thinking?"

He grinned. "Do you really want me to answer that?"

She felt heat rush to her face even though the fire burned low in the hearth. "I can't accept this." Even as she said the words, her fingers stroked the fine silk that flowed over her hand like water. She took a breath. "I won't wear it."

"Sure you will. One night for me."

That prostitute thing again. That's what he was thinking of, and all because he'd never seen a bra and thong before. She bridled. "I will not." She laid the gown down and stood up to leave.

Miguel took a sip of wine. "If you don't take it with you, I'll leave it right here for everyone to see in the morning."

She looked at him, horrified. "You can't do that to Raul!"

Miguel shrugged. "He's a boy. He'll have to learn sometime about girls."

"He's seven!"

"Then take it with you."

She wasn't going to win this one, although she wasn't even sure what she considered to be "a win" anymore. What an infuriating man he was! She snatched the package and stomped to the door of the hallway leading to her room.

"Elizabeth?"

She stopped in the doorway. He never called her that. She turned. "What?"

He set his wine glass down and walked over to her. He stopped, his broad-shouldered body towering over her, so close she could feel his male heat, his scent like an aphrodisiac.

"Just this." He pointed upwards.

She tilted her head up. Mistletoe. It hadn't been there before. And then his lips were on hers as he ran his fingers through her hair and held her head in place. He kept the pressure gentle, kissing first her upper lip, sucking lightly on the lower one, then taking her mouth fully with his.

Elizabeth felt her stomach flutter like the fast, sinking feeling she had on a downhill rollercoaster. How could a kiss be so soft and so totally sensual? And so slow? If men only knew what slow did for a woman—Obviously, Miguel did, for he was taking his time, keeping his kisses deliberately easy. And then his tongue lightly traced the outline of her puffy lips, seeking entrance.

She parted her lips and gave a low groan as his tongue explored her mouth, just as slow and leisurely as his kisses had been. And then, just as she was ready to melt into him, needing to meld with him, to press her breasts against him, he withdrew, giving her one slow final kiss before he stepped back.

Elizabeth was left gasping, her lips swollen and needy. *Why did he stop?* She opened her eyes to find him watching her.

"A kiss is all that's allowed with mistletoe," he said. "If you want more, you'll have to ask me. Nicely."

"Ask you?" She couldn't believe her ears.

"Nicely. And you'll have to wear the gown."

That did it. By far, he was the most arrogant man—Elizabeth took a deep breath to calm her wildly beating heart. "I will not ask…ask?" She held up the negligee. "And I won't wear this either!" She turned and fled down the hall, only to hear his laughter trailing after her.

"You will," he called.

"Never," she said before she slammed her door.

Chapter Seven—The Rival

Miguel mucked out Diablo's stall with more gusto than usual, tossing the trampled straw into a wheelbarrow outside. Damn, but Elizabeth got to him. Not only was she physically beautiful with her emerald eyes, creamy skin and a body that curved into a man's hands perfectly, but she had an independence he grudgingly had to admit he admired. All he'd intended to do last night, under the mistletoe, was give her a slow, luxurious taste of what might be had. Instead, he'd nearly ripped her dress off when she pressed herself against him; it had taken every ounce of self-control to step back.

But she wasn't ready for him. He felt it. Whatever had happened to her was more serious than he first thought. He didn't think he could take another rebuff from her. So—he'd keep teasing her, tantalizing her with light touches and almost-kisses, taking every advantage that would leave her breathless and…frustrated. Yes. He wanted that. He wanted Elizabeth to come to him, wet and hot and willing, wearing those black things she'd had on, begging him to take her. And he would, slowly, creating exquisitely pleasant torture as he explored every inch of her body. He'd tear that small bottom piece of cloth off her with his teeth—

"No need to hit the far side of the wall with manure," Olaf said as he stopped by the stall door. "What's got you so all fired up?"

“Nothing,” Miguel answered and forced himself to scoop up the last bit slowly.

“You don’t say.” Olaf pulled a fresh blade of hay from a bale and stuck it between his teeth. “Might be that red-headed filly that’s got you gone coon?”

Miguel straightened. “I’m no goner. She’s just…interesting, that’s all, what with her stories about not knowing where she’s from.”

“Uh-huh. I ain’t seen you look so addled since Elena first arrived and you found out she was a beauty.”

Miguel smiled ruefully. Too bad “pretty” didn’t take care of everything. His loon-craziness hadn’t lasted long once his wife showed her true colors. “Nah. It’s just that what Elizabeth was wearing when I found her— Well, she’s got to be a working girl.”

“Maybe. Maybe not. You said Lily didn’t hire her.” Olaf squinted up at him and spit out the hay. “Could be she just means ‘no.’ Maybe she doesn’t cotton to you. You thought of that?”

A muscle tightened in Miguel’s jaw and his fingers clenched the shovel. Those were fighting words coming from most men, but Olaf just laughed.

“Them are the ones to watch for, boy. She’ll have you hog-tied and hunkered down before you know it.” He started out the door, then turned and winked. “I know. Olga did it to me.”

Miguel stared after him. There was no way that would happen. Elizabeth—because she had refused him twice and rarely did a woman do so even once—provided a challenge. That was all. A challenge. And he’d win. He always did.

****

Elizabeth walked into the stables a short time later,

dressed in her boots and jeans.

Swift Hawk followed her in so silently she jumped when he spoke at her elbow.

"Fire Woman. What brings you to the barn?" His black-eyed glance traveled down her denim-clad legs. "The Spirits have given you odd choices of clothes." Then he smiled, his eyes glittering. "I do not mind, though."

"Well, I do." Miguel stepped out from Diablo's stall and towered over her. "I told you not to go around dressed that way."

Elizabeth drew herself up to her full five foot six inches, yet her head hardly reached his shoulder and she had to crane to look up at him. Not exactly the best way to establish a power base. "Why not? It's practical."

"Because," Miguel said as he looked over at Swift Hawk, "it obviously causes a distraction. I can't protect you if the ranch hands can see all of your…ah, assets."

Elizabeth raised an eyebrow at him and inwardly smirked to see him look slightly guilty. Just like Raul when he stole a warm cookie off Olga's tray yesterday. "Women from my cent—" She stopped, aware that Swift Hawk was still there. "Women I know can take care of themselves. Anyway, how can I ride if I don't wear jeans?"

"We have a sidesaddle. Olga can get the seamstress to sew you a riding habit with a split skirt."

"Great. And how will I herd cattle in that?" Elizabeth put her hands on her hips.

"Simple," Miguel said and turned to begin saddling Diablo, who was impatiently stamping a hoof. "You won't."

She stared at him. Did he think she was going to plop

into the nineteenth century, on a Texas ranch, and not take the opportunities to experience history? Real cowboys doing real wrangler things? No way was she going to miss out on a real Old West experience. Maybe she would have to wheedle just a bit.

She gave a loud sigh. “I suppose you don’t think I can ride well enough to do it. Why don’t you let me ride one of these beautiful mares—Andalusians, aren’t they?—and I’ll show you.”

He looked at her in surprise. “What do you know about Andalusians?”

She knew her history. She’d researched the horses for an undergraduate paper she’d done on Lipizzaners and the Spanish Riding School of Austria. “Andalusians were bred from the Spanish Iberian horses and the invading Moorish Barb horses in the seventh century. William the Conqueror rode one in the Battle of Hastings. From the fifteenth century, they were known as premier war horses.” She reached up to pat Diablo’s soft muzzle and the stallion lowered his head and nickered.

Miguel cinched the saddle tight and studied her. “Do you know, also, that the bloodline is always kept pure? We allow no cross-breeding.” He looked at Swift Hawk. “Chief Jim Ned even offered to treaty for the use of one of our studs, but I have refused.”

“Our mustangs are strong,” Swift Hawk muttered. “It would be a good match. You should heed the chief.” With that, he turned and walked away noiselessly.

Elizabeth watched him leave. He always gave her an uneasy feeling. Whether it was his silent approaches or the look in his eyes, she didn’t know, but she always felt better when he was not present. She turned back to

Miguel.

"I'll prove to you that I can ride. Just point out which mare I can use."

He studied her and then went to one of the stalls and led a delicate, nearly white, mare out and tied her to the indoor rail. "Her name is *Plata*."

Elizabeth stroked the satiny neck and the mare turned her head, her large, limpid eyes watching Elizabeth. "Silver," Elizabeth said softly and gently rubbed behind an ear, under the halter. The mare bent her head, her neck cresting gracefully, and touched her muzzle to her knee. 'Ah, you're liking this, aren't you, girl?"

Miguel came back from the tack room with bridle and saddle.

"Let me do it," Elizabeth said. "She needs to get to know me." She took the horse blanket and laid it across the horse's back, high on the withers. Miguel lifted the saddle, but Elizabeth held out her hands.

"I said I'd do it."

He raised an eyebrow and then shrugged. "Whatever you say."

She was not prepared for the weight. Most saddles in her century had a plastic core under the leather, but this one was solid wood. She took a deep breath and struggled to raise it over the horse. She would show Miguel she could do this!

Then he was behind her, his arms coming around on either side, enclosing her in his warmth and unique man smell. She felt a wave of heat flash through her body. He was so close…and yet, he wasn't touching her. Would she ever stop reacting like this? If she turned around, would he kiss her? Much as she didn't want to admit it, she had lain awake most of the night, remembering how his sensual mouth had felt against hers.

But he merely adjusted the saddle and stepped back. Fumbling now, Elizabeth reached under the mare for the girth. Her hand shook so much she was sure the horse would feel it. She made quick work of looping the leather belt through the ring and tightening it. There. That was better.

Miguel had already done the bridle and handed her the reins. "Leg up?"

Elizabeth shook her head. "I can do it." Dear Lord, if he touched her calf, she'd never have the strength to mount. She stretched her leg, finding the stirrup. Taking hold of the mane and horn, she pulled herself up—rather gracefully, she thought—until the mare suddenly shied as a mouse scuttled across the floor. Wildly unbalanced, her weight not over the horse, Elizabeth began to lurch sideways.

Miguel steadied her, one hand clasping each buttock. She gasped as his fingers kneaded her soft flesh as he helped her back into the saddle, knowing her face was probably as red as a desert sunset. She looked away, but she could tell from the sound of his voice that he was amused.

"You have an interesting way of mounting," he said.

"I was fine until that mouse came dashing out."

He grinned and vaulted onto Diablo. "I'll have to thank the mouse, then."

Maddening man. Was there always an innuendo with him? Elizabeth was about to touch her heels to the mare, when he put a hand on her reins.

"Let's try you out in the paddock first."

"You don't think I can ride?"

"Plata can run like a gazelle. I don't want you flying off and hitting your head again."

Elizabeth gave him an exasperated look. "Fine."

They walked the horses to the enclosed area and Miguel swung down to open the gate. "Let's see what you can do."

Elizabeth tapped lightly with her heels and was rewarded with a sprightly trot. She'd never ridden a horse so smoothly gaited as this one. No bone-jarring jog here, only a fluid one-two-three-four rhythm. She pressed her heel again and the mare moved easily into a slow, rocking-chair canter, her neck arching gracefully. She was a sheer joy to ride. Elizabeth laid the right rein against her neck and tapped her left boot against Plata's flank. Immediately, the mare spun around, not breaking stride, and loped in the other direction.

Elizabeth slowed to a trot and did several figure eights before she halted in front of Miguel. "Can we come out now? I'd like to feel her run."

He nodded. "Let's make it interesting. See the tree just at the bend of the road? Once we're through the gates, I'll race you to it."

Already she was eager to feel this beautiful animal stretch out. "And if I win?"

"Your choice of reward."

It sounded too easy. Was that a smirk she saw on his face? "And if I lose?"

The smirk widened into a grin. "I get to choose."

She stared at him. Surely, he didn't mean…he wouldn't really expect…would he? Her hands shook a little and the mare twitched her ears. He had said Plata could run—

He was watching her intently, his eyes serious above

the easy smile. Fire and ice spread through her simultaneously. She wasn't sure of anything anymore.

"Well? Are you game or would you rather play it safe? I can have a gentler mare and the sidesaddle brought."

Her chin came up defiantly. She was no coward. If this were a ticket to ride the range, she'd do it. Only thing was, she'd have to win. She *really* had to. She took a deep breath. "I'm game."

Miguel looked surprised and gestured to the road. "I'll be chivalrous and give you a head start."

Elizabeth opened her mouth to protest and then closed it. She couldn't afford to lose. Yet she wanted to win as an equal. Maybe just a wee bit of a head start, though—

"Why wait to get to the gate?" she asked. "Let the starting line be here." With that, she dug her heels in and loosened the reins, bending over Plata's neck as the mare leaped into full gallop.

She heard a muffled curse and then Diablo's pounding hooves behind her. She bent lower over the mare and urged her on. "Come on, girl, we can do it!"

Plata snorted and gave an extra burst of speed, stretching flat out, her stride so smooth it was as though they weren't moving at all. Only the wind whipping the mare's mane in her face told her differently. Diablo was still behind them and the tree loomed up ahead, slightly to the right of the road. She was going to win! *Yes*! Her reward would be to ride the range and do real cowboy things. Miguel couldn't deny her! He promised!

Then she saw a blur veer off the road. Diablo jumped a low sagebrush and slid to a stop, hooves churning up dust, directly in front of the tree.

Elizabeth reined in Plata as they approached. “That wasn’t fair. You didn’t stay on the road.”

“Was that one of the rules? Your start wasn’t exactly fair either.” He slipped down and came around to her and held up his arms. “Come here.”

A dozen butterflies left their perches in her stomach, all fluttering their wings at the same time. Dear Lord, what was he going to do? “Umm. Couldn’t we just ride a little more?”

An eyebrow shot up. “You surprise me, Red. I didn’t think you’d go back on your word.”

Ouch. Her father had always been adamant about not breaking a promise. Trembling a little, she brought her leg over the saddle horn and let him help her down.

He kept his hands around her waist as he backed her away from the horses. “I believe the agreement was winner’s choice.”

Elizabeth took a deep gulp of air. She wasn’t sure if she were shaking with anxiety or anticipation. “Yes. Within reason, of course.”

“I don’t remember that being in the rules either.”

Okay. Time to lay the cards on the table. She met his look. “What do you want, then?”

His eyes grew darker as he pulled her toward him and let his hands roam her back, fingers treading gently, then palms following in firm, broad strokes. Everywhere he caressed, her skin came alive, nerve endings tingling with warmth. By the saints, maybe the man was really Merlin, for his touch was magic.

He slanted his mouth against hers, his tongue gliding over her lips, teasing her to want more of him. Elizabeth gave an involuntary moan and he deepened the kiss, his tongue probing now, filling her mouth. Oh, the slightly salty taste of that velvet tongue! He varied the pressure, slowing down for gentle playful kisses, then building her passion again with long deep ones. He was devouring her, making love to her mouth until she was nearly senseless. She felt her resolve taking wing, like a flushed quail.

He crushed her to his chest, his erection hard against her belly. Suddenly her whole body ached with need, nerve fibers demanding more skin, more closeness, the hot wet throbbing between her legs demanding to feel him *there*.

As if reading her mind, he cupped her buttocks and pressed himself to her, gyrating his hips. Dear Lord, the sensation was like none she'd ever experienced. If he hadn't been holding her, she would have slipped to the ground because her knees had jellied. But that wasn't where she was concentrating. Oh, no. The pulsation where his shaft jutted against her repeatedly was building, getting stronger, taking over her body, her soul. And then the contraction started, deep within her, her body clenching itself onto nothing as wave after tremulous wave washed over her. Had Miguel not had complete possession of her mouth, she would have screamed loud enough to be heard in the next county.

He slowed his movements, letting her experience the aftershock, and then broke the kiss, leaning his forehead against hers, both of them panting softly.

Eventually, he straightened and leaned back. "That was a taste, Red. I want you to want me—to make love together."

What had she just done? She'd come, for God's sake. Did he know that? She looked up. He knew, all right. But he'd never believe it was her first time. She drew in a shuddering breath. “I think I’ve given you what you want.”

Miguel smiled. “No. I’ve given you what *you* wanted. I intend to have you make love to me. Of your own free will. Not here. Not now. But someday soon. Then you’ll have paid your debt.”

His statement hit her like a pail of ice water. Paid her debt. Of course. He didn’t really mean making love—he meant having sex. Sweet Mary, she’d almost fallen for him. Almost allowed herself to think his kisses held real affection. That maybe, just maybe, he was seeing her as a real person, not some slut who had been knocked in the head. He’d just given her a fantastic climax—her first—and all he could think of was that she owed him a debt?

Ah, but he was good. He’d awakened feelings in her she didn’t know she had. She would just have to be very careful not to let herself get in this situation again. She would not be used. Abruptly, she pushed away from him.

“Of my own free will? I’m afraid you’re going to have a long wait.”

His finger traced a pattern over her still puffy mouth. “I don’t think so, Red. A woman who reacts like you do can only hold out so long. I’m a patient man.” He bowed elegantly. “Allow me to help you onto your horse. You seem a bit shaky.”

He wasn’t taking her seriously. Annoyed, she said, “I can manage.” To her great embarrassment, however, she found he was right—blast it. Her legs were too shaky to mount. Smothering a smile, Miguel lifted her and set her in the saddle.

“I told you,” he said.

She ignored him and nudged Plata into a canter, but

she could hear him laughing behind her.

****

The next week passed quickly. After the incident, Miguel behaved like a perfect gentleman, not even alluding to what had taken place. He even acquiesced to her riding. He took her with him as he rode the fence line for the pasture where he kept the brood mares. He often stopped to prop up a fence post or make a note on where wires had been torn and needed replacing. Most days Olaf accompanied them and Elizabeth found his gruff, man-of-few-words personality comforting and reliable. As he'd told her, "I don't use up all my kindlin' to make a fire."

She nudged Plata to keep up with Diablo. They were nearing a dried gully full of sand and dead grass when the stallion reared suddenly, nearly slamming into the mare. As Miguel settled the horse, Elizabeth heard the menacing rattle of the snake and drew her handgun she now wore and fired into a clump of sage. The rattler sprang upward and fell back.

She hid a smile as she remembered how Miguel had balked at her shooting a gun. They'd had a terrific argument over why women should not carry guns. She'd pleaded and cajoled to no avail. Only when she challenged him to target practice, asking if he'd like to repeat the wager they'd made for the race, did he allow her near one.

She struggled now to suppress the mirth bubbling up and threatening to explode as she remembered. He'd had a smirk on his face, positive she'd make a fool of herself and he'd be able to take another of those breathtaking kisses. To be truthful, she had played with the idea of letting him win just for that, but with Swift Hawk and

Olaf watching, no way was she going to lose. Too bad Miguel didn't know her father had taken her to the shooting range, beginning when she was twelve. Winning that little contest was why she was here now.

"You're welcome," she said a bit smugly.

Miguel grunted something that sounded like "thanks" and Elizabeth bit the inside of her lip to keep from laughing outright. His male pride hated to admit a woman had bested him. It actually made him more endearing, not that he needed to know that.

"Easy, boy," Miguel crooned, his hand sliding along the horse's sleek neck as he avoided looking at Elizabeth.

She bit back another grin. Men in this century needed some enlightenment. Yet she was amazed at the special relationship Miguel had with Diablo. He talked to the stallion as though he were human and she could have sworn the horse understood. She'd never heard so many responsive sounds come from a horse. It seemed Miguel was capable of caring for the horse, anyway—and Raul and Olga and Olaf. Everyone but her. She was only a sex toy he wanted to play with, but she'd deal with that later. The day was too nice to spend on a pity party.

Elizabeth shifted her weight in the saddle and breathed in the fresh air this early January morning, enjoying being in the country, under open skies and miles of prairie. She had seen deer and antelope and, once, even a herd of buffalo, although Miguel said they were nearly extinct in this part of the country, one reason so many Indian tribes were already on reservations. This was what it looked like, before the metro-mess that was now Dallas-Fort Worth came into being. She glanced sideways at Miguel as he knelt on the ground, pushing a post deeper into the hole.

He was a different man when he was working. His men respected him and he didn't hesitate to get down and work alongside them. Usually, by the time they rode home in the afternoon, he would be covered in grime and dirt, just like his son.

She frowned. Raul would be returning to school in two days. She wondered if the same amount of time had passed in her century. What would happen when she didn't return to work?

"What's wrong?" Miguel was standing, watching her.

Elizabeth shook her head to clear it. "I was just thinking about going back to teaching. I'm going to be missed."

The look he gave her clearly told her he thought she was fantasizing again. Would he never believe her? "I am a teacher. I'll prove it to you. I'll go along with Raul when he returns to school and talk to his teacher. Education stuff. You'll see I know what I'm talking about."

Miguel mounted and they turned their horses toward the *hacienda*. "That might not be a bad idea," he said. "Miss Parsons is having a little trouble with his antics, and you seemed to have curbed that after the snake incident. Raul has been remarkably well-behaved since then."

Was he actually complimenting her? Raul was used to having his own way, probably a result of having no mother, only a nanny who had run off. Olga, as efficient as she was about running the place, had a definite soft spot for the imp. That his persuasive grin looked so like his father's didn't help matters either. Still, Elizabeth had decided to be firm with him. He'd paid for the stolen cookie by washing the dishes. Not happily, but he had done them.

"So how did you get so good with kids? Most ladies-of-the-evening don't have time—"

Her feeling of good will ground to a halt. He was back to that theory. She should have known chivalry wouldn't last with him. She had hoped they could be real friends. "I am not a prostitute. Can you not get that through your head? You saw me in lingerie from a store called Victoria's Secret. A lot of women own things like that and are not prostitutes."

His eyebrow arched. "A lot of women?" He grinned infuriatingly. "Too bad you don't remember where you came from. It would be interesting to meet those ladies."

Elizabeth thrust her chin out. "Just let me meet the schoolteacher." She dug her heels into the mare's sides, causing Plata to leap forward in surprise, and left Miguel following in her dust.

****

Snow had fallen during the night and a thin layer of ice covered water puddles as Miguel drove Elizabeth and Raul to school in the carriage. A fitting day, Elizabeth thought. The boys would be having snowball fights, for sure.

Abigail Parsons wasn't Elizabeth's picture of a nineteenth-century schoolmarm. For one thing, she was obviously more interested in Miguel than in Raul. From the moment they walked in and Raul ran to giggle with his friend, Gus, Miss Parsons had not left Miguel's side. As Elizabeth watched, she tucked her slender hand inside the crook of Miguel's elbow and smiled up at him.

"Have you thought about what I suggested?" she asked in a silken purr that made Elizabeth want to scratch her own nails on the chalkboard. "We could begin tonight."

Begin what? Elizabeth looked over the petite woman. Everything about her was golden: her skin, her hair, even her eyes. Cat eyes, slanted at the corners. Her smile was seductive and alluring even with the children present. Elizabeth blinked as the tip of Abigail's tongue protruded at the corner of her mouth. She could almost see the schoolmarm licking cream from her whiskers. Was she another of Miguel's conquests? Probably. Or she soon would be. Elizabeth didn't care if she was. Not at all.

Miguel smiled at Miss Parsons before he disengaged himself. "I think I've arrived at a solution for Raul's misbehavior," he said and gestured toward Elizabeth. "Miss O'Malley seems quite capable of controlling him. Perhaps she could give you a few suggestions."

Abigail's eyes narrowed almost imperceptibly, but Elizabeth caught the action. When those golden eyes trained on her, they were as cold and calculating as a mountain lion's and a small shiver went down Elizabeth's spine in spite of the potbellied stove heating the interior of the room. This was a person used to getting what she wanted.

Miss Parsons inclined her head slightly. "Miss O'Malley. Are you a new domestic for Miguel?"

Domestic? Servant? Elizabeth's temper began to simmer and the fact that Miguel was trying not to grin almost sent it over the edge. And why was the schoolmarm using Miguel's first name? This Miss Parsons was just a little too uppity. Elizabeth lifted her head and stood tall. "I'm a teacher, just like you are." She caught the warning look in Miguel's eyes, but she ignored it. It was about time he understood.

Miss Parsons arched a delicate eyebrow. “Really?”

“Yes.” Elizabeth glanced around the room. “Do you use groups?”

For a moment, she looked puzzled. “Groups?”

“Groups. Tables with three or four children to work together to study different topics.” She let her voice trail off as the schoolmarm’s eyes glazed.

Elizabeth looked around the room again. A blackboard, dusty with traces of erased chalk covered the front of the room. That would be a computerized smart board with power point at her high school. An old, battered wooden desk sat directly in front of the chalkboard facing the students. Rows of connected wooden desks with folding seats and inkwells were nailed into the hardwood floor. Few rooms in modern schools limited themselves to straight rows. Elizabeth smiled inwardly. She’d never seen real desks like these, although she did have a miniature old-fashioned desk sitting on a shelf in her bedroom back home. Along one wall were pegs for hanging coats, and above the pegs, wooden cubbies for sack lunches and caps. The opposite wall held a bookshelf without many books.

“Mig…*Señor* de Basque has a wonderful library. Perhaps I could bring some of the books here and read to the children,” Elizabeth said.

Again, the schoolmarm’s eyes narrowed almost indiscernibly. “I hardly think that is necessary.” She tilted her head and smiled up at Miguel. “I would love to see your library. Might I?”

For some unexplainable reason that made no sense, Elizabeth knew she didn’t want this catlike woman in Miguel’s library, her hands touching the soft leather of the rare books on the shelves. Elizabeth didn't even want Miss Parsons in Miguel's house. She bit her lip. She needed to get a grip. She didn't mean anything to Miguel. If anyone were behaving like a wanton woman, it was this Abigail person. Couldn't Miguel see it? Or maybe he liked it, since he was smiling at her again.

"We'll see," he said. "Perhaps it would give you and Miss O'Malley a chance to work together. I think we've taken enough of your time for now."

She held out her hand to him and he bent over, brushing her knuckles with his lips. Elizabeth's stomach coiled into a knot. How gallant of him. He never did that to her! Miss Parsons he treated like a lady when she was the one acting like a hooker! Her temper, which had been reaching a slow boil, threatened to spill over. And she was supposed to work with Miss Parsons?

Miguel straightened and caught her look. The corner of his mouth twitched, which didn't help her mood. Was he trying to make her jealous? Well, it was not going to work. No way.

He put one hand on her back, his fingers stroking lightly, as he guided her to the door. The touch was just enough to make Elizabeth remember how his hands had felt the day of the horse race. She tried to stanch the feeling with little success.

Miguel opened the door. "After you. Watch—"

Trying to rein her temper in as he closed the door, she didn't see the patch of ice until her foot slipped on the last step. She gave a little shriek as she lost her balance and fell backwards.

"I tried to warn you," Miguel said.

She found herself lying in his arms, partially suspended in air, gazing up at that chiseled jaw. His arms were like steel bands, supporting her. He bent his head lower, his dark eyes searching her face. A wild thought of how his mouth would feel in an upside-down kiss flitted through her mind. Sparks began igniting in her belly, shooting tiny pieces of friction into her limbs. At that moment, she felt ridiculously safe and content. He was going to kiss her. Her and not that cat-woman inside. Elizabeth closed her eyes and parted her lips.

Nothing happened. Slowly, she opened her eyes to find him watching her, his face still close.

"If you want to be kissed, you'll have to ask me," he said. "Remember?"

Flustered, she struggled to regain an upright position. "Ask you?" she sputtered as he finally set her on her feet and released her. "What makes you think—"

He stopped her by tracing her lips with his finger as he leaned down, his breath warm on her cheek. "I think you might even want more than a kiss?"

Elizabeth felt herself blush and turned away from him and walked to the carriage, carefully avoiding any more ice patches. She clambered up before he could assist her, too afraid to feel his strong hands around her waist, afraid she might actually admit that she did want him.

She did. If she were to lose her virginity, she'd rather it be with him than anyone she had ever known. In spite of his ability to trigger her temper, she liked him. He was kind and good, even if he did think she was a prostitute. But he wouldn't believe she was from the future. Until he understood who she really was and where she came from, there could be no present.

Chapter Eight—Trouble

At the sound of Miguel's spurs jingling on the back porch, Elizabeth looked up from the kitchen table where she was helping Raul do his sums by the light of the evening oil lamp. Miss Parsons had come calling, but finding Miguel gone, she had not returned, for which Elizabeth was grateful.

Miguel had been gone nearly a month. She'd no idea she'd miss him so much. The Rangers had called him to active duty to help settle a Comanche uprising some thirty miles to the northwest of Fort Worth. Olga had told her it was a favorite spot for the Comanche when they wanted to retreat. They could effectively vanish in that territory full of small mountains, deep canyons, huge boulders and cedar brakes. Luckily, he had taken Swift Hawk with him for translating if necessary.

Elizabeth hadn't even known Miguel was a Texas Ranger until Tate Johnson showed up with four of the men who had been at the dinner that night, saying that a farmer's family had been killed and their daughter kidnapped. She'd watched Miguel hurriedly prepare, sliding the crossbands of bullets over his broad shoulders so that the leather formed an "X" on his chest, then loading his Colt .44 and the Sharp's rifle. But it was when he attached the metal star within a circle to his shirt that she'd gasped, remembering the last time her father had prepared for duty—and not come back.

She tried not to show too much emotion that Miguel had returned safely. “All is well?” she asked when he came through the door.

Miguel looked grim as he hung his hat on the peg near the door and ruffled Raul’s hair. “Why don’t you go to bed, son? It’s Friday. That homework can wait until tomorrow.”

All was not well. Silently, she followed him into the *sala* where he poured a stiff drink of Kentucky bourbon. He took a deep slug and offered her the glass, but she shook her head. He refilled it and sank down on the sofa in front of the hearth. “Sit down beside me, Red.”

Elizabeth stoked the fire first, coaxing the feeble flame into something that would produce some warmth, and then she sat down. “What’s wrong?”

Miguel swirled the contents of the glass, staring into it before he answered. When he did, she had to lean closer to hear him. “We were too late. They’d already raped her.”

She inhaled sharply. The girl had been a child, just twelve or thirteen, Mr. Johnson had said. “Is she alive? How—how badly was she hurt?”

He looked at her then and she didn’t think she’d ever seen more pain and misery in a man’s eyes. “She’s alive. We managed to get there before the ceremonial ritual was completed, although I’m not sure she’ll ever thank us for that. She was tortured.”

Tears welled up in Elizabeth’s eyes. “Oh, no…” she whispered. “How?”

“They staked her arms and legs,” he said and took another strong swig. “Each of the five braves who led the attack had his way with her, then carved a power symbol into her skin and licked her blood.” He watched the fire as if mesmerized.

Elizabeth felt herself gagging and she swallowed hard. That poor child. Mary, her name was. “Why would they do something so barbaric?”

He shook his head. “Men have been raping and pillaging since the Dark Ages.”

“But why the torture? And the blood-drinking?”

“Culture is a funny thing, Red. To them, the giving of the power symbol is a mark of respect. Many of the braves receive one after their first kill.”

“Like a tattoo?” Elizabeth asked.

He frowned. “A what?”

“An ink picture. It’s made by pricking the skin with a tiny needle.”

“Ah. I think I saw one of those once, on a sailor in San Francisco.” He paused for a minute and studied her. “Is that where you might be from?”

Images of the notorious waterfront with its attendant saloons and brothels flashed through Elizabeth’s mind. It hurt her for him to think that, just when they were having a meaningful conversation. She sighed. “No. Now finish this horrible tale of what happened. Why did they drink her blood?”

“Because they draw power from it. They believe they can draw her spirit into their own bodies by absorbing her blood.”

Elizabeth shuddered. This sounded too much like a vampire story. “How much power do these braves think a child could have anyway? Is there something magical about children?”

He continued to stare broodingly into the fire and twirled his empty glass.

“Well, is there?” she asked again.

"No. Nothing magical about children," he answered and then he looked up and into her eyes. "What was magical was that she had red hair, just like yours."

Elizabeth stared at him, remembering Swift Hawk's proclamations. She felt dizzy suddenly. He said she would give him much power. Was he capable of slicing into her to take her blood? What if he caught her alone? Was she really safe?

She heard a roaring in her ears, like that of a fast train, before the world turned gray and then slid into black.

****

When she regained consciousness, she was lying in a large, four-poster feather bed, warm bricks wrapped in towels around her feet, a down quilt covering her. Tentatively, she felt her body. She was wearing a nightdress. What had happened and whose room was she in?

Something moved in the shadows of the far corner of the room and came toward her. In the dim light from the banked fire, she could see it was Miguel. He sat down on the edge of the bed and smiled at her.

"You had a nasty shock. Feeling better?"

She remembered then. The child with the red hair. She shook her head to clear it and then struggled to sit up.

"Here. Allow me." Miguel put one hand under each arm and easily lifted her to a sitting position, his fingers splayed against the soft, round sides of her breasts. He reached around behind her, his cheek grazing hers as he plumped the pillows, and then he leaned back and handed her a glass of brandy from the bedside table.

"Drink this. It will do wonders to revive you."

She pulled the quilt up under her chin, all too aware of the thin cotton of the nightdress and where his hands had just been. Had he undressed her?

"Where am I?" she asked as he took her hand and wrapped it around the glass.

"My room," he answered. "It was easier carrying you in here than up the stairs."

She took a sip of the fiery liquid and looked around. A massive black walnut wardrobe took up much of one wall, its panels inlaid with gold trim. A matching walnut table and chairs stood by the window and on the other side of the room, an overstuffed armchair sat on a soft woolen rug close to the hearth, a pile of books on the floor beside it. A simply furnished room, yet comfortable. Lived-in. Her clothes hung on a peg by the door.

She looked back at him. "Did you…" She hesitated and then took another sip for courage. She had to know. Had he actually seen her naked?

"No," he finished for her. "Olga undressed you and got you snuggled into bed. Although," he said as he picked up the thong and bra from the floor, "if I'd known you were wearing these, I might have been tempted."

She blushed furiously and downed the rest of the brandy and then gasped. She would never learn to drink this stuff.

He shook his head and took the glass from her and set it back on the table. "Slowly, Red. I can see I'm going to have to teach you something about appreciating fine French cognac."

"Never mind. About the child—can you keep this from happening again?" Elizabeth asked when she could speak again.

There was a subtle change in his expression. “I wish I could. Chief Jim Ned says it was a renegade raid, nothing he led. The braves are in custody at the brig in Fort Worth. There’ll be a trial when the circuit judge comes around.”

“What about Swift Hawk?”

Miguel looked surprised. “What about him?”

Elizabeth felt a chill, in spite of the warm bricks and blanket. “He’s always staring at me and making remarks about my hair being red. Am I safe? I wish you could send him away.”

“I can’t do that. He and Cactus Flower are our guarantee the Comanche will not raid our ranch. My part of the treaty is to expose them to the white man’s ways in hopes they will eventually become mediators.”

“That will never happen with Swift Hawk.”

“Maybe not. But it’s better to have him here, where I can keep an eye on him, then send him back to his people where he can stir up enough trouble that you *could* be in danger.”

Elizabeth felt the chill seep through her again. “So you do think I’m in danger?”

Miguel was silent for a moment. “I doubt it. You should be safe here.” Then his expression changed and he grinned. “But if it’s protection you want, the bed is big enough for both of us.”

She took a pillow and flung it at him, although not hard. “Is that all you ever think about?”

He stood. “Pretty much, with you. My promise still stands—I would give you more pleasure than any other man you’ve had.”

Of course he would. She was a virgin! She wasn’t sure whether to laugh or cry. “I’ve told you I don't...don't..."

He glanced meaningfully at the black silk that lay on the floor and she felt her face flame. She threw a second pillow at him. "Go!"

Miguel raised an eyebrow and then bowed dramatically from the waist. "As you wish." He walked to the door and then turned. "Just remember, you're in my bed. Sweet dreams."

She could hear him chuckling as he went down the hall.

He was maddening. Not to mention arrogant. He was also right. She'd dreamed of him plenty already, not that she would admit to it. She sighed and inhaled the scent of him on the pillow as she drifted off to sleep.

****

It didn't take the feline long to realize Miguel had returned. Miss Parsons arrived the very next afternoon, a still-warm apple pie in her basket.

"I baked it myself," she said as she handed it to Miguel, her fingers lingering on his hand.

Elizabeth would bet she didn't. How did she know apple was his favorite? What an old ploy to think that the way to a man's heart was through his stomach. Still, did Miguel have to act so pleased?

"I did want to see that library your domestic told me about," she purred and looked up at him with wide eyes. "Would you escort me there?"

Domestic? She was a teacher! Just as she was about to confront her, Miguel blocked the path.

"This way," he said.

Elizabeth followed them, fuming. Miss Parsons had latched onto Miguel's arm and was chattering like a magpie. She stopped, though, when she saw the vast expanse of books in the study.

"This is a real library!" She actually released Miguel's arm to walk closer and read titles. "You have classics here and," she paused, "the Arthurian legends." She turned and smiled at Miguel, totally ignoring Elizabeth. "You probably aren't going to believe this, but I knew a girl named Gwen, which is short for Gwenevere." She tilted her head to the side and studied him. "You'd make a very satisfactory Lancelot, I think."

Miguel groaned and looked at Elizabeth. "What is it with you women?"

Like she had something in common with that hussy? Elizabeth hated to think they shared any kind of the same thoughts. "It's just that you and Sir Knight have the same bad-boy image," she said flippantly. "It's a universal thought."

Miguel looked confused. "What kind of image?"

Elizabeth sighed. How could she explain the charisma that lured women to perfect-looking men who were anything but perfect for them? A man who could make a woman feel like she was the center of his universe—if only she didn't mind the fact that his universe became a bit crowded with all the other women who were centers, too.

"I think she means you're irresistible." Abigail gave Miguel a sleepy-eyed look, a small smile playing on her mouth.

Miguel raised an eyebrow, still looking at Elizabeth. "Is that so?"

Really! Asking that question just proved the point; he probably did think he was! And now he was actually waiting for an answer. She felt herself blush furiously. She seemed to do a lot of that around him. "Irresistible to Diablo, maybe," she said.

He grinned. "That's not an insult, Red."

Abigail looked annoyed. "I'm really quite thirsty, Miguel. Do you suppose Elizabeth could get me some water?"

Elizabeth felt her mouth drop open and snapped it shut. The nerve! Ordering her about! The last thing she wanted to do was leave Miguel alone with the schoolmarm, but if she refused to leave, she'd be all but admitting she was jealous. And she wasn't. She was *not* jealous. No way.

"Of course," she said sweetly, "and I'll ask Olga for some cookies, too."

Unfortunately, Raul waylaid her on her trip back. She found him at the kitchen table, grumbling over his arithmetic. She helped him with a division problem and then poured three glasses of lemonade and added some sugar cookies to the tray.

Raul swiped a cookie and popped it into his mouth. "I don't like my teacher being here," he said. "I'm not even sure I like her."

Smart boy. Elizabeth kept her voice even. "Why don't you?"

"She makes lots of mistakes. Gus corrected her once and she yelled at him." Raul shrugged. "Whenever a father comes to school, she forgets all about us and she's always asking about *Papá*. I don't like that."

If Elizabeth hadn't had her hands full, she would have hugged him. Then she realized she had been gone longer than she intended. She gave him a quick smile and walked back to the study.

And wished she hadn't. She'd left the door slightly ajar, and as she pushed it open with her foot, she saw the schoolmarm raise up on tiptoe, put her arms around Miguel's neck, and pull his head down for a kiss.

Molten lava hardened in Elizabeth's stomach. She nearly dropped the tray. She began to back out of the room hurriedly before she would be seen. The hem of her skirt caught on the edge of the straight chair next to the door. Damn skirts anyway. She balanced the tray in one hand and tugged, only to have the dress snag more. It gave a horrifying loud rip. She froze, wishing she could melt into the floor.

Miguel turned, disengaging Abigail's arms from around his neck. He walked over to her. "Let me take that," he said as he set the tray on a small table.

Elizabeth bent over, hiding her face as she tried to work the skirt loose from the rough edge that had caught it. She was humiliated beyond words.

His hand covered hers. "Let me." Gently, he wiggled the material free. "There. I'll have to get that chair sanded down." He straightened and looked at her. "Not much damage done."

If he only knew. She tried to ignore the surge of warmth his touch always gave her. She had only herself to blame. She'd let herself begin to care: first the feeling of family over the holidays, then the month waiting for him to return safely. She had let her guard down. Why wouldn't he be interested in Miss Parsons? She obviously wanted him and was willing to do something about it. Her eyes began to burn and she blinked rapidly to keep embarrassing tears at bay.

"I think Raul needs some help with his homework, so I'll leave you with the lemonade," she said stiffly. "The cookies are good."

As she turned, Miguel caught her arm. His dark eyes

were serious as he looked into her face. "I'd rather you stay."

She freed her arm. "Your son needs some help." She lifted her head and walked away, hoping her unsteady legs would support her.

She heard the front door open and close a few minutes later as she sat at the kitchen table with Raul. Miguel approached, but stopped in the doorway. She didn't look up from the problem she was helping solve. Unfortunately, it was the last one.

"Done!" Raul said and threw his pencil on the table. "I'm going outside to play."

"Don't get too dirty," Elizabeth said to his back.

Miguel sat down in the chair that his son had occupied. "You're really good with him. I've meant to thank you."

Elizabeth avoided looking at him as she gathered the supplies. She didn't want his pity or a gratuitous compliment. He might suspect something, but at least she hadn't made a fool of herself.

She stood quickly. "You're quite welcome. He's a wonderful boy. If you'll excuse me—"

"No." Miguel stood in front of her, blocking her path. "We're going to talk."

"About what?"

"About what you saw—or thought you did—just now."

Elizabeth's chin jutted out. "I hardly think I need to have a kiss explained."

He took her supplies and set them down and took her hands in his. Elizabeth tried to pull back, but his grasp was firm. And hot. How could a man have such hot, hard, yet gentle hands?

“I didn’t kiss her.”

“I saw what happened. Not that it matters, of course. You’re free to kiss whomever you choose.” How much more prim could she get? She really had to get away from him before she blubbered her way into admitting she was a little bit jealous. She tugged at her hands to no avail.

“Whomever I choose,” Miguel echoed. “Precisely.” He covered both her hands with one of his and caught her chin lightly with his other one, holding her head in place. He bent his head and gave her a soft, slow kiss and released her.

“I choose you. Now we won’t speak of this again.”

Elizabeth held on to the back of the chair as he walked away, her legs wobbly and her heart beating rapidly.

****

“Do you want to go to Fort Worth with me today?” Miguel asked as he stood up from the breakfast table in the kitchen.

Elizabeth swallowed the last bite of her eggs and brushed toast crumbs from her Levis. “Absolutely. I can be ready in five minutes.”

“Not dressed like that,” Miguel said. “I want to check with the family that’s caring for Mary, and you’ll need to be dressed like a lady. A real one.”

She wrinkled her nose at him. “You mean I have to wear a corset? I’ll need help with it and I haven’t seen Cactus Flower this morning.”

“I could come with you and draw the laces myself.” He grinned and started walking toward her. “I’ve had some practice.”

“I’ll find Cactus Flower,” she said hastily and nearly knocked her chair over as she went out the door. She knew he was laughing at her even though there was silence.

The man was unnerving. He could be such a gentleman and such a rogue. It had been a week since the incident with the schoolmarm and he'd been neutrally pleasant. The morning after her fainting spell, he had taken Swift Hawk aside and had a long talk with him. Even though the Indian boy still watched her silently, he left her alone. Miguel had stayed close to her, too, and she would feel herself gradually relaxing, only to become tense again, but for another reason. His closeness. If he got within three feet of her, she could sense his animal magnetism, the uneasy desire that lay potent, just below the surface of civility. The clean scent of him, of soap and leather and a light spice, penetrated her brain with giddiness. Only when she put some distance between them could she think straight.

She met Cactus Flower on the landing leading up the steps to her room and asked for her help. The Indian girl giggled as they stepped inside.

"What's so funny?" Elizabeth asked.

"Just that *Don* Miguel is taking you to Fort Worth," she said. When Elizabeth looked puzzled she continued. "He usually stops to visit with Miss Lily. I've heard Olga scolding him for it."

Miss Lily? The madam? Elizabeth's temper stirred. Did he intend to introduce them, in hopes she would recover her "memory" as a working girl? Was that the reason he had finally invited her to go with him? Suddenly, a chill swept through her. Maybe he intended to have this madam hire her. Elizabeth had been a guest at his house nearly two months; she hadn't allowed him to seduce her nor had she gone to him of her own free will either. Maybe he wanted to get rid of her. Maybe he wanted to make room for Miss Parsons after all.

"This dress?" Cactus Flower held out her favorite, a green silk with small yellow flowers on it and a flattering neckline.

"No." Miguel had said he wanted her to look like a lady—a real one, he'd said, as though she weren't—well, he'd get a lady all right. She rummaged toward the back of the closet for the dark gray shirtwaist with its long sleeves and high collar. It was her prim and proper go-to-Sunday-meeting dress. No way was she going to let some real hooker think she was one.

****

The team of horses trotted at a mile-eating clip, the surrey not lurching as much as the buckboard did. Elizabeth found that if she clutched the side rail of the seat, she could keep from landing in Miguel's lap. She had done that once already.

"What's that? Another town?" Elizabeth pointed toward a small settlement nestled near a stream that flowed not far from the road.

Miguel's gaze followed her outstretched finger. "That's Village Creek. It was once a gathering place for the Comanche."

"Once? Why did they leave?"

"The white man's hunger for land. The Peter's Colony established by the Republic of Texas gave three hundred and twenty acres to every couple who would farm it. This area had good water. In 1841, General Tarrant brought in enough troops to drive the Comanche westward."

"Hmmm, it doesn't seem fair to the Indians," Elizabeth said and then glanced at him sideways. "There will be a lake near here one day."

Miguel gave her a wary look. "Are you going to predict the future again?"

She had to get him to understand she was telling the truth. But how? "Lake Arlington. And there will be a freeway sign named Village Creek Road."

"Freeway?"

"Freeway—uh—big roads on which horseless carriages drive very fast."

"Horseless carriages? That's impossible." He glanced at her sideways, a troubled expression on his face. "Just when I think you're rational—a bit hot-tempered, but I like spirited women—you say something like this. Maybe the army doctor should—"

"No!" Elizabeth could have bitten her tongue. Would she never learn? "You promised me you wouldn't send me away to rot." Her hands grasped his arm, her nails digging into the skin where his shirtsleeve was rolled up.

He pulled the horses to a stop and turned to her, gently prying her fingers loose. "You'll get more cooperation if you kiss me rather than mutilate me." He let his gaze rest on her lips and then he looked into her eyes. "Want to try?"

"That's blackmail!" She tried to make her voice strong, but the sleepy, heavy-lidded look he was giving her sent waves of desire shimmying through her. She found herself staring at his wide, full mouth, so close she could feel his breath. She remembered the last slow, sensuous kiss he had given her. Her insides still went to mush at the thought. Elizabeth wet her lips and leaned toward him and then stopped. If she kissed him, he would think she was selling herself for his silence. She straightened and folded her hands in her lap. “I thought you were a gentleman.”

Miguel studied her. “I think a gentleman would bore you to death, Red.” He slapped the reins on the horses’ rumps. “You need a man who will make every inch of your body come alive, playing with you until you beg for mercy. Someone who will make you pant with desire and beg for more—”

“Stop it.” Elizabeth folded her arms across her chest and immediately felt her breasts swell and ache with the need to be touched. How could he do that to her by just talking? “I thought in the 1800s—” She stopped abruptly. “I mean, men aren’t supposed to talk to ladies like that. It shows disrespect.”

Miguel glanced at her. “Is that what you think? That I don’t respect you?”

She searched his face for some hint of sarcasm, but found none. “Do you?”

A muscle twitched as he clenched his jaw and he turned his attention to the horses, urging them into a canter. “More than you’ll ever know.”

****

They stopped off first to visit Mary. Physically, she had recovered, but she was quiet and withdrawn. Elizabeth’s heart went out to her. The child needed counseling and she’d taken counseling courses for her master’s degree. If only she could take Mary home. But that was impossible. Swift Hawk was there. The best she could do was to talk with her and listen well. Later, she talked with the farmer’s wife, Bertha, and explained what symptoms signaled depression.

“I think Bertha was quite impressed with you,” Miguel said when they were back in the carriage and headed toward the town near the fort.

"Now will you believe that I'm really a teacher?"

He gave her a long look. "When did teachers start wearing garments like those black silk ones?"

She sighed. "I told you—" The thundering of hooves directly behind and then beside them drowned out her voice. A team of six horses pulled a red stagecoach, the words "Wells Fargo" emblazoned in gold on the sides. The driver and shotgun rider swayed perilously as the big coach rocked on its through-braces, the sturdy wooden wheels digging into the road, sending gravel and sand dust flying in their wake.

Miguel's horses snorted and tried to rear in their harness braces. Expertly he sawed on the reins, speaking in a soothing voice.

"Do they always drive like that?" Elizabeth asked in a shaky voice.

"Yes," Miguel answered as they rode into town and pulled over next to the stopped coach near the saloon. "To a stage line, time is money. The faster they travel, the less chance for a robbery or Indian attack." Miguel helped her down from the carriage just as a young woman stepped down from the coach.

Elizabeth stopped and stared. The woman wore well-fitting traveling clothes that showed her slim waist and large breasts, and her hair was the brightest, most unnatural shade of red Elizabeth had ever seen. Her eyes were bright blue, enhanced by a subtle shade of blue shadow. Her lips were rosy and her cheeks tinted a delicate pink. She had high cheekbones and a full mouth which, Elizabeth noticed, Miguel was looking at appreciatively.

Just then, two men barreled out of the swinging

saloon doors, grappling with each other as they fell into the street, landing at the young woman's feet. She nimbly sidestepped the fighting men and walked over to where Miguel was standing.

She gave Elizabeth a cursory look and then smiled up at Miguel, swinging her lace parasol slightly. "Hi, handsome. Could you help a lady?"

Elizabeth gave an undignified snort. Lady? She doubted it. And Elizabeth didn't like being ignored as though she weren't even present. When she saw the corner of Miguel's mouth quirk up, it only added to her irritation. Surely, he wasn't going to fall for that line, was he?

"Would you be looking for Miss Lily?" he asked.

For a moment the woman looked nonplused and then curved her lips into a knowing smile, the tip of her tongue peeking out at the corner. "Are you well acquainted with her establishment?"

Miguel grinned. "You could say that."

Elizabeth resisted the urge to kick him in the shin. Was he going to blatantly proposition an obvious prostitute in the middle of the street? And in front of her? The woman was looking at him as though she were ready to flagrantly strip right here and now.

Several more men crowded out the saloon door, yelling angrily at each other. One hit another over the head with a whiskey bottle and a free-for-all erupted.

Miguel took each woman by the arm and moved them away from the *mêlée*. "I think perhaps we should escort you there. It seems rowdier than usual today."

Escort her? "I'm not going anywhere near that place," Elizabeth said and tried to jerk her arm away.

Miguel merely pulled her closer, until the side of her

breast was crushed against the hard muscles of his arm. "Would you rather stay here with a bunch of drunks?"

Why did he have to pick today to be chivalrous? Why couldn't he just point the way and let the hooker find her own way? Of course, she knew the answer. The girl was pretty and obviously willing.

He helped both of them into the carriage and smiled slowly as Elizabeth made sure she got the front seat next to him. He didn't need to look so cocky about that. He hiked the woman's trunk onto the rumble seat and drove them the four blocks to the edge of town.

Lily's "establishment" sat back from the main street, a well-maintained two-story house with swings on the front porch and a manicured lawn, brown now in the winter. Flowerbed patches waited for spring. A wrought-iron fence surrounded the place. It looked nothing like what Elizabeth thought a brothel would look.

As they approached the steps to the front door, it opened and the biggest man Elizabeth had ever seen greeted them. Close to seven feet tall, his skin was ebony-black and his voice a deep bass.

"Afternoon, *Don* Miguel. Come on in." He glanced over the ladies and his white teeth flashed in a smile. "I thought Miss Lily was only expecting one girl."

"She is, Clarence." Miguel answered and turned to Elizabeth. "You wait here in the foyer. I'll be back shortly."

Where was he going? She watched as he walked away with the prostitute. Surely, he wasn't going to have a quickie while she sat alone, seated off the entrance, waiting for him? She didn't like the way the woman clung to his arm, either.

"Can I help you?"

Elizabeth turned to find a gray-haired woman with glasses smiling at her. She was pleasantly plump and dressed in a shirtwaist, similar to what Elizabeth was wearing. A soft woolen shawl draped over her shoulders. Probably the housekeeper.

"I'm waiting for someone."

The woman's smile broadened. "Most of the girls here are." She tilted her head to one side. "You're very pretty. The letter of reference you sent didn't lie."

Letter? Dear God! This woman thought she was the hooker.

"I'm Lily," the woman said and held out her hand. "I can't imagine why Clarence let you sit out here. He usually takes the new girls straight to the back to get checked in."

This was Lily? She looked like someone's grandma.

"Come," Lily said. "I'll show you the salon and sitting rooms and explain how we transact business here."

"I'm not—"

"I see you've met Lily," Miguel said as he strolled in swirling a brandy.

"Miguel! What a nice surprise!" Lily grasped his hand warmly and offered her cheek for a kiss. "I didn't know you were coming. This is Sharee, my newest girl from New Orleans. Maybe later, when she's checked in properly—?"

The corner of his mouth twitched as he leaned over Elizabeth and wound a strand of her hair around his finger. "Nothing would please me more, Lily."

Elizabeth glared at him as he let the back of his hand seductively trace the curve of her cheek. Lightly, his hand dropped to her shoulder. Good Lord, was he going to touch her breast? Heat from his touch seared straight to her nipple. She couldn't bear it if he did, and she was going to hate it if he didn't. Even with Miss Lily right here.

Miguel was watching her, hidden laughter in his eyes. He knew exactly what he was doing to her! She brushed his hand away.

Miguel straightened and sighed. "Sharee's in the back. This is Elizabeth."

Lily's eyes widened. "So you're the one. Well, well." She glanced at Miguel with concern. "You may be spending the night here anyway."

Miguel arched an eyebrow. "Why?"

"We've had rumors the Comanche are massing west of here in preparation for the trial, but the more pressing problem at the moment is that the circuit judge hasn't arrived yet. Tempers are running high and there's been talk of lynching to save the judge a trip. Folks are wanting to hold a kangaroo court."

"The braves are safe in the brig," Miguel said.

"Maybe. But the military isn't enforcing civil law. What we need is a Ranger."

Miguel frowned. "I wasn't expecting this. Has Tate Johnson been sent for?"

Lily shook her head. "There hasn't been time. Most of the real trouble started brewing this morning when some hired guns rode in, offering to kill the braves themselves. For a fee, of course."

He set the brandy down. "I'll go over to the saloon and see what I can do."

Elizabeth stood. "I'm going with you. I can get a room at the hotel."

"I need you to stay here. It's a lot safer for you to

stay out of the town proper." Miguel looked at Lily. "You do have a room?"

Lily nodded. "I have one that's unoccupied."

"Good," Miguel said. "I'll take a room at the hotel across the street from the saloon. I'll be able to keep an eye on things from there."

Lily's eyes twinkled. "The hotel sold out this afternoon when the hired guns arrived." She turned to Elizabeth. "Let me show you to your quarters. I hope you won't mind sharing it with Miguel."

Elizabeth stared at her, speechless, but Miguel only grinned as he turned to leave.

"I'll be back," he said.

Chapter Nine—Life in the Old West

Miguel could feel the tension even as he swung the saloon door open. Not good. The air was as static as after a lightning strike. The hired guns—five of them—sat at a table facing the door, their backs to the wall. Not surprising for their line of work.

"What's to stop us from stormin' the fort's gate ourselves and demanding a trial here and now?" one of the locals asked. "We don't need gunfighters. We need justice."

"They raped a white girl. They don't deserve justice," someone shouted.

"Lynch the Injuns, I say," said another. "To hell with waitin' for the judge!"

Shouts of approval swelled up from the crowd and glasses clattered on the bar for more whiskey.

Miguel stepped inside, resting the butt of the Sharp's rifle casually under his arm and the long barrel over his forearm. He looked at the bartender. "The bar's closed."

Instant silence reigned. All heads turned to look at him, some with glasses raised halfway to their lips, their mouths agape.

"Who would you be?" one of the hired guns drawled, his hand drifting lower.

Miguel lifted the barrel slightly. "I'd keep my hands on the table."

The man hesitated and then slowly brought his hand

back up. “I’m still waitin’ on an answer.”

With his left hand, Miguel pulled the metal star out of his pocket and stuck it on his leather vest. “Ranger. We’re the law around here.” He looked again at the barkeep. “Bar’s closed. These men need to go home and sleep it off before they find themselves looking at the brig from the inside out.”

The tender nodded nervously and began collecting glasses. The men at the bar grumbled and others shot their whiskey down fast. Most of them, if they didn’t know Miguel personally, had seen him enough to know he meant business. The more sober of the group helped their rowdier friends to the door.

One of the hired guns stood. “Ranger, huh? Is it true what they say? “One Ranger, one battle”? There’s five of us here. From Kansas. We don’t hold to accountin’ to a *Texas* Ranger. Maybe you’ve got somethin’ to prove?”

“No…no shootin’ in my bar,” the barkeep stuttered.

“There doesn’t need to be any shooting anywhere,” Miguel answered, his eyes boring into the gunslinger’s. “Regardless of what anyone thinks, those braves will get a fair trial. If they’re sentenced to hang, they’ll hang. But it’ll be done legal. No kangaroo court. No vigilantes.” He glanced at the other four and then back to the one standing. “Now, gentlemen, I’d suggest you retire for the day, nice and peaceful.”

“And if we don’t?” The man looked at his friends. “Like I said, there’s five of us. You can’t take us all.”

“Maybe not. But I can take you.” Miguel shrugged. “Do you feel like dying?”

“Oh, hell, Bart,” one of the seated men said. “Let’s go. We came here looking to make money, not death.”

The others nodded and stood. “Yeah,” another one

said. "This town may still need us if those Comanche camping west of here don't like the outcome of that fair trial the Ranger is so sure about."

Slowly, they sidled past Miguel, the rebellious one last. "You haven't seen the last of me, Ranger, and don't you forget it."

****

Miguel let himself quietly into the room Lily had given Elizabeth. It was late, well past midnight, but he wanted to make sure the town had quieted down for the night and wouldn't erupt again. In the morning, Tate Johnson should be here with the rest of the guard.

Elizabeth slept on her side, her back to the door, fully clothed. Miguel glanced at the cotton nightgown Lily had left, neatly folded on the dresser. Obviously, Elizabeth wasn't taking any chances. But how in the world could she sleep with that dang corset on? Women could hardly breathe in them.

He hung his gun belt over one of the bed posts and sat down on the nearest edge of the mattress to remove his boots. He stripped his vest and shirt off and then hesitated at the zipper of his pants. Elizabeth would throw a fit if she woke up to find him naked in bed with her.

Wouldn't she? Or, maybe in the semiconscious state of near-waking, if she felt his cock up hard against her, she'd reach for him automatically and remember who she was or what she was, although he was beginning to have doubts. The inquiries he'd sent out had brought no results. No one seemed to know her. Clearly, she wasn't an ordinary working girl like he had once assumed. She was too educated, for one thing. But the lingerie...he hadn't seen anything like that even in the fanciest house in New Orleans. Maybe she had been a European courtesan, sent for by some wealthy man in San Antonio. The stage stopped here first. She could have gotten off to tend to needs, been abducted and hit on the head.

He thought about how different she was from other women he'd had. There was nothing contrived about her; she didn't flirt or play games. In fact, she seemed genuinely interested in conversations he and Olaf had about breeding stock and breaking horses. She rode as well as any of his wranglers, and he'd never before met a woman who could shoot straight. Elena had cringed at the sight of a gun. And then, there was his son. Raul had never warmed up to anyone else except Olga. A brief thought flitted through his mind that Raul may not even have cottoned to his own mother, as self-centered and egotistical as Elena had been. Cold where Elizabeth was warm—warm and soft and feminine.

Yes, waking up to her would be nice. She'd turn over in his arms and snuggle against him. He'd give her soft, slow kisses, then nibble his way down her neck, his hand flicking a nipple lightly—very lightly—like a butterfly's wings while he teased her awake with his tongue. He groaned, thinking of taking her breast in his mouth, suckling her until she whimpered and became wet for him.

Miguel bent over her. She looked like a child, sleeping peacefully with one hand tucked under her cheek, the other holding the edge of the blanket. She looked almost virginal. He shook his head and slipped under the covers with his pants on.

He placed a hand on her waist and felt the hard whalebone of the corset. She couldn't be comfortable. The least he could do was loosen the stays. Gently, so he wouldn't wake her, he worked the buttons open on the back of the dress. Damn, why did women's dresses have to have so many buttons? There must be more than fifty. Once she murmured and stirred and he stopped, but she just sank further into her pillow.

There. He'd gotten the dress open. He untied the bottom of the corset and then began loosening it, pulling the laces through the eyes until the corset was undone. He pushed it aside and stared at her bare back. Heat began to stir in his loins. Had he ever wanted a woman as much as he did her? He didn't want to wait until morning to find out. He leaned over and kissed the back of her neck. Just one kiss. That's all he'd do. He inhaled the sweet scent of her hair, like meadow flowers on a spring day. Just one more kiss. His lips brushed her spine and then again, his mouth firmer each time as he worked his way slowly down her back. He really should stop…

****

Elizabeth was dreaming. The bed felt deliciously soft and warm. Hands she couldn't see stroked her, the touch incredibly light as those fingers caressed her shoulder, then feathered down her arm and up along her ribcage. A slight breeze rippled along her back and then the most exquisite sensation of cool air and warm tongue, easing along her spine, slipping downward, past her waist—

Her eyes flew open, but she didn't move. This wasn't a dream. She'd recognize Miguel's touch anytime. Fire kindled along the track his mouth had taken. Sweet Mary, he was trying to seduce her while she slept! She flipped over on her back. "What do you think you're doing?"

He leaned up on one elbow and grinned. "If you

don't know, my technique definitely needs improving."

She tucked the blanket under her chin, flustered. "Trying to take advantage of me in my sleep..." Her voice trailed off as she stared at his bare chest with the hard pecs and large biceps in his arms and gulped. "You're not...naked, are you?"

The grin broadened. "Why don't you lift the blanket and see?"

Elizabeth groaned, knowing she'd set herself up for that one. The worst thing was a part of her wanted him to be. But not here, in a brothel! He already thought she was a whore. Gingerly, she nudged his leg with her foot. Ah. Levis. Good.

He caught her leg and pulled it between his thighs, inching closer until she could feel the hardness of his shaft against her hip. Sweet Mary.

Miguel slid his arm around her, turning her to him, and grasped her buttock, pressing her more tightly against what was definitely growing and becoming larger.

"Why do you keep fighting me, Red? I promise I'll give you all the pleasure you could want. However you want it."

She nearly melted when he nuzzled her neck and nibbled lightly on her ear—but she couldn't let him do this. Not here. She put her hands on his chest and pushed to no avail. He was rock hard everywhere. "Let go. Get out of my bed."

He raised his head and looked at her. For a moment she thought he would force her, but then he released her leg and rolled over.

"I asked you to get out of my bed."

"Can't do it, Red. There's no place to go."

She sat up and swung her legs over the edge of the bed. "Then I'll go sleep in that chair. I can't trust you."

His hand caught her arm like a vise and she found herself sprawled on her back. Miguel leaned over her, his eyes serious.

"If there is one thing you can do, it's trust me, Red. All I really intended to do was loosen that damn corset. I got carried away. It won't happen again." He released her and swung out of bed. "I'll take the chair. Can I have one of the blankets?"

Elizabeth nodded, not trusting her voice. She hadn't meant to make him angry, but what could she say? He blew out the oil lamp and she could hear him settling in the chair.

She sank down into the darkness. The bed suddenly seemed so cold.

****

The chair was empty the next morning when she woke. Quickly, Elizabeth dressed, struggling with the buttons, after she'd flung the corset on the bed. Without it, the shirtwaist was snug, but she didn't have anyone to lace the thing and she wasn't about to ask for help from any of Lily's girls.

She found Miguel in the kitchen, seated across the table from Lily, drinking coffee that smelled of chicory. He looked up at her warily, a tired expression on his face. She felt a twinge of guilt for making him sleep in the chair.

Lily arched an eyebrow and stood. "I think I'll leave you two alone."

Miguel stood, too. "I'm leaving. I've got to go talk to Major Arnold."

"I'm coming with you," Elizabeth said.

He shrugged. "Suit yourself. Do you want to eat first?"

She shook her head. She was hungry, but she feared he'd leave without her and leave her stranded here.

They rode the short distance from the Trinity River to the bluff where the fort stood in silence. The guard at the gate lifted the bar and let them through. He grinned when he saw Elizabeth, but quickly stopped at the glare Miguel gave him.

Once inside the walls, Elizabeth looked around with interest. She had read about the historic Fort Worth. To her right stood the hospital and dispensary, roofed with real shingles. A small office type of building stood next to them. To her left were the stables, forage and tack rooms, and smithy. The parade grounds cleared the middle of the complex and behind them, a large tent that served as a mess hall stood next to the stone kitchens. Elizabeth could smell bacon frying as they passed by and her tummy rumbled. If Miguel heard, he gave no sign. The commanding officer's house stood close to the back wall. To one side were three sets of officers' quarters made of clapboard-covered logs, roofs tar-pitched for insulation, and fireplaces made of stone. On the other side were the enlisted men's barracks, long rows of log cabins daubed with mud. Only slim tin chimneys poked through the rooftops.

They walked up the steps to the porch, but before they could knock, the door opened. A young soldier ushered them into the parlor.

"Major Arnold will be with you shortly. Please have a seat."

Elizabeth sat down on a brocaded chair while Miguel stood by the mantel of the fireplace. Her fingers traced the smooth rosewood of the arm of the heavy Victorian piece. She looked around. Currier and Ives prints hung above the horsehair sofa along one wall, heavy velvet curtains framed the large front window. The wood floor had a soft Oriental rug covering most of it. Obviously, commanding officers didn't lack for comfort, even at a far outpost like Fort Worth.

"Miguel! What brings you here at this hour?" Major Ripley Arnold walked through the doorway, wiping his hands on a linen napkin. He had on a regulation shirt, breeches, and boots, but had not donned his jacket. He looked surprised when he saw Elizabeth. "Is this social? I'll call my wife."

"No," Miguel answered and quickly relayed the events of the past night. "Middleton should be arriving with the other Rangers in an hour or so."

Major Arnold nodded. "We can install a military curfew, too. I'll have the captain assign double shifts on watch, as well." He ran a hand through his hair as he began pacing. "Having those Indians here hasn't done a lot for morale with my troops either. I fear some of them share the townspeople's ideas."

Miguel raised an eyebrow. "Won't they be facing court-martial if they disobey orders?"

"It's the only thing that's holding some of them back," the major replied, "but we don't need bickering within the ranks, not with Chief Jim Ned's warriors sitting out there, waiting for the outcome."

Miguel frowned. "So what the hired guns said was right. Do you think the Comanche will go on the warpath?"

The major shrugged. "Don't know. I've sent an envoy to tell the chief he can send representatives to be present during the trial. They'll have safe conduct."

"Any news as to where the judge is on the circuit?"

"Nope. Last I heard, his health had turned puny. I hope he doesn't come down with the lung fever."

"Pneumonia?" Elizabeth interrupted. "There is medicine—"

"The sooner the judge can get here, the better." Miguel cut her off. "We'd better be getting back so I can meet up with Middleton."

The major cleared his throat. "There's something else you should know."

Miguel stopped halfway to the door. "What?"

"Well, some of the soldiers have been talking to the townsfolk. They've gotten kind of fired-up that those two hostages you have aren't under guard."

"The Rangers treated with Chief Jim Ned about that," Miguel said evenly. "They've not caused trouble in town the four years they've been with me."

"Yes, well. Having gunslingers in town to stir things up doesn't help. They got wind that you don't fence your land, that you let the Comanche use it for grazing." The major looked uncomfortable. "They're saying you're an Indian lover."

Elizabeth sputtered, her Celtic temper rising. "How dare they! Miguel has done nothing to endanger any of the townspeople. No, he doesn't keep Cactus Flower or Swift Hawk under lock and key; he respects them. They're *people.* How are we ever going to have peace with the Indians if they're treated like second-class citizens?" She stood and began to pace. "And whose business is it what Miguel does with his land? He owns it. If getting along with the Comanche and sharing land that once was theirs is considered wrong—"

"That's enough, Elizabeth." Miguel took her arm and gently tugged her toward him. "Don't kill the messenger here."

"Fiery little hellcat, isn't she?" the major said wryly.

"That she is," Miguel said. "Never a dull moment."

Elizabeth looked up at him, expecting him to be angry at her outburst. Instead, he had the strangest look on his face, as though he were seeing her for the first time.

The major escorted them to the door and soon they were once again headed toward town. Elizabeth looked with interest south of the road. The notorious Hell's Half Acre would be located there in another twenty years or so. She wanted to tell Miguel about it, but one look at his face made her decide not to.

"Do you really think the Indians will attack?" Elizabeth asked. "What will the townspeople do?"

"The townspeople can seek shelter within the fort," Miguel answered. "It's well- built enough to stand a hundred years."

"You won't believe me," Elizabeth said, unable to stop herself this time, "but where the fort sits now…in my century there will be a county courthouse."

Miguel looked heavenward, but his voice sounded patient. "We aren't even a county. Do you want me to stop off and have the army doctor check you out?"

She clamped her mouth shut and remained silent until he dropped her off at Miss Lily's. She turned around as she walked up to the porch. "You will be," she said.

"Will be what?" Miguel asked, holding the horses in check.

"A county. Tarrant County, after the general who

fought at Village Creek." She turned and walked inside before he could answer.

****

Miguel returned to Miss Lily's later that afternoon for a bath and a shave. Elizabeth was only aware of it as she came downstairs and saw him getting ready to leave again. Sharee stood behind him at the door, holding a wet washcloth and bar of soap. She gave Elizabeth a self-satisfied smile.

Elizabeth didn't return it. Had he let that woman give him a bath? No doubt, considering where they were. She didn't even want to think about that wanton soaping him down, dribbling water over his magnificent nude body, touching him— Miguel could have had the decency to at least take his own bath!

"Are you leaving?" she asked. "Can I come along?"

"No. I'm on watch. Tate Johnson's men are posted all over town. I'll be stationed by the stables for the evening. I'll see you in the morning and take you home."

In the morning? Did that mean he was going to spend the night in Sharee's bed?

"I'm going crazy here. I've been cooped up in that room all afternoon since I don't want to be taken for one of the…working girls."

Miguel turned to Sharee. "Would you excuse us?"

She pouted and then purred, "Come see me later."

He waited until she had gone. "These girls have to work for a living. You could at least try to show some respect."

"Respect? For prostitution?"

She didn't catch the warning that flashed in his eyes. "I've shown you respect, haven't I?"

Elizabeth felt her face flush at the tired implication,

but her temper still rose. "I'm not a whore! And you'll never catch me giving you a bath!"

He stopped his retort and studied her. Then he grinned. "I think you're jealous."

"I most certainly am not!"

He moved closer and she caught the clean scent of him. Her heart beat faster as he tilted her chin up with one finger and looked deeply into her eyes. She refused to look away and hoped he didn't feel her trembling. Must his touch always send quivers racing through her?

"Hmmm. I think I'm going to look forward to that bath." He turned away and stepped through the door. He was at the iron gate before he turned back. "Oh, just one other thing, Red."

"What?"

"I always return the favor. Just think about my bathing you. We could—"

She slammed the door shut, trying to block out the sound of his chuckling as he walked away.

****

The weather turned bitterly cold with the arrival of a sudden front shortly after Miguel left. Lily had fires lit in all the hearths and her cook mulled wine for the customers.

To avoid boredom, Elizabeth found her way to the kitchen and offered to help the cook, Carmen, with the big cauldron of *carne guisada* she was making for supper. The older woman eyed her suspiciously at first, but Elizabeth explained she really was only a temporary guest and needed something to do out of sight of the parlor and visiting rooms.

Most of the girls ate an early meal, as regular visiting hours began at 8:00 p.m. Sharee had a smug smile on her face when she came through the kitchen. Elizabeth clenched her teeth, not wanting to think about when Miguel would be visiting her.

To be fair, she had all but kicked Miguel out of her bed last night, clearly letting him know she did not welcome his attention. Well, that wasn't quite true, she thought, as she remembered his soft tongue winding its velvet way down her back. She did want him, but she wanted him to *care*…and to believe she wasn't a prostitute. She rubbed her temples, hoping a headache was not coming on.

Elizabeth helped Carmen clean up the dishes and watched as the woman poured some of the still steaming stew into a pottery crock and seal it.

"There," she said as she set it on the counter. "It'll still be hot for *Señor* Miguel when he comes in. "*¿Esta muy frío, a al aire libre, no?*"

"Yes, it is getting chilly," Elizabeth said. The woman reminded her of a Spanish Olga. And Lily wasn't what she'd expected either. How did Miguel manage to charm these women into coddling him?

Carmen folded several corn tortillas in half and wrapped them in a clean towel. "He'll be wanting these too. He loves my *tortillas masas*."

"Does he come here often?" Elizabeth asked casually.

Carmen stopped what she was doing. "He and Miss Lily have been friends a long time." She looked Elizabeth over appraisingly. "Or is it *las señoritas* you're wanting to know about?"

Elizabeth blushed. "No—I mean—I don't care about that."

"Then you'd be the first not to. More than one

woman has tried to lasso him, as the *vaqueros* say, but he always manages to slip the noose." She laughed lightly. "*Él es un caballo…salvaje y libre*."

A wild and free stallion. That fitted him. As a young girl, Elizabeth had watched a stallion mount a mare once, on her uncle's ranch, before someone had quickly taken her away from the breeding barn. She'd never forgotten the sounds the horse had made or how big his organ was. Unbidden, a throbbing began between her thighs. Sweet Mary. Why were these thoughts invading her brain?

She decided to change the subject. "Why don't you go home, Carmen? I can finish up here. It'll give me something to do."

"*Muy bueno,*" the Spanish lady said gratefully. "*Tengo una familia.*"

After she had gone, Elizabeth hung the damp towels near the hearth to dry and wiped the countertops. She stacked clean plates and looked around the kitchen. Everything was done. She could hear the evening "visitors" begin to arrive, which meant she couldn't be seen. She hated the thought of sitting in her room with nothing to do.

Her gaze landed on the crock of stew. Why not take it to Miguel? She could make amends. The night was cold and the stew would warm him from the inside out. He said he'd be on watch near the stables and that was only a few blocks from here.

Quickly, Elizabeth took one of the capes from its peg near the back door and threw it over her shoulders. She wrapped the crock and tortillas in another towel for insulation and slipped out.

Thankfully, it was dark. She skirted around the fence without being seen and walked the caliche path leading to the main street of town. It was lighter there, with oil lamps swinging from the rafters of the buildings. She stepped up on the wood sidewalk as a horseman trotted by.

Ahead of her, five men left the saloon and looked her way. She stopped momentarily as they noticed her, suddenly aware she was alone. Elizabeth breathed a sigh of relief when they moved in the other direction into an alley beside the saloon.

Carefully, she passed the saloon, remembering the men who had come hurtling out fighting the day before. Someone was playing the piano badly and some even worse singing was going on, but it was definitely quieter tonight, probably because of the Rangers. She could see the stable now, a couple of blocks away, and picked up her pace.

She didn't have time to scream as a hand clamped over her mouth and she was pulled roughly into the alleyway. Her cape was torn off. She couldn't see the faces in the dark, but the hands mauling her breasts and tearing her skirt were harsh. Too many hands. Dear Lord, it must be those five men she saw earlier!

"What have we here?" one of them asked. "A prize filly, I think."

"Move over, Bart," another of them said to the man who had his hand over her mouth. "Let's all have a kiss first before we take her some place where we can take our time with her."

"Nah. She's mine first," he answered. "Just get that damn thing she's holding out of my way."

Elizabeth fought desperately to hang onto the crock and fingered the lid, struggling to get it open. Her eyes had adjusted to the lack of light and she could see outlines now. She wasn't that far away from the street, if only— The lid suddenly gave way and she turned the pot upside down, spilling the hot contents down the front of the man's pants.

He howled as the steaming stew penetrated through the cloth and burned his groin. Elizabeth gave him a push and he fell back against the other men. She picked up her tattered skirt and lunged for the street, screaming like a banshee.

The men bounded after her, Bart grabbing her again. "You'll pay for that."

She wrapped her arms around a hitching post, refusing to be dragged back. One of the men grabbed her waist, lifting her off the ground, and pulled. She wrapped her arms tighter around the post and clung for dear life. Surely, someone would hear her scream, even with that racket coming from the saloon.

She heard the thud of a fist make contact with crunched bone before she saw him. Miguel drove Bart down to the ground, knocking him senseless and pounding his face to a pulp. He only leapt up when the second man approached and tackled him. By that time, a crowd was spilling out of the saloon, eager to put wagers on the fight.

The third and fourth men circled Miguel while the second one pulled a knife. Miguel reached into his boot for his dagger. The gunslinger sliced at him, but Miguel parried. They pressed close before springing apart. A well-placed kick from Miguel landed man number five on the ground groaning. His knife fell and Miguel snatched it. The others started to close and Miguel crouched, pivoting, a weapon in each hand. Number two lunged again and Miguel sidestepped. The man hurtled past and impaled number three on his knife. Number four dropped his weapon then and raised his hands.

From nowhere, other Rangers appeared, dispersing the crowd. Within minutes, the five gunmen were rounded up and on their way to the brig.

Miguel took some heaving breaths, bent over, his hands on his knees. Then he looked at Elizabeth.

She tried to pull the bodice of her dress together, suddenly aware that her breasts were almost completely exposed and the skirt had a tear up to her hip. Miguel straightened and came to her and wrapped his arms around her. For the first time that night, she felt safe and warm.

He held her so tightly she had difficulty breathing. She turned her head to the side against his chest and could feel his heart hammering. He murmured her name as he laid his head on top of hers, nuzzling her hair, his hands coursing up and down her back, kneading her toward him in long strokes.

"Are you all right, Elizabeth? Did they hurt you?"

Her arms slid around his waist and she clung to him, grateful for his solid strength. She burrowed into his shoulder. "I'm all right."

Someone handed him her cape and he draped it over her shoulders and brushed her forehead with his lips before he stepped back and fastened the cape for her. "Let's get you back to Lily's, then."

He kept a protective arm around her on the way back and Elizabeth wished she could stay cocooned in his embrace for the rest of the night, but he turned her over to Lily once they arrived.

Lily took over, ordering a hot tub and briskly stripping her of her torn clothes. Elizabeth didn't even try to protest, realizing suddenly how sore she was going to be the next day. Already, bruises were forming on her arms. Lily added lavender salts to the water.

"This will help you relax," she said, "and I have a eucalyptus salve for those marks. You'll be fine in a day or two. You're sure nothing else happened?"

"I wasn't raped," Elizabeth said weakly and inhaled the soothing fragrance.

"Good. Well, we have something for that too, as you might suspect," Lily said with a smile. "My girls don't have babies unless they want to."

In no time, Elizabeth was clean, warm, dressed in a soft cotton gown, and tucked into the bed. It amazed her how efficient Lily was. And how wrong Elizabeth had been about her. Maybe she had been wrong about the girls who worked here, too.

As Lily dimmed the wicker on the lamp, Elizabeth wondered where Miguel was. She wanted him with her tonight. In bed. What he thought she was didn't matter anymore. She felt safe with him. More than that, she wanted to give herself to him completely.

Chapter Ten—Resistance

What the hell had she been thinking? Miguel stomped angrily toward the alleyway. No woman wandered alone at night, especially with tension so high. He had told her to stay inside Lily's where she would be safe. Why didn't she listen? Damn! She was the most stubborn woman he'd ever met.

And by far, the most sexy. To think of those hired guns' hands pawing at her, tearing her clothes, infuriated him. *His* hand should be caressing her breasts, slowly teasing the nipples into an aching need for him. *His* mouth should be the one covering hers, bringing exquisite sensations to her as he varied the pressure and strokes. *Thank God they didn't have a chance to rape her.*

His emotional response to her, though, had him confused. That he wanted her physically, he knew. He hadn't been prepared for the tenderness he had felt when he held her trembling body in his arms. A need to protect her from harm nearly overwhelmed him.

He entered the alleyway and stopped when his boot struck something hard. He bent down and picked up part of the broken crock. He sniffed. Carmen's *carne guisada.* His hand found the linen napkin holding the tortillas. Had Elizabeth been bringing dinner to him? Even though she'd turned him out of her bed, did she care about his welfare? His brow furrowed as the unfamiliar feeling of tenderness swept over him again. He sensed danger ebbing from every pore of his skin. Getting emotionally involved was something he took care not to do. He didn't need the problem of a woman clinging to him, making demands. Pleasuring a woman—and he always made sure he did; he owed them that—was one thing. Loving one was another. He had been prepared to give his heart to Elena. He wouldn't take that chance again.

He made his way back to the stable and leaned back on the wall for the rest of his watch. What he needed was to satisfy his lust, that's all. To plunge himself into a willing woman who would accept what pleasure he could give and not expect anything more. He thought about Sharee's offer. She was pretty enough and, undoubtedly, well-experienced. And yet that thought did nothing to stir his desire. The image of Elizabeth, copper hair spread over a satin pillow, writhing beneath him passionately, legs wrapped around him, nearly took away his breath. He slammed a fist against the wood. Damn. The best thing he could do was keep his distance from her until he had his emotions in check. With a sigh, he decided he'd sleep in the barn tonight.

****

Elizabeth dozed fitfully, waiting for Miguel's step on the stairs. Finally, in the wee hours of the morning, she fell asleep. When she woke, sunshine flooded the room.

He hadn't come to her. She glanced at the other side of the bed hopefully, but the cover was smooth. He had gone to Sharee. She felt a sharp ping in her chest. How could he? Had she been wrong in thinking he might care? He had held her so protectively and called her name—

her real one, not Red—and she could have sworn there was worry and concern in his voice. Why hadn't he come to the room when his watch was over? Last night, he'd said there was no other place to go.

But there was. Sharee. Elizabeth bit her lip, remembering the smug smile on the the girl's face at supper. She was sure of her feminine hold over him, sure she could lure him to her room instead of Elizabeth's. Miguel liked experienced women. He'd made that clear enough. She felt her body flush all over. Dear Lord, she wouldn't even know what to do with him—to him. He was used to women who knew exactly what to do, where to touch him, how to excite him. Miguel would find her inept, after bedding a skilled courtesan—which, according to Carmen, Lily's girls all were.

A hysterical bubble rose in her throat. What would he do if he ever found out she was a virgin? Laugh at her?

Well, he wouldn't find out. Never. She balled her fists into the mattress. Better to remember her resolve about good-looking men. Too many women chased after them. She wasn't Irish for nothing; Celtic women were strong and independent. They didn't need a man.

Then why, she wondered, did she feel so miserable?

****

Miguel was waiting for her when she came out of the kitchen after breakfast. Self-consciously, she tugged at the neckline of the dress Lily had lent her. It was a pale gray silk, modest by working-girl standards, but the neckline was still low and the bodice form-fitting.

Miguel glanced briefly at the swell of her breasts and then looked away. "Are you ready to go? The carriage is outside."

She nodded. His obvious avoidance of looking her in the eye was probably because he was remembering his night with Sharee. He didn't look rested at all. Had they made love all night? Well, Elizabeth didn't care. She lifted her chin and walked past him and out the door.

Middleton Tate Johnson and the other Rangers were waiting. He helped her into the carriage and Miguel climbed up beside her.

"We have an escort today," he said.

She looked at him. "Are you expecting trouble?"

"Probably not. The Comanche will wait for the trial. The town's secured, with the military curfew and the hired guns in the brig. We all have our own work to do."

He didn't say much else to her on the long drive back, speaking mainly with whichever Ranger rode beside them, and Elizabeth fell silent. There was a coolness to Miguel this morning, and he hadn't even mentioned the incident of the night before.

The Rangers left them as they turned onto the private road leading to Miguel's ranch and Elizabeth waited for Miguel to say something, and he finally did.

"I hope you've learned your lesson. Women don't go wandering around unescorted unless they want to be waylaid."

"Waylaid? I was bringing you some supper!"

"You made yourself a target. In the future, I will not let you go around unescorted. This time you will obey me."

His unemotional tone made her angry. He could show a little concern over the scare she'd had! "In my century, women are free to come and go as they please. They don't need a man."

"It seems you did last night."

Elizabeth paused. He was right. What if he hadn't come to her aid? She remembered how safe she had felt with his muscular arms wrapped around her, his strong hands stroking her back, holding her close. But he went to Sharee's bed last night, so he had only done the decent thing by rescuing her. She straightened and held on to her side of the seat, careful not to brush against him. "Thank you," she said stiffly and heard him grunt for an answer.

Swift Hawk came to meet them as they drove up to the *hacienda*. His black eyes lingered on Elizabeth's neckline and then he looked into her eyes. "The color becomes you, Firewoman." He held out a hand to help her down.

She was loath to take it, but Miguel made no move to descend. Lightly, she put her fingers into Swift Hawk's palm, but his hand closed around hers and then he circled her waist with his other arm, lifting her down. His hand lingered on her side not quite long enough for her to protest, but long enough to make her uncomfortable, as always. The Indian was too intense. His eyes glittered as if he could read her thoughts.

"*Papá! Papá!*" Raul ran to them, waving a white envelope. "It's a barn-raising over at Marrow Bone Spring. Can I go with you, please? Last time you said I was almost old enough!"

Miguel stepped down, retrieved the sack with Elizabeth's torn dress, and handed the team over to Swift Hawk, then turned and ruffled his son's hair as he took the envelope. "We'll see."

"Please?" Raul begged and then turned shining eyes on Elizabeth. "Please make him take me, Miss Elizabeth. I've done all the chores you asked and even my schoolwork." He looked back at his father. "And I ain't scared Miss Parsons once."

As if anyone could scare that predator, Elizabeth thought. "Haven't," she corrected. "What goes on, in this barn-raising, that you want to go so much?"

Raul puffed out his chest as they walked into the foyer. "The big boys—I mean the really big boys, ones who don't have to go to school anymore—get to help their fathers build the barn. It means I'm almost a man."

Elizabeth suppressed a smile, careful not to hurt the child's ego. "That's pretty important, then. Why don't you let your father think about it?" Over Raul's head, she noticed Miguel looking at her with a peculiar expression, almost one of wariness. Now what did she do? She was trying to be diplomatic.

"Good idea," Miguel said. "Why don't you find Olga and tell her we're home?" He watched as his son scampered off and then turned back to Elizabeth.

"It seems you're making quite an impression on him."

Was that wrong? Ever since the day of the snake incident, she'd been helping Raul with his schoolwork and sometimes even played games with him when Miguel was gone or too busy. She thought Miguel appreciated it. She decided to try a neutral approach. "I hope I've convinced him to leave the schoolteacher pranks for someone else."

His dark eyes studied her. "I don't remember him ever asking Katy to persuade me of anything."

Elizabeth bit her tongue not to say Katy probably had her own methods of persuasion. After all, what did she care? Still, Miguel's coolness all morning made her uneasy. Before she could answer, Olga bustled out.

She eyed Elizabeth's dress and looked questioningly at Miguel.

He handed her the sack with the torn dress. "There was some trouble in town and I told her she would be safe at Lily's, but as usual, Red didn't choose to follow my instructions. Perhaps that can be repaired." He turned to go. "If you'll excuse me, I've got chores."

Olga watched him go and then held up the tattered dress. She gave an exclamation of dismay. "What happened, child? Come into the kitchen and I'll make you some tea."

Until that show of motherly concern, Elizabeth had felt strong. Now she felt her knee buckling and she began to shake. Olga guided her into the kitchen and seated her at the table, then busied herself with the tea and set some chocolate chip cookies she had just made in front of Elizabeth as she sat down.

"Tell me, dear. Don't hold back."

Elizabeth drew a ragged breath and then unburdened herself, telling Olga everything from meeting Miss Lily and Sharee to how she decided to bring Miguel his supper and made herself vulnerable to attack. "And now," she concluded and tried not to sob, "Miguel acts like he hates me. I don't know what I did."

The housekeeper patted her hand. "Don't you worry about Miguel. More likely he's angry with himself for placing you in danger. He cares for you."

He cared for her? He only wanted to take her to bed—or he did before Sharee. But she couldn't tell that to Olga.

"Did you have fun?" Cactus Flower interrupted them as she walked in and helped herself to a cookie. She sat down beside Elizabeth and her eyes widened at the new dress. "Did *Don* Miguel actually take you to Miss Lily's?"

"Sometimes you ask too many questions," Olga said briskly. "Do you know where Raul is?"

Cactus Flower nodded, her eyes still on the gray silk. "He's polishing Diablo's saddle, I think. I saw him talking to Swift Hawk a little while ago and they both were headed to the barn."

Elizabeth smiled. "He's probably trying to soften up his father to let him help at the barn-raising."

Cactus Flower clapped her hands excitedly. "I can hardly wait myself."

"Oh?" Elizabeth wrinkled her forehead. "Are women supposed to help, too?"

The Indian girl looked at her as though she were daft. "Some of the women cook during the days it takes the men to build the barn. It's the dance afterwards that's fun."

"Dance?"

Olga nodded. "Before the animals are placed in the barn, while it's still clean and the floors slippery with sawdust, there'll be a dance. They'll have fiddlin' and guitars."

"And maybe even *mariachis*," Cactus Flower added. "*Don* Miguel hired some from San Antonio one time."

It did sound like fun, but Elizabeth doubted she'd be going. She had no gowns suitable for dancing. Her dresses were made for everyday wear. She wasn't about to ask Miguel for new clothes, not in his present mood. "I wouldn't know what to wear."

Cactus Flower giggled. "We'll come up with something."

****

Since Miguel had decided to stay at Tate Johnson's for the duration of the barn-raising and Olaf joined him when he could get away, Olga decided to take them a home-cooked lunch one day.

Elizabeth held the big basket on her lap in the surrey. The smells of fried chicken, still warm yeast bread, and a pungent potato salad wafted up, making her hungry. The cinnamon spice from the apple pie didn't help matters either. Even the two wranglers who rode as their guards sniffed appreciatively.

She hadn't seen Miguel in nearly ten days. His original excuse had been that he needed to be able to make plans with Tate Johnson on handling the Indian trial when the circuit judge came to town, but Elizabeth suspected he was staying away for a different reason. She wasn't sure what it was; he had just been cool and distant toward her since the attack in Fort Worth. She had played the event over and over in her mind, wondering what could possibly have gone wrong. The only conclusion she came up with was that Sharee had been so good he had decided to quit bothering with Elizabeth. Not a conclusion she liked at all.

Olaf came to meet them as they drove into the barnyard. She watched as he helped Olga down and kissed her cheek. Roughshod he might be, but there was love between the two of them. Elizabeth sighed. Would a man ever treat her like that?

Then she saw Miguel. Shirtless, his tanned body gleaming with a light layer of sweat, he wielded a hammer as though it were nothing more than a kitchen fork. Yet his biceps contracted and his back muscles rippled as he nailed the two-by-four into place. Raw, semi-naked man. Would she ever get tired of the sight of him?

He tossed the hammer down and reached for his shirt and she saw him walk toward a small grove of shade as he buttoned it. Then she stiffened.

Abigail Parsons was sitting on a blanket, a picnic spread on a linen cloth. As Elizabeth watched, Miguel dropped down beside her. She handed him a thick sandwich and a napkin. Even from where Elizabeth stood, she could hear the woman's laughter. Only, to her, it sounded more like the screech of a cougar about to pounce.

Olga followed her gaze and made a hissing noise. "Ach, child. Pay no attention. He'll come over when he can."

Which really wasn't the point. How often had the schoolmarm been coming? Miguel had been gone two weekends and one day school was closed because, supposedly, Miss Parsons was ill. Had she been spending all those days bringing Miguel lunch? A burning sensation began in Elizabeth's stomach as if she'd swallowed hot coals. So maybe it hadn't been Sharee at all. Maybe the reason for his staying away was really to rendezvous with the cat-woman. He had said he didn't kiss her that day in the library, but she had kissed him. Maybe he liked it and decided to go for more. By all the saints, the schoolmarm had made it known she was willing.

Miguel looked up then and his hand paused halfway to his mouth. He smiled and nodded his head. The schoolmarm immediately followed his gaze and her own eyes narrowed as she put a hand possessively on his arm and leaned closer.

Elizabeth turned away and found herself looking at Beauregard Cartier. Surprisingly, he didn't look like he'd worked up a sweat at all. His white linen shirt was clean and his dark wool trousers neatly creased. Even his boots weren't dusty.

"What are you doing here?" she asked.

He smiled. "Just delivering some paperwork to Tate Johnson. I must say, my dear lady, the food smells as absolutely delicious as you look, begging your pardon for my taking such a liberty as saying so. Might I impose my company on you?"

Elizabeth considered. She knew there was plenty of food—Olga believed in Scandinavian smorgasbord cooking. And Beauregard was definitely a handsome man with his blond hair and blue eyes, although he reminded her too much of Edward. A pity the Predator didn't put her claws out for this one. No matter. If Miguel planned on acting chivalrous and all gallant toward Miss Parsons, Elizabeth could play the game too. Beauregard was Southern, so she summoned up her best image of Scarlett.

"My, but you do flatter me," Elizabeth said and almost choked on the words. How did women say stuff like that? "I'm sure Olga won't mind." She allowed herself a small side glance and was rewarded to find Miguel staring at them. Good. Let him.

The meal seemed to stretch into eternity, although Beauregard kept up a running conversation and politely made sure Olga and Olaf were included. Finally, Elizabeth saw Miguel escort the schoolmarm to her carriage. Damn. Did he have to help her into it? She wasn't surprised to see that Miss Parsons had driven alone; Elizabeth had a feeling any self-respecting wolf, coyote, or rattler along the way would avoid the woman.

Then she saw Miguel say something to one of the teenage boys. He passed him a coin and the young man grinned and nodded and ran for his horse. She watched as he galloped after the schoolmarm. So Miguel sent an escort and was protecting her after all.

Elizabeth plastered a smile on her face and turned her full attention to the lawyer, not hearing a word.

****

Miguel sauntered over to them, wondering what he was going to say to her. Having not seen her in over a week, she nearly took his breath away in those form-fitting jeans. The ones he had told her not to wear. He sighed. He doubted she would ever listen to him. Just another reason not to let himself get emotionally involved. A man had to have some respect from his woman. He stopped short. Elizabeth was not his woman. But what the hell was that dandy lawyer doing here today?

And, of all days, Abigail Parsons had to show up, too. He knew Elizabeth wouldn't believe him if he said it had been the first time she did and he'd had no idea she was coming. That beautiful, wild, red hair of Elizabeth's was also reminiscent of the legendary temper of the Celts.

He dropped down to the ground on the other side of her and reached into the basket for leftovers.

"Still hungry?" Elizabeth asked coolly.

Ouch. He forced himself to look into her eyes and then let his gaze linger on her mouth. Full sensual lips that he longed to kiss. He looked back into her eyes. "As a matter of fact, I am." He was rewarded with a blush that swept across her face before she looked away.

Grinning, he helped himself to a chicken thigh.

"Beauregard was just telling us about his life in Virginia," Elizabeth said quickly and somewhat breathlessly. "I find it fascinating. Did you know he's a writer?"

"No. What brought you to Texas?" Miguel asked languidly.

The lawyer paused. "I guess I wanted to see what the Wild West was like. Thought I might try writing some of those dime novels like I've been reading. They're quite the rage in the East."

"We're pretty tame here, since most of the Indians are on reservations," Miguel answered. "The real adventure lies in California's gold. San Francisco is full of intrigue. Maybe you should go there."

Beauregard shook his head. "Texas is fine with me. Tate Johnson and my father were both Masons. The families go back a way. And, I think I can establish a good practice here, with Fort Worth growing."

"Economic growth is important," Elizabeth said. "Just suppose—say in another hundred and fifty years or so—that Fort Worth might have several hundred thousand people living here!"

Miguel sent her a dark look. He wished he could convince her not to talk about the future—someone was going to assume she was truly addled.

Beauregard laughed. "You do have a delightful sense of humor, my lady."

Little did he know she was serious. Miguel changed the subject as he accepted a piece of pie from Olga. "Did you make the pie by any chance, Red?"

"You know very well that's Olga's pie," Elizabeth snapped. "Didn't Miss Parsons bring you dessert?"

He looked into her eyes. "She offered dessert, yes. I turned it down." He watched as the implication sank in and was pleased to see the blush spread again. "Would you like some of mine?" He tried not to grin when the blush deepened.

"No. Thanks." Elizabeth turned away and Miguel was forced to listen to her ask Beauregard more about life in Virginia. At least, she wasn't comparing it to the twenty-first century. But when she asked the same somewhat general question for a third time, he suspected she might not be all that interested in life in Virginia.

Miguel brushed against her arm as he put the empty pie plate down and heard her sharp intake of breath. He moved slightly closer, although he did not touch her. Just enough for her to be aware of him, even if she pretended she wasn't.

Trouble was, it was a damn lot disturbing for him too.

****

Tonight was the dance.

In her room Saturday morning, Elizabeth tried to decide what to wear. She finally settled on the gray silk, even though she felt the neckline a bit low. She could wrap one of Olga's softly woven shawls around her shoulders. She had just finished her bath in the oaken tub in her room when there was a knock on the door.

Cactus Flower entered at her summons. "I thought you might want to wear this."

Elizabeth gasped, looking at the most stunningly beautiful gown she'd ever seen. The fabric was emerald green silk, which would set off her eyes and hair. She slipped it on. The bodice was fitted with an embroidered circle under the bustline. The gathered material spread out like flower petals, making the neckline scalloped, exposing just a hint of cleavage. The skirt hugged her hips softly and hung in soft swirls to the floor, eliminating the need for a crinoline. The fashion was very European.

"Where did you find this?" she asked.

"Among some trunks in the attic," Cactus Flower answered. "I was looking for something for myself, but everything is too long."

Elizabeth narrowed her eyes. Could this be Katy's dress? She probably left a lot behind when she ran off with that drifter. Cactus Flower had told her Miguel brought Katy fancy clothes.

"Was this Katy's?"

Cactus Flower frowned. "I don't know. I never saw her wear it. But she was tall, like you are."

Could she wear something that belonged to Miguel's former mistress? It was so beautiful, though, and the fit was perfect. Her diamond sparkled brilliantly at her throat, catching the green fire of the silk. Elizabeth twirled and felt the fabric swing out and then settle softly. Ummm. Miguel had been so cool to her…and then she discovered that hussy with him… Maybe letting him see her in this would stir his interest again. As much as she hated to admit it, she did want his attention. She hadn't been able to get the rescue out of her mind. She wanted to feel his arms around her again, and maybe that did make her as much of a hussy as she was blaming Miss Parsons and Sharee of being, but she had felt lonely and cold with Miguel gone This dress should spike his interest. At least, she hoped so.

****

She stood with Cactus Flower just inside the double

barn doors that evening, her cloak wrapped tightly around her to keep the evening chill away. Inside, oil lamps hung suspended on ropes which stretched the length of the barn on either side. Braziers burned along each wall, bringing a cheery, bright warmth to the building.

Miguel approached them. “Your wraps, ladies?” He took the one Cactus Flower handed him. “Swift Hawk chose not to come?”

Cactus Flower shrugged. “He said he wouldn’t, but Elizabeth may have changed his mind.”

Miguel gave her an odd look. “You asked him to come?’

“No,” Elizabeth said quickly. “You know I don’t like the comments he’s always making about my red hair. Here.” She handed him her cloak.

Miguel stiffened. His face blanched, leaving his dark eyes stark in contrast. The cloaks slipped from his hands. “Where—where did you get that dress?”

Elizabeth had hoped it would get his attention, but she hadn’t expected anything like this. Did he really think her that beautiful in it? She spun around for him, the skirt gently sweeping his leg. “Do you like it?”

As if the material had scorched him, he sprang into action, bending to retrieve the fallen cloaks. When he straightened, color was high in his face and his eyes gleamed with a strange light. “You have no idea,” he managed in a waspy whisper that was nearly inaudible before he turned and walked away.

Elizabeth watched him, puzzled. It wasn’t exactly the reaction she’d expected.

“May I have this dance?” Beauregard asked with a courtly bow.

Before she knew it, Elizabeth was spinning around and around to a sprightly polka. She danced another dance with him before other men started cutting in. Each one gave in none too graciously as another would claim her.

The evening was a blur. She caught sight of Miguel several times, always well away from her. What bothered her more than his refusing to meet her eye was Miss Parsons clinging to him. Or did she? Maybe Miguel had invited that slinky feline for lunch that day. He seemed to be laughing at her jokes and he certainly was not keeping her at arm's bay.

They lined up for the Virginia Reel. At any other time, Elizabeth would have been delighted to participate in a dance she'd always thought so courtly and romantic. At least, as the two lines facing each other crisscrossed their dancers and started down the center, he would be forced to acknowledge her. But his touch, when he took her hand in his and twirled her and retreated, was impersonal. What in the world was wrong with him?

The dance finished and Abigail Parsons plucked at his sleeve. "I'm so thirsty after that. Would you fetch me some fruit punch?" She purred and gave Elizabeth a satisfied smile. Elizabeth could almost see her licking her whiskers.

Luckily, Beauregard asked her for a dance and she readily accepted, glad not to be there when Miguel returned. When the dance was finished, she excused herself, needing to get some fresh air.

She was standing near the door, her back to it, when someone brushed her arm. Turning, she stumbled back in shock.

Swift Hawk stood there, a strange smile on his face.

For once, he wore western clothes. All black from his boots to his pants and shirt. He'd tied the raven-blue hair back with a strip of black leather, but the hawk's feather dangled from it. His black eyes looked like ebony in the firelight and his dark face was a series of hard angles. He was not unhandsome, Elizabeth thought remotely, but he had a dangerous air.

"Dance with me, Firewoman. *Don* Miguel appears to be occupied."

She glared at him. "Why should that matter to me?"

He shrugged. "It shouldn't. You have been watching him."

"How long have you been here?" She would never get used to the Indian's silent stealthy approaches. Always, he nearly made her jump out of her skin.

"Long enough. Ah." He tilted his head to listen to the music. "Is this not what the white man calls a waltz?" He took her hand in his and brought the other arm around her waist, pulling her close. Too close.

"Let go of me," Elizabeth hissed.

He spun around, surprising her with his grace. "Not this time. Not until this dance is over." His hand slid along her back toward her buttocks. "I intend to make you mine, Firewoman. The son of a chief never backs down."

****

A lot of good it did Miguel to stay away from Elizabeth. Seeing her at lunch that day and now tonight in that dress, he wondered if he were a blithering fool. On the way back from Fort Worth, he'd deliberately avoided looking at the swell of her breasts pushing against the bodice of the gown Lily had lent her. He imagined her nipples becoming taut buds as they pressed for release against the fabric. Even better, he could see himself stopping the team and ripping the thin fabric from her and suckling those pink tips himself, bringing her to the edge of ecstasy and then pausing, making her beg for more.

He thought he'd gotten himself under control these past days and could revert to his easy teasing of her. And then she'd shown up wearing that dress.

How had she found it? And why had she gone to the attic anyway?

His hand shook as he poured the punch for Abigail. The woman clung to him like a cornhusk to a tamale, but for tonight, he threw his usual precaution about such women to the winds. Anything to keep from looking at Elizabeth, dancing with man after man in a green swirl of fine silk.

The dress had been Elena's. He had ordered it from Paris when he'd learned she was pregnant, hoping to appease her anger. He knew how she loved fine things, and he'd prayed that once the baby was born a mother's instincts would take over. By the time the dress arrived, she was too large to wear it, but she had promised him, with shining eyes, that it would be the first one she'd wear once she was through with childbed. She had been so delighted with his gift that it had made him hope the marriage might work.

She never did get to wear it.

He should have burned the damn thing, he reflected as he watched Elizabeth covertly. His eyes narrowed as the dandy lawyer dipped her low. He hoped Elizabeth was sensible enough not to believe those flowery Southern phrases dripping like honey from the man's mouth. He sighed as Elizabeth pirouetted across the floor. The dress would never have done Elena the justice it did Elizabeth. The color, the style, the way it molded to her slim curves…everything made it hers. He just wished it didn't stir the memories of his guilt, trying to buy his wife's affections.

He returned to Abigail and handed her the cup. Her fingers lingered on his hand and she tilted her head and looked up at him through long eyelashes. She took a sip of punch and licked her lips, her eyes not leaving his face.

If there was ever an invitation from a woman, this was it. A thought flitted through his mind that Miss Parsons should be working for Lily, not teaching school. Then again, maybe he needed to feel another woman in his arms. All he could think of was enveloping a frightened Elizabeth that night in Fort Worth and how soft and vulnerable she'd felt. Damnation. Another woman was what he needed. He was about to offer to take a walk outside when movement near the door caught his eye.

He turned and straightened. Swift Hawk had arrived and was talking to Elizabeth. He saw a look of near terror flashed across Elizabeth's face when Swift Hawk put an arm around her for the dance. Why did the Indian frighten her so? Lily must have been right; perhaps a Comanche had abducted her from a wagon train. As he watched, she tried to push free, but Swift Hawk pulled her closer.

"Excuse me," Miguel said to Abigail, and left her standing there with a look of shock on her face. All he saw were Swift Hawk's hands sliding down to where they had no business being.

"This waltz is mine, I believe." Miguel put a hand

on the young man's shoulder and spun him off Elizabeth so quickly she nearly lost her balance. "I've told you, Hawk—leave her alone."

The Indian glared at him, balling his fists. Miguel held his gaze unwavering. With a snarl, Swift Hawk turned and stalked out the door.

Miguel took Elizabeth into his embrace and moved away. By God, she felt good. Her fingers were soft and slender in his, her back smooth and straight beneath his touch. He wanted to take the hand she rested on his shoulder and move it to encircle his neck. He wanted to feel her fingers playing with his hair, her breath sweet on his cheek as he nibbled her ear and trailed kisses down her throat.

She was looking at him strangely. Had his intentions been so obvious on his face? "What is it?" he asked.

She gave him a mischievous smile. "The music's stopped."

"So it has." Reality returned abruptly and he released her. "Walk with me. I think you have some explaining to do about that dress."

****

Elizabeth felt, more than saw, the aloofness engulf him again. One minute he was holding her in his arms, looking like he wanted to devour her, and the next, he was as cold as ashes.

He grabbed her cloak from near the door and handed it to her. "It's cool out."

Suddenly, she realized he wanted her dress hidden. Obviously, her plan to arouse his interest hadn't worked. Had he cared so much for Katy that he couldn't stand to see the dress?

Elizabeth followed him outside and around a small

hill to an apple orchard, hidden from the crowded barn. He leaned against a tree, arms folded across his chest.

"You're a guest in my house. What were you doing in my attic?" he asked.

"I wasn't in your attic."

"No? It's not polite to snoop."

Elizabeth bristled. "I wasn't snooping! Cactus Flower went up there looking for something to wear to the dance, and she found this." She watched as the hard lines in his face eased a little. "I guess I should have checked with you first."

"You should have."

She felt her temper simmer. "You weren't home, remember? You've been avoiding me ever since that visit to Fort Worth, and I don't know why."

He stared at her, his dark eyes reflecting the moonlight that filtered through the branches of the trees. His full mouth softened and, for a moment, she thought he was going to kiss her. The thought of his lips on hers made muscles deep inside her ache and contract. Her anger melted into desire. She hadn't been this near to him in two weeks. She laid her hands on his folded arms and thought she felt him tense. "I'm sorry. I didn't know wearing Katy's dress would upset you so much."

His voice sounded husky. "Katy?"

Elizabeth nodded. "Your mistress. If you bought it for her, I thought maybe wearing it would make you—" She stopped.

His expression changed and a corner of his mouth quirked up. When he spoke, he sounded like the Miguel she knew. "What is it you want to make me do, Red?"

She shook her head, thankful he couldn't see her blush in the moonlight. "It's—nothing. Forget it."

He lifted her arms around his neck and encircled her waist beneath the cape with his hands, pulling her against his chest. “Something like this, maybe?”

For a moment she struggled with the idea of pushing away from him or giving in. In spite of herself, she found her fingers curling through his hair where it touched his collar. His hair was softer than she’d imagined and she inhaled the clean scent of him.

“Tell me what you want me to do, Red.” His voice was raspy. “In detail.”

In detail? How could she explain she wanted to have his hands on her naked body, stroking her breasts and stomach and the insides of her thighs until his fingers found the very essence of her? How could she tell him she wanted his mouth to follow the path, sucking her breasts until she cried in ecstasy and then, moving downward— She felt a warm gush of fluid between her legs. Oh, God, she couldn’t tell him *that*.

“Kiss me,” she whispered.

Obligingly, he lightly brushed his lips against hers and leaned back. “Like that?”

“No. More—” He was going to make this difficult, standing there with a smirk on his face. Why couldn’t he just take over? “More like— Well, whatever you’d have done with her.” There. Now let him take charge. He was the one with experience.

His voice changed imperceptibly. “You want me to do with you what I did with Katy? All of it?”

Again, she was thankful the moon was in shadow. “Um. Yes. I mean—” She didn’t get the chance to finish for he’d covered her mouth with his, his lips crushing hers, sucking on her upper lip then her lower one before probing with his tongue. She separated her lips willingly, enticed by the taste of him as he explored her mouth.

His hand kneaded a breast gently as he trailed kisses down her throat. With his other hand he pulled back a petal of the neckline, exposing a nipple which immediately budded under his touch. Elizabeth whimpered as he flicked his tongue over it, flaying it from right to left and back, like exquisite torture, and then he began suckling as he pressed her hips to his groin.

She felt the length and thickness of him through his jeans as her hips began to undulate against him instinctively. She pressed his head closer to her breast, wanting more of him.

He broke away with a small groan and tugged the dress up, covering her breast with the silk. "Ah, it's too cold here to be naked," he said, "but when I return home tomorrow, we'll rectify that. You please me, Red. I knew you would once you remembered what you know how to do."

Remembered? Elizabeth dully came to her senses. He still thought— "I won't be your mistress!" she said, trying to hold back tears.

"No? You said you wanted to be like Katy."

"I did not!"

"You wore the dress, thinking it would arouse me. Isn't that true?"

Elizabeth cringed. It had come across like that. But the last thing she wanted him to think was that she was willing to be kept and used.

"You can't say you didn't want me as much as I wanted you, just now." He pulled her toward him again. "Come to my room tomorrow night. You'll see."

She pushed away and pulled the cloak tightly around

herself. “Not as your whore!”

His face darkened and he frowned. “Don’t trifle with me, Red. ’Tis not wise to tease. Didn’t you learn that?” He turned to walk away. “And don’t wear that dress again unless you want me to follow through on what I started.”

“Did you love her?”

He stopped and turned back. “Who?”

“Katy. Is that why this dress bothers you so much?”

Several emotions warred across his face and in the dim light, Elizabeth wasn’t sure if he was angry or sorry or depressed, but his voice sounded strangled. “No. I didn’t love Katy. I did love my wife, in my own way. It’s her dress you’re wearing.”

****

Much later, Elizabeth lay under her quilt, quietly sobbing. She had managed, in a single evening, to destroy any kind of budding relationship she might have had with Miguel. She should have known better than to wear clothing found in his attic. To flaunt his dead wife’s gown in front of him was unforgivable. No wonder he’d ignored her all night. And he still thought she was a prostitute. She’d nearly proved the point to him, brazenly asking for sex. She curled into the fetal position. What his hands and mouth had promised on her body was exactly what she wanted. So, was she any different from those women she’d turned her nose up at? Dear Lord, how had she gotten into this mess?

He’d be coming home tomorrow. How could she ever face him? What was she doing in this century anyhow?

Chapter Eleven—To Be or Not to Be

Miguel arrived home late in the afternoon and Elizabeth kept busy with Olga in the kitchen, unsure of what to say to him. At dinner that evening, she wore another of the shirtwaist dresses with a high neckline and long sleeves.

His dark eyes swept over her and she thought she saw amusement in his glance. She tried to avoid looking at him. Did he really think she wanted to be his mistress? Did she? She wasn't sure—she wasn't sure of anything anymore. The nineteenth century was feeling more and more like home, and memories of her empty apartment and the world of the future were fading rapidly. There was love here: Olga and Olaf and Miguel and Raul. She wanted to be a part of that. Wistfully, she wished there had been more warmth in her childhood. If only her father had lived—but would she be able to go back home if he had?

She sighed. On the other hand, she was getting nowhere with convincing Miguel who she was, and with each passing day she felt herself being drawn more and more toward him. Was it only a matter of time before she gave in to him and accepted that being his mistress was better than having nothing?

Suddenly, she heard her father's voice in her head and recalled a conversation they'd had when she was an awkward teenager and had just discovered boys. The most popular one in class had asked her to do his homework. She'd been desperate to please him. Her father caught her, and the look of sadness on his face haunted her for weeks. "Darlin' o' mine," he'd said, "how proud of your wee self will you be in the mornin'?" Then they had "the talk" about respect and she'd made her promise to wait for true love.

"Bad news," Miguel said, breaking into her thoughts. "The circuit judge has been laid low with lung fever. Chances are we won't be seeing him before Easter."

Swift Hawk looked up from his seat at the end of the table. A muscle twitched in his jaw. "That means my people will stay locked inside the white man's jail."

"No harm will come to them, Hawk," Miguel said with certain weariness. "The Rangers will be standing watch."

Elizabeth turned to him. "Does that mean you'll be gone again?"

His eyes twinkled. "Will you miss me?"

Somehow the fiery retort she wanted to give him didn't emerge. "I was merely asking a question."

"How long will you be gone?" Swift Hawk asked in a careful monotone.

Miguel studied him before answering. "I don't know. My job is to convince Chief Jim Ned to take his warriors home to the hills. Having them camped outside Fort Worth just stirs up trouble. I hope to put his mind to rest that those braves will be safe until trial."

Swift Hawk's smile gave Elizabeth the shivers. It was hard and calculating and didn't reach his eyes. His slow gaze traveled from her face to her breasts and back to her face and did nothing to alleviate a sudden dread that swept over her. Hopefully, Miguel would take Swift Hawk along.

The young man pushed back his chair with wolfish grace and turned around at the door. “My people will not rest. They wait.”

****

To complicate matters further, Abigail Parsons arrived the next morning—the plague that kept returning, wearing something looking like it belonged on one of the girls at Miss Lily’s.

She brushed by Elizabeth and Raul with scarcely a glance. “You dropped this at the dance,” she said as she handed Miguel his watch fob. “I thought I’d better bring it to you personally rather than send it with Raul. You know how small boys are.”

Elizabeth didn’t miss the sudden redness that spread over Raul’s face, even though he looked quickly away. How could a teacher be so insensitive?

“Actually, Raul is quite responsible,” Elizabeth said. “He was the man of the house while Miguel was barn-building, and he checked each morning with the foreman on what work needed to be done.” It was true, too. Raul had been so disappointed when Miguel had told him he couldn’t miss that much school for the barn raising. She had suggested Miguel give him some responsibility at home.

Raul scuffled the toe of his boot on the floor, a sure sign that, while he might be embarrassed, he was also pleased with the compliment.

Miguel placed a hand on Raul’s shoulder and looked at the schoolmarm. “Miss O’Malley is correct. I have a great deal of confidence in my son.”

“Well, of course.” Miss Parsons looked somewhat

disconcerted. “I didn’t mean to imply otherwise. The watch looked expensive. I thought you’d appreciate having it returned as soon as possible.” She pouted, her lower lip trembling a bit.

Oh, great. Put on a show. What’s she going to try next? Elizabeth glanced at Miguel and found him looking confused. She hoped he wasn’t going to fall for that trick.

“I do appreciate it,” Miguel said. “It was very kind of you.”

The pout turned into a brilliant smile. “Well, I did feel somewhat responsible for its coming loose since I was ever so clumsy and nearly fell. I think it may have dropped when you caught me.”

Tripped? Elizabeth had seen the whole thing. A cleverly contrived act was what it had been.

“Might I share a cup of coffee with you before I leave?” Abigail asked.

“We have work to do,” Raul interrupted.

Miguel frowned at him. “Don’t be rude. Apologize.”

Raul looked down and his lip trembled, but he muttered, “I’m sorry.” Then, when Miguel grimaced, he reluctantly added, “Would you like some coffee?”

“Thank you, Raul. Yes, I would,” she said prettily and slipped her hand into the crook of Miguel’s arm.

He sent Raul to the kitchen and led them to the parlor. Miss Parsons sat down on the sofa and Elizabeth settled on the other end for the duration of the visit. If Miguel allowed a kiss this time, Elizabeth would have her answer, although she wasn’t quite sure she really wanted it.

Miguel strategically took an armchair and left the sofa to the ladies. A wise move, Elizabeth thought wryly.

Olga had just finished pouring the coffee when Swift Hawk appeared in the doorway, shirtless as usual.

The schoolmarm's eyes widened as she looked him over appraisingly. When her gaze met his, she smiled slightly.

Elizabeth nearly dropped her cup. Swift Hawk's eyes lit and a corner of his mouth turned up. Whether in sarcasm or amusement she couldn't say, but it gave his usually sardonic face an actual friendly look. Slowly, he looked Miss Parsons up and down, his eyes lingering on the low neckline—and why was a schoolmarm dressed like that anyhow?—before he nodded at Miguel.

"One of the mares is foaling. I thought you'd want to know."

Miguel stood, looking relieved. "I'll come at once. Will you ladies excuse me?"

"Well," Miss Parsons said as she set her cup down, "I really must be going."

Elizabeth almost grinned. So much for girl-talk, not that she would have kept the conversation going long. Anyway, she didn't want to miss the foaling.

They saw Miss Parsons out and Elizabeth rushed upstairs to change into her jeans. She nearly collided with Miguel as she raced out the kitchen door.

"Why aren't you in the barn?" she asked. "What are you doing here?"

"Waiting for you, Red. The mare's in the pasture. I figured I'd not hear the end of it if you came looking in the barn and no one was there."

"That was really nice of you," Elizabeth said with genuine feeling. Maybe there was hope that he'd think of her as a real person.

"You're the only woman I know who would enjoy

this." He grinned suddenly. "Did I ever tell you that you're unique?"

She smiled back. "You have no idea."

'Hmmm," he said.

****

Miguel had been gone over a week making sure the brig in Fort Worth was secure. Elizabeth grew restless as she brushed Plata. Miguel had told her never to go out riding by herself and Olaf had been too busy overseeing the ranch to accompany her. Today the sun warmed the hardened winter ground and the sky was a bright blue: a wonderful day for a wild gallop over dried, brown grassland.

"We'd be perfectly safe," she grumbled to the mare. "No one would bother us."

True, the ranch hands always stopped what they were doing to stare at her when she appeared in the well-defining Levis and shirt, but Miguel had made it quite plain that they were to leave her alone.

She really couldn't understand the fascination males in this century seemed to have with being able to see a woman's shape. She supposed it was because the "fashion" of the time covered respectable women from head to toe. Even the future Annie Oakley would wear a split skirt when riding.

Elizabeth hung the brush on its hook and looked around for evidence of Swift Hawk. He was nowhere to be seen. The only person she could see was Tomás, a young man Miguel had recently hired, mucking out stalls at the far end of the barn.

Maybe she could ride into Johnson Station and pick up whatever mail had been delivered this past week. It would save Olaf a trip while he was busy taking care of things in Miguel's absence. Elizabeth eyed the mare. "Want to go for a run?"

Plata stamped a hoof and nickered.

"Good girl. That's what I thought." Quickly, she saddled the horse and led her out the back door of the barn. Johnson Station wasn't that far. She'd be back before Olaf even noticed she was gone.

The wind felt wonderful as it swept her hair behind her. Plata's mane whipped in her face as the mare stretched out to her full gallop, seeming to enjoy the run as much as Elizabeth did. What a glorious day to be alive! Eventually, they slowed and she walked the mare to cool her down.

She reined in at a clump of mesquite near the fork leading to the Trinity River and slipped down, allowing the horse to drink her fill of the cold water. There were boulders near the bank and Elizabeth sat down on the warm stone and turned her face to the sun, closing her eyes. There was definitely more than a hint of spring in the air.

She heard a horse cantering up the road, but paid it no heed until she realized the animal had stopped. Elizabeth opened her eyes as a momentary flicker of alarm swept through her mind. She was only halfway to town and this was lonely land. Too late, she wished she'd brought a rifle.

She craned her neck, but could see nothing but the bushes and small trees. Perhaps the rider had taken the other fork and she had not noticed the hoofbeats fading.

Plata's head came up suddenly and her nostrils flared as she scented the air, ears pricked forward. She gave a low whinny and Elizabeth heard a corresponding one from behind the boulders. Someone was here, nearby.

Before she could get up to look, strong hands were on her shoulders, holding her down.

"We are finally alone," Tomás whispered in her ear as he squatted beside her and pressed his head aside hers.

Elizabeth clawed at him and tried to get up, but his grip was like steel.

"Go ahead and scream. No one will hear." One hand caressed her cheek and fisted a handful of her hair. "I'll not hurt you."

"Take your hands off me!" Elizabeth hoped he didn't feel her tremble. Her stomach attempted to twist itself into a square knot. "Miguel will be furious with you for following me."

"Do you think I care?" His laugh was not pleasant. "By the time he finds out, I will be far gone from here." His lips grazed her cheek. "The *don* is not the only man who can please a woman."

His hands slid down toward her waist and Elizabeth moved with a speed she didn't know she was capable of. Rolling from the cowboy's grasp, ripping her shirt in the process, she leapt to her feet, kicking out instinctively with her heel. She heard a satisfying "thud" as she made contact with Tomás's jaw, temporarily unbalancing him. She ran for Plata without looking back.

Behind her, Tomás howled in rage and rushed after her, but she had one foot in the stirrup and, half-lying over the saddle, she gave the mare her head.

Hooves pounded behind her, but she didn't dare look back. Plata seemed to sense her urgency, for the mare galloped a straight line, ignoring the curves in the trail, leaping tumbleweeds and crashing through sage.

Finally, they reached the main road. With relief

Elizabeth sighted Olaf riding toward her. Even as she did, she heard the horse behind her slow and the *vaquero* turned to ride swiftly in the other direction.

"I've never been so glad to see anyone," she said shakily as Olaf came to a stop beside her huffing horse.

He frowned at the condition of the animal and then looked at her, taking in the torn shirt. "You all right?"

Elizabeth nodded as they turned their horses around and headed home. "I got away from him, but he was closing on me. If you hadn't come—"

The foreman reddened. "What in Sam Hill are you doing out here by yourself?" he asked gruffly.

"I was going to town to pick up the mail."

"Didn't Miguel give you orders not to go alone?"

"Yes, but—" She let the sentence trail off.

"Miguel's going to be mad as a peeled rattler."

"At me? He should send men after that near-rapist he hired."

Olaf slid a look toward her. "He told you not to go out alone."

Elizabeth stuck her chin out defiantly. "I'm not a child. I don't need his permission to go to town!"

"Humph," Olaf said off-handedly as they rode on. "Only a fool argues with a mule or a cook." To himself he muttered, "And you're both mules."

****

"She did what?" Miguel glared at Olaf as he unsaddled Diablo and put him in his stall. He'd succeeded in getting the chief to retreat temporarily, but that treaty was fragile. If anything incited a riot, the Comanche would be on the warpath. He was bone-tired, having ridden nearly twelve hours in the saddle to get home tonight. And now this. Confound it. Could

Elizabeth not heed him in anything?

"I warned her you'd be all horns and rattles," Olaf said.

"I'm sure that put the fear of God into her," Miguel said wryly. He seriously doubted if anything could. He'd never met a more obstinate woman in his life.

"Well," Olaf said with a shrug, "she didn't seem too upset. Something about not needing permission from you."

Miguel raised an eyebrow. "Is that so? Perhaps a small lesson in obedience might be in order."

Olaf snorted. "That I want to see."

"You don't think I can do it?"

"I think you'd be barkin' at a fence post, son."

"Well, then," Miguel said as he turned toward the door, "I'll just have to prove it to you, too."

"Like I said before," Olaf muttered to himself, "two mules. Yep. Two mules."

****_

Elizabeth had heard Miguel ride in late last night, but she'd stayed in her room, letting him think she'd retired. She'd rather face his wrath over her escapade after a good night's sleep.

She slipped out of bed and freshened up with the warm water from the pitcher Olga always left for her in the mornings. There was even a fresh bar of scented soap this morning and satin hair ribbons on the dresser. Strange. Olga knew she didn't wear hair ribbons.

She opened the drawer for her jeans and shirt and then stared. The drawer was empty. Surely, Olga wouldn't have taken them to the laundry. They were clean. Quickly she put on a ready-made dress and descended the stairs and made her way to the kitchen.

Miguel was already there, sipping coffee.

"Good morning," he said pleasantly.

Elizabeth hesitated for a moment. She had fully expected a lecture on her foolishness, but he seemed unfazed. Maybe he didn't care what happened to her. That thought hurt. She warily said a pleasant good morning and turned to Olga. "Where are my jeans?"

Olga set a plate of bacon and eggs in front of her and didn't answer. She simply looked at Miguel.

Elizabeth followed her gaze and then narrowed her eyes. Miguel had the same smug look on his face that Raul used when he thought he'd done something particularly clever. She had the uneasy feeling this was not going to bode well for her.

"Do you know anything about this?" she asked suspiciously.

Miguel buttered a piece of toast and took a bite. "Yes, I do. I have them."

"Why?"

"Because you obviously are not willing to listen to me. You put yourself in harm's way yesterday by going out alone, so I decided to take your riding clothes away."

The arrogance of the man! Did he think she needed to be punished like a child?

"You can't do that!"

"No?" He tilted his head. "I already did."

"Give them back, Miguel." With an effort, Elizabeth controlled her temper.

He pushed his chair away from the table, stretched his long legs out in front of him, and folded his arms across his chest. "I might barter them back to you."

"Barter? What are you talking about?" Somehow, she wasn't going to like this.

"I think it's time you showed some appreciation for another gift I've given you."

Warily, she asked, "Which is?"

"Those dresses I purchased from Godey's. You know, the black dress and the red one. The ones you think are indecent. You've not worn them for me."

God, she'd hoped he'd forgotten them. They were in the back of her wardrobe. Forcing a smile, she appealed to what she hoped was his courtly side. "I'm not comfortable in them. You wouldn't want to embarrass me, would you?"

His eyes glittered with amusement and a corner of his mouth twitched up. "I've seen you in less, if you'll remember."

So much for gallantry. And he had played at being King Arthur as a child! "Those dresses will make me look like I'm one of Lily's girls."

He arched an eyebrow and Elizabeth was prepared to kick him in the shins if he made one more comment about her being a working girl, but he merely shrugged. "Suit yourself. Wear one of them at dinner for me and you'll get your jeans back."

She stared at him incredulously. He was actually blackmailing her! And where had Olga gone off to? She'd hoped for the housekeeper's support. "That's not fair. You know how much I like riding."

For a moment, hesitation flitted over his face, and then he shook his head. "That's the way it is, Red. You won't obey my orders; you will allow me this."

That was the limit. "Obey?" Elizabeth sputtered. "Women in the twenty-first century don't "obey" men. We're equal—"

He was on his feet in a flash, bending over her,

pulling her up from her chair. "It tires me, Red, to hear this craziness about the future. That will also stop. You are in the nineteenth century. Flesh and blood, like me." His hands stroked her arms and he palmed her face, thumbs sliding slowly across her cheekbones. "Do you feel me?"

How could she not? Even with the anger she sensed seething in him, his touch was gentle. The look in his eyes was not. They were blazing. She forced herself not to look away. "I feel you. Now let go of me."

He held her a moment longer and then released her and raked his fingers through his hair. "You have no idea of how men react to seeing you in those jeans, with every curve obvious. Christ, Elizabeth, you were nearly raped yesterday. I can't protect you if you won't abide by my rules. How can I keep you safe?"

She stared at him. Was he admitting he cared? That he was really concerned about her? She thought about the many warnings he'd given Swift Hawk. He didn't have to do that. And the rescue from the gunslingers. She was sure that his reaction had been genuine, but then he hadn't come back to the room that night. Maybe she should relent about the dress—she did need those jeans.

"If I agree to wear the dress for you, will Swift Hawk have to be there?" She didn't think she could bear his eyes on her neckline throughout dinner.

Miguel stepped closer and tilted her chin with his finger. He looked deeply into her eyes. "I promise you we'll be alone."

Which could lead to other dire circumstances. She swallowed hard. "That won't be necessary. I wouldn't want to deprive Olga and Olaf and Cactus Flower of the dining room."

Miguel laughed. “I wasn’t thinking of us being in the dining room for long. Just wear the dress tonight—with no corset—and you’ll have your jeans in the morning.”

Elizabeth tore her gaze away from that lush, firm mouth and met his eyes. “You drive a hard bargain.”

He bent his head, his lips slowly brushing hers, lingering just long enough for her to taste him, leaving her wanting more.

“Tonight,” he said.

****

Olga served an early supper and everyone was leaving when Miguel escorted Elizabeth to the dining room. She was self-conscious in the red satin and had draped a shawl around her shoulders, but even so, Swift Hawk paused mid-step to stare at her. Elizabeth was grateful that Cactus Flower urged him along. Olaf looked surprised and then gave Miguel a big grin before he followed the rest of them out.

“What was that about?” Elizabeth asked as Miguel held her chair for her at the end of the table.

“He was probably surprised to see you wearing the dress,” Miguel answered as he lit the candelabra and took the chair to her right. He poured two glasses of wine from the crystal decanter on the table and handed her one. Then he reached over and slid the shawl off her shoulders, the tips of his fingers grazing her bare skin.

“I want to appreciate you in the dress,” he said. “You’re an attractive woman.”

Elizabeth felt herself blush and was grateful when Olga brought in their food. Then she stared at the plate. Roast pheasant with orange marmalade sauce and wild rice, and a medley of freshly steamed vegetables, along with warm yeast rolls and newly churned butter. "You've outdone yourself, Olga. Thank you."

The older woman beamed and went back to the kitchen, leaving them alone.

"How did you find fresh vegetables this time of year?" Elizabeth asked Miguel.

"Tate Johnson has been experimenting with a structure made of glass panes. The sun warms the earth inside and allows the plants to grow, even in the wintertime." He raised his glass in toast. "Is everything acceptable?"

Elizabeth sipped her wine, unsure of the gleam in his eye. "Yes. Quite."

She became uneasy as they ate, since Miguel benignly kept the conversation neutral and she had expected at least some ogling of her neckline, but there was none. He seemed genuinely interested in the conversation. When he mentioned the taffy pull, though, her attention became more focused.

"Miss Parsons thought it would be a fun thing for the kids to do for Valentine's," Miguel said. "There'll be other games, too, and dancing for the adults."

Elizabeth tried not to frown. When had he seen that slinking feline? She and Olaf usually went to get Raul from school and the schoolmarm had definitely not mentioned any of this to her!

"Will we be going?" she asked.

"Of course. Try and keep Raul away from candy." His eyes swept the fitted bodice of her gown. "Only don't be wearing this. I would like to keep intimate knowledge of your body to myself."

Elizabeth blushed. "You have no such thing."

He grinned. "The night's not over."

He was impossible. Even as she prepared a retort, she felt herself weakening. The argument she had been having with herself for the past weeks raised itself.

What was she waiting for? She wanted him, he wanted her.

He thought she was a prostitute.

Did it matter anymore? He didn't believe she was from the future either.

She wanted respect.

But didn't he treat her well?

Did she really want that cougar in the classroom to have him?

Abruptly, Elizabeth held out her glass, the decision made. "I think I'd like some more wine," she said and then nearly gulped the glass when he poured.

He shook his head and stood. "Come," he said, "let's retire to the study. I think I have something there you'll enjoy."

The room was dimly lit, as before, but this time the lamb's wool rug had been rolled up, exposing the smooth wooden floor. As Miguel went to retrieve something from the corner, Elizabeth poured herself a stiff cognac from the decanter and winced as the heat of it seared her throat, but took another swallow. If she were going to give away her virginity, she needed a little liquid courage. She hiccupped slightly.

Miguel set something on the counter that looked like a phonograph. Elizabeth blinked. Edison wouldn't invent the phonograph for another quarter century. Had someone else had the same idea?

"Where did you get this?" she asked as she squinted and peered at it.

"France. A new invention that plays music." Miguel

cranked the handle and set the needle carefully in the record groove. The tune of a waltz wobbled out.

Elizabeth stared at it in fascination. A genuine antique that pre-dated Edison! Then she remembered that in the nineteenth century this would have been the very latest in technology. A far cry from iPods and streaming music off the Internet.

Miguel walked over to her and set her empty glass down. “Shall we dance?”

He took her hand and put an arm around her waist, leading her into a skillful turn. Elizabeth quenched a wave of dizziness and inhaled the male scent of him. To be this close and yet their bodies weren’t touching was both agonizing and stimulating. Dreamily—the booze really did make her feel relaxed—she let her hand drift upward on his neck and tangled her fingers in his hair. His response was to tighten his hold and draw her close. That was better. She liked having her breasts pressed against his broad chest, his hand caressing her back, making her spine tingle. Provocatively, she rotated her hips against his and was amazed at what she felt. His erection was immediate, ramrod hard, long and thick.

And then both her thoughts and her breath were gone. Miguel covered her lips with his, the kiss harsh and demanding. His tongue sought hers and hungrily he explored her mouth, teasing her with an in-and-out thrusting motion, making her swollen lips even more sensitive.

He nibbled at her ear and licked his way to the nape of her neck, sending quivers of sensation down her back. His hand leisurely stroked her breast through the thin fabric of the gown and she shuddered. Elizabeth felt a sudden swish of cool air and was only dimly aware that somehow he had managed to undo the back of her gown with his other hand. She felt him give a little tug and the top of the dress fell away, leaving her breasts exposed to him. She giggled. Wasn't this supposed to feel indecent? What it felt was very, very good.

"My God, but you're beautiful," Miguel said as he flicked a thumb over a pink, hard bud. He lowered his head, his tongue warm and velvet smooth as he circled the nipple, his teeth just grazing the tip. Elizabeth arched toward him, wanting him to suckle, to fill her aching need for him. If only she didn't feel so woozy.

Agonizingly, he bedeviled her breasts, cupping them together with his hands, his mouth moving from one to the other, teasing, lightly tasting, making her groan at the torturous slowness with which he fed her arousal. Elizabeth was ready to scream; she ran her fingers through his hair and tried to press his head to her breast, but he resisted.

"Ah, no," he said. "I'm not satisfying you that easily. I want you panting, Red."

Like she wasn't already? And what was he doing… Miguel dropped to his knees, taking the dress along with him, crumpling it in a heap around her feet. Holding her hips in place, he kissed her stomach with long, slow, wet kisses and Elizabeth felt her insides contract and turn to mush. Her knees would barely support her.

He took the corner of the thong strap in his teeth and pulled it down, uncovering her mound of bright, coppery curls, sliding the thong lower on her thighs. His hands slowly stroked their way downward and Elizabeth gasped when he slipped a finger between her legs, fondling a spot that sent tantalizing pinpricks of pure pleasure ricocheting throughout her body.

Elizabeth didn't know such feelings were possible. Just when the throbbing was subsiding, he pressed his face into the vee of her thighs and his tongue lapped at the engorged folds of her womanhood, sending her once more to unknown heights of sheer exquisite delight.

Miguel tugged again at the thong, bringing it to her ankles. He lifted one foot to remove it as Elizabeth tried to balance. Maybe she shouldn't have had so much to drink. She shook her head to clear it.

Miguel looked up at her. "If you liked that, you'll enjoy this more." He lifted one of her legs to place over his shoulder, opening her completely to him. It was then that she lost the battle and toppled over.

He caught her before she hit the floor. "Are you all right?"

She peered at him. Suddenly there were two of him where a minute ago there had been one. Which was real?

He watched her eyes shift back and forth and realization struck him. "I think you're drunk, Red."

"So whath if I amm?" She blinked, trying to focus and giggled again. "I like whath you…you're doing."

With a sigh, he lifted her and stood up, bringing the gown along with him. He slipped the straps back over her shoulders. "Turn around. I'll fasten it for you."

Elizabeth swayed slightly and blinked somewhat owlishly. "Why? I want you…"

Gently, he turned her. "I don't take advantage of drunken women, Red. And I won't have you accuse me tomorrow morning of forcing you."

"But I won't…I prommisse…"

Miguel shook his head and helped her up the stairs, opening the door to her room. "Sleep it off, Red. One day—and it will be soon—I'll show you that tonight was only a beginning. I want you to remember each and every thing I plan to do."

****

Elizabeth awoke with a colossal hangover the next morning. She groaned as the beams of sunlight streamed across her bed and struck her face. Sitting up, she held her head, hoping the pounding would stop. Painfully, she made her way to the window and drew the curtain. Blessed darkness fell, curbing the pulsations in her brain. Ah, just to stay in bed all day—or at least for a little bit longer. She crawled back into bed and pulled the covers up. No use trying to get breakfast; her stomach was too queasy to hold down food.

She awakened again several hours later to a light rapping on her door. She pushed herself up in bed, aware now she was not wearing any clothes. She pulled the sheet to her chin. "Who is it?"

Miguel opened the door, holding a tray with a bowl on it. "I brought you some *menudo*," he said as he started toward her.

"Stop! I'm not wearing…"

He came to sit on the edge of the bed and placed the tray with the steaming soup on her lap. "I saw you naked last night, but you may not recall."

Elizabeth blushed. Had he really done all of that to her with his tongue? Vaguely, she could remember urging him on and she felt her face flush even more.

"Here," Miguel said and spooned some of the broth to her lips. "Don't look so stricken. I took no advantage."

She swallowed the spicy broth and then accepted another spoonful of the hominy and tripe mix. *Menudo* was invigorating; she actually felt like she might live. She couldn't tell Miguel she wished he had taken advantage of her. This hang-up with her virginity had gone on long enough, and if what he had done with his tongue was any indication of what he would do with his other member… She knew her face was probably the shade of sunset—it was the bane of having fair skin—and couldn't meet his eyes. Instead, she grabbed the spoon and began eating hungrily.

"Did you enjoy it? Miguel asked when she finished.

"Yes, it was very tasty. Thank you," she said and handed the bowl back to him.

He placed it on the table beside the bed. "I meant last night. What do you remember?"

She cast her eyes down. "Dinner. We danced. I think we kissed."

A corner of his mouth lifted and he tilted her chin up. "We did. What else?"

"Not much," she said feebly and hoped he would believe her.

"Liar."

So much for embarrassing herself. "Ummm. Maybe you touched my breasts? I think I let you do that. I'm not sure."

He laughed and stood up. "You're hurting my male pride. I can see I'm going to have to repeat the whole thing so your memory will be refreshed." He picked up the bowl and moved to the door. "But next time, Red, you'll be sober. And I can assure you, you'll remember."

She burrowed down under the quilt after he left, her body reliving every shudder of delight he had given her. How much better could he make her feel?

****

Elizabeth felt like her normal self the following morning. She rose early and slipped out to Plata's stall.

Her jeans had been returned just as Miguel had promised and she wasn't going to miss out on an early morning ride on a sunny day that was already warm for February. And then, maybe tonight—

She was in the stall, combing the mare when she heard the men walk in.

"If that don't beat all, Miguel," Olaf said, "I opined she'd pitch a conniption fit about you takin' them pants away. But no, thar she was, just as pleasin' and ladylike as could be."

Elizabeth heard Miguel's easy laugh and her hand stilled on Plata's coat. She stood motionless as a statute.

"Did you really doubt me, Olaf?"

She could hear the awe in the foreman's voice. "Dang, if you didn't have her eatin' out of your hand just like Diablo does. Gettin' that filly to obey you—"

Swift Hawk interrupted them and, for once, Elizabeth was grateful for his presence, even though she was hidden. What did Olaf mean—getting her to obey Miguel? Obey? That was an obsolete word in her vocabulary. She leaned against the horse as her knees buckled. Had everything Miguel done to her—even arousing her like he did down *there*—had it all been nothing but a ploy?

The men changed the subject and were talking now about the big Valentine get-together. Miguel was urging Swift Hawk to attend, telling him he had to be more sociable. Swift Hawk's reply startled her.

"I will attend only if I am allowed to dance with Fire Woman."

"I won't let you do that. She doesn't want you anywhere near her, Hawk." That was Miguel, his voice not condemning, just stating the fact. "I think she's made it clear; she's afraid of you."

"She has nothing to fear from me." For once, there was no arrogance or defiance in the Indian's tone. He actually sounded almost hurt.

Elizabeth frowned. Was she really *afraid* of Swift Hawk? He made her uneasy with his near-worship of her red hair. He was young enough to be one of her high school students. If she did allow him to dance with her, she could control the situation. Maybe even get him to see she was human, after all, and not sent by the Great Spirits. Maybe she had been approaching this situation all wrong.

As for Miguel saying he had her eating out of his hand… Well! Not only would she dance with Swift Hawk, she'd encourage Beauregard, too, and whoever else caught her fancy. And since Miguel wanted to see her in those satin dresses he'd bought, she'd oblige him. She'd wear one to the dance. The black one would set off her copper hair nicely. And, while she was at it, she might just refuse Miguel a dance at all.

He wanted her to *obey* him? Not hardly.

Chapter Twelve—Disaster on the Chisholm Trail

Elizabeth was still irked at the idea of obeying any man when Valentine's and the big day of the candy pull and dance arrived. For two weeks she had managed to avoid being alone with Miguel—not that it had been difficult since he wasn't exactly pounding on her door. Still, he flashed her that lopsided smile of his that was so enticing—and the box of chocolates that arrived by stagecoach yesterday had mellowed her a little. Maybe more than a little, if she wanted to be honest. Still, she was going to wear the black dress.

She lifted it from its hanger in her wardrobe and called for Cactus Flower to come help her. Another drawback to not wearing jeans and shirts was all those tiny buttons up the back she couldn't reach, although Miguel had unfastened them with one hand. She blushed, remembering. Such strong, adept hands, yet so gentle a touch.

Cactus Flower's eyes went wide when she saw what Elizabeth intended to wear.

"*Don* Miguel will never let you out of the house!"

Elizabeth sniffed. "He can't tell me what to wear."

"No?" She looked doubtful. "He'll take your jeans away again."

"I've hidden one pair. He'll never find them. Now help me."

Eventually, they had fussed with each other's

dresses and hair and were ready. Elizabeth took a deep breath before she descended the stairs.

Miguel looked up from where he was waiting with Olaf, Olga, and Swift Hawk at the door. Raw desire flashed across his face and was replaced quickly with a grim look.

“That dress is for my eyes only. Go back and change.”

Elizabeth stepped down and walked toward him. “No.” There. Obey him indeed. She had defied him. Only did he have to look so good? Tonight he was wearing a supple, soft black leather jacket that contrasted with the snowiness of his shirt and the golden tan of his skin and set off his dark hair and eyes.

He folded his arms across his chest. “That wasn’t a request.”

She looked archly at him, although it didn’t help that she had to tilt her head up to look at him. “The answer is still the same. No.”

“Then you’ll be staying home.”

For a moment, she faltered. He could do that. But Johnson Station wasn’t that far. She could ride Plata sidesaddle if necessary. She opened her mouth to retort when Swift Hawk stepped forward.

“I will gladly stay home with her.”

Dear God. That was the last thing she wanted. To be alone with Swift Hawk. She shot Miguel a troubled look. He sighed and looked at the young Indian.

“I’ve told you. You need to become more socialized. You will go.”

Swift Hawk expanded his chest and lifted his head, his black eyes locking with Miguel’s. For a moment, Elizabeth had a vision of Swift Hawk in full native regalia, including a feathered warbonnet and paint on his face. It was a fearsome vision. She blinked rapidly to remove the illusion.

His voice was low, but hard. "I go only if Fire Woman attends also."

A muscle twitched in Miguel's jaw. Elizabeth knew he was aware of how Swift Hawk frightened her. Surely, he wouldn't leave her alone. For a moment, she almost gave in to his order for her to change her clothes. That would eliminate this standoff. Yet, if she were to acquiescence, she'd be doing exactly what Olaf and Miguel had laughed about. She would be obeying him. And Irish Celts "obeyed" no one. She lifted her chin.

"If I had time, Red, I'd carry you up those stairs and change your dress myself," Miguel said, "but Raul's waiting in the buckboard and I don't want him to miss the children's events." He made an elaborate bow. "After you," he said sarcastically, lifting his arm toward the door.

As she swept past him, she heard Olaf chuckle. "Who's winning, did you say?"

****

The first person she saw was Abigail Parsons. Actually, Elizabeth was all but brushed aside as the schoolmarm rushed over to them in the pretense of being worried that Raul would be late. Like the woman cared. Raul struggled out of her hands and ran off to find Gus, but the Predator only smiled and linked arms with Miguel.

"You're just in time," she said with a purr. "The taffy's been pulled until it's hard." Her feline gaze moved slowly across Miguel's chest and then toward his belt before she looked back up at him. "We're about to start the competition. I could use a strong man to help me."

"I'll be glad to," Miguel said with a smile and turned to the group. "You'll excuse us?"

Elizabeth snapped her mouth closed. Ouch. He really was angry with her. And now she'd have to be treated to watching that woman clawing her way all over Miguel tonight. She sighed.

"I'd be honored to have you be my partner." Beauregard joined her and held out his arm. "The pair that can make the longest pull wins."

Elizabeth put on her best Scarlett O'Hara smile. Or at least she hoped it was coquettish. She really wasn't practiced at this. "The pleasure would be mine," she said.

Miguel won, of course. Elizabeth barely endured the sight of Abigail throwing her arms around his neck and she didn't dare let her gaze linger on his hands on the teacher's slim waist. Hands that were so capable of arousing her with a soft touch or a long, smooth stroke—

The evening got worse. The schoolmarm hellcat decided to join the children in bobbing for apples, insisting that Miguel hold her hair back for her and then handing him the towel to dry her face.

Elizabeth dreaded the dancing when it began, knowing Abigail would press her body against Miguel's every chance she got, enjoying the feel of his strong arms wrapped around her. Elizabeth shut her eyes, remembering their own private dance in the study. How it had almost ended.

But she smiled brightly and chattered away at her ever-changing partners. The dress worked on that account. The men nearly stood in line for a chance to dance with her. All except for Miguel. In fact, he seemed quite taken with Miss Parsons. Elizabeth was beginning to doubt it was an act any longer. When Swift Hawk finally cut in, Miguel glanced over to her, but made no move to disengage from the vixen.

Well, at least she could use this opportunity to put an end to Swift Hawk's obsession, once and for all.

He twined a curl of her hair around his finger. "The lantern light makes your hair pure flame. The Great Spirit has blessed me."

She jerked his hand away. "Stop this nonsense, Swift Hawk. No "spirit" sent me. Lots of Irish women have red hair."

"You are from Ireland? Miguel said you didn't remember—"

"No," she interrupted. "My ancestors were Celtic. A very ancient tribe, much like your people. But we're human just as you are. I am no goddess."

Swift Hawk looked thoughtful. "You look like one called Dream Catcher."

In spite of her misgivings, Elizabeth was intrigued. "Dream Catcher? You mean like the totems you hang over a child's bed to keep bad dreams away?" Elizabeth remembered the one her students had given her; that life seemed so far away.

He smiled and the lines of his hard face softened momentarily. "Dream Catcher is a powerful spirit. The shaman is the only one in our tribe who speaks directly to her. Sometimes, though, others can see her in the haze of the sacred pipe. She dresses always in white leather."

Hallucinations? Elizabeth tried to remember: Peyote, Jimsonweed—no, that was done most often in California—Mescal. Did Swift Hawk take these drugs? Was that why he was so obsessed with her hair?

Did Miguel know? She glanced across the dance floor, but the Predator had him firmly engaged in conversation, tilting her head to expose her bare neck to him. Even from here, Elizabeth could see her body language just begging for a kiss.

"She has fire hair, too," Swift Hawk said.

"Who?" Elizabeth reluctantly brought her attention back to Swift Hawk.

"Dream Catcher. I often dreamt of her when I first came here. Always, she told me I had her protection. And then you came."

Elizabeth stared at him. "You can't think I'm Dream Catcher!"

He shrugged, about to make a reply when Beauregard tapped his shoulder.

"This waltz was promised to me, I believe," he said and swung Elizabeth away.

As glad as she was to no longer be dancing with Swift Hawk, Elizabeth had a strange feeling that she was still trapped in his embrace.

****

"Damn!" Elizabeth swore the next morning as she pulled her empty hand back from beneath the bed. The jeans and shirt she'd hidden between the leather webbing and the mattress were not there. How could Miguel have known? Another thought came to her. *When* had he taken them? She'd put them there just before Cactus Flower helped her dress and they'd gone directly downstairs from here. He wouldn't have had a chance to come to her room.

She pulled on a robe and stomped down to the kitchen. He was alone, sitting and sipping coffee. Waiting.

"Where are they?" she demanded, her hands on her hips.

"I assume you mean your clothes? In my room." Miguel let his gaze wander over her and he grinned. "Since you're not dressed, maybe you'd care to go there and do some negotiating?"

Elizabeth pulled the robe closer. "Hardly. You ignored me all night."

"I didn't feel like standing in line." He poured another cup. "Coffee?"

She accepted it grudgingly and sat down. "Okay, you've had your fun. What do I have to do this time to get my jeans back?"

Miguel studied her. "You could come to my room tonight. I seem to recall buying you a lace sleeping gown at Christmas that I haven't seen you wear either."

He really was infuriating. If he thought she would trade her body for her clothes— She felt tears start to burn and blinked them away. Of course that's what he thought. She was still a working girl in his mind. He probably wouldn't think of talking like that to the schoolmarm. *Her* he would respect.

"Why don't you give it to Miss Parsons? I'm sure she'll be glad to wear it for you," she snapped and immediately regretted her words.

Surprise flickered in Miguel's eyes. He leaned forward and grasped her hands before she could pull them away. He stroked lightly down her fingers to their tips. "I think your claws are showing, Red."

"My claws?" she sputtered. "I'm surprised you don't have scratch marks all over your body after last night."

He eyed her a moment and a corner of his mouth

twitched. "You don't know that I don't. Would you care to examine me?" He stood and came around to where she sat. Slowly, he began to unbutton his shirt.

"Stop it!" Elizabeth felt her face grow hot. Just a glimpse of his bare chest inches away from her face sent her blood racing through her veins like a flash fire. If his shirt came off, she would follow him to his room, God help her! And by all the Irish saints, she shouldn't want to—didn't want to—but she would.

The shirttails came out. "Well? Would you like to assure yourself that I don't have a mark on me?"

She shook her head mutely, looking down at the table. Never had she met a man so arrogant. And so sexy. She knew, beneath the shirt, he was all rippling muscle, tight abs and flat obliques. More than anything she wanted to run her hand across his torso—

As though he read her mind, he flipped the shirt back, lifted her to her feet and brought her arms around his bare waist. "Feel my back, Red. I don't think you'll find any welts."

His skin was warm and smooth, and she felt his back muscles tighten as he wrapped his arms around her, holding her against him. She squirmed, aware that somehow her robe had fallen open—all that was between them was the thin cotton of her nightshift. She became painfully aware of the hardness of his shaft straining against her belly.

"How badly do you want those jeans back?" he whispered as he nibbled on her neck and breathed softly into her ear. "It could be easily arranged."

She pushed away from him. "You dare to force me—"

"Force?" He looked at her steadily. "I could have

taken advantage of you last night, had I wanted to."

She frowned. "What do you mean?"

"When do you think I got your clothes? You were sound asleep, lying there on your side with no covers, your shift hiked to your waist…Ah, it would have been an easy thing to bring you awake with me inside of you."

Fever sizzled through her body, exploding in a fiery gush of warmth between her legs. Sweet Mary. He had been there. Watching her. Seeing her near naked. Again.

"How do I know you didn't take advantage of me?"

He laughed and stuck his shirt inside his waistband as Olga came into the kitchen. He bent over and whispered to Elizabeth, "Believe me, Red. You would have known."

****

She got her clothes back the next morning, but only after Miguel left for the spring roundup. Olga delivered them to her room along with the news.

"How long will they be gone?" Elizabeth asked.

"Three weeks, maybe four," Olga answered. "They have to ride the whole range, even though there are several branding stations about the land. Then, they'll be bringing the cattle they wish to sell back to the pens northwest of Fort Worth and Miguel will arrange for a cattle drive."

On what would become the Chisholm Trail. Elizabeth remembered her history: it wasn't until the advance of the railroad that ranchers would try to drive large herds great distances, but nearly a million and a half cattle were moved up the Chisholm Trail in just four years and that was before the heyday of the cattle markets in Dodge City and Wichita and Laramie. How she would love to be a part of that drive! And of the roundup. She had told Miguel weeks ago that she wanted to go. It was probably the real reason he'd taken her clothes. To keep her home.

"Are they working from the farthest points first?" she asked.

Olga nodded. "They always do. Then they start driving the cattle back."

"Which camp will they arrive at last?" Elizabeth asked casually.

That got her a suspicious look. "There are cattle pens near Bird's Fort on the upper Trinity. Why?"

She hoped she looked innocent. "Just curious. Did Olaf go with Miguel?"

"No. He'll run things here and then meet Miguel at the fort with any business that needs taking care of before the cattle are driven north." She studied Elizabeth for a minute. "And if you're planning on going along, think again. Miguel would be furious."

Elizabeth shrugged. "Maybe. But what could he do once I'm there?"

The housekeeper gave her one long look before she left. "Sometimes it's better not to try Miguel's patience, young one."

****

"Dad-burn. My brains ain't addled to have brung you here," Olaf said. "Miguel will be mad enough to swallow a horned toad backwards when he sees you."

Elizabeth hardly paid attention. They had just arrived at the pens north of Bird's fort and the scene in front of her could have been out of a western movie.

Longhorns milled, churning up the ground, their calves skittish as the *vaqueros* rode between them, the twenty-foot lariats whistling through the air, settling on a dogie's neck. The trained horses drew up short, but the wrangler was already on the ground, hog-tying the calf for the branding. Elizabeth wasn't close enough to smell the flesh roast or feel the sizzle from the iron, but she heard the calf's bawl and for a moment she winced. Yet it had to be done.

The dust was so dense that she didn't see Miguel until Diablo emerged from a cloud of it next to her.

"What in blue blazes are you doing here?"

Elizabeth had decided on the ride over she would ignore his wrath. She smiled sweetly. "You don't think a twenty-first century Texas girl would miss a real roundup, do you?"

"Stop it. I've had enough problems on this roundup without that craziness." He looked for Olaf and glared at him as the man sidled his horse closer. "Is there an explanation for this?"

"Not really. I was halfway here when one of the boys thought we were being trailed. I circled back after we made camp and found her bedding down for the night in a thicket of scrub oak. I figured it was easier bringin' her than turnin' around."

Miguel turned to stare at Elizabeth. "Have you gone daft? You were riding alone for two days? Apart from human vermin, there are rattlers and wolves out here. Did you think of that?"

She refused to look away. No way was he going to know how scared she was the first night when she heard the coyotes howl. "I had a gun. I've done some camping. I built a fire."

Miguel groaned. "And what if that fire had attracted a drifter? He'd have had a fine time with a single woman. The gun wouldn't matter. Why won't you listen to me,

Elizabeth, for your own safety? A roundup is no place for you. Especially this one."

Olaf lifted his head. "Trouble?"

"Not sure," Miguel answered. "The Comanche have been following us. They haven't stolen any cattle, so I think they're leery about the braves still in the brig. Swift Hawk disappeared for a day too, and I'm pretty sure he met with them, although he denies it."

Swift Hawk. Elizabeth had been so glad Miguel had taken him along, and now she'd forgotten he would be here. She never had gotten a chance to talk to him after that dance to make sure he understood there was nothing magical about her. Well, there certainly were enough cowboys around that he'd leave her alone.

"I'm just glad this is the last of the branding," Miguel said. "Tomorrow we'll start the herd north. I'll ride as far as the Red River where our cattle will merge with some Tate Johnson has waiting and I'll turn everything over to his trail boss. I should be home in a week or two." He turned to Elizabeth. "I don't have a tent for you. The men sleep in the open with their bedrolls and I do the same. You'll have to tough it out for tonight, and tomorrow Olaf will start home with you. There is a boarding house at Bird's fort where you can spend tomorrow night."

She nodded demurely. This was not the right time to tell him she fully intended to ride the cattle drive with him.

* * * *

Miguel found her the next morning near the chuckwagon, deftly scrambling eggs in an iron skillet over an open fire. Cooky had a big grin on his face and from the expressions of the cowpunchers standing around with empty plates, Miguel felt an uneasiness settle over him.

“Now if you’ll just hand me the cheese you sliced,” Elizabeth said to Cooky, “and those peppers and onions I chopped, I’ll have the making of an omelet here. Much tastier than those boiled eggs you’ve been eating.” She stirred the ingredients in, watching the cheese melt. “Oh, and check those potatoes.” She pointed toward a second skillet nestled between two rocks above part of the fire. “They should just about be fried.”

Miguel stepped through the crowd and the cowboys fell back. “What do you think you’re doing?”

“Making myself useful.” She dished some eggs and potatoes on a plate and held it out to him. “Go on. Try it.”

He took the plate. He couldn’t even begin to imagine Elena cooking for a crowd if she had lived. “You should be getting ready to ride out of here.”

“Oh, I am,” she said and continued to serve the line of men.

“Then why aren’t you with Olaf? I just saw him finish saddling the horses.”

She served the last man and filled her own plate. “Because I’m riding with you.”

“You’re what?” He was so surprised he nearly dropped his plate. Had she not understood his position yesterday? The woman was the most exasperating female he’d ever encountered.

“I’m riding with you.” She leaned closer and whispered, “History is being made even though you won’t believe me. I’m not missing this.”

He tried not to let the sweet scent of her hair or the closeness of her lips to his ear deter him. “You most certainly are *not* coming on a cattle drive."

She sighed and turned back to the men who were greedily finishing their breakfasts. "*Don* Miguel wants to send me home. Apparently he doesn't think you deserve tasty meals."

Miguel grimaced as he heard the men mumble. The sly wench was trying to turn his men against him!

"Not," she said hastily, "that Cooky can't do the same, since I brought this food with me. I was thinking if I could ride with you for several days I could show him some other recipes." She looked at the men hopefully and then lowered her head. "But I must obey *Don* Miguel."

Obey? Since when had she decided to do that? She was using his own words against him. The men were giving him baleful stares, as though he had totally dishonored her.

"I could use the lessons," the young cook said, and the men started laughing.

"You sure could!" one of them said.

"Ah, come on, Boss." One of the older men who had been with him for years spoke. "We'll all protect her. What harm could come of it?"

Miguel looked around at his men. There were twenty of them and not one had been with him less than five years. His glance fell on Swift Hawk, standing in shadow at the far end of the group, observing silently. The Indian had watched Elizabeth last night, but had drawn early duty. As far as Miguel knew, they hadn't even spoken.

"It'd be mighty nice to have somethin' other than jerky and beans," another voice said.

Not only was he losing this battle, but he had no

weapons to win it with. The little minx had managed somehow to turn these brawling, independent men into schoolboys. And there she was, standing at his side, looking for all the world like a subdued, compliant woman who wanted nothing more than to serve a good, hot meal. She didn't fool him. Not for one grasshopper-fast minute.

Still, it was nice having her lying near him last night, even though he'd left plenty of respectable room between them.

"All right," he said at last, "but if you're going to ride, you're going to have to do your share of herding as well. This isn't a ladies' touring trip."

He got the distinct impression she was about to throw her arms around his neck, but she refrained. "Of course," was all she said.

****

The afternoon of the third day of the trip, Miguel dropped back from point position to ride beside Elizabeth. So far, even though he hated to admit it, things had gone smoothly. The men were happy eating good meals and Swift Hawk left her alone. Miguel frowned. Hawk had slipped off again last night, which made him uneasy, wondering what the Comanche were up to.

He looked over at Elizabeth. She hadn't complained when he'd assigned her to the flank near the rear. It was a dusty position, following the slow-moving herd, and the part of her face not covered by her bandana had been filthy. What other woman did he know—had ever known—who would put up with that? Still, she hadn't whined. She'd just washed up in a basin like the men did, and gone on to help Cooky. He had to admire her for that. He was feeling a little guilty.

"We'll be camping by a river tonight," he said. "I'll make sure you have some privacy for a bath if you want one."

She slanted him a look. "Will you be standing guard?"

His mouth quirked on its own accord. "Well, someone will have to." He could tell she was smiling behind the face cloth because her eyes lit up mischievously.

"Are you sure—" she started to say and suddenly something exploded near the head of the herd and off to the left side, near a pile of boulders. The cattle began to bawl.

"Dynamite!" Miguel said just as a second charge went off. The stock shoved against each other, beginning to mill.

A third rumble rattled the earth. The longhorns started to run, gaining momentum with each yard.

"Stampede!" Miguel yelled as he spurred Diablo forward. "Turn 'em to the right! Circle around!"

He had no idea why anyone would be using explosives out here. This was not mining country and the railroad wasn't even doing any surveying yet. He only hoped Elizabeth kept to the rear where she would be safe from the half-crazed cattle. Then he had no more time to think. Clouds of dust billowed around him as clods of earth flew up from the churning hooves of panicked cattle. He lost sight of Elizabeth and prayed for once that she'd obeyed him. He gave Diablo his head, moving in a great arc around the surging herd, trying to reach the point rider.

Nearly an hour later, the herd had been contained. They were on a hillside with plenty of grass and a small creek nearby. Miguel decided they would hold off and camp there for the night. No sense taking spooky cattle farther than needed today.

Elizabeth could still have her bath, but they might have to go upstream around the hill. Miguel felt a smile begin. That would be better anyhow. Maybe then he could join her, soaping her down, running his hands over the silky flesh of her body, tasting her again. Where was she, anyway? He hadn't seen her near the chuck wagon.

She wasn't in the area where the men had put the bedrolls either. He walked to the river, but there was no sign of either her or Plata. Miguel checked the picket line when he came back to camp, but the mare wasn't in it.

Thirty minutes later, he was trying not to give in to panic. Dusk was falling. Every wrangler who could be spared from keeping watch on the cattle was out searching. No one had seen Elizabeth or Plata since the stampede began.

To add to Miguel's misgivings, Swift Hawk was missing as well.

Chapter Thirteen—Comancheria

Elizabeth tried to quell the panic slowly rising to hysteria in her throat. One moment she had been talking to Miguel, the next the stampede had started. For once, she heeded his orders to stay at the back of the herd, even though the churned-up dust choked her.

Swift Hawk appeared out of a cloud of brown haze.

"This way," he yelled and pointed toward a cedar brake to the right. "We can flank the herd as it's turned."

She hesitated but a moment. It made sense. They would be away from the swirling chunks of debris and be ready to corral the front cattle as the herd was turned. She barely made it past the stand of trees when a muscular bare arm reached for her reins, jerking them from her hands and bringing her horse alongside.

In another moment, a band of Comanche, stripes of red and black war paint on their faces, brandishing war shields and spears, surrounded her. She half-expected them to let out traditional war whoops, but they were strangely silent, intent on leaning over their horses at full gallop.

Swift Hawk rode beside her, having taken Plata's reins. "Don't worry," he said earnestly, 'you'll be safe."

A cold knife of fear cut through her that had nothing to do with the speed of the horses racing over uneven ground. "What kind of craziness is this? Where are you taking me?"

His intense look brought another shiver to her soul. "I'm taking you home. To *Comanchería*. To be with my people."

She glanced over at him in horror. She'd known he was obsessed with her red hair, but to kidnap her? "Let me go! You know *Don* Miguel will come for me."

"Probably," he answered, "but by the time he finds us, it will be too late. You will already be my woman. No more talking now. We ride."

****

They rode through the night. Fresh horses waited for them and Elizabeth realized then that Swift Hawk had planned well. The dynamite had been set intentionally to throw the herd into panic. Elizabeth fell silent as they rode through the next day, entering the canyon land to the west that Olga had told her about. The Comanche seemed quite familiar with these surroundings and she had no doubt they were skilled at hiding in the many caves in these hills.

They finally arrived at the camp, hidden well in a gulch behind huge boulders. It was near dusk when she was thrust inside the tepee with orders not to leave. Elizabeth looked around the inside of the tepee in which she was being held captive. The tanned buffalo hide stretched over four angled poles, thick and rough, the edges held to the ground by large rocks. A circle of stones in the center of the tepee held a small fire, the smoke curling upward toward the hole where the poles met. To one side, piles of hides made for a sleeping pallet. Soft wolf fur pelts replaced traditional blankets.

Sometime later, an elderly squaw brought her a bowl of steaming succotash, a mixture of boiled corn and beans along with flatbread. In spite of her circumstances,

Elizabeth was ravenous and the food tasted surprisingly good.

If only she could have faith in being rescued. She realized now why Swift Hawk had always made her uneasy—afraid even—the feeling had been a premonition. His infatuation with her hair had been far more than that. He actually meant to keep her as his woman. Elizabeth felt a hysterical bubble of laughter arise in her throat at the irony. She wasn't willing to let Miguel, her most virile fantasy, "keep" her and now it appeared her worst nightmare would be doing just that. What could be worse than to have Swift Hawk rape her? For that's what it would be. She would never willingly consent to become his woman.

She had no more than finished that thought when Swift Hawk appeared at the entranceway. He had never seemed particularly tall to her before—certainly not as tall as Miguel—but now he loomed large in the small entrance, blocking the fading light totally with his body. He had returned to his native dress, and in the dim firelight his bare chest glistened with some sort of oil that gave off a faintly pungent aroma. He had also painted red and orange circles on his face and outlined his black eyes with the same colors. It gave him a demonic appearance and Elizabeth shrank back against the furs.

Swift Hawk smiled. "That's just where I want you."

As if the pelts had singed her hands, Elizabeth scuttled away from them toward the fire and looked for a burning stick or something she could use to keep him at bay. Her eyes scanned the embers. Nothing.

As though he read her thoughts, he kicked dirt over the dying fire, leaving them in near darkness. In two strides he was squatting beside her.

"This is marriage paint. Tomorrow, the women will prepare you." He brought both hands to her shoulders and lifted her hair. "Comanche women cut their hair when they marry and give it to their man." He fisted a handful and Elizabeth nearly cried out in pain. "I will weave it into my braid, Fire Woman, and it will bring me both recognition and power." Abruptly, he released it and pulled her closer to him. "But tonight, I did not come for that."

Elizabeth fought her rising nausea. She managed to turn her face away and his lips brushed her cheek instead, then suddenly she felt his hands cradling her head roughly, forcing her to look at him.

"You are mine. Do not think you can avoid me."

She tried to push away from him, but his arms were like steel. She had handled emotionally disturbed students before. What would work with Swift Hawk?

"Do you truly care for me, Swift Hawk?" she asked in as neutral a voice as she could muster.

"Yes. Why?"

As much as she hated to cower, she had to appeal to his male pride. "If I am to become your wife, would you grant me a small favor first?"

A look of wariness crossed his face. "Maybe. What is it?"

"Well." She forced herself to relax and managed to put a little space between them. "In the white man's world, a virgin bride is considered valuable. Is it not the same with your people?"

He stared at her and then grinned. "You are a virgin? Don't tell me the *don* wasn't able to seduce you."

She shook her head vehemently, thinking of all those times he nearly had. "No. Not once." She widened her eyes and hoped she looked guileless. She was so not good at acting helpless. "I have always wanted to save myself for my husband."

"Then I'm glad you did. All the more reason you will bring me luck." His fingers began to fondle her breast.

Definitely not the direction she wanted this conversation to take. Quickly, she caught his hand. "What I meant was—was I had hoped to save myself for my wedding night." If she could just buy some time!

He seemed to consider, and then he shook his head. "It matters not which night it is. I have wanted you for too long. I shall make you mine tonight. Right now." His other hand began to unbutton her shirt.

She caught it too. "I didn't think a Comanche could be so weak."

His eyes narrowed. "Weak? Be careful, Fire Woman, or I will show you—"

"I don't mean physically," she interrupted, trying to sound calm and rational. "I know how strong you are. I've seen you working the horses. I know you can force me to do your bidding. I'm too weak to fight you." She tried to look demure and biddable. She hated feeling vulnerable, but she *was* vulnerable. "All I ask is that you honor my wish to remain virginal until my wedding night. Surely, the son of a chief has been taught patience?"

He lifted his chin, straightened his back and stared beyond her. The illusion of thc warrior shimmered in the air. Elizabeth could almost see the horned buffalo head on his, the stream of war feathers trailing down.

"I have both strength and patience. I will wait." He rose lithely and silently moved to the flap door. "In two nights there will be the *Comanchería* moon. We will wed then."

Elizabeth found herself trembling after he had gone. At least, she had bought herself some time. Maybe in the daylight she could find a means to escape. She had no idea of where she was, but this was spring. The weather was not too hot or too cold. She would be able to scavenge her way to civilization somehow if she could just get away.

She had serious doubts Miguel would be able to find her in this wild country. Another thought struck an even deeper fear. What if he didn't even bother to look? They were deep within Indian territory, she knew. Would he even risk riding this far in? She'd caused him so much trouble, maybe he would just be glad to be rid of her.

A young Indian maid lifted the flap and slipped inside. "I am Little Fox, Swift Hawk's sister," she said, gazing in awe at Elizabeth's hair. "He asked me to bring you this," she finished shyly, dipping her head.

"This" was traditional Indian dress. The smooth doeskin of the fringed skirt was softer than velvet and beads had been intricately woven into patterns on the tunic. Fur-lined moccasins completed the outfit. Even to Elizabeth's untrained eye, she knew the clothing was special garb. All she needed was to braid her hair and attach feathers, she thought ironically. She would not wear it.

"Tell him I'm comfortable with what I have on."

The girl's eyes widened. "You must not refuse. You are to see our father, the chief, soon."

The chief. Miguel had said Chief Jim Ned spoke English. Maybe she could persuade him to release her from Swift Hawk's obsession. She lifted her head. "Very well, then. I will meet the chief as he wishes. I'm sure he wants Swift Hawk to be happy. When I tell him I have no wish to marry your brother, he'll let me return home."

Little Fox furrowed her brows. "Marrying Swift Hawk would be the best thing you could do."

Elizabeth kept her face neutral. Of course his sister would feel so. For that matter, probably all of the unmarried girls in the tribe would feel fortunate to marry the chief's son. He was young and strong and, in his own somewhat diabolical way, handsome. "It is our custom to love the man we marry," she answered as gently as she could. "I don't love Swift Hawk. Surely, any of your women would be honored."

"They would," she said, "and Father had already chosen the daughter of Chief Feathertail for him. He is not pleased with these arrangements."

Elizabeth restrained herself from showing the elation she felt. If the chief didn't want this marriage, she was all but home. She'd be ready to leave tonight. But Little Fox was still frowning—something wasn't right. "So if your father has a bride for Swift Hawk, why do you say it would be the best thing I could do to marry him?"

The Indian girl turned soft brown eyes toward her. "He could protect you."

"From what?"

"From the shaman." Her voice was barely audible.

Cactus Flower's father? How would she be in danger from a healer? Considering Cactus Flower's sweet disposition, he was probably a kind and gentle man. "I don't understand," she said.

"It's your hair," Little Fox whispered. "The shaman believes Sky Father sent you to save us from being sent to a reservation."

That magic stuff again. She may not know how she arrived in the nineteenth century, but Elizabeth knew she didn't possess any magical powers. She'd just have to explain that. She tried to remember her history. The Comanche were one of the last holdouts, fighting the reservation to the bitter end. "Why is red hair so important to your people?"

Little Fox shuddered. "It is the color of blood. Blood replenishes Earth. Your blood will bind us to this land."

Blood always had. From the druids through Biblical times to the present Middle-Eastern turmoil. Apprehension began to give Elizabeth an uneasy feeling. She suddenly recalled Mary, and the ritual the braves who were still sitting in the fort's brig had tried. But the chief had said they were renegades. Surely, he wouldn't allow something like that to take place.

"Blood?" she asked shakily. "Do you mean the shaman wants to carve a symbol into my skin and collect the droplets?"

"Oh, no." Little Fox looked miserable. "He says Earth Mother requires much more to make the binding permanent. He intends to sacrifice you to Morning Star."

****

Miguel swore a string of oaths as the realization of what Swift Hawk had done hit him like another dynamite charge. Quickly, he dispersed two of his most trusted men—one to round up the Rangers and gather Cactus Flower, for he could use her as a negotiating hostage, and the other to inform Major Arnold that he wanted the cavalry behind him. The chief would not be so foolish as to incite a war with the U.S. Army.

"You don't mean to ride alone into Indian territory,

do you?" his trail boss asked. "I don't have any choice," Miguel answered. "I can't take any more of you away from the herd. They're spooked, so they'll be hard to handle for a day or two. And if I'm going to track the Hawk at all, I can't afford to stall." Lord, if Elizabeth had already been harmed… He checked his rage. What he needed now was a calm head.

"What if they're waiting for you? You know how hard a Comanche is to spot; they smear leaves, mud, and ashes on themselves to blend into the landscape. Hell, the cowdogs couldn't even pick up their scent with the ashes."

"I don't think they'll leave anyone behind. The idea was to get Elizabeth away as fast as possible. Anyway, it's a chance I'll have to take." He accepted the hastily prepared sack of food and canteen of water from Cooky and looked back at the trail boss. "I'm leaving you in charge, José. If anything happens to me, Olaf has my Will. Get back to him as soon as you can." With that, he turned Diablo and gave him his head. The stallion leaped forward into a dead gallop as though he knew his master's mind.

Miguel picked up the trail easily enough since the Comanche had not taken the usual trouble of dragging brush behind them to erase any tracks. And there were too many of them. Miguel counted at least ten horses and he recognized the distinct nail pattern of the shoes Plata wore on her hooves.

"Damn you, Hawk," he said and then silently cursed his own foolishness for allowing Elizabeth along. He should have defied both her and his men. What had he been thinking? He knew what he had been thinking. Sensible or not, he wanted her with him. When he was in her presence he felt different. Somehow whole, as though she completed a part of him that had always been empty.

He reflected as Diablo covered the ground in a mile-eating steady canter. Elizabeth. Stubborn, argumentative. Yet she had defended his peace treaties with the Comanche when a lot of people would have agreed with the major. He admired that. Elena would never have done it. So what if Elizabeth had some silly notion she was from the future? Suddenly, he didn't care anymore. If she was a bit off in the head, what did it matter? She was rational and intelligent in all other respects…and physically, her responses to him promised much, much more. Just running his fingers down her arm could give him a harder erection than Katy ever did. What's more, he didn't give a damn if she was a prostitute, although the idea seemed more and more remote. Someday she'd remember, but he didn't care. He wanted her, and not just for a night or a month or a year. He needed her. The thought that had been niggling at the back of his mind came forward with such intensity that he felt dizzy and nearly lost his balance. He loved her. Loved her more than he had Elena—had he even really loved Elena to begin with? Elizabeth was the woman he wanted to share the rest of his life with.

There was no more question about it.

He prayed he would not be too late.

****

After Elizabeth had changed into the clothes Swift Hawk had sent, she had been led to the Council and now stood before them, her hands bound behind her. Some way to treat a goddess or whatever she was supposed to be. There was no place for her to run either— two Indian braves with spears stood with her, one on either side. Elizabeth frantically looked from the chief to his shaman, trying to understand what they were saying, but most of the conversation was in their native tongue.

She prayed Miguel would rescue her, although she knew knights in shining armor only came riding out of nowhere in fantasies—and *this* was no dream. If he did come, through some miracle, she would never again doubt him, even if he did think she was a prostitute. Her mind and body and soul would be his. Miserably, she wished she had let him take her. She would have known exquisite pleasure at least once before she was either made Swift Hawk's property or worse. She refused to take the thought beyond "worse."

Swift Hawk was angrily defying the shaman. Had he not been the chief's son, Elizabeth had no doubt he would have been beaten senseless. Even so, the stern faces of the council told her they did not approve his argument.

"Flame-colored hair brings much magic," he said with deadly quiet. "If our children bear red hair, think of the power and respect we will have among our tribe."

The shaman shrugged. "Even so, it is her blood that will seal our fate to this land. The spirits spoke to me this afternoon in the sweat lodge."

"The smoke of your pipe speaks to you," Swift Hawk answered bitterly as he paced in front of his father and the shaman. "I brought her here to be my woman."

"That will not be," Chief Jim Ned said severely. "You have been chosen for another. I will not risk war between the tribes because you dishonor Feathertail's daughter."

"Risk war?" Swift Hawk turned on him. "What do

you suppose will happen if Fire Woman is killed? I have learned the white man's ways only too well. De Basque will have the whole damn U.S. Army invading us."

Elizabeth felt a glimmer of hope at those words. Would Miguel do it? How many soldiers were at Fort Worth? And how many more could he muster? Enough to take on the Comanche? She felt a slight warmth toward Swift Hawk in the way that deprived prisoners often learned to cling to their captors. At least, he was trying to defend her.

"Tomorrow night is the *Comanchería* moon," the shaman said. "The Sun Dance will be done during the day to pay respect to Sky Father." He paused. "If you wish it, son of the chief, she will spend the day in the medicine lodge. The sacred weed will allow her to feel no pain."

Swift Hawk gave a feral howl and from beyond the gully, a lone wolf answered.

The shaman nodded. "The wolf is a good omen." He continued in English, "Tomorrow night, as Dream Catcher raises the moon, we will give the blood of the woman to our Earth Mother. When Morning Star appears, it will be finished."

The words were like a stake through her heart. She was going to die. Her blood turned chillingly cold. There was no way Miguel would arrive in time.

****

Elizabeth refused to eat the next morning. She did not want to take the chance that peyote or mescal had been mixed with her food and that she'd be dragged to the medicine lodge to spend the day—her last?—in some stupor. She needed her wits about her if she were to survive—and she intended to survive.

She sat outside in the sunshine later with Little Fox and most of the women from the camp. Her leg had been tied to a strong stake and anytime she moved to scratch at the rawhide binding, one of the squaws would slap her hand away. Fat chance she had of escaping. And the green leather was tightening as the sun rose.

Still, it wasn't as bad as the ghastly sight she was being forced to witness. She had read about Sun Dances and War Dances, but had never imagined they would be so brutal. A tall pole rose to her left and green rawhide thongs with wooden skewers at their ends dangled from it this morning, much like a Maypole. She didn't realize what the intent was until seven braves, including Swift Hawk, stepped forward.

The skewers were thrust through the skin of the brave's chest. Once the point had protruded, it was wrapped in thin rawhide and its end also attached to the long ropelike thong. The braves stepped back until the tethers were taunt and then a rock was placed by each Indian's foot. He would not be able to step forward of that stone as the sun gradually tightened the new hide until muscle and skin were strained and tearing. The object, from what Elizabeth could tell, was to test the bravery of the young men as they struggled to free themselves without the use of their hands, which were bound behind them. Swift Hawk had managed to place himself where he had a direct view of her and throughout the day, his eyes did not leave her face.

"Why is he willing to endure such pain?" Elizabeth asked Little Fox.

She looked surprised. "It is a test of manhood for our people. When our braves go on the warpath, they must know the one who rides beside them has courage."

It was barbaric. And to think she had all but told Swift Hawk he was weak. Then a word Little Fox had used halted her thoughts. “Warpath?”

“Yes.” The Indian girl hesitated. “There will be war for what the shaman plans to do. Our father knows this, so we prepare.”

Elizabeth shivered even though the sun was warm. “Little Fox. Help me escape. Then there will be no war.”

“I would like to, but I cannot.”

“You can. Say I’m not feeling well. The sun is too hot. I need to lie down.”

“Maybe you should go to the Medicine Lodge, after all.” Little Fox’s eyes were troubled. “The sacred weed will help you to accept what must be.”

“No.” Elizabeth clasped her hands to still the trembling. If she were going to die, she would do it in her right mind. But. She. Was. Not. Going. To. Die.

A short time later, an older woman who bore a striking resemblance to Cactus Flower brought them a rich venison stew. Although it smelled delicious, Elizabeth pushed hers away.

“You must eat,” Little Fox urged.

“I don’t want to be drugged,” Elizabeth said.

Little Fox looked sympathetic. “Would you like to exchange? Here, have mine; I haven’t touched it. I’ll take yours.”

She hesitated. If the girl were ready to trade, the stew should be fine. But that might be a ploy. Her stomach growled loudly, reminding her she hadn’t eaten since yesterday afternoon. She would need her strength if she managed to escape. She looked at the bowls. “All right. Let’s switch.”

Little Fox lost no time in cleaning her bowl and after

a minute, Elizabeth did the same. The stew had a heady flavor, full of sweet herbs and spices. Sated, Elizabeth gave the bowl back to the woman and gave her thanks.

Ten minutes later, she slumped to the ground, smiling dreamily about Miguel.

****

Elizabeth sat up on her pallet, holding her throbbing head. Damp heat stifled her. In the center of what appeared to be a cave a pit had been dug. A grate holding large, flat stones was laid over the fire beneath. No wonder it was so blazing hot in here! She suddenly realized someone had undressed her, leaving her naked beneath a thin blanket.

She started to throw the blanket off, when a woman entered and threw a pail of water over the hot stones, causing more steam to rise. The Sweat Lodge. As the flames hissed angrily, she became aware that she was not alone.

On pallets around the fire lay the braves from the Sun Dance, the smell of the eucalyptus poultices on their chests flavoring the room. They seemed to swim in and out of her vision. She had been drugged. If the braves were through with the torture, did that mean the sun had set? What time did the moon rise? How much longer did she have to live? She looked wildly around for Swift Hawk, hoping that he might yet help her escape, but he was not there.

She blinked to focus. There was another woman in the room. Where had she come from? The flap to the lodge hung still. Elizabeth rubbed at her eyes for the woman suddenly seemed to be floating in the mist from the steam. She had red hair like Elizabeth's, but hers was braided and beaded. She wore white leather and it was difficult to tell her age. Elizabeth shook her head to clear the effects of the drugs.

“Who are you? Can you help me?”

The woman smiled and it seemed to Elizabeth’s fogged mind that rays of light radiated from her.

“He comes.”

“Who? Miguel?” Elizabeth asked hopefully and then frowned. She was speaking to air. The woman had disappeared. Probably an hallucination. She was so desperate for rescue she was conjuring up images. Stifling a sob, Elizabeth struggled to think more clearly, but the effect of the drugs had not worn off and her eyes began to close.

Sometime later, she awoke to the sounds of war whoops. Sweet Mary! What time was it? Were they coming for her? It could not be time already. How could she have actually slept? More shouting ensued and she heard a horse’s hooves clattering on the rocky terrain. The noise grew louder and the men outside the cave entrance grew silent. And then she heard him. Miguel.

“Where is she?”

Elizabeth whisked the blanket around her in one stroke and staggered for the door. One of the braves stood and she bared her teeth. “Don’t try to stop me.” She didn’t know if it was something in her voice, or perhaps he was still too weak, but he sat down abruptly and nodded. She raised the flap and tottered outside.

“Over here, Miguel,” she called weakly. Please God, he has to be real and not an hallucination. She shook her head to clear it.

He was beside her in an instant, one strong arm around her waist supporting her. She closed her eyes and laid her head against his chest, listening to the steady beat of his heart. Nothing had ever felt so good as being held in his arms.

"Thank God, Elizabeth, you're safe."

She struggled to open her eyes. "They want to kill me, Miguel. How many men did you bring?"

"I'm alone," he whispered.

"Alone?" She could have wept. "Then they'll kill you too. Oh, Miguel, why did you come alone?"

"I had no time to waste. Don't worry." Slowly, he led her back to where Chief Jim Ned waited with the shaman. He addressed the chief, ignoring the medicine man. "You don't want war over this. Your braves still sit in a white man's jail."

The chief narrowed his eyes. "You show courage to come by yourself."

Miguel shrugged. "The Rangers and the U.S. cavalry are less than a day behind me. If you kill me, it will only incite them." He finally turned to the shaman. "I still hold your daughter hostage."

For the first time, Elizabeth saw softness in the shaman's face. "I haven't seen Cactus Flower in four years. She is well?"

"You can see for yourself. She rides with the Rangers. I will exchange her life for Elizabeth's."

The shaman's gaze lingered on Elizabeth's hair. "She will bind us to this land."

"You won't have the land if you don't let her go," Miguel said. "Those of you who survive will be carried off to a reservation before you can pack your tepees." He turned back to the chief. "I have always allowed the Comanche the use of my lands for grazing. We have lived in peace when others warred. Is this the thanks I get?"

The chief glanced at his shaman. “He speaks truth. Many braves’ lives have been spared because of this man.”

“But the land—”

“What about Cactus Flower?” Miguel demanded, his arm tightening around Elizabeth. “Do you wish her returned to your people?”

The woman whom Elizabeth had thought looked like Cactus Flower burst through the gathered crowd. “Gray Eagle,” she said to the shaman, “I want my daughter back.”

The women gasped and the men looked stunned. The woman put her hands on her hips and stared at her husband. He gaped at her. “Know your place, Running Water.”

“I honor you in all things, my husband, but if you deny me this, I will leave my people and go to her.” Running Water stepped over to stand beside Miguel.

“Perhaps,” Chief Jim Ned said quietly, “an arrangement can be made. *Don* Miguel, do you love this woman?”

He did not hesitate. “Yes.”

Elizabeth shook her head, sure that the drugs had affected her hearing. Did Miguel just say he loved her? She must have misheard. She was having an auditory delusion. For a moment she panicked. Maybe this whole thing was an hallucination brought on by the drugs. Maybe Miguel wasn’t even here. She was in denial because of impending death. That must be it. She looked up at him—

The look on his face could not have been more tender or real. “I love you, Red.”

“Oh, Miguel!” She threw her arms around his neck,

the blanket parting to bring her bare skin against him.

He gave her a smoldering look as he carefully pulled the blanket close around her. “You might want to hold that shut for now.”

The chief cleared his throat. “Since it seems Fire Woman feels the same way,” he said, “you should not mind our keeping the Andalusian mare and your stallion as well. I have wanted to breed that stock into mine for years. A fair trade, I think.”

Oh, no! Not Diablo! He treats the horse like a brother. She could feel Miguel’s arm tense around her and a muscle in his jaw twitched. Silently he glanced over to where Diablo waited. The horse nickered in response.

“Done,” he said.

“No!” Elizabeth said. “You can’t give him up.” She turned to the chief. “Maybe another horse. You don’t understand what Diablo means—”

The chief’s wise eyes told her he did. He understood exactly what pound of flesh he was extracting, although Elizabeth was sure he’d never heard of Shakespeare. But Miguel knew, and he was willing to do this for her. Love for him filled her until she thought she would burst. A tear trickled down her cheek.

“Hush. It’s done,” Miguel said. “Now go put on some clothes.”

“No.” She clung to him. “I want to get out of here right now. Before they change their minds.”

Miguel nodded and looked at the chief. “I will have to borrow a horse.”

The chief gestured and a moment later, a pair of well-matched paints was led out. One of the braves unsaddled Diablo and put the gear on the pinto. Miguel watched mutely as Diablo was led away and Elizabeth felt him take in a gulp of air.

"I'm sorry," she whispered.

He looked down at her. "He'll be well cared for. The Comanche have always appreciated their horses."

"I'll have the mare's saddle brought for the second horse," the chief said.

"No need," Miguel answered and lifted Elizabeth sideways onto his horse and swung up behind her, gathering her into his arms.

"I am taking two of your animals," Chief Jim Ned said. "I repay in kind."

"Not this time," Miguel answered. "I'll have this horse returned when I meet the army." He looked at Running Water as he turned the horse. "Cactus Flower will be home tomorrow. You have my word."

As he set the horse to a swift canter, Elizabeth saw Swift Hawk being restrained by two braves at the edge of the crowd. He managed to break through and started running after them. As the distance grew, he stopped and gave her a mock salute. Elizabeth hoped she'd never see him again.

She felt the awkward position of riding sideways surprisingly comfortable as the miles rolled away. Miguel's right arm was supporting her back and her legs were draped over his left one as she leaned against his broad chest. She wrapped her arms around his waist and the wayward blanket slipped down to her waist. Vainly, she tried to pull it up, but it wouldn't stay unless she held it, and she'd much rather be feeling the hard muscles of Miguel's back.

He grinned. "Why is it I'm always rescuing you when you're half-naked?"

For an answer, she burrowed more tightly against him and felt his shaft thicken and harden under her. She gave a wicked little wiggle.

"Stop that," he commanded, "unless you've a mind for me to stop the horse before we leave *Comanchería*."

She smiled slowly. "I wouldn't mind."

He reined in the horse. "You're sure?"

"I'm sure."

His hand began to gently stroke her breast. Then he broke off and swore.

The U.S. Army was headed toward them at a full gallop.

Chapter Fourteen—The Trial

They had no time for private talk after that. The Army made camp for the night, and the next morning Elizabeth, clothed in one of Cactus Flower's dresses, bade her a teary farewell.

"I know you're going home," Elizabeth said, "but I'll miss you."

The Indian girl nodded. "There is much of the white man's life that I like." She looked up as Miguel led the paint horse toward her. "I'll make sure Diablo and Plata are cared for."

"Thank you," Miguel answered as he helped her mount. He pulled a small bag from his pocket and handed it to her. "Sugar cubes. Diablo likes one after he's been brushed."

Her doe eyes were soft. "I'll see to it. You've been good to me, *Don* Miguel."

They watched as she rode away with her escort. Tate Johnson joined them, leading two army mounts. "Major Arnold's troops will wait for the escort to return. The Rangers had better get back and make sure there's no trouble in town."

Elizabeth took the reins he handed her and contemplated mounting in a dress. The skirt was full enough to cover her legs, once in the saddle, but how to get there? She stole a glance at Miguel only to find him watching her with that lopsided smile of his. "Maybe I should ride with you," she said teasingly.

"Nothing I'd like better, but that position puts your derriere in a location I will not be able to resist for the whole day's hard ride we have ahead." He leaned down and kissed the tip of her nose. "I doubt Tate Johnson would mind if we lost ourselves in the brush on a rest break, but it wasn't what I really had in mind for our first time."

Elizabeth blushed and felt warmth flooding through her body, culminating with a pulsation between her thighs. Sweet Mary. If his words could have this physical effect on her—

He laughed as if reading her thoughts and then put his hands around her waist, lifting her into the saddle. His fingers found their way under her skirt and he caressed her thigh and calf before spreading the folds of the dress to cover her properly. "Until tonight, then," he said.

****

Both Olga and Olaf were waiting up for them when they arrived late that night. Miguel knew immediately something was not right. He had pushed the horses to near their limit, hoping to be able to finally claim Elizabeth as his own. Now he sensed that would not happen.

Olga took one look at Elizabeth's drawn face and whisked her away, muttering something about a hot bath and a good night's sleep.

Miguel watched them leave and then took the horses to the barn. Elizabeth had been through an ordeal and she was looking tired and exhausted. A few hours' sleep might be just what she needed. He'd enjoy waking her up slowly with soft kisses.

"What's wrong?" he asked later when Olaf joined him in the kitchen as he was having some leftover stew. The older man had been too quiet since their return.

"The townsmen are all fired up," Olaf said as he sat down. "Elizabeth getting carried off makes them want to string up the braves still in the brig. The few soldiers Major Arnold left behind have had a time of it, pullin' double shifts and all."

A few minutes later, Miguel sat back and wiped a hand over his tired eyes. "I'll ride out at dawn and collect the Rangers. We can spell the men until the Army returns." When Olaf didn't reply he glanced over at him. "There's more?"

Olaf nodded reluctantly. "It ain't just Johnson Station men. Village Creek heard too, and this afternoon, men arrived from Bird's fort, all of them in a mood for lynching. They remember Mary. Now this."

"Damn." Miguel stood. "Get me a fresh horse. I'll be ready to leave in five minutes. Just let me check on Elizabeth."

"Elizabeth? Not Red? What happened out there anyway?"

Miguel gave him a slow grin. "She's still Red. It's just that—"

"It's just that you finally came to your senses and figured out that you love her," Olga finished for him as she came through the kitchen door. "About time, the way you two have been carrying on, always arguing with one another and both of you wanting each other so bad the air's fair thick with the smell of it…"

Miguel hoped he wasn't turning red. He hadn't blushed since he'd lost his own virginity. Had his lust been that obvious? Wait—*both* of them wanting each other? Did Elizabeth really feel the same way about him, too? She'd responded to his hands and his mouth readily enough, but he'd supposed that was because of her not-remembered profession, even though she always held him off. "I've got to see her," he said and turned to go, but Olga put a restraining hand on his arm.

"Your mother isn't here, Miguel, so you listen to me. This time there's not going to be any sneaking around at night, hiding from Raul, like you did with Katy. Do the right thing. Make Elizabeth your wife. She loves you."

He stared at her. "She loves me? She said that?"

Olga snorted and took the cups to the sink. "Didn't have to. It's all over her face plain as handwritin' on paper." She shook her head. "A person would think you're both daft not to see it."

"Five minutes," he said to Olaf and turned to run up the stairs.

He opened the door quietly not to startle her, but she was lying on her side, her copper hair spread over her shoulder, one hand curled around the pillow, sound asleep.

He bent over her and inhaled the clean scent of her skin from the bath. Gently, he brushed back the silky strands of her hair. He wanted to wake her and take her right then: to fill her mouth with his tongue, to let his hands roam every inch of that soft flesh, to taste her juices before sliding himself into that hot, wet sheath that was the very essence of her. Yet he knew Olga was right. His feelings for Elizabeth were different from any he had ever known. Besides the ever-present lust that raged continuously, he trusted her, he realized with surprise. After Elena had turned on him, trust was the one thing missing from all of his relationships. Yet this woman—wherever she came from—would not let him down. Her defense of him with the major should have been a clue. Bull-headed as he was, he hadn't seen it.

His wife. He liked the sound of that. Yes. He would make Elizabeth his wife. And, if she were willing to have the wedding soon, he might be able to make himself wait to claim her. It was an idea he'd never entertained, but it felt absurdly right. He sighed and gave her cheek a light kiss before he rose and went to the door.

****

Elizabeth awoke the next morning feeling more refreshed than she had in days. She allowed herself the luxury of stretching fully and then curling languorously under the covers. Sunlight splashed across her bed and she could hear the first robins of spring singing in the tree outside her window. Miguel had said he loved her. And she loved him. She had never been so sure of anything in her life. What could be more right in her world?

Was the nineteenth century her world? She tried to push the thought away, but the voice was persistent. She sighed and reached over to open the drawer to the little table beside the bed. Picking up the fetish, she rolled it between her fingers, once again wondering how it had enabled her to time-travel.

The first two or three weeks she had obsessed over it, trying to remember exactly what her last words were before she'd gone to bed the night before Christmas. She'd repeated what she could remember, over and over, thinking it would send her back.

Gradually, though, she lost the desire to try. More and more, Miguel's century felt like home to her. Horses, not cars. Clean air that still smelled of sage and mesquite. No pollution. Talking to people, not Facebooking. No smart phones permanently attached to people's ears. Real cooking, not take-out. Real family…Olga, Olaf, Raul and Miguel. Especially Miguel. A man of honor. A man who did the right thing because it was the right thing to do, not for any other reason. A man who had risked his life to rescue her. A man who said he loved her.

Miguel loved her. There couldn't be anything more wonderful than that. Would she want to return to the twenty-first century, even if she knew how? No, she realized, she wouldn't. Modern conveniences weren't that important. This was her home now, and she would make the most of it.

She tossed the fetish back into the drawer and hopped out of bed. If she hadn't slept too late, maybe she could catch Miguel in the kitchen before the day's work began. Just to feel his arms wrapping around her, drawing her body hard against his, his sensual lips brushing hers, then becoming more demanding—

She nearly bowled Olga over as she swung through the kitchen door. "Where's Miguel?" she asked as she steadied the older woman.

"*Ach*, child. Sit." Olga turned to finish scrambling the eggs in the skillet. "Miguel's been gone most of the night."

"Gone?" Elizabeth felt a sharp pang of disappointment stab through her.

"*Ja*. There's been trouble at the fort on account of those Indians and what happened to you. He'll be back as soon as the Army returns. Don't you fret yourself."

She spooned eggs onto a plate and heaped sizzling bacon beside them. "Now eat."

Elizabeth dutifully took a forkful of food. There was never any winning with Olga when it came to eating. Elizabeth had so wanted to see Miguel this morning. She wanted to make love. At long last. She sighed with pleasure at the thought, an intense passion kindling deep within her, ready to ignite into a blazing inferno. When was he coming home?

****

Miguel rode into the ranch yard the next afternoon, the side of his face bruised and his eye swollen.

Elizabeth rushed out to him. "What happened? How badly are you hurt?"

He dismounted and gave her a kiss. "It's nothing. Just a little skirmish with some men who didn't think the Rangers were the law. They've joined the braves in the brig now." He looked around for Olaf. "I'm leaving again. I just came to get cleaned up and get some clothes. Word came that the circuit judge is on the mend. Tate Johnson thought it best if some of us rode to escort the judge here as quickly as possible. Trouble is brewing. The sooner we can decide the fate of those braves, the better."

Elizabeth sighed. So he wouldn't be home again tonight. A thought crept into her mind, making her blush. He was going to take a bath. Why should she wait any longer? She leaned on tiptoe and kissed the good side of his face. "I love you," she whispered shyly. "I'll bring you some salve for the bruises."

His eyes turned darker and she could sense his desire, but he only gave her an affectionate smack on her rump as she turned to go. "Do that."

She waited until she'd seen him return from talking to Olaf and seen the servants hauling buckets of water to his room. Then she turned the knob to the door and entered.

Miguel stood with his back to her, water glistening on his bare skin and dripping from his tight buttocks. Thick muscles defined his thighs leading down into well-shaped calves. Elizabeth let her gaze sweep upward noting the narrow waist expanding to his broad shoulders and hard traps and deltoids. He reached for a towel and she watched the muscles ripple in his back.

She must have made some sound, for he turned slowly, the towel still in his hand. Her eyes dropped and she gasped at the size of his manhood. It would never fit inside of her! Elizabeth let the jar of salve slip to the floor. She knew she should look away. Sweet Mary. Did he have any idea of her reaction? Apparently he did, for his shaft was extending itself, becoming more engorged. Mesmerized, she continued to stare.

"If you keep on looking at me like that, I'll not be responsible for my actions," he said and wrapped the towel around himself, tucking the end in at his waist before he held out his arms. "Come here."

Elizabeth flew into his embrace, circling her arms around his neck, her lips parted for his kiss. He did not disappoint. His hands stroked her back and slid down to cup her buttocks against his hardness while his tongue explored her mouth thoroughly, deepening the kiss only to withdraw and tease her lips with his, applying more pressure until she sucked his tongue back into her mouth and whimpered.

He nibbled his way down her throat to the nape of her neck causing her to quiver. Elizabeth gyrated her hips against him, seeking more contact. Never had she felt this urge to actually meld with someone. She heard him groan, low in his throat.

"Make love to me, Miguel."

He leaned lower to kiss the tip of her breast through the fabric of her shirt and then straightened, separating them. "Not now. There's not time."

She looked at him, her lips swollen from his kisses and her eyes glazed from desire. "There's time. How long does it take anyway?"

Miguel laughed and pulled on his Levis. "The rest of the afternoon and all night. Until you are so satisfied you beg me to stop. Or so exhausted you can't say the words." He zipped the pants and reached for his shirt. "Besides, there's no need to rush. We can wait."

Elizabeth stared at him, exasperated. The man was impossible. "Wait? You've made it clear since I got here that you wanted me in your bed. Now you tell me we can wait?" Hands on her hips, she asked, "Are you playing some kind of game with me? Just to see how long it would take before I said yes?" She closed her eyes. Sweet Mary. Maybe he didn't want her. Maybe he just said he loved her to get the chief to agree to the release. Had she been foolish to tell him she loved him too? Maybe that's all he wanted to hear and he could go on to his next challenge. Her eyes flew open. "Is it the schoolmarm you really want?"

"What?" Miguel reached her in two strides and put his hands on her shoulders. "I thought my body had made it perfectly clear I wanted you. Don't tell me you didn't understand."

No doubt he was the most infuriating man she had ever known. "Then why, now, when I want to go to bed with you, you don't?"

"I do, love. Never think I don't. I just thought—" He

paused and tilted her chin up with his fingers. "I thought you might want to wait until your wedding night."

Wedding night? She felt a swish of dizziness sweep over her. She clutched at him, her eyes wide. "Are you saying—?"

"Yes." Miguel seated her on the edge of the bed and knelt beside her. "Let me do this as properly as any knight of the Round Table would." He took her hand in his and turned it over, kissing the palm softly. "I love you, Elizabeth. Will you marry me?"

She stared, committing to memory the sight of him, on bended knee, his shirt open, exposing his broad chest, the dark hair falling forward over his forehead. Just a hint of a smile quirked at the corner of his mouth. How could she not be in love with him? A fleeting thought from nowhere flitted through her dazed mind. Round Table? Ironically, the two most gallant of its knights—the pure Galahad and his father, Lancelot, the adulterer—had never proposed marriage. And yet Miguel—*her* knight—he'd certainly earned the title, riding after her!—was doing just that. With a start, Elizabeth came out of her reverie.

"I…do you still think I'm a prostitute?" Well, that really wasn't what she meant to say. Why did it still niggle at her? Miguel loved her!

Miguel shrugged. "It has never mattered to me what you were or where you're from. If your memory returns, we'll deal with it." He caressed the side of her cheek with his fingertips. "I'm not in the habit of asking women to marry me. Are you going to answer my question?"

"Yes." Elizabeth threw her arms around his neck. "Yes. The answer is 'yes.' "

Miguel stood, bringing her up with him, and pressed

her body against his as their lips met again, the kiss deep and intense. The hunger of their mouths built into throbbing desire until both of them were nearly too weak to stand.

"If that's any indication of what sharing a bed with you will be like, Red, maybe we should set a wedding date soon."

"Tomorrow," Elizabeth answered. "Stay home and send for a priest."

"Olga would kill me if I denied her enough time to get ready for this wedding." Miguel grinned. "Anyway, aren't brides supposed to be excited about a wedding dress and all of the preparations?"

Bride. What a wonderful sound that word had! Suddenly, she felt overwhelmed. She wanted nothing more than to say, "I do," and be done with the ceremony, but Miguel was an important person. There would have to be invitations, a reception, and political correctness. And, of course, a dress. As a teenager, she had poured over *Bride's Magazine* looking at designer gowns. How many years had it been since she'd given up the fantasy of a white dress and all the pomp that went with a big wedding? And where, in the nineteenth century, was she going to find something? She turned to him. "There are a million things to do. Material to buy, a feast to plan, seating arrangements—"

He laughed and kissed her nose. "I'll be glad to leave you to it. I think escorting the judge and keeping order at the trial will be a lot easier than planning this." He picked up the satchel he would be taking with him and went to the door. "Just keep me in mind during all the hoopla. After all, it's you I want, lying naked beside me in our bed."

****

The month it took for the Rangers to escort the judge to Fort Worth and hold the trial was spent in a flurry of activity. Olga badgered the owner of the general store in Johnson Station to order French silk from New Orleans and the finest tulle netting for a veil. She'd thought of and scrapped a dozen menus before deciding to include it all. "A true smorgasbord," she'd said.

Even Raul got caught up in the excitement. He had a suit specially tailored for him. He complained about the necktie, but Elizabeth knew he was pleased to be included. She had heard him bragging to Gus that he would be responsible for the ring his father would be giving her.

Elizabeth wondered about that, since there were no jewelry stores within a week's ride from them, but she decided not to worry about it. She didn't really care if she got a ring. It was Miguel she wanted.

At night, she lay in bed thinking of his solid, muscular body lying naked beside her. Of the ability of his hands to excite her at just the merest touch, and the way her blood kindled into a raging inferno when his hands or mouth found more intimate places. Not to mention how his erection had jutted out at her from the nest of black curls, thick and long and hard. Her body trembled in anticipation of having *that* slide into her. And she would have that pleasure, over and over. Miguel was hers, now and forever.

It was the "forever" part she worried about. One morning after she'd had a fitting for the gown, she went back to her bedroom and took the fetish out of the drawer. She studied the smooth carving on the wood, wondering again what power it had and how it had brought her here. There was only one way to make sure it didn't send her back.

She walked down the steps and out the front door. A patio was attached to the west side of the house and with it was a small pit for grilling steaks. Elizabeth gathered twigs and small branches from a nearby mesquite tree and lit a fire. It didn't have to burn long. She whispered a small prayer of thanks for the gift and for arriving in the nineteenth century and then laid the fetish amidst the flames. As she watched it disintegrate, she hoped it wouldn't bring bad luck.

Elizabeth pulled an oak chair close and waited for the fire to die out. As the ashes cooled, she felt a sense of relief. She had done the right thing. Destroying the fetish assured her a permanent home in the nineteenth century. Now there was nothing that would send her back to her own time.

****

Miguel could almost smell the tension in the saloon that also served as a courtroom when the circuit judge was in town. Even though the liquor was locked up until the trial was over, the restless, shifting crowd was spoiling for a fight. The slightest bit of jostling made men spin round with their fists up. He'd already intervened in several disputes.

Major Arnold had the five braves under heavy guard behind the barrier of the bar. It didn't help their cause that they all looked surly and contemptuous. At least the major had gotten them to wear western clothes, even though their hair was in ceremonial braids.

Miguel had no doubt the outcome of the trial would result in a guilty verdict. Finding an impartial jury was nigh to impossible. He'd tried to convince Major Arnold to send an invitation to Chief Jim Ned to be included at the trial, but at the last minute the major had declined, saying if an angry mob decided to take its fury out on the chief, there would be no stopping the Comanche. Miguel had countered that without some representation from the tribe, they would be inclined to believe the trial was a hoax. He had even toyed with the idea of asking Cactus Flower to return to serve as a witness to the proceedings. but as much as Western men held most women in high regard, he couldn't guarantee her safety either. There were rabble and scum in the crowd, bullies who would encourage a riot for no other reason than to see others injured. Emotions were running too high. Folks remembered Mary's scarred arms and her total reticent demeanor—it was enough to have the lunatic fringe screaming for vengeance.

Miguel listened to the opening statements Beauregard made regarding the crime and wondered what kind of defense the lawyer they'd brought with the judge would make. They'd had to ride all the way to Houston to find a lawyer willing to represent Indians. Miguel was just glad Major Arnold was sending troops to escort the man back. He didn't want to be gone from Elizabeth another four weeks for that round trip.

The defense attorney was surprisingly articulate and well-versed in Indian culture. He made no attempt to deny what the braves had done, but slowly and patiently parceled out the significance of the rituals, adding that there had never been any intention of killing Mary, only of taking that small amount of blood to infuse them with power in the eyes of their great spirits. The rapes, he contended, were ceremonial, and he quoted history from a time when goddess worship still celebrated the Great

Marriage, the ritual of uniting a priestess with the king to insure fertility for the people, livestock, and crops.

Miguel blinked and shook his head. For a moment, an image of an ancient white-robed druid with a sickle in his hand super-imposed itself on the attorney. That couldn't be. For the slightest moment, he almost thought he heard chanting. He glanced around the room quickly. Nothing had changed. Men's faces were still hardened, their bodies tense with the need to lash out.

He sighed. He hoped the jury would decide on life in prison, which the lawyer had pled for, rather than hanging. The Comanche would not take kindly to having five of their tribe killed by the white man for any reason.

His hopes were dashed when the jury returned with a verdict less than fifteen minutes after they'd adjourned. Death by hanging, the sentence to be carried out immediately. A roar of approval went up as the crowd pressed forward, hands grabbing and dragging the Indians forward out toward the gallows which had been built in anticipation.

The Rangers shouldered their way through the angry mob and surrounded the braves, brandishing the cudgels Tate Johnson had insisted they carry. Now Miguel understood why.

"The verdict's been given," he said. "Let these men die with some dignity."

"They didn't give Mary any!" someone shouted. "I say we draw and quarter them first!" More shouts of approval swelled from the crowd.

Major Arnold's troops formed a barrier line as the braves were hustled up the steps. Five nooses waited. Miguel wondered if, indeed, this had been merely a kangaroo court. The gallows should not have been built until the verdict was in.

He glanced up the hill to where Chief Jim Ned sat astride his horse, motionless as a statue, the feathers in his war bonnet the only thing swaying in the wind. Beside him, Swift Hawk sat equally still. A dozen warriors lined up on either side of them, forming a formidable silhouette against the sky.

Reluctantly, Miguel removed his red bandana and waved it over his head, signaling the verdict was "Death." The white handkerchief in his pocket would have signaled the braves' lives were saved.

The line of horses along the hill's crest remained immobile for a minute. Then the chief stabbed his spear into the ground and turned his horse around. The warriors melted away with him.

"Well," Tate Johnson said as he came alongside him, "at least, Chief Jim Ned is retreating. I was afraid he wouldn't accept the outcome."

"He hasn't," Miguel replied. "He only waits. He'll put out a call to other tribes."

"Why do you say that?"

"Because his response to my signal should have been a raised spear. All he did was throw down a challenge." Miguel looked up to the empty horizon. "Comanche on the warpath, and now we have no hostages to stop them."

Chapter Fifteen—Wedding Bells

Elizabeth waited up late into the night for Miguel to return. She had only briefly seen him when he returned from Houston and stopped by on his way to the trial in Fort Worth. She had wanted to go with him, but after her abduction, her presence would only incite an already emotional crowd to riot.

Finally, she heard the steady cadence of his horse's hooves pounding the road. With relief, she went to the door and opened it as he dismounted and came toward her.

Miguel wrapped his arms around her and kissed her thoroughly before leading her to the sofa, keeping her in his embrace. "What are you still doing awake at this hour?"

"Waiting for your kiss," Elizabeth said as she snuggled against him. "You've been gone too long."

He rubbed a hand over his eyes and for the first time, Elizabeth noticed how tired he looked. She sat up. "They were found guilty, weren't they?"

"Yes. Guilty, and hanged on the spot."

Elizabeth was shocked. "Without waiting for an appeal?"

Miguel gave her a strange look. "An appeal?"

She bit her lip. Death row appeals were automatic in the twenty-first century, but not in the nineteenth. Frontier justice was carried out immediately. When would she remember not to keep bringing up the future? That was only a memory now. “Never mind.”

He pressed her head back to his shoulder and stroked her hair. “It’s okay if you have a quirk about the future. I love you anyway.” He paused. “Maybe I’m a little crazy, too. I thought I saw a druid priest during the trial.”

It was the first time he had even mentioned the possibility of a parallel time period. “How did that happen?” she asked.

“The lawyer—the one from Houston—delivered an emotional speech about ancient rituals and tolerance of others’ belief systems. It wasn’t enough to convince the jurors, but he believed in what he said.” Miguel shook his head. “Ah, well. I’ve been on the road too long, and there was a lot of tension in that courtroom. They wanted a lynching. I guess stress just made me think I saw the lawyer dressed as a priest.”

“Maybe you caught a glimpse of him from another life,” Elizabeth said. “Some people believe in reincarnation.” If only Miguel would accept a little bit of the paranormal, maybe then one day he would believe that she really was from the future.

“Okay, Red. Stop trying to convince me to accept something that’s impossible.” He brushed his lips across hers slowly. “How are the wedding plans coming along? Have we set a date?”

She recognized the diversion, but the wedding was something she was happy to talk about. “May Day,” she said, “the heralding of spring.” Brooke would have reminded her that it was also Beltane, the ancient festival of fertility. Well, she hoped she’d be fertile. Raul needed a brother or a sister.

“Did you post the banns while I was gone?” Miguel

asked.

“Banns?” She hadn’t even thought of the old practice of putting their intention to marry in writing and having the clergy read it to the public. “I—I thought it would be better to wait for you.” That was true. It would have been awkward to ask the priest to announce their wedding without the groom present.

“Tomorrow’s Sunday. We’ll do it then,” Miguel said as he rose from the sofa and brought her with him. He nuzzled her neck, one hand gently kneading a breast. “How am I going to wait three more weeks to bed you?”

She let her hand trail down his chest, across his flat belly and then lower until her fingertips touched the increasingly hard bulge that was growing. “You don’t have to.”

He made a growling sound low in his throat. “Keep doing that and I won’t wait.” Briefly, he pressed himself against her and then he took her hand. “I promised Olga, on my mother’s grave, that I would do the honorable thing and wait.” He sighed. “It’s getting late. We have to be up early. Now go, before I change my mind.”

As Elizabeth left, she thought of Abigail Parsons. The schoolmarm no longer posed a threat, but she’d be at church in the morning. Elizabeth would have given nearly anything to have a twenty-first century camera with her to catch the look on her face when the banns were read.

****

Elizabeth had just finished purchasing some fabric Monday morning when the door to the general store burst open and Abigail Parsons swept through. She had a copy of the banns that had been posted yesterday in her hand and she slammed it down on the counter and glared at Elizabeth.

"You think you've won, don't you?"

Elizabeth stifled a grin. She *had* won, but there was no sense in enraging a scorned woman who was already angry. Abigail hadn't been in church yesterday, but she obviously had heard the news.

"Miguel is marrying me, yes."

The schoolmarm's golden eyes slitted, giving her the appearance of a feral cat. "Don't be too sure about that."

"There isn't anything you can do about it, Miss Parsons." Why didn't she just give up? Miguel had never really encouraged her and he had made his choice.

The schoolmarm snarled and Elizabeth almost stepped back. Almost. Instead she managed to inquire, "I'm assuming that means you aren't going to wish us well?"

Abigail made a strangled noise and picked up the paper only to crush it in her clawed hand. Elizabeth noticed for the first time how long and sharp the schoolteacher's nails were. For a brief moment, Elizabeth had the impression the woman was going to crouch and spring, as coiled as her body was. Elizabeth tensed. She had always detested breaking up cat fights at the high school. Girls fought dirty. Those nails could do some damage, and the timid young woman behind the counter would be of no help. Miguel was down the street at the smithy, but Elizabeth was not about to run out of the store looking for help. Suddenly, Miss Parsons loosened her grip on the paper and smiled.

"I'm going to ruin you."

Elizabeth took a deep breath and pulled herself up to her full height. "How are you going to ruin me?"

The schoolmarm's smile twisted. "I'm going to make sure everyone in this town knows the truth about you."

The truth? That she'd time-traveled? How could she know that? Elizabeth decided to fish. "What are you talking about?"

"Your little secret. You know."

Miss Parsons couldn't prove anything. "Refresh my memory, will you?"

The schoolmarm smirked. "Very well. I'll tell you what you already know. Swift Hawk found you nearly naked in Miguel's barn, did he not?"

"How do you know that?"

A knowing smile appeared. "The Indian is a lonely man. I got him to talk."

Swift Hawk? Elizabeth remembered the looks they'd exchanged that day in the library. Okay, so Miss Parsons had cornered him. Maybe more than that. Swift Hawk thought Elizabeth was some kind of spirit dream-catcher person.

"Yes, Miss O'Malley, he talked. He says you speak of strange things in distant places. That you have knowledge of future things. Of course, he thinks it's because his gods sent you; I say you're either a witch or you're mad. Either way, once I start spreading the rumors that there's something odd and possibly dangerous about you, people will shun you. It's amazing how little it takes to get people to believe what you want them to—a subtle suggestion here, a little allusion there. Built slowly, the rumors will ruin you. Miguel is a Ranger and also influential. He can't afford to be saddled with a lunatic."

Elizabeth stared at her. In a way, it was exactly what

Miguel had warned her about—that people would think she was crazy. Why had she not learned to keep her mouth shut?

Abigail smiled sweetly as she turned to leave. "I intend to have Miguel, and I always get exactly what I want."

****

Two days later, Elizabeth was still shaky over the encounter, even though Miguel had assured her he would be able to quell any rumors that might get started. He also sent an inquiry out about Miss Parsons' background. The knots in Elizabeth's stomach twisted even more when an army soldier came galloping into the yard on a nearly spent horse.

"Major Arnold asks you to come quick!" he said as he slid down from his blowing, heaving mount.

"Comanche?" Miguel asked even as he signaled for fresh horses.

The young soldier nodded. "Fur trapper named Cockrell was returning from his trap lines and he nearly ran into Chief Jim Ned's camp. He heard them talking of meeting up with Chief Feathertail, so he rode to warn the garrison."

"Feathertail. That means the southern Comanches are joining forces with Jim Ned. You're talking several hundred warriors."

And all of them hungry for revenge. Elizabeth remembered the Comanche were horrific fighters and had even managed to push the fierce Apache tribes farther west. Feathertail was ruthless. And now the blood lust flowed through them for what had been done to the braves.

Miguel turned to Elizabeth. "I'm sorry, I've got to

go. I know Jim Ned better than any white man. He must be stopped before Feathertail reaches him."

She nodded dumbly and watched him mount. He leaned down to give her a quick kiss. "Don't worry about anything."

"Be careful," she said. Why did the Army need him anyway? Couldn't they fight their own war? She sighed. She knew the answer. Miguel was a Ranger. He would no more shirk his duty than her father had done.

Elizabeth shivered suddenly, although the sun was warm. A feeling of dread inched its way through her. What if something happened to Miguel? She wouldn't be able to stand it. Then she heard her father's voice in her mind. *"You have to trust, daughter. We each have our time."*

Elizabeth shook her head to clear it. Miguel would be all right. She was just being silly. She hoped.

****

Miguel knew, as soon as he entered the major's office late that afternoon, that there would be no negotiating this time. The major had maps strewn all over the table with defense tactics scribbled over them.

Arnold acknowledged him with a nod but didn't stop giving orders. "We'll attack from three directions." He turned to his officers. "Captain Maclay, you'll head north. Lieutenant Street, you'll go south and swing around. Be careful Feathertail's not on your back. I'll take my troops and head directly west. Jim Ned will be flanked on three sides. He'll either fight without Feathertail or he'll retreat. Miguel, you ride with me."

"When do we leave?"

The major frowned. "As soon as we've eaten. It's a *Comanchería* moon. Jim Ned will move tonight. I want to be waiting for him."

Miguel sat on his horse, several hours later, peering into the darkness. The full moon had just risen and there wasn't enough light yet to see far ahead. The Comanche were stealthy, but they were mounted. It would be hard not to hear their approach, but his concern was for Indian scouts who could count *coup* and flee before anyone knew someone was dead.

One of their own outriders returned just then. "You were right, sir," he said to the major. "They're on the move, less than a half mile from here."

The major nodded and dispatched two riders for his captain and lieutenant. "Here we go," he said and urged his horse forward.

The initial clash did not last long. Surprised and outnumbered, the Indians had no choice but to turn back. Miguel saw Swift Hawk hesitate, tomahawk in hand, but a terse command from Jim Ned made him follow. The chief was no fool and this wasn't over yet, even though they left thirty-seven dead and fifteen more wounded.

Major Arnold rode up to Miguel. "Not one casualty on our part. Not bad for a night's work."

"What are you going to do about their wounded?" Miguel asked.

The major looked around. "We should just shoot them."

"That'll incite even more trouble," Miguel said. "We don't want the entire Indian nation coming off the reservations."

"You have heard of taking no prisoners, I assume?" he answered.

Miguel clenched his jaw. *God!* He was glad he'd never joined the Army. All he wanted to do was go home and hold Elizabeth. Beginning a range war would not make things safe for her or anyone else.

"Then don't take prisoners," Miguel finally said when he could speak civilly. "Leave them here. The Comanche will come back for their dead once we're gone. Let them take their wounded, too. Maybe it will mend things with Jim Ned. War can be prevented."

"You think so? I was trained to stand and fight. I wouldn't be here if I weren't." The major frowned as he spoke, appearing to be fighting an internal battle. "But Washington wants peace. The sooner we can convince the Comanche to move to the reservations, the better." He sighed and signaled the retreat. "I sure hope you're right."

They camped by the Brazos River that night, anticipating the path that Feathertail's warriors would take. At dawn, just as the first red streaks lit the sky, the Indians appeared on the horizon.

Spotting the army, Feathertail let out a war whoop and broke into a gallop.

"They've got us outnumbered this time," Captain Maclay said grimly, "and our men haven't had much sleep."

"Bah." The major snorted and patted his sidearm. "We have five bullets riding on our hips and we have these." He raised his rifle. "This will be over as quickly as last night was."

But it wasn't. Miguel knew last night had been a fluke. Jim Ned had no way of knowing the trapper had overheard him. His braves were not even painted for battle, which meant they had planned to wait for Feathertail.

Feathertail fought fiercely—making charges, firing

arrows, and then quickly retreating to form another line. The infantry held its ranks in a double line, the first line firing, then dropping to their knees to reload while the second line above them fired. The cavalry counter-charged, trying to flank the Indians, but they were too spread out.

It was midmorning when Feathertail led a suicidal charge, infiltrating the army lines and bursting through. Miguel wheeled his mount around and found himself face-to-face with the chief. He raised his hand and asked for peace in the Comanche tongue.

Feathertail sneered at him and raised his tomahawk, bringing it down in a felling swoop. At the same time, the chief arched his back, his eyes opening in surprise as a bullet found its mark. The arm with the tomahawk wavered, missing Miguel's chest and imbedding the heavy blade in his thigh.

Dimly, through the haze filtering over his eyes, Miguel was aware of the Indians retreating now that their chief was dead. The pain in his leg seared like a knife through the rest of him. The world was becoming darker, as though the sun had set. He felt himself being eased from the saddle—and then he knew no more.

****

Miguel woke groggily in the infirmary to pain and blurry vision. The scent of lye disinfectant assailed his nose and the whitewashed walls and white sheets covering him made him think he was drifting in a cloud. A woman faded in and out of his consciousness. At times, she looked like Elizabeth, but then she shifted into traditional Indian dress, although her braided hair remained red. She placed a cool hand on his fevered brow and the pain receded. He blinked his eyes hard to bring her into focus, but she was gone.

"You're awake." Elizabeth came to his side quickly from the chair where she had been dozing. "How do you feel?"

"The pain…it was there and now it's gone." He tried to sit up, but Elizabeth pushed him down and held onto his hand. He gave her a feeble smile. "Did you just touch me a minute ago?"

She shook her head, looking puzzled. "No. I've been dozing in the chair. Why?"

"""Well, someone did. She made the pain go away."

"There's been no one in here but me, Miguel. Maybe you're still delirious."

"Still? How long have I been here?"

"Four days. The wound got infected and you were burning up with fever. The medic didn't know if you'd make it. That's when they came and got me."

He brought her hand to his lips and kissed it. "I'm glad you're here." Then he frowned. "But you didn't see a red-haired woman with braids, dressed in fringed white leather and moccasins?" Elizabeth looked startled and Miguel asked, "What is it? Did you see her too?" He pushed himself up against the headboard. "Not my imagination, then. I'd like to thank her, if you can find her."

"I can't Miguel. I…I may have seen her, too—in the Sweat Lodge—but I thought she was just a vision." Elizabeth wrinkled her brow in thought and then widened her eyes. "There was another time—" She looked at him apprehensively. "It was in a dream. Just before I found myself in your barn and the nineteenth century."

****

Miguel wasn't strong enough to travel for another week, and even then he walked with a slight limp, although he was determined to go home.

When they returned to the hacienda, Cactus Flower was waiting for them.

Elizabeth hugged her. "What are you doing here?"

"Chief Jim Ned sent me. He's returned your horses. He said he angered the Great Spirit since you took nothing in return. My father said it was the reason Chief Feathertail was killed." She looked at Miguel. "I am to remain your hostage."

"You are free to go," Miguel said. "Having Diablo back is all the token I need for peace."

She gave him a shy smile. "I would prefer to stay, if that's all right."

"Of course." Miguel studied her. "The white man's ways appeal to you, then?" When she nodded, he went on. "Perhaps you can be the ambassador that we've wanted. Someone who understands both cultures. You could relay messages from time to time."

"That would give you an opportunity to see your mother, too," Elizabeth added.

Cactus Flower smiled gratefully. "I would like that. It was the only sadness I felt when I offered to bring the horses back."

"And you can help me with the wedding plans. Olga did tell you?"

Cactus Flower giggled and Miguel grinned. "In that case, I'll leave you two ladies to it. I've got a meeting with an old friend I haven't seen in a while." Whistling, he headed off toward the barn.

Arm in arm, the women headed toward the house, both talking at once.

****

The wedding day dawned with blue skies, sunshine, and a zephyr breeze. The ranch wives decorated a maypole with fresh prairie grasses, meadow flowers and ribbons. Olga had persuaded farmwives from neighboring homesteads to help her with the food. From the kitchen came the smells of fresh bread and country pies, and from the massive pits near the patio, Olaf oversaw the roasting of steer, javelina, and deer.

Guests began arriving in midafternoon, even though Elizabeth had opted for a candlelight ceremony. While the garrison remained on alert, every soldier not on duty had been invited, as well as the townsfolk of Village Creek and Johnson Station. The Rangers were there, of course: Tate Johnson, and Echols, Parker, Turner and Farrar. To Elizabeth's surprise, the grandson of José Antonio Navarro, who had signed the Texas Declaration of Independence from Santa Anna's Mexico, arrived from San Antonio. Governor Bell sent his regards, as well.

Lily arrived with several of her "ladies" late in the afternoon and checked into rooms above the saloon in Johnson Station, much to the delight of the single men in the group. Miguel sent word to Elizabeth not to be shocked when she arrived at the church. She smiled when she got the note. She knew how much Miguel valued Lily's friendship, and she had grown fond of the older woman too.

Outside the hacienda was a blur of movement. Elizabeth watched the activities from her upstairs window, for both Olga and Cactus Flower were adamant Miguel should not see her before the service. She stepped away from the window as Miguel looked up from the courtyard.

Just a few more hours and he would be hers. The rumors that Miss Parsons had tried to start had been quickly squelched, as Miguel promised. A little talk from the school board had convinced the schoolmarm to cease her efforts. Still, Tate Johnson was going to make sure she didn't attend the service, although there wasn't much they could do about the wedding dance in town that evening.

Elizabeth soaked in the warm, rose-scented water, hoping to calm her jittered nerves. Thoughts of lying naked with Miguel sent rivers of fire jettisoning through her body and yet—she had *seen* the size of his manhood. Would she really be able to take all of him? She desperately didn't want him to be disappointed. Virginity was expected in the nineteenth century but, ironically, Elizabeth wished she were more experienced.

Cactus Flower interrupted her thoughts to do her hair, and she had no more time to worry. Olga arrived to help her slip into the yards and yards of filmy ivory silk, trimmed with Venetian lace. It was an exquisite gown that two of the town's most skilled seamstresses had spent days on, but Elizabeth was not quite sure how she would breathe in it, for Cactus Flower had managed to cinch the corset an extra two inches so her waist looked nearly as small as the legendary Scarlett O'Hara's. But when the veil was placed on her head and she looked in the mirror, she decided the torture was worth it. Her dream was finally coming true.

They walked down the stairs to where Olaf waited with the surrey. Miguel had ridden on ahead to wait for her at the church. Just as Elizabeth was opening the door, Cactus Flower halted.

"I almost forgot. Just a minute." She rushed up the stairs to her room and returned moments later, holding a dream catcher.

"This is for you. My father made it himself as a peace offering."

"Thank you," Elizabeth said as she held it up. It was larger and heavier than the one her students had given her and done in dark leather with black and red beads. Three black raven feathers hung from the bottom part of the ring. Overall, it had almost an ominous feel to it. She gave herself a little shake. That was ridiculous. Dream catchers were supposed to catch bad dreams. The shaman had crafted it to make amends. She smiled at Cactus Flower. "It's beautiful. Just let me put it in Miguel's room and I'll be right back."

A short time later, as the carriage wheels crunched to a stop near the church, Elizabeth drew a shaky breath and peered out the window. Where was Miguel? There were so many people. She couldn't find him anywhere. She spotted Lily and some of her girls, already being friendly to the men.

And then Miguel was there, helping her down. He looked magnificent, dressed formally in broadcloth black breeches and spats, a gray pinstripe waistcoat, stiff collar shirt and silk ascot. He could have stepped off the cover of *Esquire*, although his shiny dark hair still fell stubbornly across his forehead. She reached up and brushed it back.

He stared at her for a moment with something akin to awe. "You're beautiful, Elizabeth," he said as he offered his arm. "I don't suppose I could give you a taste of what's to come when we can get these clothes off later?"

She knew she was blushing. “Behave yourself.”

He grinned. “Only for a little while.”

Together, they entered the church. To Elizabeth, the ceremony was surrealistic, the priest speaking in Latin, which she didn’t understand. Brooke would have said it had a Faerie feel, the day being Beltane and all. Perhaps there was magic in the air. Elizabeth knew she’d never been happier. In just a little while, she would be kissing her new husband. Husband! Nothing would ever take her from Miguel’s side.

Thank goodness the priest switched to English for the vows. She wanted to make sure she heard Miguel say the “until death do us part” thing. That would make it real.

She needn’t have worried. The look Miguel gave her as he slipped his mother’s gold wedding ring on her finger said what no words could. She knew from Olga that he hadn’t made the offer of his mother’s ring to Elena.

“I pronounce you man and wife,” the priest said. “You may kiss the bride.”

Miguel raised an eyebrow at her, mischief in his eyes, as he lifted her veil. She knew that look—

He lowered his head to hers and whispered, “Do you want a real kiss, Red?”

She stared at him. Was he talking tongue and all? Here? In church? Out of the corner of her eye, she saw Lily’s girl, Sharee, watching them. How far would Miguel go?

She handed her bouquet to Cactus Flower and put her arms around Miguel’s neck. “You were saying earlier—”

He wrapped his arms around her waist and drew her

to him in one crushing sweep, his mouth covering hers, ravaging her lips, probing them open for his tongue. His kiss was thorough and deep and he lingered at the parting. Thank God he was still holding her up, for she had no breath left.

She saw the shocked look on the priest's face. Olga was trying to look stern, but Olaf was grinning like a schoolboy. "Wow," Raul said and then the crowd broke into good-natured applause. Miguel kept his arm around her as they ran toward the doorway, getting showered with rice along the way.

Outside, he kissed her again, more respectably, and then grinned. "I can see I've made a good choice. Perhaps there are some things you can teach me tonight."

She kept the smile on her face, but her stomach fluttered as anxiety filled her. She'd forgotten how experienced he was and what he would be wanting. Would she know what to do?

Perhaps holding onto her virginity all these years while other women were gaining experience wasn't such a good thing, after all. Even Edward had not gotten as far as Miguel did the night she was drunk. She entertained a wild notion of trying to find Lily and get a crash course.

She realized Miguel was looking at her quizzically. "You have the strangest expression on your face," he said. "It makes me think you're planning on doing all sorts of delicious things to me later."

She smiled weakly. *Oh, dear.*

****

Rangers clapped Miguel on the back and told Elizabeth it was about time there was a woman in his life, and then the reception line continued. Olaf and Olga beamed with the joy that blood parents would have shown. Lily hugged them both and whispered to Elizabeth that Miguel would treat her right. Elizabeth wasn't sure if she meant in bed or otherwise and found alarmed butterflies battering their wings in her stomach again.

Sharee approached and took Miguel's hand. "A pity we never got to know each other," she said and then looked at Elizabeth. "I think you're a lucky woman."

"I know I am," Elizabeth answered with a big smile. She felt almost giddy. Miguel hadn't spent that night with Sharee after all! And then Beauregard was there offering congratulations. Sharee gave him a big smile. He promptly extended his arm to her and Elizabeth watched them walk away.

"I don't think she'll miss me too much," Miguel said with a grin.

Elizabeth swatted his arm and they moved on to the dance. The Grand March consisted of one circle of the rather small Town Hall and then Miguel swept her into his arms for a waltz.

"This is one dance when I'm going to have you all to myself," he said. "No one's going to cut in."

Elizabeth sighed contentedly. She could have danced all night, as happy as she was. Unfortunately, a short time later, she felt a tap on her shoulder.

Miss Parsons. Did the woman never give up? Miguel had made his displeasure well known, so what was she doing standing there and smiling at him in the middle of a crowded dance floor?

"I know what I did wasn't right," she purred to Miguel. Elizabeth was surprised cream didn't dribble out of her mouth. "Would you forgive me and let me have one dance?"

"I think not, Miss Parsons. I prefer dancing with my wife."

"Abby! What are you doing here?" Sharee asked as she and Beauregard stopped dancing close to them. "I thought you had followed the gold miners to California."

The schoolmarm looked decidedly uncomfortable. Miguel frowned. "Do you two know each other?"

"No," Abigail said.

Sharee looked puzzled. "Of course we do. We worked together at *Le Céleste* in New Orleans, remember?"

"I think you must be mistaken. You're a prostitute, aren't you? I don't associate with them. If you'll excuse me." Miss Parsons walked away quickly.

Sharee stared after her. "What's got her so hoity-toity? Like she's suddenly too good to talk to me…"

A corner of Miguel's mouth twitched. "Are you saying that you—uh—were in the same profession in New Orleans?"

"*Oui*. The house was well known." She patted her bright hair and then smiled at Beauregard. "She wasn't as popular as I was, but Abby was much sought after."

It was too much. Elizabeth nearly doubled over with laughter. All this time that *creature* had been pretending to be a schoolteacher—Abigail had been a prostitute. And Miguel had thought *she* was one when she really *was* the schoolteacher. What delicious irony! Elizabeth dabbed at her eyes, trying to control another fit of giggles.

Miguel glanced at her, trying to look stern. "It seems we've been deluded, then. She's our schoolmarm."

"Not for long," Elizabeth tittered and then cleared her throat. She really needed to take this seriously—and then giggled helplessly again.

Sharee gave her a doubtful look and then turned back to Miguel. "I'd no idea Abby had gotten out of the business. I wouldn't have said anything."

"I'm glad you did," Miguel said. "Arrangements will have to be made. For tonight, though, everyone needs to enjoy themselves."

He watched as Beauregard swept Sharee away and then turned to Elizabeth. "Am I going to have to kiss you into behaving?"

"Please do," Elizabeth said as she smothered another fit of laughter.

Miguel took her at her word, leaving her barely enough air to breath as he conquered her mouth.

****

Finding out the truth about Miss Parsons had been most gratifying. The dinner and reception had been lovely, and Olaf had hidden the surrey and horse so she and Miguel could steal away and come back to the hacienda while everyone else was still enjoying the dance in town.

In their bedroom now, she slipped on the black silk and lace gown Miguel had bought her for Christmas and looked at herself in the mirror. *Dear Lord.* The lace barely covered the lower half of her breasts, and the silk was so fine that it clung to her body, leaving little to the imagination. She felt suddenly shy—this was *it*. She really *was* going to lose her virginity. Wrapping a thick terry robe around herself, she stepped out from behind the dressing screen that Olga had put in Miguel's bedroom.

He was lying propped up against the headboard, the corner of the sheet draped casually over his nude hips.

The long muscular legs were bare, as was his broad chest. Elizabeth tingled in anticipation—and a little dread—of what that bit of cloth covered.

Miguel raised an eyebrow at her attire. “It took you that long back there to put on that?” Then he grinned. “Come here.”

Elizabeth fidgeted with the robe’s belt and her eye caught the dream catcher lying on the dresser. She needed just a little more time to calm her nerves before she got into bed with him. She picked it up. “Let me hang this first.”

“It won’t be catching any dreams tonight, Love. I don’t intend to let you sleep until you’re fully exhausted.”

Elizabeth blushed and tried to ignore the fact that as she knelt on the bed and removed a small picture to replace it with the dream catcher, Miguel was nearly beneath her. Her fingers were shaking. “There,” she finally said as the dream catcher swung from its hook. “All done.”

“We’ve yet to start.” Miguel’s hands circled her waist and brought her down across his lap, cradling her shoulders with one arm as she leaned against him.

He undid the robe with his other hand and slipped it off her shoulders, and for a moment he just looked at her, a teasing smile lifting a corner of his sensual mouth. “I knew you’d wear it for me, Red. I was hoping it would be tonight.” He fingered one of the delicate straps. “We’ll play with this later.”

He tilted her chin with his hand and began kissing her face, light butterfly touches to her forehead and eyelids, tracing a pattern along her cheek and down her throat. Elizabeth mewled softly as he nipped gently at the lobe of her ear and moved to the nape of her neck. He brushed her lips with his, teasing her again and again, until she ached to feel his mouth hard on hers and demanding. She tried to put her arms around his neck and pull him to her, but he caught both hands in his and held them to his chest.

The first kiss was slow and soft and sensual. He lingered, his mouth playing with her upper lip, then nibbling at the corner before taking her lower lip and sucking it between his. A thousand flames flared in her veins. She needed his tongue. *Now*.

Sensing her need, his tongue teased her lips before he began to fully explore her mouth, playing with her, pretending to withdraw so she would pursue him, the pressure steadily increasing. Could a man actually make love to a woman's mouth? Elizabeth panted softly. Apparently he could.

Somehow, he had lowered her to the bed and was leaning over her. Elizabeth had no idea of when that had happened, but the touch of his hand through the lace sent more tingles pulsating through her. He kneaded a breast, his thumb flicking over the nipple, causing it to bud immediately. Miguel caught the hard tip and rolled it between his fingers, bringing her to another peak of delight.

He slipped one of the straps down and exposed her breast. His warm tongue circled the nipple and darted back and forth across it, the friction sending another wave of sensation washing over her. She shivered slightly as the cool air fanned over her and that adept tongue moved to where her other breast lay exposed. *When did that happen? How had he gotten her gown off?* He teased the nib slightly, then covered it with his mouth and began to suckle.

Elizabeth whimpered and felt a gush of wetness between her legs as a parallel throbbing began there. She pressed his head closer to her breast, urging him on, not wanting that delightful feeling to stop.

Miguel cupped her breasts and brought them together, alternating his attention between them. His hand began the long, slow stroking of her torso, the fingers gliding lower to bring the most feathery of touches to the mound of auburn curls and then trailing upward again, only to wander intimately over her ribs and belly and below again. Her body began to tremble. It couldn't get any better than this!

Could it? Sweet Mary. He kissed a trail down her stomach, stopping to nuzzle and kiss the sensitive area on the abdomen just above her curls. Elizabeth's stomach did a roller-coaster drop, but before she could gain her breath, he lifted her knee toward him, exposing her womanhood, and nibbled his way down her inner thigh. Virginal instinct kicked in—she brought her other knee over to close her legs.

"Uh-uh," Miguel said catching her leg and shifting his weight so that he was kneeling between her legs, facing her. "This is where it gets interesting."

Gets interesting? Gets? She was already weak as a kitten. *How—? Oh!!!* Miguel spread her legs slowly and then lowered himself to his feast. Gently, his fingers opened her swollen folds and he lapped at her juices, swirling his tongue deep inside of her. He began to lick her with long, slow, flat strokes. The velvety roughness of it made Elizabeth writhe, a moan escaping her lips. Then she gasped as he nibbled her nub, his mouth hard against her as her body flexed to meet him. She was spiraling upward, lost in sensation, the throbbing between her legs growing in urgency until she felt she was going to explode. And still he did not stop. She was trembling in earnest now, crying out for him to stop and not stop. What unbelievable, exquisite torture! And then, just when she was sure she could stand no more, he suckled deep on that jutting tip. Spasms rocked her body as the volcano inside her erupted and spread through her veins like molten lava.

Elizabeth lay panting, feeling her heart pounding harshly. Would she ever be able to breathe normally again? She felt Miguel slide up beside her, his hands caressing her body, and then lightly fondling a breast. As sated as she was, her traitorous body flared to life, the nipple hardening instantly.

"Don't look so sleepy," he said with a grin. "We haven't consummated the marriage yet."

Dear God. He was right. She was still technically a virgin. Elizabeth became aware of something really hard pressing against her thigh. Something hard and really long. She ventured a glance and then swallowed hard. And thick. His manhood was even more engorged than when she had seen him after his bath. It would never fit inside her. What if he tore her apart?

Panic began to bubble up and for a crazy moment she wished she were back in her own century, safe in her own bed. Alone. *By all the saints—no, by the Irish patron saint, Brighid…*she needed a woman's help at the moment—she said a quick prayer for help.

Oddly enough, it came, stopping her trembling. A voice, soft and faint—comforting.

"Relax, my child, and welcome your womanhood. You've waited centuries—"

Elizabeth took a deep breath. Maybe if he let her hands play with it, it would go down or something. She reached out and touched him. He felt like velvet-covered steel.

He caught her hand. "Not tonight. I'll have no control left if you do that. And I want to make this last as long as possible."

She had to tell him. "Miguel—" But her words went unfinished as his mouth covered hers, this time harsh and demanding, the heat from his body permeating the air, filling her with the masculine scent of him.

"Ah, Elizabeth," Miguel whispered as he straddled her and splayed her legs. "I've waited so long for this."

She flung her arms around his neck and felt the rounded head of his shaft probing her, finding her entry, pushing. Elizabeth closed her eyes, clung to him, and bit her lip.

Nothing happened. He wasn't moving. She was pretty sure he was supposed to move. After all, she'd read her share of romance novels. She opened her eyes slowly to find him raised on his elbows, staring at her, his dark eyes inscrutable.

"What's wrong?" she asked.

"You—you're a virgin." His voice shook.

"Yes."

"Not a working girl."

"No. I tried to tell you."

"Oh, God, Elizabeth! Can you ever forgive me?" He rained kisses on her face and the tip of her nose. "All those times when I assumed—when I tried to take advantage— No wonder you were angry with me. You were right. I am an arrogant—"

"Hush," Elizabeth said and gave him a long,

melting, deep kiss. She looked into his eyes. "It's just that—well, I don't think—" She paused.

"You don't think what? That you want to make love to me?" He held very still.

"No. I mean yes. I do want to make love to you." She was finding this more and more embarrassing, especially since he was still a little bit inside of her. "I just don't think you'll fit," she blurted. "You're too big."

The relief on his face was obvious and he stifled a laugh. "Thank you for the compliment, but I can assure you I'll fit." Then he sobered. "I'll try not to hurt you, but there will be some pain the first time, sweetheart. I'll make it as easy as I can."

Miguel's head was reeling. All of this time—when he had been so sure she was just holding him off to arouse him even more, that she was really adept at the game—she had been pure. And she was his. His wife. No man had claimed her before and no man ever would. His heart swelled with pride and love.

He ignored the pulsing of his painfully rigid erection and spent some time using his fingers to pleasure her again while stretching the opening. She was tight and hot and so wet. Everything a man could want, and after tonight, he could ram into her as hard and deep as he liked and bring her to heights she didn't know existed. But for now—

Miguel eased himself on top of her and nudged his cock to the edge of the barrier inside her. He felt her muscles involuntarily contract. "Relax, Love. It won't hurt so much if you do."

"I'm…I'm trying."

He covered her mouth with his, his tongue leisurely playing with hers, sliding in and retreating, mimicking the action that would soon follow. Gradually, he felt the tension ease around his shaft. He deepened the kiss and with one fluid motion plunged through the barrier and filled her.

She shuddered, gave a scream swallowed by his kiss, and dug her nails into his shoulders. He lay perfectly still, giving her time to adjust to the feel of him. He nibbled her neck. “Does it still hurt?”

She took a shaky breath. “It’s easing.” She wiggled a little. “You feel strange.”

He grinned. “That won’t last long.” He experimented with a slow partial withdrawal and then full penetration again. Her eyes widened. “Does that feel good?”

“Ummm.” It did feel good. More than just good. The throbbing between her legs started again and this time it was demanding movement from him. She arched her back and could feel the tip of him pressing against her womb. “I think I might like this.”

Miguel’s grin widened and he began a slow, rhythmic thrusting, forcing himself to stay gentle with her until her responses became urgent. When she began to buck under him, he finally allowed himself to drive deeper and faster, grinding his hips against the slick wetness of her, loving the snugness that hugged him as he withdrew and lunged into her sweet depths. He felt the tension mounting in her, even as his own fire surged upward, threatening to become a blazing inferno. She gave a shrill cry and then came that blessed contraction, gripping him, letting him know that the world had shattered for her.

With a final forceful thrust, he gave in to the luxury of finding his own release and spilled himself inside her.

Elizabeth curled into his arms and nuzzled his neck. “And to think I was afraid. I want to do this every night for the rest of our lives.”

Miguel kissed her forehead and pulled her closer. “We will. Believe me. We have our entire future before us.

Chapter Sixteen—Back to the Future

Elizabeth rolled over in bed, extending an arm, groping for Miguel. Her hand felt empty space. Sleepily, she blinked her eyes open against the morning sun streaming in the window. The pillow beside her was plump and untouched.

Untouched. Vaguely, the thought wandered through her mind that the comforter on the bed wasn't Miguel's quilt. She stared at the blank pink wall. The walls in her old bedroom in Arlington had been pink. And what was that noise? Cars?

Elizabeth shot to a sitting position, her heart pounding. It couldn't be. She ran to the window and then gripped the sill to keep herself from falling as she gazed in horror at the cars parked in the apartment complex.

She was back in the twenty-first century. Her mind reeled and she felt light-headed. She grasped her arms with icy fingers and eased herself into an upholstered chair, gasping. She forced herself to breathe deeply and slowly and tried not to panic.

What had happened? Was it all really a dream? She remembered going to bed just before Christmas, after the fight with Edward, and wishing she'd been born a century earlier. Could she really have dreamt it all? Miguel, Raul and the ranch? Swift Hawk and the abduction? She glanced at the window again and shook her head. The trees had new leaves on them; it was spring, not winter. The month of May, if reality hadn't totally left her. And the pleasant soreness between her legs was real. She couldn't have dreamed *that*. Not all of it anyway. She hadn't even known there were so many sensitive areas on her body nor imagined how many ways pleasure could be taken.

It had to have been real. She twisted the ring on her finger and then realized what she was doing. The ring was still there. Miguel's mother's ring of soft eighteen-karat gold encrusted with tiny dazzling diamonds. Elizabeth breathed a sigh of relief. She wasn't crazy—and then she felt a hysterical bubble rising in her throat.

How had she time-traveled again? She'd burned the fetish. This wasn't supposed to have happened. And where was Miguel? Trapped in the nineteenth century?

Ironic that Miguel had thought her a bit off at first and now, if she told anyone in today's world she'd time-traveled, they'd probably pack her off to John Peter Smith hospital in Fort Worth for a psychiatric examination. What was she going to do? More importantly, could she return to Miguel?

****

"Have you seen Elizabeth this morning?" Miguel asked as he walked into the kitchen and kissed Olga's cheek and helped himself to a cup of coffee.

He'd been disappointed when he'd awakened to find her side of the bed empty. All he'd wanted to do was repeat last night's marathon performance. In fact, he was surprised Elizabeth had the energy to be up and about. They hadn't finally rested, in total exhaustion, until dawn was breaking.

"I haven't seen her." Olga set his steaming oatmeal in front of him with a thoughtful look. "You didn't have one of your fights, did you? On your wedding night?"

"Of course not." Even if he'd wanted to, which he didn't, he could not have found a single fault with Elizabeth last night. After her initial fear, she had opened herself to him without hesitation, begging him to take her deeper and harder, as eager to please him as he was to please her. And she was a fast learner. Just remembering the slow, long strokes she had given his shaft gave him an erection, and when she'd covered the tip of him with her mouth and sucked—Miguel groaned, instantly hard.

He pushed the bowl aside and stood. "Maybe she's decided a game of hide-and-seek will pique my interest." He grinned at Olga. "Not that it needs it."

He returned to the kitchen nearly an hour later, a worried expression on his face. "I've looked everywhere. Plata is in the barn. Olaf hasn't seen Elizabeth. The gardens are empty." He frowned. Women didn't just disappear from his bed. If Swift Hawk had still been there, he might fleetingly have entertained the thought that the Indian had really counted *coup* and stolen her away. He was stealthy enough, but Miguel had checked with the guards that had been posted since Chief Jim Ned's uprising. No Indians had been spotted anywhere.

"Have you sent for the Rangers?" Olga asked as she down beside him.

He nodded wearily. "Olaf went for them. They'll search, but I can't imagine where she could have gone on foot. I've sent our ranch hands out to scour the surrounding areas. No one has returned yet." He refused to face his worst fear: that she was lying hurt somewhere, or worse.

Miguel went over the events again in his mind. They had finally finished making love—he'd lost count of the times—and were lying entwined in each other's arms. The last thing she'd murmured to him, half-asleep, was that they would be together for the rest of their lives. Not something a woman would say and then sneak out of bed to run away. He shook his head. He *knew* Elizabeth loved him. Not only had she said it, she'd shown him in every way she could. He trusted her; she had built that trust with everything she did—caring for Raul, helping Olga, taking an interest in livestock, even in standing up to him.

An uneasy thought niggled its way into his brain. Elizabeth had never stopped insisting she was from the future. He hadn't believed her any more than he had about her not being a working girl. Yet she had proved to be a virgin. If he could have been so wrong about that—what if Elizabeth hadn't been imagining?

The idea was disturbing. It made no sense to his logical brain. People were born on earth and people died, all in one lifetime. They didn't travel through time. They didn't come back from the grave. He paused, remembering the conversation he'd had with Lily about the girl who called herself Gwenevere. Did they?

Cactus Flower interrupted his reverie. Her face was unusually pale and her normally quick steps slow.

"What is it?" he asked as she sat down at the table. "Do you know where Elizabeth went?"

She shook her head, but she looked miserable.

"It's okay to tell me. I have to know, Cactus Flower, even if the news is bad."

She looked up at him, her large doe eyes wet with tears. "I don't know for sure. I think maybe the dream catcher was cursed."

Miguel wrinkled his brow. Dream catcher? Ah. The

one Elizabeth had hung before they went to bed. He had hardly noticed, intent as he was on what would follow. "Cursed? What do you mean?"

"My father. He said he made it to make peace, but—"

"But what?" Miguel leaned forward.

"Swift Hawk went in to visit him while he was making it," Cactus Flower said softly. "I remember seeing the raven feathers in his hands and I thought the colors my father had chosen were odd for a dream catcher. Red and black are used for war."

"Go on."

"The last thing Swift Hawk wanted was for you to marry Elizabeth. He still had some notion he would get her back somehow, even though his father told him to stop thinking about her."

"So you think the Hawk asked your father to place a curse on the gift?" Miguel asked, puzzled. "Even so, it couldn't have made her disappear."

Cactus Flower took a deep breath. "My father has strong magic, and Swift Hawk provided the feathers. If he touched the dream catcher while it was being made, the strands of his hate for you and his desire for Elizabeth would be woven into its threads. It would be a powerful dark charm, especially if he convinced my father to put a demon inside the web."

Miguel leaned back and studied her. He knew the shaman was well taught from his ancestors in the use of medicinal herbs, some of them both potent and dangerous. The Indians held strong beliefs in totems and fetishes, but this sounded more like the ancient voodoo practiced in New Orleans. Lily had hired a quadroon once who claimed to be a daughter of Marie Laveau. The girl had managed to make most of the others ill so she could have the choice of men—or maybe it was a particular man—before Lily sent her on her way. Still, that had probably been as simple as poisoning the food. If one didn't believe in voodoo, it held no power. Did it?

"In the white man's world, that would make your father a sorcerer, not a healer."

Cactus Flower shrugged. "My father has learned many things from many people. He has even tried to learn to bind spells from the Great Spirit our people know as Dream Catcher, but so far, she has not favored him."

Miguel almost smiled. "How do you know this spirit is a woman?"

"That's easy. When she is summoned in the sacred smoke, she always appears the same. Several of the elders have seen her, dressed in white doeskin, her hair in braids…her hair is the same fire-color as Elizabeth's," Cactus Flower finished slowly. "That is why Swift Hawk wants her. He thinks the power of Dream Catcher lives in Elizabeth."

The woman he'd seen in the army hospital. A slight chill spread along Miguel's spine. She had seemed so real that he'd even asked about her. She had a healer's touch, making his pain recede. He had not sensed evil about her. He grimaced, thinking he was letting his imagination run loose. A spirit could not have whisked his wife out of bed.

"That's crazy," he said.

"To you maybe, but not to my people," Cactus Flower said gently. "My father has called on the spirits before, to shield our warriors from human sight."

Miguel stared at her. How many times had he heard

the army say settlers had no warning of death raids? And Swift Hawk was able to count *coup* before anyone knew he was there. Could Elizabeth's disappearance be an illusion? That somehow some sort of smokescreen was concealing her? He cringed inwardly, thinking of those times when he'd wondered about her sanity. His own thoughts were going loco.

"Perhaps you should take the dream catcher to the priest," Cactus Flower said. "Does your religion not have a way to remove…devils, I think you say?"

Miguel raised an eyebrow. "An exorcist? Elizabeth has disappeared, not gone mad."

"Still," Cactus Flower insisted, "a holy man might be able to take the evil out of the charm. Once that is removed, we may find her."

She might have a point there. Everyone in his graduating class at Harvard had to take one course in religious philosophy. He remembered reading a theory about something like that. If they didn't find Elizabeth soon, it wouldn't hurt to try. Yet he knew the elderly priest who ministered to them here had no such training. He would have to make the month-long trip back to "civilization" as Elena had always called it. New Orleans. Bishop de Neckère, who had performed that marriage, was no longer there, but an archbishop had been appointed to the newly built St. Louis Cathedral. Perhaps he could give some direction. Miguel didn't know what else he could do. Silently, he whispered, "Elizabeth, I love you. Somehow, we will be together again."

****

Brooke looked worried. Elizabeth could hardly blame her as her friend sat across the living room in a chair whose sheet cover lay on the floor. She'd just told her everything that had happened.

"We thought Edward had taken you to Europe," Brooke said shakily. "He left town just about the time you did."

"I would never have quit my job without warning," Elizabeth said. She had called the school administration earlier, only to be told she had been replaced and would have to reapply if she wanted to teach in the fall. The secretary's cold tone had implied they didn't think much of people who just stopped coming to work. Not that Elizabeth blamed her. She had always prided herself on being reliable.

"I know," Brooke said. "When I hadn't heard from you and you weren't answering the phone, I called the police. They didn't seem too concerned since there was no sign of a struggle or forced entry."

"But all my stuff was here! My purse and car keys—"

Brooke nodded. "I pointed that out and they finally agreed to put out a bulletin. They tried to question Edward, but when they found out he'd gone to France, the idea grew that you'd eloped with him. The manager of his condo said you'd been there two nights before."

Elizabeth groaned. Too bad no one had seen her leave after she'd discovered Edward with the Barbie doll. "Did anyone call my mother?"

"I did. She seemed to accept the elopement rumor too. In fact, she said it was about time you found someone to marry and if you were in France, so much the better. She wouldn't have to be in a hurry to come home and could continue her project in Navarre."

"Miguel's people were from there," Elizabeth said

and caught the look of dismay on her friend's face. "Brooke, you've got to believe me. This happened. I am married to a man I love very much. A gorgeous hunk of real Texas cowboy—someone who would rival those knights in shining armor you love so much."

"If it did happen," Brook said, patting Elizabeth's hand, "Miguel would be nearly two hundred years old now."

Tears sprang to Elizabeth's eyes. Brooke was right. Miguel was long dead. One night of passionate love, now a widow. Her life stretched out ahead of her, decades of emptiness. No one could replace Miguel. No one would believe her, either. Her sorrow and grief must remain secret unless she wanted to be committed to a mental institution, and then she wouldn't be able to teach again. "Do you think I'm crazy?"

Brooke studied her. "No. You know me—I'm an incurable romantic and I think it would be exciting if I could go back to the days when knights rescued damsels in distress." She looked wistful. "It might be better if you didn't tell anyone else, though."

"And how am I going to explain disappearing for five months?"

"If I were you, I'd go along with the story that you eloped. Things didn't work out and you're back."

Elizabeth drew a shaky breath. She didn't know how she was going to survive without Miguel, but she didn't want to be committed for psychiatric evaluation, either. She looked around the bare apartment. Brooke had boxed all her personal items and stacked them in the spare room.

"Who paid the rent while I was gone?"

"I did. I had the feeling that you'd be coming back;

I just couldn't believe you might be dead." She wiped a tear away. "Besides, I didn't know what to do with your stuff. I'm just sorry your car was repossessed."

Elizabeth hugged her. "Thank you. I could be on the streets now if it weren't for you." Irish practicality set in. She would grieve when she was alone later. She had to find a job and repay Brooke. Arlington had no bus line, but she hoped she still had enough in her bank account for a down payment on an older secondhand car. She pushed away the thought of Plata waiting for her in the stable, nickering her welcome and waiting for her apple treat.

"I have to go," Brooke said as she stood. "I will come back later."

As Elizabeth closed the door after her friend, she looked into the hall mirror. "Oh, Miguel! Why did I have to lose you? The one man I could trust to take care of me for the rest of my life. By all the saints, why?"

And then she burst into uncontrollable wails of anguish.

****

Miguel squinted in the bright Louisiana sunlight of Jackson Square and gazed up at the three large, white spirals of Saint Louis Cathedral. The cathedral had recently replaced an older one. It was a fantastic rendering of European architecture, only it had been built with wood instead of stone.

He wiped traces of sweat from his face and pushed the hair off his forehead. The sweet smell of magnolias almost overpowered him. He had forgotten how humid and sultry New Orleans was in June. He felt like he needed another bath, although he had taken one this morning.

The entrance to the large rectory was cooler while he waited for his audience with Archbishop Blanc. He felt rather foolish now, bringing the dream catcher here like some superstitious illiterate. But they had not found any trace of Elizabeth and he had to exhaust every possibility.

A servant appeared in the doorway. "The archbishop will see you now."

He followed the man down a long corridor, its polished wooden floor glistening. The servant pushed the massive oak door open silently and gestured for him to enter. The archbishop was seated in one of the two overstuffed armchairs on either side of an unlit hearth.

"Excellency," Miguel said and bowed.

"Have a seat, my son." Archbishop Blanc looked at the waiting servant. "Chilled coffee, if you please." He turned back to Miguel. "We still have some ice preserved in straw in the stone sheds. It makes the heat bearable."

Miguel nodded thankfully and wished he could remove his frock coat or at least loosen the bat's wing from around his throat. He was already wishing for the wide-open skies and dry wind of northern Texas. How the clergyman managed to not sweat with all those robes and vestments was beyond him.

The archbishop accepted the drinks when they were brought and handed him one. "The season comes early this year," he said by way of conversation. "The blood-biters are already out. I hope we won't be plagued with the yellow fever again." He looked at Miguel. "But you haven't come to discuss our weather."

Miguel took a sip of the strong, black coffee, appreciating the pungency of the chicory the Creoles loved, and then set it aside. He pulled the dream catcher out of his satchel and handed it to him. The archbishop listened as Miguel told him what had transpired. He turned the dream catcher over in his hands thoughtfully.

"The Church, of course, does exorcisms on people," he said finally. "There is nothing written in canon that addresses curses on objects." He handed it back. "I am so sorry. I wish I could help."

Miguel tried to hide his disappointment. He'd ridden all this way! He started to put the dream catcher back in his satchel.

"Wait! Maybe there is someone who might help you."

Miguel's hand froze in midair. Was there hope? "Whom?"

"A woman called Marie Laveau."

"The voodoo queen?" Miguel asked, startled. "As a holy man you condone that?"

The archbishop smiled at his expression. "It might surprise you to know that Marie is a devout Catholic. She attends Mass nearly every day."

He was stunned. "Forgive me, but the rumors I always heard were that she dabbles in the black arts and is feared by many."

The older man's eyes twinkled. 'She may be feared, for she has friends and informants all over this city. An advantageous thing to have. Sometimes "overheard" knowledge can be made to seem supernatural." He shook his head. "But black arts, no. Marie is a healer well-versed in herbals and potions. She has uncanny senses."

Miguel hesitated and the archbishop smiled. "Tomorrow is St. John's Eve. Marie holds religious rituals on the banks of Bayou St. John every year. Why don't you attend and judge for yourself whether you want to talk to her?" He picked up a small bell and rang it. Instantly, a servant appeared, and Miguel stood, realizing he was being dismissed.

"Thank you for your time, Excellency," he said. "I'll think about it."

****

He was still thinking about it the next evening when he found himself in the crowd that had gathered on the bank of the bayou near dusk, waiting for Marie to appear. The fetid stench of decaying matter in a nearby swamp assailed his nostrils and he felt he was breathing liquid air, so heavy was the humidity. Cypress trees hung over the still water, and Miguel half-expected to see an alligator crawl out at any time.

He looked around. People of all cultures were here—black slaves, mulattos, quadroons, Spaniards and Frenchmen, dandy-dressed businessmen and farmers.

A tall, dark-haired man accompanied by an attractive, auburn-haired woman stood near him. Even in this crowd, the man stood out. He was dressed simply, in soft leather breeches and riding boots, a white linen shirt open at the throat, the sleeves rolled up. He carried no gun, but many men in New Orleans didn't. Instead, he wore a magnificent long-sword at his side, the huge ruby in its pommel sending streaks of fire in the twilight. Even in the fading light, the sword looked to be very old and valuable. Miguel's gaze traveled to the man's angular face and he didn't think he'd ever seen eyes so penetrating, as though the stranger was anticipating each individual's action around him. He stood very still and Miguel had the distinct impression he missed nothing. Perhaps he was a lawman. Certainly, he exuded authority.

The woman at his side laid her hand on his arm and whispered something. Miguel blinked at the sudden transformation in him. The man bent down to her, his dark eyes smoldering and nuzzled her throat, his left hand caressing her back. She arched her neck for him, clearly giving him liberty. Miguel felt a jealous pang and turned away. The woman, although older, reminded him of Elizabeth, and he would have done just what the stranger did, had he the chance.

Marie Laveau appeared on the far bank, a large snake wrapped around her torso. From behind her came soft chanting, different from the Gregorian chants, its volume and tempo increasing as she began to dance. Some of her followers on Miguel's side of the water began to do the same. The smell of sandalwood incense came wafting across to them.

She stopped suddenly, and to Miguel it seemed she looked right at him. Then she turned away and raised her hands to begin the ritual. Miguel watched in silence, surprised to feel the emotion that was pouring out of her devotees. He could find nothing "devilish" throughout the service, either. When it was over, Marie circulated through the crowd, hugging small children, who certainly showed no fear.

The worshippers finally drifted away into the warm, sticky night and Miguel had just decided to go back to his hotel when he heard his name. He turned around.

"Did you not come to see me, *Monsieur de Basque*?"

Up close, Marie Laveau had a certain beauty that was ageless. Her skin was bronze-colored and smooth, her dark hair curly and her eyes a rich hazel-green. High cheekbones, a straight nose and a full mouth gave her a youthful appearance, yet Miguel knew she must be at least in her fifties.

“How did you know my name?”

She smiled. “A woman does not give away her secrets, *oui*?” She held out her hand. “Do you have the item with you?”

Miguel nodded, wondering how she knew. He had not wanted to leave the dream catcher in the hotel room. He took it from the satchel and handed it to her.

She closed her eyes, her hands caressing the dream catcher as lightly as though she were stroking a butterfly. She hesitated at the feathers and opened her eyes. “The man who put these here wanted you separated from someone you love.”

Miguel tried not to show his surprise. How could she have known that? Was there a spy in the archbishop’s quarters? But no, they had been alone when he had poured out the story. Hadn’t they?

Her smile widened. “You don’t trust me.”

“No! That isn’t it,” Miguel said quickly. “It’s just—”

She held up her hand for silence. “No matter. There is powerful magic in this.” She pulled the three raven feathers from the totem and nodded to a boy standing nearby holding a torch. He came forward immediately. “We will take the three feathers and burn them, one at a time.” Marie said and held up the first one. “Think of the person who wishes you ill and know he is gone.” They watched it burn and she picked up the second feather. “Feel yourself free of the curse.” As she lit the third she told Miguel to close his eyes. “In your mind’s eye, you must see the one you love.” She held the dream catcher high and mumbled words in a language Miguel had never heard, and as he opened his eyes to watch the last of the ashes turn to gray dust, her face contorted with pain. Finally she took a deep breath and looked at him. “The spell is reversed.” She started to hand the dream catcher back to him and then stopped, frowning.

“Your love. She is not here in this lifetime.”

Miguel felt as though a mule had kicked him in the stomach. “You’re saying she’s…dead?”

“*Non.* I am saying she has not been born. Her soul is only spirit, not flesh.”

The mule’s other hoof found his chest. “She said she was from the future. The twenty-first century. But that can’t be. Such things aren’t possible.”

Marie’s eyes widened and she glanced around to where some of her followers still lingered. “Ah, *Monsieur. Je suis désolé.* I am sorry. I do not know how to help.” She handed him the dream catcher. “Return this to the one who gave it to you. *Peut-être*—maybe?—you may yet find her.”

He watched as she left. Disheartened, he turned to go back to the hotel and found himself face to face with the dark-haired stranger with the magnificent sword. The man’s smoke-colored eyes held a contemplative look, but the woman beside him smiled at Miguel.

“We could not help overhearing your conversation,” she said with an accent that Miguel could have sworn was British. “Perhaps we may be of help.”

“The name’s Lance,” the man said and extended his hand.

A Frenchman from his accent, Miguel thought, as he shook hands. “Don’t tell me you believe someone can time-travel from the future to the past?”

“Time-travel?” He seemed to weigh the words. “I

am not familiar with the term. But once, long ago, a…friend…of ours was killed in battle and a mage foretold he would return one day to lead the people."

"You mean reincarnate?" Miguel asked.

The stranger shook his head. "No. He would return as himself." He touched the hilt of the sword. "This was his. I hope to be able to return it to him one day." He seemed to sense Miguel's confusion. "What I am trying to say is that you may find the person you seek. I have learned over many years that the impossible can happen." Momentarily a look of pain flashed across his face, but then the woman squeezed his arm. He smiled and covered her fingers with his hand. "If you believe in the future, then maybe the future will open its doors for you."

The lady nodded. "No one believed me—" She hesitated and then changed the subject. "We really must go, but do think about it."

Miguel watched them walk away, the man's arm protectively around the woman's shoulders. What a strange conversation and yet, he had felt almost a kinship with them.

Lance. Miguel pondered the name as he strolled toward his rented carriage. It seemed as though there were pieces of a puzzle that needed to be put together. The woman was probably English and well-bred from the sound of her voice. The man equally so, although French. He'd mentioned a friend killed in battle who would return, and also a Mage. What an old-fashioned word to use; it belonged more to the Middle Ages. There was something else—what had the Mage said? That his friend would lead the people. Lead the people. Like a king or something.

He stopped dead in his tracks and his heart began to race. The Arthurian legends. He had practically memorized Mallory as a child when he was running around with his wooden sword. Merlin had predicted King Arthur would return. *Jesu*! Could he just have met—no, it was impossible—but could it be? Could he have just met the great knight Lancelot du Lac? The man had been from Brittany—little France. If so, then the woman had to be no other than Gwenevere, Queen of medieval Britain. And the sword—the real Excalibur!

Miguel shook his head. He really was going loco, leaping to totally illogical conclusions, so desperate he was to find Elizabeth. Another thought hit him with the clarity of a lightning bolt against a night sky—his conversation with Lily about the woman who said she was Gwenevere. The stranger fit the description Lily had given and so did the woman. And there had been the stranger at Plum Creek with a fantastic sword—

Por Dios! If this were true, then time-travel *was* possible. Elizabeth was alive somewhere. What had Lancelot said? Believe in the future—

And suddenly, Miguel did. With all his heart he knew Elizabeth had told the truth, that she had never lied to him. In his arrogance, he had not believed her.

He sank to his knees in prayer beneath one of the cypress trees. "What I wouldn't give to go to her," he whispered. "By all the saints and gods and goddesses—" He looked down at the dream catcher he still clutched and, for a moment, he thought he saw the Indian maid in white leather looking back at him. "What I wouldn't give to go to Elizabeth," he whispered. "What I wouldn't give to go to her."

Chapter Seventeen—Home

Elizabeth parked the car on 26th Street, glad to find an opening so close to the historic Fort Worth Stockyards. She walked down Main Street and joined the hordes of people headed either for Booger Red's Saloon with its saddle-chairs and famous Anita-Ritas or for the White Elephant, equally well-known. A little early in the afternoon for beer, she thought, but tourists take little stock of time.

She had just finished teaching the remedial summer school class in history and had decided to drive in from Arlington to do some research for her students on the cattle industry, comparing the Chisholm Trail in its heyday to how ranchers bid on cattle now.

As she made her way to the Livestock Exchange Building, she reflected on the past two months. Since her conversation with Brooke the first day back, her life had fallen into a plodding, dull routine. She'd managed to convince the school district that she was indeed repentant for her foolishness in eloping with a man who did not have her best interests at heart. Brooke suggested trying tears, but she couldn't do that. It was bad enough to lie about where she'd been. Luckily, the district had an opening in summer school.

She'd talked with her mother, too, only to hear that Jacqueline was put out with her for not coming to the south of France to visit. Her mother had dismissed her so-called divorce as minimal. “At least you don’t have kids,” she said.

Jacqueline couldn’t have any way of knowing what hope had sprung in Elizabeth’s heart at that thought. She hadn’t even considered she might be pregnant after only one night, even though they had made love numerous times. She’d confided in Brooke when her period was late and together they had waited for the results of the home pregnancy test. As tough as it would be to raise a child alone, it would have been Miguel’s—a sort of replacement for him and Raul. She cried when the test came back negative and her flow began. There was nothing of Miguel left for her. Only memories.

But the memories were good, especially the more erotic ones. Only two days ago, on midsummer’s night, she’d had the best dream. She’d felt his spirit calling to her and then she had *felt* him.. She recalled his kisses, those warm sensual lips on hers, playing with her, teasing her, his hands roaming her body, making every inch of skin tingle in anticipation, suckling on her breasts until she was wet with desire and then slowly prolonging the exquisite throbbing between her legs with his mouth and tongue until she shuddered and spasmed and shattered. Only then would he enter her and bring her to even greater heights of frenzied passion. She awoke, sure they were together again, but the other side of her bed was empty.

Elizabeth thought she saw Miguel everywhere. Oncc at the mall and again in a public library. She’d even followed one tall, dark-haired man on foot in Sundance Square in downtown Fort Worth, only to be disappointed when he turned to look into a store window and his profile was different. She knew she was being foolish.

She had no idea of how she'd time-traveled to 1849 or home again. What were the odds that Miguel would or could? Or that they'd find each other again? She'd be luckier wagering on the lottery.

How ironic she couldn't tell her students she'd been where they read about. She had *lived* history. She gave herself a little shake as she turned into the old building in a quieter part of the yards. One of her students even looked like Raul.

She sighed. She'd cried enough tears to last a lifetime, and even now she felt them welling up inside again. She wiped at her eyes before she went inside.

Sweet Mary. She missed him.

****

"Are you all right, sir?" The gray-haired police officer gazed anxiously into Miguel's face. "A tourist found you sitting on the ground here, leaning against the wall."

"What?" Miguel felt lightheaded, as though he'd been dancing the reel at double speed. He looked up at the lawman. The man wore a badge and carried a gun, but it was unlike any Miguel had ever seen, the grip more squared, the barrel short. His clothes were unusual too. "A what?" he asked again as he slowly stood up.

"A tourist. Are you sure you're all right?"

Miguel had no idea what a tourist was. He glanced at his surroundings. Ah. Cattle pens. He was familiar with those, even though these were paved in bricks. What looked like an auction area was to his right. Both were empty. No animal smells emanated from them. He frowned at the noise coming from a building behind him. It sounded like amateur musicians were trying to play guitars or fiddles, but they had a metallic sound and someone was pounding drums far too loudly to help their poor attempt at music, if that's what it was.

The officer laughed at his expression. "Someone's left the door open to the saloon again." He shook his head. "Young folks' music takes some getting used to. It's not exactly Willie Nelson anymore."

"Who?" Miguel felt more and more disoriented. Some other noise was bothering him too, a steady rumbling that seemed to come from some trail he couldn't see.

"You've never heard of Willie Nelson?" The man asked incredulously. "You look like a cowboy. Where are you from anyway?"

Miguel started to say Texas and then thought better of it. Until he could figure out where he was, it was better not to offer too much information. He certainly didn't want to be hauled off to a brig somewhere. "*Mi familia es desde España.*"

"Spain, huh? Are you here with a tour group?"

"*No. Con mi esposa.*" He needed to get himself away from this lawman so he could think. "I guess I'd better go look for her."

The officer nodded and pointed. "If you'll go by the Stockyards Museum and cross East Exchange, there's a Visitor Center. They can help you find her."

"*Gracias. Eres muy amable,*" Miguel said and turned to walk in that direction. He had just passed the large building with its cupola and was about to cross the street when he glanced to his right and stopped in his tracks. Another street crossed this one and metal boxes on wheels were moving past the intersection at incredible speeds. People were inside them, but he could see no train tracks or how they were driven. There wasn't a horse in sight. The constant noise he'd heard seemed to be coming from them. Where on God's earth was he?

The street was crowded with people. And the women! He tried not to stare, but even at Lily's the girls didn't walk around showing their entire legs in something that looked like cut-off jeans. Some of these younger ones hardly had their breasts covered and their backs were bare, except for a thin string tied in a bow. The men with them didn't seem to care. How could anyone not notice so much skin? Briefly, he wondered if they were all wearing underwear like Elizabeth's.

Miguel became aware that maybe he had arrived in the century that Elizabeth had talked about. He wasn't sure how he'd done it. The last thing he remembered was praying and thinking he'd seen another vision of the red-haired Indian maid. She had held out her hands to him and nodded and he remembered a blinding white light…

He still had his saddlebag slung over his shoulder and he opened it now. His money was all there, but he must have dropped the dream catcher somewhere. He knew he'd been holding it when he had the vision. He wondered if he'd blacked out.

Miguel began to smile. If this was Elizabeth's century, that meant she must be here. He'd just ask those people at the Visitor Center to find her. Easy enough. He straightened his hat, crossed the street, and opened the door.

The room was lit oddly with little squares in the ceiling. People milled around, some of them with pamphlets in their hands. Others held small boxes to their ears and talked into one end of them. Very strange, yet no one seemed to take notice that these people were all talking to themselves.

Someone official-looking stood behind a counter and Miguel made his way to the young man. “I’d like to find Elizabeth O’Malley, please.”

“Is she visiting the stockyards, sir?”

“I don’t know. She lives here.”

The clerk raised an eyebrow. “No one lives at the stockyards. Do you mean she lives in Fort Worth?”

Fort Worth—is that where he was? “Well—I think—is there some place called Arlington?”

The young man gave him a wary look and Miguel wondered what he’d said. Maybe he should switch to Spanish again. This boy was blond, though, and probably didn’t understand a word of it. “*No soy desde aqui, lo siento*.”

A pretty Hispanic girl joined the clerk. “He’s not from here, Harrison.” She smiled at Miguel. “*¿De donde son?*”

He smiled back. This might work, if only they thought he was foreign and not loco. He needed to find Elizabeth. “*España*. I am looking for an *amiga*.” He’d almost said wife. “She lives in Arlington.”

The girl pulled a huge book out from under the counter and turned it to him. “You can look in the phone directory and see if she’s listed.”

He had no idea what a phone directory was, but obviously she expected him to look for Elizabeth’s name. He thumbed through the O’s. Yes, there it was! “Here!” he pointed it out. “That’s her.”

“If you don’t have a cell,” the girl said as he stood there waiting, “you can use our phone.” She turned a square object on the desk toward him, separated the top part, which seemed to be attached by some kind of cord, and handed it to him. He took it gingerly and looked at it. He jumped slightly when an identical box next to it started ringing loudly.

"Excuse me," she said and lifted the top half of the other box. She spoke into it. "Visitor Center. How may I help you?" Miguel listened in fascination. She appeared to be answering questions, but he could hear no one else speaking. What sort of things were in these boxes? Were the other people who had them on their ears answering questions?

She put the box together again and looked at him. "Go ahead, dial the number."

Dial? He glanced around and noticed some people were holding their boxes in their hands and punching them with their fingers. He looked back at the one in front of him. It had little pads with raised numbers. Somewhat apprehensively, he tapped out the numbers from the phone book, not sure what would happen. The girl had put the top half to her ear to talk, so he did too.

He heard a ringing on the other end. Then a voice startled him. "The number you have dialed is out of service or has been disconnected. Please check your number or try your call again." Click. Silence. It wasn't Elizabeth's voice.

He handed the instrument back to the girl and told her what he'd heard. She shook her head. "I'm sorry," she said, "your friend must have moved."

"How can I find her then?"

"I don't know. You might go to Arlington. It's only a few miles from here."

He brightened. "Is there some place I could buy a horse?"

"A horse?" she asked and behind her, the blond boy stifled a laugh. Miguel was not amused. If he'd had

Diablo, he wouldn't even be here now.

"Yes. A horse."

"You might try the Superior Livestock Auction across the street," she said, "but they don't have live animals."

He stared at her. What on earth would he want a dead horse for? But he wasn't making any headway here; he might as well wander around and see if he could find a horseman. He'd seen plenty of men walking around in jeans and boots. Maybe one of them might help him. He thanked the girl and headed back the way he'd come. Dead horses. Elizabeth's world certainly was strange.

****

Elizabeth huddled in front of a television monitor in the corner, her back to the door, watching a video auction. This was the high-tech way to purchase breeding stock. Via satellite the auctioneer would start his pitch and ranchers across America could turn on the televisions and see which animals were on sale. If they were interested, they called in their bids to the operators manning the phone lines.

She knew this was economical; cattle didn't have to be delivered to market, they stayed fattened, their muscles remained tender. Still, the romantic in her yearned for the cattle drives, especially since she had been on one. The chuck wagon, the cowboys singing low tunes to quiet the cattle as they rode, the harmonicas and campfires at night, sleeping under the stars—the modern world had lost so much.

"How do you get animals in that machinery?" she heard a male voice ask. "And how do they have room to move around?"

The man sounded like Miguel. Maybe she really was

slipping from sanity. Not only did she think she saw him everywhere, now she was hearing him too.

"What are you talking about?" one of the telephone operators asked. "Those animals are on tape."

"Tape?"

Elizabeth closed her eyes and bit her lip. In a minute she would turn around and see that this man was not Miguel. Just like the others. But for a few seconds, she could fantasize. She listened as he continued.

"Well, I want to buy a horse. A live one."

"I don't know that we're offering any horses for sale," the woman replied. "This is a cattle auction."

"Where are the cattle?"

She sounded exasperated. "On tape, sir. You're looking at them. Check with the auctioneer and see if there is a horse listed."

He pitched his voice lower, much like Miguel did when he'd had about enough. "I don't want a *picture* of a horse. I need one I can ride to Arlington."

This time there was no mistaking the sarcasm in her voice. "Wouldn't it be better if you'd rent a car and drive there?"

His voice dropped lower and Elizabeth strained to hear, hugging her knees and keeping her eyes closed. For this blissful moment, it was as though he were here.

"Are you going to sell me a horse or not? I have gold."

"Gold? You want the currency exchange then, sir. It's down—" Before she could finish, he thundered at her.

"*¿Tu eres loco? Queiro un caballo. Ohora!* I have to find my wife!"

Elizabeth stifled a sob. Now she was really

becoming delusional, thinking this man was trying to find her. She was putting words into her head that he wasn't saying.

"*Señor*. I'm going to have to ask you to leave." Elizabeth heard boots stomping toward the door and she turned, needing to see the man who sounded so much like Miguel, but the door had already shut. The hallucination was gone.

And then she caught a familiar scent. Soap and leather and Miguel. *All* of her senses couldn't be deceiving her, could they? Sweet Mary. She rushed to the door, stubbing her toe in her haste to get through it.

The street bustled with people. Frantically, she looked above their heads, hoping to spot a tall, dark-haired man. There! She started running, only to have the man stop and hold out his hand to a small child. He turned and she saw it wasn't Miguel. She searched up and down Exchange Street, trying to think where he might have gone. She even checked the bars, although she hardly expected to find Miguel there.

Dejected, she went back to the auction and picked up the notebook she had dropped on her way out. She decided to avoid the crowds on Main Street and cut through the cattle pens area toward Stockyard Boulevard and 26th Street.

That's when she saw him. He had his back to her, arms folded across the top of one of the fences, one boot on the bottom rail, staring into space.

"Miguel?" Did she dare to hope it was him?

His head snapped up. Slowly, he turned and looked at her as though not believing what he saw. "Elizabeth?"

She thought she screamed, but she wasn't sure. He reached her side in four strides and then she was in his arms, his hands caressing her back and pulling her tight against him as his mouth covered hers in a deep and hungry kiss.

When he finally broke the kiss, it was only to stroke her hair and face before holding her close again. Elizabeth laughed and reached behind her for his hands as a crowd began gathering.

"I don't know how it happened and I don't care. You're here. Let's go home."

They stopped on the sidewalk of Main Street and Miguel stared in fascination at the traffic. "What are those?"

"Cars. It's what we use instead of horses," Elizabeth said as the light turned green. "Come on."

He balked. "I'm not walking in front of them."

"It's okay," Elizabeth tried to soothe him. "They've stopped for us." She took his arm and tugged. "We have to cross before the light turns red."

"Why?"

"Because they'll all start moving again. Trust me."

He gave her a desperate look, but she finally got him safely to the other side of the street. When they reached her car, she unlocked it and opened the door. "Slide in."

"You expect me to *sit* in that?"

"You have to," Elizabeth said. "It's how we're getting home."

"Can't I buy a horse?"

She laughed. "I know you won't believe me, but under that hood, there's the power of three hundred horses."

His look was incredulous. He tapped the metal with his fingertips. "Impossible. There isn't even one horse in there."

She sighed. That probably hadn't been the wisest thing to say, considering how he'd fumed about cows on the television monitor. "Never mind. I'll explain later. Right now, I need you to get in the car."

Dubiously, he eased himself in. She went around to the other side and slid behind the wheel. She leaned over and tugged on his seatbelt. He grinned as her hand brushed against his groin.

"At least that's something I understand," he said and reached for her.

"Not here," Elizabeth said and yet lingered over his kiss. She finally pulled back and started the car.

Miguel gripped the door handle. "What are you doing?"

"Relax, sweetheart," Elizabeth answered as she eased out into traffic. "This is called driving. You'll get used to it."

Miguel closed his eyes. Elizabeth suspected he might be praying. By the time she reached Interstate 30, he had opened his eyes. Then they widened in alarm.

"Watch out! It's a runaway train!"

She dared not laugh. "That's an eighteen-wheeler," she said. "They carry all sorts of things, like wagons did in your time."

Miguel closed his eyes again. Elizabeth sympathized. To him this century must seem terrifying; at least, she had *known* what history held in store when she went back in time. She tried to think how she would feel if she were catapulted into the twenty-third century. She'd be equally anxious and alarmed. If she could just get him home where there would be peace and quiet… He needed some time for things to sink in.

Finally, after what seemed like an eon, she pulled

into the apartment complex and parked. Miguel sprang out of the car quickly and looked at the ground. She wondered if he were going to stoop down and kiss it. He really did look grateful to have arrived in one piece.

Elizabeth opened the door to her apartment. "This is it," she said and snapped on the light switch.

Miguel looked from the switch to the lit lamp and back again. "I'm not going to ask," he said. He proceeded through the living room and poked his head into the kitchen. "Some of this looks familiar. Sink. Is this a stove? And icebox, no?" He frowned when he opened it. "How does it stay cold? There's no ice block."

"Electricity," Elizabeth said. "It's something I'll explain later. Let me show you another room." She took his hand and led him to the bedroom. "Recognize this?"

Miguel grinned and she could see him visibly relax. "Your world is very confusing," he said, "but I think I know what to do in here." He wrapped his arms around her and brought her against him. Elizabeth felt his erection harden even as his tongue plunged deeply into her mouth. Eagerly she sucked on it and then plied him with her own, her senses arousing to a searing pitch.

She was on the bed and naked without being aware that he'd undressed her. His hands kneaded her breasts while his lips moved adeptly from one hardened nipple to the other, lapping gently and then suckling hard, afterward blowing cool air on the hot, deliciously tender swollen tips. He moved downward, his tongue blazing a trail of heat to where her nub throbbed and vibrated with its own ache. Elizabeth groaned.

"I need you inside of me."

Miguel raised his head and looked at her, his dark eyes like orbs of ebony fire. In one motion, he was astride her, spreading her legs, thrusting his shaft deep to the hilt.

There was nothing gentle or easy or slow about their lovemaking this time, only a fevered need to complete each other. Elizabeth opened herself to him fully, feeling him ram against her womb, savoring the fullness of him, whimpering at his near-withdrawal only to gasp with pleasure at the renewed vigor of his second thrust.

Miguel ground his hips against hers, increasing their tempo to a frenzied thrashing like a ship tossed between swells of a stormy sea. Elizabeth lurched wildly beneath him, her back arching to take more of him. Her nails scraped across the hard muscles of his broad back even as her tongue frantically found his, their movements in unison to the rhythm of their lovemaking.

Elizabeth shuddered, her body cresting on a wave of undulating sensation before plunging into a trough of momentary calm, then rising again in ever-increasing surges of rapture. Small spasms grew into one long convulsing contraction as she peaked, screaming Miguel's name in the wake of her climax, and then she felt him flooding her with his own release.

They lay exhausted and panting in each other's arms. Finally, Miguel lifted a damp curl off Elizabeth's forehead. "With lovemaking like that, I may get used to living in this century."

She nestled further into the curve of his arm. "Promise?"

He grinned and rolled her over on top of him. "I could be persuaded. Why don't you try to convince me?"

Elizabeth smiled and leaned down, brushing his chest with her breasts. "This time, we'll take it slow."

Hours later, she sat facing him in the bathtub, her

legs over his thighs. She squeezed soapy water over his shoulders and then let her fingers slide down the slick wet skin to tease his nipples. She loved the way his eyes turned even darker with desire.

He gave a little growl as her hands slid across his flat belly to find their prize. Elizabeth giggled as she felt his member grow hard again under her hand.

"Insatiable wench," he said lazily.

"Only with an incredible lover," she said.

Miguel lifted and settled her on top of him so that his now-throbbing shaft probed her entrance. "Remember I once told you I was going to enjoy your giving me a bath?"

"Uh-huh," she murmured and nipped at his ear.

He lifted her buttocks then and brought her down hard as he filled her completely. "And remember," he said as he established their rhythm, "that I told you I always return the favor?"

She didn't have time to answer before his mouth covered hers. With a low moan, she clung to him, merging once more, not sure where her body ended and his began. Not that she cared at this particular moment as she soared to the summit of rhapsody.

Chapter Eighteen—Real World

Elizabeth found Miguel in the kitchen the next morning, switching the light on and off with an incredulous look on his face.

"Good morning," she said, rising on tiptoe to kiss him. "Having fun?"

He shook his head in amazement and then opened the refrigerator door. "It lights up, too. How does that work?"

She laughed. "Twenty-first century magic, you might say. It's called electricity. Just about everything in the apartment uses it. Would you like some coffee?"

"Where is the fire for that? Is it this?" He pointed to the stove. "I turned a knob earlier, and it glowed red."

"We use that to cook. I use this," she said as she clicked the switch on the coffee maker. She took two breakfast entrees out of the freezer, unwrapped one and popped it into the microwave. "This will be thawed and ready to eat in three minutes."

Miguel looked skeptical when she set it in front of him. He sniffed and then poked at it. "It's hot!" Tentatively, he took a taste of egg. "And good. How does that thing work?" He picked up the second entrée. "I want to try."

An hour later, he had microwaved several potatoes, warmed up soup, and popped corn, fascinated by the speed of it. Elizabeth was beginning to think she would run out of food for him to experiment with.

"Are you ready to venture out into your new world?"

Miguel looked up from extracting a warmed-up piece of apple pie from his new toy. "Just give a minute to savor this." He took several bites and then stood. "Ready."

He was still wary of the car. Elizabeth coaxed him into it. "I'll teach you to drive soon. Most men fall in love with their cars."

"I prefer Diablo. Him I can trust," Miguel answered as they melded into traffic. "Why does everything move so fast in your century?"

"I don't know," Elizabeth answered, "you would think with all the modern technology we have to help us with our work, we'd slow down, but we don't."

A few minutes later, she parked the car at the mall and took a deep breath, hoping Miguel wouldn't be overwhelmed. "This is what you might call a marketplace."

Once inside, he swiveled his head from side to side, trying to take in all the different shops as they walked. More than once, Elizabeth had to steer him out of someone's way since he wasn't watching where he was going.

"There are so many people," he said when she had nudged him out of the path of a group of teenagers texting while they walked.

Elizabeth stopped a few doors down, in front of a men's clothing shop. "Let's get you some clothes."

Miguel caressed her cheek with a fingertip. "Just like I did for you. This isn't exactly like the general store at home, is it?"

Elizabeth frowned slightly. "You are home,

Miguel." As a sad expression crossed his face, she realized how much he must miss his son, and her heart went out to him. She squeezed his arm. "I miss Raul too."

"I wish…" He stopped, squared his shoulders, and took a deep breath. "Home it is, as long as you're with me." He gave her a brief kiss before they stepped inside.

They were greeted by a thin, elegantly suited salesman who straightened his silk tie, cleared his throat and then clasped his pale hands together before he approached. He gave a slightly haughty glance at Miguel's cotton shirt and jeans, but his expression changed when he noticed the soft leather hand-tooled boots. "May I be of some assistance, *Monsieur*?"

Miguel looked down at him and nodded. "*Oui. Je voudrais acheter une veste, une chemise, un pantalon et une cravate*."

Elizabeth almost giggled at the man's puzzled expression. She would bet he didn't know much more French than *merci* and *s'il vous plaît*. Pompous ass. "I think he wants a suit, shirt and tie," she said.

The man tried to look down his nose at her, but she was too tall. He gave a slight sniff instead and gestured. "Of course. This way."

Elizabeth sank down into a comfortable easy chair while she waited for Miguel to try on clothes. T-shirts and jeans they could pick up elsewhere. Then she heard a bellow from the dressing rooms.

The little salesman scurried out in fright, followed by a shirtless Miguel. "What do you think you're doing, walking in on a man like that?"

The man sniveled. "I was bringing you some more choices in shirts, that was all."

Perhaps it was time to intervene. Elizabeth didn't

like the way several female shoppers had stopped what they were doing to stare unabashedly at Miguel's bare chest and well-muscled shoulders and arms. One rather young, curvy blonde started to smile at him.

Predators. They were present in every century. And, Elizabeth reminded herself, a lot bolder in this one. She tucked her arm into Miguel's somewhat possessively and turned him around, which might have been a mistake, for now the ladies had a view of his rippling back as he walked, not to mention his tight buttocks.

"I think I'll stand guard," she said.

He grinned at her seductively. "Why don't you come inside and help me?"

"Dress or undress?" she quipped.

"Your choice," he murmured as he pulled her against him and slid the curtain back into place.

"Mmmmm," Elizabeth said.

****

"I thought you might find this interesting," Elizabeth said as she parked the car in the 300 block of Main Street in Fort Worth and they entered the Sid Richardson Collection of Western Art. "It'll seem more like home."

A pleased expression appeared on Miguel's face as he wandered through the collection of paintings by Russell and Remington. He stopped by one titled *Buffalo Bill's Duel with Yellowhand*. After several moments, he said softly, "This reminds me of the Texas I knew. The hills in the distance, the prairie, sage, and cactus."

"Even a cowboy and an Indian," Elizabeth said with a smile. "My students always teased me about that."

Miguel draped his arm around her shoulder. "Who was Buffalo Bill?"

"Long story," Elizabeth answered, "but he was the epitome of the Old West. Pony Express rider, army scout, buffalo hunter, Indian fighter—" She paused and looked at the painting. "He scalped Yellowhand in retaliation for the massacre at the Battle of Little Big Horn."

"Little what?"

She patted his hand. "I forget the time difference. 1876. It hadn't happened yet in your world, but a general named Custer made a big mistake and didn't follow orders. It cost the U.S. Cavalry its biggest Plains defeat at the hands of the Indian chiefs Crazy Horse and Sitting Bull."

Miguel lifted an eyebrow. "Sitting Bull I have heard of. Chief Jim Ned spoke of him once. From the Dakota land, wasn't he?"

Elizabeth nodded. "That's where the action in this painting took place. After everything was settled, Buffalo Bill became an actor and traveled with a Wild West show. Quite a stretch from his younger days, but in a way, he helped keep the Old West alive. He actually employed Indians and used buffalo."

They moved on quietly until they came to a painting called *The Puncher*. Miguel laughed. "He looks like the vaqueros I hire." The rider wore a *sombrero* and bandanna and a Spanish *bolero*. A rifle was tucked into the side scabbard. Miguel sighed. "I guess there aren't too many working cowboys anymore."

"Some," Elizabeth answered, "especially on the big ranches in South Texas. We could drive down and enjoy the beach someday." She looked back at the painting. "Remington was a friend of Teddy Roosevelt's—whoops, a president from your future—anyway, he once said the wild riders of the range were the final players in the American frontier." She took a wistful breath. "Sometimes I wish that frontier had never disappeared."

Miguel hugged her and she put an arm around his waist as he asked, "You miss the 1800s as much as I do, don't you?"

She rested her head on his shoulder. "Yes, but I don't know what to do about it. We'll just need to keep trying to figure out how time-travel happens."

He smiled and kissed the top of her head. "We may have ended up in the wrong century, but we still have our memories. We have each other. That's all that matters. Let's go home."

****

Elizabeth tried to keep the grin off her face. She'd known Miguel would impress Brooke, but her friend was sitting beside them on the sofa now, just staring at him.

Well, he was a hunk. *Her* hunk. But she trusted Brooke more than any other person she knew. This was not flirtation; it was awe.

"And you have no idea of how you got here?" she asked for the fourth time.

Miguel shook his head. "I thought I saw a vision of a woman with braided hair and wearing white leather, sitting in a tree. Crazy I know, but I was so disappointed when Marie Laveau told me—"

"Wait! The voodoo queen? You *talked* with her?" Brooke's blue eyes widened. "Did she put a spell on you? Is that maybe what worked?"

"No. She removed a curse from the dream catcher I was holding, but that's a long story. Actually, I didn't even believe in time-travel. If I hadn't met Lancelot, I'd probably still be there."

Brooke sat as still as a statue and Elizabeth knew what was coming. Mention *anything* medieval and Brooke went into tailspins, but Lancelot was her hero. Well, Elizabeth couldn't fault her on that anymore—she'd married her own bad boy and he had turned out really good. *Really* good.

"Lancelot?" Brooke asked in a breathless voice, "as in Gwenevere and King Arthur? You *met* him?"

Miguel shot an amused look to Elizabeth and then looked back at Brooke. "That I did. Gwenevere was with him.'

Brooke's mouth gaped and for a moment Elizabeth was afraid her friend was actually going to drool, but Brooke made a concentrated effort and spoke.

"What did he look like? Was he enough to take your breath away?"

Miguel grinned. "Not mine, although Gwenevere seemed equally as smitten with him as he was with her."

"*What did he look like*?"

"Stop teasing, Miguel." Elizabeth smiled at her friend. Brooke might appear even-tempered most of the time, but when she wanted information, she was as tenacious as one of those huge medieval wolfhounds she was so fond of. And her temper could equally rival Elizabeth's own, for Brooke was Celtic, too.

"Ah. Well. Tall. Muscular. I guess a lady would find him attractive."

"*Specifics*," Brooke said clearly. "*Hair? Eyes*?"

"Dark hair. Penetrating eyes."

"What color were they?" Brooke asked.

He shrugged. "I'm sorry, I didn't pay that much attention to him—kind of smoky-colored, I think. I could describe Gwenevere in more detail…"

Elizabeth threw a pillow at him and he ducked, laughing.

Brooke was not to be sidelined. “Tell me about her, then.”

“Just a moment.” Miguel pulled Elizabeth to him and wrapped his arms around her, effectively pinioning hers to her side. “I don’t want to get hit in the head when I do.”

Elizabeth responded by giving him a sharp nip on the side of his neck.

“Very pretty,” he said and leaned away from Elizabeth’s teeth. “Well, actually, she looked a lot like Elizabeth, only older. What amazed me was how she and Lancelot looked at each other, I could practically feel the sizzle in that humid, wet air.”

“*Ooooh*,” Brooke sighed softly.

“Kind of like what happens with us, huh, Red?” Miguel grinned down at her.

She snuggled into the crook of his arm. “You got yourself out of that pretty easily, smooth talker that you are. You still haven’t told us how Lancelot helped you time-travel.” She was as curious as Brooke was, for if she could grasp some small hint, maybe they could go back.

“He only said that sometimes you have to have blind faith and just believe. It wasn’t until they’d left that I put the pieces of the puzzle together. Then it was easy. If they had come from the past, why couldn’t I go to the future?”

“And can we go back?” Brooke asked, a faraway look in her eyes.

That was the question Elizabeth would have given any twenty-first-century thing to have answered.

****

"I wanted to show you something," Elizabeth said several weeks later as she pulled into a small graveled lot of an old cemetery on the corner of Mayfield and Cooper Street. "I think it will help make the transition easier."

Actually, she was proud of the way Miguel had adjusted. The hustle of the malls and the abundance of food and restaurants amazed him. Anything electric fascinated him. He'd made countless baked potatoes in the microwave. He found the Internet incredible, but he didn't trust the car. He was a horseman, he said, and it was too bad this world moved too fast for them.

She knew he missed Raul terribly. He didn't talk about it much, but she'd see him looking at other fathers and sons when they went out. It was the one thing she couldn't fix with an explanation. It was also one of the reasons she had brought him to this place.

"Johnson Station Cemetery," she said and pointed to the sign as they got out. "Just north of here, your town once stood."

They entered through the gate of the wire fence. Even though the traffic flow was heavy on Cooper Street, it was strangely quiet beneath the large oak trees which provided shade for the old markers. Many of them were tilted and a few were broken, but as they walked through the oldest part, Miguel read the names silently.

"Elizabeth Robinson. Died November 15, 1863." He looked up. "I knew her."

"That's the oldest marker here. Remember I told you about her?" Elizabeth hesitated. "I don't think any of your family would be here, but we could look."

Miguel shook his head. "We had a family plot at the hacienda. You remember where Elena was buried. All the family members would be there."

"Did you want to try to find it?" she asked. Over the past century and a half, the land he had once owned was now covered with suburban sprawl and they had not been able to find any direct descendants. She had hoped this trip might bring some closure.

He gazed into space for a long time, holding her hand. Then he gently squeezed her fingers and wiped an eye. "I don't think I want to know what or when things happened. I miss the Texas I knew, but I have you and I don't want to jeopardize that." His hand traced the Robinson marker. "It's goodbye to one century and hello to another. There's no point in looking back any longer."

****

"Here." Elizabeth turned the heavy history book around and pointed to a page. "April, 1861. Fort Sumter. The beginning of the Civil War."

It had been several days since they'd visited the cemetery and Miguel had decided maybe he did need to fill in some gaps. They'd come to the public library to do that.

"Actually," Elizabeth said, "it began before then. South Carolina seceded first and successfully repulsed a supply ship to Fort Sumter earlier that year. It was only when a second ship was sent and the commander, Robert Anderson, refused to surrender that shots were fired." She thumbed through the pages. "Look here. The battle of Shiloh: 24,000 casualties. Antietam: 19,000 wounded, 5,000 killed. Then Sherman's march to the sea, which destroyed just about everything that was still left in the South. And in the end, a president was assassinated."

She closed the book and leaned back. "Do you remember the dinner with Tate Johnson when I said the slaves would be freed?"

Miguel fingered the cover of the book soberly. "Yes. And no one believed you. Yet this is going to—did—happen only eleven years from the date of that dinner. What a horrible time it must have been for families to be so torn apart. Was this the worst war our country's been in?"

"Casualty wise, probably. But we've been involved in two massive world wars in the twentieth century and conflicts in the Far East as well. Viet Nam nearly divided this country as much as the Civil War did. Even now, there's constant strife in the Middle East: Jews against Muslims, Muslims against Christians. The ironic thing is that each side calls the other "the Infidels."

Miguel looked up from tracing the cover of the book with his fingers. "That war is centuries old, from the time of the Templars. You're telling me that skirmishing is still going on?"

"I'm afraid so," Elizabeth said. "it's a pity we can't just tell nations to play nice, like we would naughty children."

Miguel smiled a little. "I don't know what they're fighting about now, but originally, the contention wasn't so much over religion as it was treasure."

Elizabeth frowned. "Are you talking about Solomon's treasure that was supposedly buried under the temple? The rumors were that the Templars who escaped prosecution made off with it and that's why they became such successful bankers."

"More than just rumors, perhaps."

She stared at him. "What do you know about it?"

"My French ancestors left records that were passed down and translated throughout the centuries," Miguel said quietly. "Tate Johnson thinks there may be veiled clues or even a map in code, if I'd ever get the papers deciphered."

Elizabeth shook her head in confusion. "What does Tate Johnson have to do with the Templars?"

"He's a Mason," Miguel answered. "They've always had an abiding interest in anything to do with Solomon's Temple. But it's a moot issue; the papers are hidden in the hacienda a hundred fifty years in the past."

She sat there for some minutes, trying to make sense of what Miguel was saying. She thought of her mother, still in the south of France, researching. Treasure that was supposed to be buried at *Rennes-le-Château.* She felt herself getting a headache. It was too much to absorb.

"This is way too complicated," she said as she got up and put the book back. "Let's go to lunch and talk about the 1800s. Life was so much simpler then, with only the Comanche to worry about."

Miguel stood too. "I'm with you," he said. "It seems we haven't learned our lessons well, does it?"

"Nope." She took a deep breath and gave herself a shake. "But enough gloom. The sun is shining outside and the sky is blue. It's good to be alive, whichever century this is. And," she added mischievously, slowly and seductively wetting her lips, "after lunch, when we get home, I have a special dessert planned for you."

Miguel's eyes grew darker and he grinned. "That's what I love about you, Red. Do we really need to stop for lunch?"

She gave him a wicked look and walked out the door, swinging her hips in a most decadent fashion.

****

They were leaving Fort Worth's Water Garden one

evening just after sunset when they heard the scream. The cascading water nearly drowned out the sound, but as they moved away, they could see a woman struggling with a man over her purse.

"A mugging," Elizabeth said, reaching for her cell phone and dialing 911.

Miguel sprinted in the woman's direction and took hold of the man's shoulder to spin him around.

What happened next was to be forever jumbled in Elizabeth's memory. She saw a flash and heard a series of pops and then Miguel was lying on the sidewalk covered in blood. The woman screeched and the mugger ran away.

"No!" Elizabeth screamed as she dropped to her knees beside him and cradled his head in her lap. He was bleeding from both lower stomach and upper thigh wounds and there was a streak of blood on his face where a bullet had grazed the side of his head. He appeared to be unconscious. Elizabeth tore at the slip she was wearing and stuffed it on the wound on his abdomen, trying to stanch the blood.

"Help me," she said to the still-stunned woman. "Use your jacket to stop the leg's bleeding." The woman just stared. "Do it!" Elizabeth said in her teacher-voice, not even realizing the authority in the tone.

It worked. The woman dropped beside her, sobbing, and held the cloth against the leg. "I'm so sorry," she repeated over and over.

In the distance, Elizabeth could hear the ambulance. Thank God for cell phones. "Hang on, Miguel, help is coming."

He groaned and opened his eyes slightly. "I'm shot?"

"Yes, my love. Don't talk. Save your strength." She brushed the hair back from his forehead and applied both hands again to his stomach.

"Eliza…beth. I…love…you." Miguel closed his eyes and went still.

For a brief eternity, she stared and then yowled. "Don't die on me, Miguel. Don't die. Not after all we've gone through to be together."

"Move over, ma'am, please." The paramedic took hold of her shoulders and gently pushed her aside to take vital signs. The portable EKG machine was hooked up and all Elizabeth could see was a flat line.

And then Miguel was surrounded by med techs performing CPR, getting the defibrillator ready, inserting needles, hooking up fluids, applying a tourniquet.

Please God! He can't die! It was the only phrase she could think of and she muttered it over and over like a mantra as Miguel was placed on the stretcher and taken to the ambulance.

"Can I ride with him?" she stuttered.

"Sorry, ma'am," the medic said. "It's going to be crowded in there if we're going to save him. We'll be going to John Peter Smith."

"I'll escort her." A very solid-looking police officer appeared at her side. "Don't you worry about anything."

She turned to him in gratitude as the ambulance left, lights flashing, sirens blowing. "He—he'll be all right, won't he?"

"I don't know. I'm Captain Vargas. My car's this way."

As they quickly walked toward it, he spoke into his radio. Between the crackling noise and the code words,

Elizabeth couldn't really make out what was being said, and her mind was too dazed to think rationally anyway. All she could think of was that, only moments before, they had been laughing and talking and planning a trip to visit the King Ranch in South Texas. Miguel had been vibrant, full of energy. Alive. And now…she looked at the blood that covered her hands and most of her skirt. "Oh, God. Please. Don't let him be killed like my father was," she pleaded silently.

"We've apprehended the suspect," the captain said as he opened the door to the squad car. "The man's got a twenty-nine—a warrant for his arrest—on another assault charge as well. Seems like he has a history of priors, too."

Elizabeth nodded dumbly. That figured. Way too many scumbags were released on parole only to turn around and commit more crimes.

The captain escorted her to the ER where she was told Miguel had been taken into surgery. All she could do was wait.

"Is there someone you can call?" the officer asked.

Before she could answer, a hospital employee approached. "I'm sorry," the young woman said, "but the media is asking for an interview. They want to do a "Good Samaritan" clip for the ten o'clock news."

Elizabeth shook her head. Unbelievable. Here she was, not knowing if her husband was dead or alive, and someone wanted her to go on camera and talk?

The captain looked at her sympathetically. "Call your friend. I'll talk to the reporters for now and give them the basic details."

"Thank you," she murmured as she shakily dialed Brooke's number.

Time did a distorted space thing. It seemed to her hours elapsed before Brooke appeared, somewhat disheveled, and yet when she glanced at her watch, only minutes had gone by. Less than an hour ago Miguel had been teasing her about what he planned to do with her in bed that night, raising all sorts of delicious shivers. Now she only hoped she wouldn't be sleeping alone for the rest of her life. She prayed again, "Please God. Don't let him die."

She was dimly aware of the captain handing her his card, telling her they would be in touch and if she needed anything, to call. Brooke sat patiently holding her hand.

"He really was a hero," she said.

Elizabeth tried to ignore the "was." Miguel was in surgery. No news right now might be good news. "I wish he'd waited for the police."

"I don't know if this helps," Brooke said, "but he protected a woman in distress, just like a real knight would. It's nice to know there are still men who act like that."

Elizabeth nodded numbly. She supposed Miguel had always had that trait of chivalry. She'd just spent so much time defending her silly belief that he'd "use" her that she hadn't seen it. Could she ever make it up to him? She sighed. "Did I tell you he was a Ranger in the other life? That instinct kicked in." Her father had said it often enough—it didn't matter if he was in uniform or not, he was always on duty.

Brooke's eyes widened. "A Ranger? They're legendary. All the stories about—"

"Mrs. de Basque?" A surgeon stood in the doorway, still in scrubs, the mask down around his neck.

Elizabeth swallowed a lump in her throat. "Yes?"

"I think he's going to be okay. He has a slight concussion from the near hit to his head, and he's lost a lot of blood. The bullets didn't really hit any vital organs—" The surgeon hesitated and Elizabeth looked up quickly.

"What is it?"

The doctor took a deep breath. "With two bullets so close to the groin area, I can't guarantee that no damage has been done. There may be some dysfunction—"

She stared at him. "My husband could be impotent? Is that what you mean?"

He nodded. "We don't know for sure. Time will tell. He's in ICU, but we can give you five minutes, if you'll follow me."

A big whoosh of air left Elizabeth's lungs. She hadn't even realized she'd been holding her breath. "Yes, please."

Miguel looked paler than she'd ever seen him, but he seemed alert as he weakly squeezed her hand. "I guess I'll have to cancel those plans I had for you."

Tears sprang to her eyes and she didn't know whether she was going to laugh or cry. He had to be in pain and yet, *that* was what he was thinking about? She pushed the thought out of her head that those plans might be permanently canceled.

"You've got a one-track mind, do you know that?" she asked.

He grinned feebly. "Can't help it. By the time I get out of here, it'll be even worse. You'd better be ready, Red."

She leaned over to kiss him, careful not to let him see the worry she felt. Obviously, no one had told him, and she wasn't going to do it either. Time to deal with that later. He was alive. "I'll be more than that. You'll see."

****

Miguel wasn't released for five days, and when he did come home, he was still weak and needed bed rest.

"You made the news for several nights," Elizabeth said as she plumped the pillows so he could prop himself against the headboard.

"Why?" he asked. "Any man would have stepped in."

"Ah, no. Not in the twenty-first century," Elizabeth said. "Years ago, a young New York woman named Kitty Genovese was attacked and murdered on the street. She screamed for help and her neighbors stood by and watched, too afraid to do anything."

"That can't be true." Miguel looked thoroughly disgusted.

"It is," Elizabeth insisted. "This is a "me, me, me" society; there is no Code of Chivalry, as Brooke would say."

"Why would a man attack a woman anyway?" he asked.

"Drugs," Elizabeth replied. "Far too many people are addicted. They wake in the morning needing a fix and the goal for the day is to rob someone to get the money to feed the habit."

He looked puzzled. "What's wrong with doing an honest day's work?"

"They're not interested in working. All they want is the high the drug gives them. That man was a scum bag."

"The man needs to pay for his crime."

Elizabeth almost laughed. Miguel truly believed that. Well, times were a lot more black-and-white in his era. How she wished they could go back to that time.

****

Miguel gained strength quickly once he was home. Although he kissed her and held her against his side at night, he had not initiated anything more than that. Elizabeth hoped it was because his wounds were still healing.

Then one night she had to know. He turned his head away from her when she asked, and Elizabeth felt like a leaden brick had settled in her stomach.

“I don’t know,” he answered and put an arm up behind his head. “I just haven’t been able—”

“Shhh,” Elizabeth whispered. “It’s all right.” She nestled down on his shoulder and his other arm went around her. Slowly, she began to stroke the underside of his arm with her fingertips, lightly brushing the skin.

“That tingles,” he said into her hair.

“Do you like it?”

“Uh-huh.”

She burrowed closer and barely grazed his arm again, then let her hand slide gently down his ribs and up again over his chest and then down, letting her palm massage his belly, taking care not to touch the mending scar. She repeated the movements until she could feel him physically relaxing under the sensual massage.

Her hand traced the hard muscles of his thigh, then trailed softly to his testicles. She felt his sharp intake of breath as she gently kneaded them and let her fingers stroke lightly up his shaft. She was beginning to feel it move, a quiver here as she sought the underside, a decided nudge there as she touched the sensitive foreskin, and a most definite push as her hand glided the full length of him. She formed a ring with her thumb and forefinger and began to slide his phallus through it. Miguel moaned and she provided more friction and speed.

Ah, that was better. He was growing—really growing—under her hand. With one fluid movement, she slipped down and took him in her mouth, her tongue circling the head before she began to suckle.

Miguel growled and she felt herself suddenly being turned, her backside to him. One hand found her breast, the other the little nub that was the center of heaven. Her upper leg came over his and then she felt his now-hard erection plunge into her from behind, filling her completely, thrusting while his hands pleasured her as well. Three sensitive areas being stimulated at one time was too much. The crescendo of passion rose quickly, the need to have him deeper and harder caused her to counter his movements; the other throbbing between her legs where his fingers tortured her threatened to overcome her first. Her toes curled as she arched against him, the tremor starting slowly…slowly building until, with a wild cry, she felt that primal contraction that would hold him prisoner inside her until her climax stopped.

And it did not want to stop. Wave after contracting wave swept over her until she was nearly senseless and then, as she gasped for air, she realized why. He had not stopped, only slowed down to allow her to enjoy her coming. His hand still played with the swollen folds, his fingers still rolled a nipple between them. The thrusting had taken on a slow, rocking cadence, almost like a canter, that was causing a second achy build-up of need. The very nerve tips of her skin cried out for release and, in one final bucking motion, he ground into her. Her body convulsed into spasms.

She lay panting on her side, too weak to turn to him, and felt his sweat-drenched body press against hers, his arms securely wrapped around her.

"Well, you've answered my question," Elizabeth whispered, but when she moved her head, she saw Miguel was fast asleep.

Just as well. A third trip like that and she might end up in the ER too.

Chapter Nineteen—Home Again

As he continued to recuperate, Miguel became more and more interested in the history gap between his time and the present.

"Do you think we would be able to change history if we went back?" he asked one crisp fall evening as he and Elizabeth sipped glasses of wine in front of the fireplace.

"I don't know," Elizabeth answered. She picked up tongs and carefully turned a slow-burning log. "The question may be…*Should* we change history?"

Miguel poked at the history book lying on the coffee table. "A lot of lives could have been saved if shots had never been fired at Fort Sumter." He thumbed through the part on the Civil War and then looked up. "What if someone from the twenty-first century who knew what disaster lay ahead had coached Douglas and he won the debates? Lincoln wouldn't have been elected President and there would have been no war."

"But the slaves would not have been freed, either," Elizabeth said. "The war was the price for dignity and respect for all humans."

Miguel sighed. "You're right, of course. I never did believe in owning slaves." He glanced over the material pertaining to Lincoln. "Hmmm. He's quoted as saying, "A house divided against itself cannot stand." That sounds like Lincoln didn't want to split the country, he wanted to unify it."

"Sure," she said, "but I still stand by my question of whether someone has a right to interfere with history. The consequences have a domino cause-and-effect. Captain Kirk always claimed the moral code of the Federation was they could not interfere, morally or ethically."

"Captain Kirk? Federation?"

"Starships. The galaxy. Life beyond this planet." Elizabeth took his hand, a mischievous smile on her face. "I'll have to try and find some copies of *Star Trek*. If you think this century is strange, wait until you see where no man has gone before."

"I don't know that I want to," Miguel replied. "I'd still prefer the wide open spaces and my horse and maybe a simple romp in bed with my wife."

She caught the glint in his eye. "I can't do much about the first two right now," she said as she slid her hand under his T-shirt and across his tight belly, "but about the third thing—"

He cut off the sentence, claiming her mouth with his. The only galaxy he was taking her to was his own.

****

Full autumn arrived with all the fury a blue norther could muster. Brooke shivered as she took off her coat and handed it to Miguel. "Nothing like cold weather to put me in the mood for Halloween," she said.

"Come on in," Elizabeth said. "I've got all the stuff laid out on the coffee table." They were planning a costume party, since Halloween fell on a weekend this year. "It's too bad we can't celebrate at school," Elizabeth grumbled as they picked out decorations.

"Why can't you?" Miguel asked as he joined them on the sofa.

Brooke rolled her eyes. “It’s no longer politically correct. A few religious zealots think it’s devil worship. If they only knew the real meaning.” She sighed. “It really spoils it for those of us who would like to commemorate the more medieval tradition of Samhain.”

“Remember I told you that Brooke likes anything medieval,” Elizabeth said to Miguel with a wry smile.

He inclined his head. “I would have laughed at that once. Since I’ve time-traveled, though, and actually spoke with Lancelot and the queen of ancient Britain, I believe anything’s possible.”

“Ah, to go back to those times,” Brooke said. “Did I tell you I’m coming to the party as Gwenevere?”

“You didn’t,” Elizabeth said, not that it surprised her.

“Who are you going to be?” Brooke asked.

“An Indian maid.” It had been Miguel’s idea that she order a fringed tunic and skirt in white leather, along with white moccasins. “I need to find that dream catcher my students bought me last year for Christmas. It’d make a good accessory.”

Brooke nodded. “What about you, Miguel?”

He grinned. “I’m going as a Spanish *empresario*. Appropriate, no?”

She laughed and he excused himself to finish some research about the twentieth century on the web. After he’d gone, Brook sighed. “You certainly are lucky, Liz, that you’ve found him. And not once but twice.”

“I know,” Elizabeth said and lowered her voice. “I think I’m pregnant. I haven’t told Miguel yet.”

“Why on earth not?” Brooke asked in surprise.

“I want to be sure. He misses Raul so much that this would be too much of a disappointment for him if I were just late." If Brooke knew just how often they made love, she'd be even more envious.

Brooke was quiet as they finished their planning, and Elizabeth knew she was thinking that she had no steady relationship. For a moment she felt guilty. Marriage was so wonderful for her. Her thoughts were confirmed when Brooke got ready to leave.

"Do you think I'll ever find my knight in shining armor?" she asked softly.

****

Things were hectic at school the next week or two, and Elizabeth tried not to think too much about being pregnant. She had missed her second period. The home pregnancy test had been positive and she'd scheduled an appointment with her gynecologist, but she was afraid she'd hex the possibility if she dwelled on it too much. By the time of the party, she'd know.

Her costume arrived a day before Halloween. Elizabeth had already begun to think of an emergency substitute, so she breathed a sigh of relief.

A hint of frost was in the air the night of the party, but it only made the stars shine like brilliant diamonds against a black velvet sky. The moon rose full and orange just after sunset.

"A *Comanchería* moon," Miguel said, looking out from their bedroom window.

Elizabeth padded over to him in her soft moccasins. "Why is it called that? I've always wondered."

He put an arm around her, but continued to gaze out the window as he answered. "Because the Comanche only raid when the moon is full; they believe it will light the darkness for the spirits of their warriors who are killed."

"The shaman wanted to sacrifice me on that night," Elizabeth said softly.

Miguel squeezed her shoulder. "Don't think about that."

"I guess people have always had superstitions about the full moon," she said and then deliberately put some brightness into her voice. "Perhaps it will light the way for Brooke's faeries and spirits as well."

Miguel nodded and turned to her. His eyes widened.

"What?" Elizabeth asked and smoothed the soft leather of the skirt.

"It's just that—" He paused and then said softly. "I had no idea you would look so much like her."

"Her?" Elizabeth asked and lifted an eyebrow. "Is there something you haven't been telling me?"

"No." He grinned. "Where would I find the stamina for another woman anyway? With your hair braided, you just look so much like the maid in the vision—the one I told you about when I was wounded and whom I thought I saw again just before I arrived here. I wonder…." He let his voice trail off.

Elizabeth turned back to the mirror. She did look like the woman she too had seen in the sweat lodge—the one Swift Hawk called Dream Catcher. She had always thought that was only an illusion. "Do you think she's real? That she had something to do with our time-travel?" Elizabeth had always felt that somehow the fetish she'd put around her wrist that night had done it, although it didn't explain how she'd returned.

"I don't know," Miguel said softly, just as the doorbell rang with the first of the guests. "Let's think about it."

Elizabeth nodded and opened a drawer to pull out

the old dream catcher. “Look what I found? It’ll make a good conversation piece, don’t you think?” She attached it to the slender leather belt that was bound around her tunic. “Shall we go?”

****

The party was a huge success. Someone had dressed as a Knight Templar, which appealed to Brooke almost as much as King Arthur would have. Miguel shook his head in amusement when Elizabeth mentioned it.

“A little different time period, but the Templars were certainly no saintly monks.”

“I know,” Elizabeth answered. “Remember, my mother is in southern France researching. If she even uncovered a hint of treasure—”

“Ah, the Code again,” Miguel answered, “but forget that for now; tonight is for fun. Let’s dance.”

And they did. Elizabeth’s moccasins were so comfortable her feet weren’t even sore after all the guests had gone. Back in their bedroom, she slipped them off as Miguel removed his clothes and sank down on the bed. He watched with interest as she removed her tunic and tugged at the skirt until it slid down.

“Did you order your costume too small?” he asked and added quickly, “not that you’re fat, my love.”

The humor of the situation struck her and she tried hard not to laugh. Elizabeth crawled on top of him and leaned down for a kiss. He lingered with it, teasing her with his tongue, his hands brushing lightly over her breast.

“I’m going to get a lot fatter, I think.”

He paused and held her slightly away. “What’s that supposed to mean?”

She was suddenly shy. “I’m…I’m going to have

your baby."

Miguel stared at her. "You're sure?"

Elizabeth nodded. "The doctor called this afternoon. I know Raul can't be replaced, but—"

She never got to finish. Miguel crushed her to him and rolled over, pinning her beneath him.

"A baby," he breathed, between showering kisses on face and ears and throat. He rested his hand gently on her stomach, slowly stroking it. 'I'm going to have to be extra careful with you."

"We've got a few months until then," Elizabeth said mischievously as she brought his hand to her breast again. "For tonight, I want you to make wild, passionate love to me so this baby will know who his father is."

Miguel groaned low in his throat and slanted his lips across hers, his tongue delving into her mouth, tasting, teasing, titillating. He trailed wet, open-mouthed kisses along her neck and over her shoulders and to her breasts. He laved her nipples, his tongue circling one before suckling lightly on the other.

Elizabeth whimpered and pressed his head closer, needing him. Miguel sucked harder, taking half of her breast in his mouth then nipping at the hard bud with lip-covered teeth. She strained toward him, tips tingly. He cupped her breasts together, kissing the cleavage, sliding his wet tongue between them and under them, nibbling at the soft sides of her breasts before consuming one of them again with his mouth. All sensation centered in her breasts, hot and heavy and swollen.

And then the sensation sank lower as Miguel licked and kissed and nipped his way across her torso and lower belly, leaving tiny pricks of flame on her heated skin. He lifted her legs over his shoulders and spread her wet, silken folds open with his fingers. The feeling of exposure sent wild pulsations to her center. Yet he teased her, kissing her inner thigh softly from the knee toward the juncture of her thighs where there was an aching need to be satisfied. But his lips just brushed against the soft hair there, tickling her and sending her desire to new heights, as his tongue lightly ran up her other thigh and then down and across again, tongue just grazing the swollen lips of her womanhood.

Had the man no sense of easing her torture? She wanted him, hard and deep. Elizabeth moaned and arched her hips.

"Something wrong, Red?"

She opened her eyes to find him grinning at her. How could he be so rational at a time like this? He shouldn't be. She wished she could see his erection, for that would tell the true tale, but he had his body angled so that she couldn't.

He flicked his thumb over her inflamed nub and she mewled, muscles constricting deep within her.

"I want you," she said with clenched teeth.

"Like this?" he asked as he slowly licked the length of her, the tip of his tongue just touching her throbbing center.

Elizabeth began panting. If he would just suck! Her climax was a millisecond away. Her legs began to tremble involuntarily. "Please…no…more…teasing…"

Miguel reached up to gently pinch her nipples as he mashed his lips against her slick wetness, his tongue pulverizing the taut, jutting little tip that for the moment was the center of her universe. With a wild cry, Elizabeth felt her entire body clench, one gigantic spasm rolling over her and subsiding into multi mini-tremors.

She gasped for air and then he was inside her, plunging deep, ramming himself home, savagely claiming her body with his. Elizabeth arched her hips upward, matching his fierce rhythm, taking him completely, feeling the head of his penis jutting against her womb. The feral growls that emanated from him unleashed her own primitive instincts and, with a frenzied scream, she came again, her body shuddering uncontrollably, just as Miguel ground into her one final time and she felt the hot release of his seed deep within.

For moments, they lay entwined, their bodies sleek with sweat, damp hair matted, breathing in great gulps of air. Finally, Miguel nuzzled her neck.

"Do you think our son knows who his father is now?"

Elizabeth curled into his shoulder. "Maybe we'll have twins after this."

"All right by me. Would you like to try for triplets?"

She gave a fake groan. "I probably won't be able to walk for a day as it is." She eyed the dream catcher where she had tossed it on the bedside table and picked it up. "We really should hang this for good luck."

Miguel gave her a quick kiss and reached over her to take it. A strange expression crossed his face and he sat up thoughtfully. "Elizabeth, what if the dream catcher is really the answer?"

Elizabeth frowned and propped herself against the headboard. 'Explain."

"Well, what if the dream catcher is the portal through Time? And the Indian maid in the vision—what if she is the one that made it happen?"

"Go on."

"You hung this the night before you arrived in my

barn," he said. "The black one from the shaman had a curse on it to send you back to your own century. When Marie Laveau removed the curse, I remember holding it and praying on my knees. And I thought I saw the Indian maid. You thought you'd seen her, too, that first time." He turned to her, his dark eyes glinting with excitement. What if we hold this together and call on her? Do you think she could transfer us back?" He stopped suddenly. "Or is that not what you want? You have many conveniences today that I couldn't offer you, like modern hospitals and medicine when the baby arrives."

"Birthing is a natural process, and Olga will be there to help." She took his face in her hands and kissed him. "I'd give all this up in a minute for us to be back on the ranch with Raul and Olga and Olaf."

He beamed at her and returned her kiss soundly. "Then we'd better get dressed."

Elizabeth nodded and climbed out of bed and dressed quickly. "I'm going to write a note to Brooke first. If this works, I want her to know I won't be coming back."

Her fingers trembled as she composed the note:

Dearest Brooke. We think we've found the method through which we can traverse Time. It's in the dream catcher, which must be some sort of totem used by its namesake, the spirit the Indians call Dream Catcher. She may go by other names as well, for she is said to have come here in ancient times."

Anyway, if you don't hear from me and find this letter, know that I am gone. Explain as much as you can to my mother and take whatever of my things that you want.

I want my child to know his brother.

I will love you always, my friend, but I know that I belong in a different time.

Always, Elizabeth

She folded the note and placed it in an envelope on the dresser, then quickly wrote a second note for her mother. Taking a deep breath, she turned to Miguel.

"Are you ready?" he asked.

She nodded and lay down on the bed beside him, snuggling into the crook of his arm. Together, they held the dream catcher.

"Do you think it'll work, Miguel?" Elizabeth clung to him. "I don't want us separated again. I couldn't bear that."

He kissed the top of her head and tucked her closer. "Shhh. Sleep now. Just hold on to the dream catcher."

She closed her eyes. "Okay, cowboy. Let's go back to where the West began."

Softly, so she nearly missed it, he answered, "Whatever century we wake up in, know that I will always love you."

Epilogue

Arlington, Texas - Summer 1876

Elizabeth sat on the wooden, covered porch that Miguel had added to the ranch house, sipping lemonade in the late afternoon and watching their grandchildren play. Maria was six and quite bossy toward four-year-old Antonio. Elizabeth knew she should intervene and make them play nicely, but Miguel always said that as mischievous as Raul had been, he deserved to handle their discipline. Trouble was, he was usually away, supervising the long cattle drives that had sprung up with the abundance of Longhorns roaming the ranges after the Civil War.

She leaned back and let her mind drift. So much had passed since Dream Catcher had returned them to this century. Cactus Flower replaced the schoolmarm. Swift Hawk had eventually married the daughter of Feathertail, but only after being wounded in the last raid that Tate Johnson led, in 1860. Olga and Olaf were still healthy, refusing to let age stop them. When Miguel had suggested Olaf hand over the foreman job and take time to enjoy life, the old man had simply spit and said he hadn't been born in the woods to be scared by an owl.

This was the year gold had been discovered in the Black Hills. She'd read in an old newspaper that the mining town of Deadwood stirred up almost as much trouble as the California gold rush had done. In a way, the Dakota impact was greater than that of the Sutter's Mill discovery which caused the 49ers to settle California. This find had led to the great Indian Plains battles. She sighed, wishing they could change history. General Custer would die tomorrow at the Battle of Little Big Horn.

The children's mother, Mary, called them into the house just as Miguel joined her on the porch swing. She offered him her glass and he took a sip. "Were there any letters from Beth or Joaquin?" Their daughter was attending a boarding school in the East and their son worked for Governor Coke in Austin as an apprentice lawyer.

Joaquin had taken the old French papers with him that might hold a code for the Templar treasure, too. Elizabeth thought how ironic it would be if that mystery were solved long before her mother began researching her project.

Miguel shook his head. "No, but there's other news. Santa Anna died in Mexico City a few days ago."

"I can't say I'm sorry," Elizabeth answered. "He cut a lot of lives short at the Alamo. Maybe if Travis or Bowie or Crockett had lived, Texas wouldn't have joined the Confederacy."

"I doubt they could have changed anyone's minds. Tate Johnson participated in the Secession Convention and wasn't able to do any good."

"And then what did he turn around and do? Led the 14th Texas Cavalry Regiment and took you with him."

Miguel put his arm around her shoulders and pulled her to him. "It's in the past. We've survived Reconstruction, the railroad is here, business is booming." He paused. "I wonder what Bell would say if I told him that his telephone invention would wind up as cell phones." Miguel shook his head and then grinned. "Now if someone could just invent the microwave a bit earlier—"

Elizabeth was not about to be sidetracked or mollified. "You were wounded in the war."

He leaned over to nibble her ear. "That was blockade running. Someone had to do it, and I had the sources in both Spain and France."

"Still," she said, "you almost lost your leg on that ship."

"Shhh," he answered and nuzzled her throat. "I don't want to talk about it anymore. I can think of more interesting things for us to do."

"In the middle of the afternoon?"

"Why not? Come on." He stood and pulled her up with him. "What good is having some retirement time if we don't use it?"

She smiled as she followed him along the corridor to their bedroom. Streaks of silver burnished his sideburns now and she'd found another gray hair of her own this morning. Their laugh lines had deepened, but she was as strongly attracted to him as she had been the first morning she'd seen him in the barn so long ago. And he was just as virile and insatiable as he'd always been.

He closed the door behind them and bolted it. She giggled and put her arms around his neck.

"Show me what an old man can do," she said.

"Old?" Miguel raised an eyebrow. He wrapped muscular arms around her and pressed her against his still flat belly, his erection hard and straining at his jeans. "How often and in what way do you want me to show you?"

"Mmmm. Let's start with this." She pressed her lips against his, opening.

He responded with a tease, allowing her a taste of his tongue and then withdrawing, only to apply pressure, gently at first, letting it build to a passion that left both of them panting and devouring each other's mouths hungrily.

His hands caressed her breasts and back and buttocks and as he turned to lay her down, she realized she no longer was wearing a stitch of clothes.

Elizabeth smiled to herself. Someday, she was going to find out how he did that.

A word about the author...

Cynthia Breeding lives on the Gulf Coast of Texas with a very non-spoiled poodle-mix and enjoys walking and horseback-riding on the beach, as well as sailing.

www.cynthiabreeding.com

Thank you for purchasing
this publication of The Wild Rose Press, Inc.

For questions or more information
contact us at
info@thewildrosepress.com.

The Wild Rose Press, Inc.
www.thewildrosepress.com

www.ingramcontent.com/pod-product-compliance
Lightning Source LLC
La Vergne TN
LVHW020528100826
845148LV00010B/1390

9781509264704